Hat Trick

CHELSEA CURTO

Copyright © 2025 by Chelsea Curto

Proofreading by April Editorial

Copy editing by Britt Tayler at Paperback Proofreader

Cover by Chloe Friedlein

All rights reserved.

No part of this book may be reproduced in any form or by any electronic or mechanical means, including information storage and retrieval systems, without written permission from the author, except for the use of brief quotations in a book review.

*For the ones who fight even when they want to give up.
I'm rooting for you.*

*(And for the readers who love a hockey player that wears slutty glasses…
Riley is for you)*

AUTHOR'S NOTE

If you're new here, this is typically the place where I'll write a long, drawn out note that explains my insights into why I wanted to write this story, and this book is no different.

I have not suffered a limb loss myself, but someone very, very, *very* close to me has (for the sake of her privacy, I'm not naming who). They've been an amputee for forty years, and throughout my time on this earth, I've seen them exhibit nothing but perseverance, unwavering optimism, and a zest for life that's hard to find in anyone else. I'm in a constant state of awe of their ability to not slow down, to not stop doing what they love, and they've been a constant inspiration to me.

When sitting down to write Hat Trick, I knew Lexi, an athletic trainer, had to end up with someone who would undergo a serious rehabilitation process for her story to be believable (yes, I know it's fiction, but work with me here).

With the renewed interest in the Paralympics last summer, including a spotlight on athletes like Hunter Woodhall, a double-amputee track star, and other decorated athletes, the idea came to me.

A hockey player who suffers a limb loss, begrudgingly

starts his rehabilitation process, and finds out who he is away from the ice.

In the early days of this story, I thought I was going to have to rely on some heavy imagination. Is it even possible to skate with a prosthesis? Has it been done before?

Then I read about Craig Cunningham, a former member of the Boston Bruins and the Tucson Roadrunners, an AHL team in Arizona. He went into cardiac arrest on the ice, and after developing an infection due to poor circulation, his lower left leg was amputated.

But guess what? He can still skate, and the videos of him on the ice is *unreal*. I really recommend you check them out, because it's the most inspirational thing I've ever seen.

Riley's story differs slightly from Craig's. Craig lost part of his leg, while Riley undergoes an AKA—an above knee amputation. It's a much more complicated rehabilitation process, and you'll see it takes many, many, *many* sessions for him to be comfortable with his new body.

Because of the length of his rehab, you'll notice the occasional time jump for readability. Additionally, some hockey elements have been altered as well (there are more than six guys on a team, but I don't want to overwhelm anyone with a list of twenty-one names).

My DMs on Instagram are always open if you want to chat more, and I hope the research, care, love and consideration I put into Riley and Lexi's story comes off the pages.

Xoxo,
Chelsea

CONTENT WARNINGS

Hat Trick is a romantic comedy full of laughs, spice, and swoon, but I want to share a few content warnings that some readers might want to be aware of.

-explicit language
-alcohol consumption
-multiple explicit sex scenes
-mention of infertility (not the main characters)
-loss of a limb by a main character (off page, detailed)
-mention of depression and suicidal thoughts had by a main character
-mention of a drunk driver
-car crash depicted on page
-rope play
-breath play
-continuous rehabilitation of an amputated limb

As always, take care of yourselves and protect your heart. If you have any questions about any of the things listed above, please know my DMs are always open (@authorchelseacurto on IG).

CHARACTER CATCH UP

Hi, reader!

I do my best to write my books as standalone novels even though they're part of a series, but some of the characters mentioned have their own books. I never want anyone to feel confused while reading, so I created a quick character catch up so you can know who is who before diving in.

If this is your first book of mine, welcome! I'm so glad you're here.

If you're a big DC Stars fan, I hope you're excited to be back with the boys.

For timeline purposes, Hat Trick takes place **immediately** after the end of Slap Shot (as in the same night), but *before* the epilogue.

Maverick Miller and **Emmy Hartwell** have their own book, **Face Off,** which is book one in the DC Stars series. It's a dislike to lovers, rivals with benefits, black cat x golden retriever story full of banter and spice.

Piper Mitchell and **Liam Sullivan** have their own book, **Power Play,** which is book two in the DC Stars series. It's a grumpy x sunshine, goalie x rinkside reporter, teach me, accidental marriage story.

Hudson Hayes and Madeline Galloway have their own book, **<u>Slap Shot</u>**, which is book three in the DC Stars series. It's a single mom x hockey player, sunshine x sunshine, slow burn story.

Maven Lansfield, the team photographer has her own book in a different series. **<u>Behind the Camera</u>** is a single dad x nanny, roommates, NFL story.

As always, I've left lots of clues about upcoming books. I can't wait to see if you find them!

DC Stars Roster

Maverick (Mavvy) Miller - right winger
Liam (Sully) Sullivan - goalie
Hudson (Huddy Boy) Hayes - defenseman
Riley (Mitchy) Mitchell - defenseman
Ethan (Easy E) Richardson - center
Grant (G-Money) Everett - right winger
Connor McKenzie - center
Ryan Seymour - defenseman

Brody Saunders - head coach

Glossary

I'm a big believer that sports should be for everyone, which means readers might not be familiar with every term and acronym. Some of the hockey related terms you'll find in this book are listed below.

PWHL: Professional Women's Hockey League
ELC: entry level contract
LTIR: long term injured reserve
ECHL: East Coast Hockey League (third highest professional league in North America)
AHL: American Hockey League (second highest professional league in North America)
NHL: National Hockey League (highest professional league in North America)
Sweater: hockey jersey
Hobey Baker Award: annual award given to the top collegiate hockey player
Duster: player who doesn't get much playing time
G League: the developmental league for the NBA
Barn: slang term for a hockey arena
Five-hole: a shot that goes through the goaltender's legs

ONE
LEXI

IF THE MAN next to me doesn't get his goddamn hands away from my ass, I'm going to break his fingers.

He's trying to be sly. Every few seconds he'll move closer to me. He'll lean to his left and shift his feet. The last time he did, his pinky grazed against my leather skirt.

The fucking *nerve*.

I turn and face him, not surprised to find a blond-haired guy looking at me.

The worst ones are *always* blond.

I am surprised by the polo he's wearing. It's striped, the collar is popped, and I thought we left that horrendous style behind in the early 2000s.

There's a silver chain attached to his belt loop, for god's sake, and I'm half expecting to hear the dialup tone from AOL replace the EDM song playing from the club's speakers.

What's next? Is someone going to ask for my screen name rather than my phone number?

"Hey!" he yells over the loud music, grinning when our eyes meet.

He steps toward me, and I wrinkle my nose. He smells like

stale beer and rotten cheese, and it's impossible not to gag. I need to get laid, but I'm not *that* desperate.

"Do you always touch random women without their permission?" I ask. "Or am I just lucky?"

"You're hot."

"I know I am."

"Thought I might introduce myself."

"I can't wait to hear what your name is." I roll my eyes. "Let me guess. Is it Brayden? Braxton? Some other combination with letters tacked on the end that don't belong?"

"Close." His grin stretches wider. There's a piece of food stuck between his teeth, and I'm noticing he has a very punchable face. "It's Bryce."

"Of course it is." I sigh and curse myself for having done something in another life to piss off the meet-cute gods. There are dozens of attractive men here, and *this* is the one I end up talking to? It's not fair. "Did you need something?"

"Want to go somewhere quiet? We can get to know each other. Or we can go back to my place. I have stuff to eat. Food, ya know? Do you cook?"

I wish I had the balls of a mediocre white man who thinks he's hot shit. I'd be unstoppable.

"I know all I need to know about you. Next time, use your words to get my attention, not your hairy fingers, douchebag." I smile at the bartender bringing me a drink. I drop a ten in the tip jar and spin on my heel. "And blonds aren't my type."

"I bet I could be your type," he says in some last-ditch effort to keep me hanging around.

"And I bet you couldn't find my clit even if I pointed it out to you," I say sweetly, and the bartender snorts. "It's never going to happen, buddy."

I disappear into the crowd to escape the creep and make my way to the VIP section of the club the DC Stars, the newly crowned Stanley Cup champions, reserved to celebrate their big win earlier tonight. I smile when I spot my girlfriends sitting in the booth we claimed when we got here and beeline it for them. Grant Everett, a second line forward on the Stars, waves at me when I pass. He's still wearing the victory goggles he donned in the locker room three hours ago when someone popped a bottle of victory champagne.

"Lexi!" he screams, holding up a handle of whiskey. "We're the best of the best!"

"I know you are G-Money." He drinks straight from the bottle and I laugh, jealous of how easily his early-twenties body is going to recover from the alcohol consumption. My ass is going to be in bed until noon tomorrow. "No driving tonight, okay?"

"More like no sleeping. We're raging till the break of dawn, baby!"

He takes off for some of the other players, stumbling as he goes.

They deserve to let loose after repeating as champions and being the ninth team in NHL history to accomplish the back-to-back feat. They fought like hell in the postseason, overcoming a shitty Eastern Conference Finals series and going on to beat the Los Angeles Bulls in an electric game seven.

"There you are!" Piper Mitchell, the Stars' rinkside reporter, tugs on my arm. I take a seat in the booth next to her and smile. "What took you so long?"

"I had to give this dude at the bar an earful. He kept trying to touch my ass." I take a sip of my gin and tonic and feel my shoulders relax as the alcohol works its way into my bloodstream. "Fucking men."

"Fucking men is right." Emerson—Emmy—Hartwell, the first female to play in the NHL and another one of my best friends, smirks. "Please look at what they're doing."

I shake my head at the conga line some of the guys have started. Half of them have ditched their shirts, and they're taking turns passing the Cup around.

Maverick Miller, the team's captain and Emmy's husband,

screams when one of the rookies drops the trophy. He dives to the floor and catches it before it can fall, then lifts it over his head a second later to a round of applause.

"I like seeing them happy." Piper scans the overpacked room, giggling when her eyes land on Liam Sullivan. The goalie and grumpy asshole extraordinaire—and Piper's accidental husband after a drunken night in Vegas but very real boyfriend—is standing in the corner with a scowl on his face. "I told him he has to socialize for an hour before he's allowed to leave."

"He looks like he'd rather be anywhere but here," Maven Lansfield, the Stars' team photographer, says. "That's a cute crown he's wearing."

"Isn't it? I'm going to make him keep it on when we get home later."

"Thatta girl." I pat her thigh. "It's nice everyone is having a good time. The guys worked hard this year. I wonder if they'll be able to go for the three-peat next season. If anyone can do it, it's this group."

"You helped with that, Ms. Head Athletic Trainer," Maven says to me, and I smile at one of my best friends. "Keeping them healthy isn't easy."

"It's not, but I wouldn't change it for the world."

"They're the greatest team of all time." Emmy sighs when Maverick grabs the DJ's microphone and yells *world champions!* and *fuck LA and their overpriced grocery stores!* "You can't help but love them."

I finish off my drink and stand, tugging on the hem of my miniskirt. "I'm going to run to the bathroom. Does anyone need anything while I'm up?"

"No, but we're dancing when you get back. Hoes before bros tonight," Piper declares.

"Bring me another drink," Maven calls out, and I give her a wink over my shoulder as I saunter away.

The music is loud. The lights are low. To my right, people

are grinding against each other on the dance floor and running their hands up and down sweat-soaked bodies. I manage to dodge a waitress carrying a tray of bottles going to one of the players' tables, but I stumble on a discarded lime.

"*Shit.*"

Before I can face plant on the hardwood floor stained with god knows what, an arm loops around my waist. A palm settles on my hip. I turn and find Riley Mitchell, our star defenseman, looking down at me.

"Hey, Mitchy," I say, relieved it's not the loser from earlier.

"Lexi." He smiles, and I can make out the hint of a blush on his cheeks. "Are you okay?"

"Yeah. Just lost my footing. I love adding limes to my drinks, but I never thought a half-eaten one would be my downfall." I gesture to the piece of citrus in question. "All is well. Thank you for saving me."

He unravels his arm and takes a step back, pushing his thick framed glasses up his nose. "Happy to help."

"How's your night?" I ask.

"Good. Are you having fun?"

"Oh, yeah. Everyone's rowdy, but it's allowed. Are *you* having fun?"

"You didn't see me dancing earlier?" he asks.

"Shoot. I missed it. Will you show me?"

"It's not nearly as impressive without music. I'd probably look like a gyrating robot."

"Sounds like a sex move," I say.

Riley chuckles. "I hope no one breaks an ankle trying to climb on the bar. Wouldn't want you to spend your summer having to heal our dumb asses."

I laugh and lean against the wall. I'm warm. My insides are a fuzzy from the alcohol I've been sipping, but I'm not drunk. I'm pleasantly buzzed, teetering on the edge of tipsy, and having a good time. I'm enjoying standing here and talking with him. It's a nice break from the loud noise and celebratory chants.

I'm not supposed to have a favorite player on the team—and I love all the guys I work with—but Riley takes the top spot.

He's nice, courteous, and cute. Quiet in an easygoing way, and unbelievably sweet. He's bashful, almost, whenever he talks to me. There's always a hint of shyness in his tone, and no matter how many times I shrug off my friends when they say he has a crush on me, it's pretty obvious he does.

He's younger than me, and I'm betting he's a relationship guy when all I want to do with a man is have fun for a few hours before I go on my way. I doubt we'd be compatible, and I'd never get involved with anyone I work with.

There's nothing wrong with flirting with him for a minute though, and that's what I intend to do.

"Make sure everyone is on their best behavior, will ya?" I joke.

"Please. You know the guys. That's impossible. Pretty sure Ethan tried to roll a hot dog cart in here."

"God. So predictable. World peace would be easier to accomplish than keeping you all under control." I brush a piece of hair away from my face, and his eyes follow my hand. "What are you doing over the offseason? Any fun plans?"

"Nah. My parents are in Chicago. I'll go visit them for a week or two. Some of the boys are planning a trip to the Bahamas. I might learn how to golf." He shoves his hands in his pockets and shrugs. "The possibilities are endless."

"And what are you going to do with the Cup on the day you get it? Please don't tell me you're going to eat something out of it."

"That's why we're all so big and tough, Lex. Because we eat and drink out of a trophy that hasn't been cleaned in years."

"That's revolting."

"It is, isn't it?" Riley laughs and mimics my pose against the wall across from me. "I think I'll do cheese curds this time. Last year, I ate the world's largest ice cream sundae."

"Now we're talking." A group of women walk between us. One of them eyes Riley with an appreciative glance, but he doesn't look at her. He keeps his focus on me, and the heat of his attention makes me shift my feet. "I should get back to the girls. I don't want them to think I'm being harassed by another man wearing a polo."

He peers down at the plain white T-shirt stretching across his chest. It's more casual than the suit and tie he wore when he walked into the arena earlier tonight, and when he lifts an arm to survey his outfit, his biceps flex. The constellation tattoo he has on his left arm peeks out from under his sleeve, and I wonder what stars make up the cluster.

"I'm not that drunk, am I?" he asks. "This isn't a polo."

"Not you, knucklehead." I laugh. He's cute all the time, but he's even cuter with a confused look on his face. With glasses falling down his nose again and jeans that sit low on his hips. "There was a guy at the bar earlier who tried to touch my ass. He was wearing a polo."

Riley's gaze flicks to my thighs. He hums. Scratches his jaw and nods. "Right," he says to my knees before bringing his eyes up to meet mine. "If another polo-wearing prick tries to bother you, let me know. The trophy weighs thirty-five pounds. I'm happy to lob it at someone."

"My hero." I pat his chest when I scoot past him for the bathroom. "Have fun, Mitchy," I add, biting my lip to fight a smile when I catch him staring at my ass. He's not doing a very good job of hiding his crush tonight, and I like it. "Don't party too hard."

"I'm a good boy, Lex," he tosses back. "You don't have to worry about me."

TWO
RILEY

OUR STANLEY CUP celebrations moved from the arena, to an apartment, to a club downtown, and the night shows no signs of slowing down.

It feels like the whole city is alive and buzzing with excitement. We're back-to-back champs after years of shitty seasons, and it's fucking *fun* to celebrate our hard work.

Months of practice, early mornings, eighty-two regular-season games and four hard-fought playoff rounds have finally paid off, and when Maverick Miller, our devoted leader and wickedly talented right wing, stands on the bar and holds the Cup over his head, I can't help but laugh.

"He's insane." Hudson Hayes, my defensive pair, shakes his head. "Ten bucks says he tries to crowd surf."

"I'll bet you thirty he says to hell with his no-alcohol pact, pours a handle of vodka in the Cup, and drinks out of it," I counter. Maverick always turns down invitations to go out with some of the younger guys on our nights off to hang out with his wife at home, but now I watch him gesture at a bartender. He waves his platinum credit card around and points to the row of bottles arranged in a neat line, and I grin when Hudson slaps three bills in my hand. "Pleasure doing business with you, Huddy Boy."

"How long are you going to stay?"

"Don't know. Depends when everyone else heads out. Probably not too much longer."

"You can come back to my place if you want," he offers. He looks absurd with a light-up necklace hanging from his throat. It's some bedazzled thing Ethan Richardson, our center, threw at him in the locker room earlier. I'm shocked it survived the journey here. "Madeline said Lucy fell asleep on the ride back to the condo after the game. Her parents are in town, but we could have a few beers and play a video game or something. It would be quieter than here."

Madeline Galloway, his girlfriend, and Lucy, her daughter, are recent additions to Hudson's life. He's joining my other friends who are settling down, and I don't know when everyone on the team went from perpetually single playboys to blissfully betrothed.

It's hard to keep up.

"Are you hitting on me, Hayes?" I joke.

"See if I ever invite you over again. Maddie made a cake, but now you don't get any," he says.

I whine. Her affinity for cooking and baking is dangerous to the top-tier shape I keep my body in during the season, but it's summer now. I can eat whatever the hell I want without Coach getting on my ass about nutrition.

Plus, some quiet sounds nice.

It's getting pretty loud in here.

"Not fair. You should've led with that. I would've had a different answer."

"Too late." He stands when he spots Ethan taking off his shirt and waving it around his head. Hudson is a responsible guy, one of the oldest on the team and a veteran who's spent years mentoring the younger players. He's about to slip into dad mode, and I can't wait to see who gets in trouble first. "You okay?"

"Hell yeah, I'm okay. We're champions." I grab my cigar off the table in front of me and take a puff. "I'm on top of the fucking world, man."

"I'm going to put out a couple fires. See you soon?"

"Don't worry about me." The alcohol I've been nursing all night to keep up with everyone else is starting to seep into my blood. I feel loose. Light. *Good*. "I'm a big boy."

Hudson smirks and beelines it to the bar. He grabs the trophy from Maverick before any damage can be done and I relax in my chair, surveying the club.

Grant is tucked away in a corner with his phone out, grinning at something on the screen. Liam is glaring at everyone like he's secretly planning our murders. He probably is. Connor McKenzie, one of our second line guys, has his arms draped over the shoulders of two women, and Ryan Seymour, my backup, is dancing with his wife.

Even Coach came out tonight, but he disappeared an hour ago. He mumbled something about being under the weather, but it's probably for the best. He'd kick our asses if he saw how we were acting, and we'd be skating laps until next season. Fuck if we won tonight or not.

My attention can't help but drift over to the booth where Emmy, Piper, Maven, and Lexi are, and I frown at the man squeezed in next to Lexi. He's chatting her ear off. Touching her shoulder and laughing at something no one else finds funny. Her eyes meet mine, and she gestures at the dude. It's a *can you believe this guy?* move, and no, I fucking can't.

Anyone with half a brain can see she's not having fun. She's trying to distance herself, to not giving him any attention, and it reminds me why I hate men who think every woman in the world wants to listen to them talk about something boring like the goddamn stock market.

I grab a napkin and flag down a server, asking to borrow a

pen. I scribble on the folded paper, holding it up so Lexi can see.

HELP? it reads.

I'm awarded with a smile. She reaches for her own napkin and borrows a marker from Piper's purse. I laugh when I see her answer under a smudge of lipstick.

GOING 2 SAY IM MARRIED. WANT 2 BE HUSBAND?

Turning the napkin over, I write out a response.

HONORED.

Lexi gives me a thumbs-up. I take another puff from my cigar and tap the ashes into the ashtray, then stand and make my way across the club.

"Ladies," I say, grinning when I get to the girls' table. My gaze bounces to the brunette with mischievous brown eyes. "Lexi."

"Hey, sugar," she purrs, and I should be embarrassed by how easily I blush.

I can't help it.

She's attractive. Out of this world sexy with her long, toned legs and sly grin. I'm pretty sure I've had heart eyes for her since the minute we met, but I've never tried to cross that line.

I'm twenty-six. She's thirty-two.

She's the team's trainer, and I don't want people to assume she got her job because a player called in a favor.

I'm quiet; she's loud. The life of every party and vivacious as hell with witty comebacks and a laugh that would bring any man to his knees.

And if it were me down there, I'd wear a collar and crawl if she asked me to.

There are a million reasons why I've kept that boundary in place, but it makes me feel good as hell that out of all the guys here tonight, she's asking *me* for help.

"Thanks for taking care of my favorite girls, man," I say to the guy who finally looks my way. "I think you're done here."

"Oh. Is this a group-sex thing?" He glances around the table and lifts his arm, trying to give me a high five. "That's hot. They're all smoking. You're lucky."

"A *what?*" I shake my head and lift an eyebrow. "I don't have a death wish, but you might because the one who's not giving you any attention? That's my wife, and I don't like when people touch what isn't theirs. Any other questions?"

"*Shit*. Sorry." He slides out of the booth and almost falls on the floor. "She didn't say."

"It's a game we like to play." Lexi smirks in my direction with bright red lips. She grabs the toothpick from her drink and wraps her mouth around the speared lime. "I do something bad, then he punishes me."

Christ.

She's always flirty, but it never means anything.

I wish that line did, even if admitting it would get me in a world of trouble.

The guy apologizes again and practically sprints to the bar and his group of friends. He's replaced by Maverick a few seconds later, who drops into Emmy's lap and buries his face in her hair.

"There you are." He wraps his arms around her waist and sighs. The dude is an absolute machine on the ice, but whenever he's around his girl, he's calm. Finally at peace after years of being unsettled. "I've been looking for you everywhere."

"I'm right here. Exactly where you left me." Emmy kisses his forehead and brushes a piece of hair out of his eyes. "And almost having an orgy with Riley."

"Yeah?" Maverick turns his chin my way. "Did you tell him about the dream you had? The one with me, him, Hud—"

"You're cut off, Miller." Emmy puts a hand over his mouth. Her red cheeks match her hair. "One more word and you're on the couch tonight."

He folds his fingers around her wrist and pulls her hand

away. "A fair punishment, but if you're going to invite anyone in from the team, Mitchy and Huddy Boy are the only two I'd be okay with."

"I'm flattered, Cap. And now that you all have Mavvy here as your bodyguard, I'm going to head out." I nudge Lexi's heel with my sneaker. "You good, Lex?"

"I'm great. I don't like to be rescued, but I don't mind being a damsel in distress if it means getting saved by a guy like you." She looks me up and down, and it's mortifying how hot my skin is. I'm pathetic. "See you on Wednesday for the parade and rally?"

"Yeah." I bump my fist against Maverick's and give them all a wave. "See you then."

I make my way around the club and say goodbye to the boys after turning down another offer from Hudson to go back to his place. I know he's eager to celebrate with his girl after scoring the game-winning goal tonight, and I don't want to be in the way.

I might be bordering on lonely, but I draw the line at hearing my friends have sex with their significant others. I deal with that enough during the season thanks to thin hotel walls, and I'm not in the mood to listen to orgasm after orgasm when I'm not on the receiving—or giving—end of one.

Finally finishing my rounds, I step outside, waiting for my rideshare to pull up. The June air is nice, and I nod at a few of the boys who are leaving the club to keep the party going at some speakeasy up the road. When I spot a white SUV, I check the plate and step off the curb.

"Lamar?" I ask, bending to talk through the window.

"Yup. Climb on in," the Uber driver tells me, and I hop into the back seat. "Looks like a fun night. Are you celebrating something?"

"Yeah." I smile and buckle my seat belt. I pull out my phone, starting to scroll through my notifications. My Instagram account is frozen from all the comments and DMs flooding in. The video I uploaded of Maverick on the bar with the trophy already has half a million likes and counting. "Something."

"Life is short. We need to celebrate the small stuff." Lamar shifts the car into drive, and we take off down the road. "Otherwise, what's the point of living?"

"Good sentiment, man." I click off my phone, not in the mood to answer messages from people I haven't talked to in a decade. They like to pop up after major victories in my athletic career, and I like to keep my circle small. "What are you doing out so late?"

"Trying to make some extra money. My wife and I just found out we're having a baby. Her first pregnancy was rough for her, so I told her I'd do some extra driving during the week so she can stay home. I don't want her on her feet all day."

"What's your wife's name?"

"Aliyah." He smiles when he says it then looks at me in the mirror. "You got a girl?"

"Nah."

"A guy?"

"Just me."

"Ah." Lamar flicks on his blinker and checks both ways before turning right at a stop sign. "Do you want someone?"

"Yeah. Guess the timing has never been right."

"Timing is a bitch. You're a good-looking guy. You seem smart, from the three minutes I've spent with you. You'll find someone."

I laugh and close my eyes. My buzz is wearing off. Exhaustion is hitting me, and I can't wait to crawl into bed. I can't wait to sleep until early afternoon and finally drag myself back to a world where I don't need to be at the rink at the crack of dawn.

I love my job. Wouldn't pick anything else to do if I had the choice, but some time off is going to be fucking marvelous.

"Thanks, Lamar. Is your first born a boy or girl?"

"He's a boy. Three, and an absolute fucking menace." He snorts, but nothing about it sounds annoyed. The dark skin around his eyes crinkles with admiration. Joy and pride. "I love him. He's a good kid."

"And your second. Do you know yet?"

"No. My wife is hoping for another boy, but I'm holding out for a girl. I've always wanted to be a girl dad."

"Girls are the best. I work with some women who are incredible. We need more of them in the world." I reach into my pocket, grab my wallet, and dig out a wad of cash. I count out ten hundred-dollar bills and lean forward, setting them in the cupholder next to Lamar's right elbow. "Go home after you drop me off. You shouldn't be busting your ass at two in the morning. Not when you've got people waiting for you to get back safe."

"Shit." He stops at a light and stares at the money. "I can't accept this. No way."

"I'm not taking it back."

"You can't be serious."

"I'm very serious. Keep it." I smile. I'm earning eight million a year to hit a puck. It's not right to keep that all to myself. "It's yours."

"Wow, man. Thank you. Are you an angel or something?"

"Nothing like that," I say, and Lamar shakes his head. "Just a guy trying to do his best."

"I can't tell you what this means to me." The light turns green, and he accelerates. "My family and I, we're—"

I don't get a chance to hear what he has to say.

One minute, I'm looking out the window at the night sky and wondering what kind of trouble the boys are getting in. They'll probably be out partying until sunrise, and I won't be surprised if they show up to the parade with tattoos of the Cup on their arms.

The next, our car is in the air. Flipping three, four times in what feels like slow motion.

There's a moment of panic. Of not knowing what's going on and not knowing what to do. There's yelling from the front seat. The sound of glass shattering and something sharp nicking my cheek.

My vision is hazy. Everything around me is blurry. I try to reach for my glasses so I can see, but they aren't there. Pain like I've never experienced before races up my right leg and I scream. I grab my thigh. My fingers touch something damp and sticky.

When I look down, I find my hand covered in blood.

It's the last thing I remember before everything goes black.

THREE
LEXI

I SHOULD GO HOME, but home is too far away.

And way too fucking lonely.

My friends left an hour and a half ago, holding hands with their husbands on their way to celebrate the end of the season more privately.

I watched them go, plastered on a smile when they asked if I wanted to spend the night at their place, and told them I was fine.

Fine, fine, fine.

I love being alone. I always have. I crave freedom and the independence to do what I want, when I want. But sitting at the bar and wondering how much longer I can stay while simultaneously dreading going home to an empty apartment sounds miserable.

And I don't want to be miserable.

"Another round?" the bartender asks, snapping me out of my sad thoughts.

I eye him. He's the same one who laughed at my joke earlier. Cute, with an arm covered in tattoos and dark, shaggy hair… he definitely has my attention.

"No." I smile. "I'm all set."

"Haven't seen that blond guy again." He grins. "He looked like a tool bag, didn't he?"

"Such a tool bag. The polo? I mean, come on, dude."

"His name is probably Chad."

"It's Bryce, actually, and it's a horrible fucking name."

"Hey. My name is Bryce."

"Oh, shit. Is it really?"

"Nah." The bartender smirks and uses the dish towel slung over his shoulder to wipe up a ring on the counter. "It's Seth."

"Wow. That was smooth. What are you doing after this, Seth?"

"Seeing if I can find your clit better than that guy could."

I throw my head back and laugh. I like his energy. I bet he likes to have a good time in the bedroom, and I love when a guy is both hot and funny. "How long until you get off?"

"With you, it'll probably only take me a few minutes."

I smile at the compliment. "You have a lot of game, Seth."

"Figured I might as well shoot my shot. Couldn't stop looking at you all night. My shift is over in thirty minutes."

"I'll wait for you to finish." I cross my legs, glad when his eyes flick to my bare thighs. "If you want."

"I do want. Sure I can't get you another drink?" Seth points at the half-full glass I haven't felt like finishing. "Women aren't usually so sober when they flirt with me."

"Uh-oh. Should I be worried about a tiny dick? Is that why you're trying to ply me with alcohol?"

"Nothing to worry about in that department." He chuckles. "I showed you mine, are you going to show me yours? What's your name?"

"Lexi," I say, not bothering to come up with a fake alter ego to get him off my back. I can tell we're going to have a good time together. "And I'll be right here when you're finished."

"Glad to hear it."

Seth goes back to the lingering patrons waiting to close out their tabs. I pull out my cell phone for the first time in a few hours to distract myself, frowning when I see two dozen missed calls from Piper. There's another from Hudson. Four from Emmy, and panic rises in my chest.

My friends know I hate talking on the phone. If you need to get a hold of me, texting is always best, but the fact that my inbox is empty while my call log is full makes alarm bells ring in my head.

I hit Piper's name first.

"Hello?" she answers on the fourth ring. I hear a door open on her end. A handful of voices and deep breathing. "Lex?"

"Piper? What the hell is going on?"

"Oh, thank god." A sob escapes her, and I sit up straight. I climb off the barstool and grab my purse, running for the door. Something is very, very wrong. "There was an accident."

"An accident? What kind of accident?"

"A car accident."

"A car—you didn't drive to the club. Are you safe?"

"It's not me. It's"—she gulps down another breath while I'm not sure I'm even breathing—"Riley. I'm at the hospital. They aren't sure if he's going to make it, Lex."

The world stops spinning when I burst outside.

I tilt sideways, close to falling over, and I brace myself on a light post.

Riley.

Not going to make it.

This can't be happening. He's too young.

Too talented.

Too much of a *nice fucking guy*.

I just saw him. I laughed with him. I made him smile.

What the *fuck*?

"Which hospital?" I ask. My tongue is heavy in my mouth. My hands shake. I'm close to throwing up. "Where are you?"

"MedStar."

"I'll be there as soon as I can."

"I'm not sure there's—"

"I said I'll be there," I almost yell, as if the louder I talk, the more of a chance he has. "Call me the second anything changes."

I hang up with Piper, not listening to what else she says. My fingers tremble. I try to pull up my Uber app but accidentally click on a food delivery service instead. Tears blur my vision. I look up at the sky and the millions of stars above me.

"Don't do it," I whisper to whoever—*whatever*—might be listening. I've never been religious. I've never prayed to anyone or anything before tonight, but right now seems like a damn good time to start believing. "He's not... let him be okay. *Please* let him be okay. I'll help him get better. Just... *let him be okay.*"

No cars pop up on the app, and I want to scream. I want to break a window, but I can't stand here and wait for something to magically appear.

Fuck that.

I slip off my heels and head west, sprinting down the sidewalk as fast as I can.

THE WHOLE TEAM is in the emergency room.

Maverick is standing in a corner with his head in his hands while Hudson whispers to him. Grant stares at the wall, a glazed-over look on his face. Ethan is walking in circles, his hands in fists at his side and his cheeks stained with tears. Liam and Coach are crowding the check-in desk, and I make my way over to Emmy and Piper.

"Hi," I say.

"You're here." Piper wraps me in a hug. "I'm so glad to see you."

"What—" I swallow. I'm not sure I want to ask this question, but I need to know. "What happened?"

"He was in an Uber and their car was T-boned by someone running a red light. The police estimate the driver was going at least seventy miles an hour based on the impact."

"Are you fucking kidding me?" I seethe.

"The police also said the driver was impaired and hit the back of the car where Riley was sitting head-on then kept on driving. His Uber driver miraculously walked away unharmed." Emmy points to a man pacing around the lobby looking dazed. He glances up every few seconds to check the doors that lead to the ER hallway, then puts his head in his hands. "He called 911, found Riley's phone, then got a hold of Maverick because he was at the top of Riley's call log. By the time we got here, Riley was already with surgeons. None of us had a chance to see him."

"Thank you for bringing me up to speed. Has anyone checked on his driver?" I ask.

"No. I think he's in a state of shock," Emmy says. "I tried to go up to him, but he ignored me."

"Okay. I'll give it a try. I'm a new face." I squeeze Piper's hand and kiss the top of Emmy's head, making my way over to the man. "Hi," I start. It's the only word that seems easy to find right now. "Were you—"

His chin jerks up. He doesn't look much older than some of the guys, and that makes me even sadder. "I didn't mean to do it. It happened so fast. My light was green and I—"

"Hey." I wipe away my tears. "Of course you didn't. It's not your fault."

"He was a nice guy. He gave me a wad of cash and—" He shakes his head. There's dried blood on his hands. A dark red stain on his shirt. "I should've checked both ways. I *always* check both ways."

"He's a nice guy, isn't he? His name is Riley. Riley Mitchell."

"Mitchell. Why does that—" He frowns and looks around the room. Understanding dawns when he spots Maverick, one of the most recognizable guys in the city, then the Stanley Cup sitting on the ground next to an artificial plant. "No. No. No. No. *No.* He didn't mention he was—"

"I'm not surprised. Riley is humble. He doesn't like attention. Sometimes when I hang out with him, I forget he's a hockey player." I laugh like saying these things is going to make everything right in the world. "What's your name?"

"Lamar. I watched the game before I started driving tonight. Saw the game-winning goal and everything."

"You don't have to stay," I say gently.

"I don't want to leave. Not until I know…" Lamar trails off. He pinches the bridge of his nose and sighs. "I'm so sorry."

"You have nothing to be sorry for." I give his shoulder a gentle pat. "You're not responsible for anything, and Riley would tell you the same thing."

I've seen hundreds of injuries over the course of my career, everything from gashes to the head and dislocated shoulders to missing teeth that required emergency dental work.

None of them were ever this severe.

None of them ended with—

I refuse to finish that thought.

The shock of what's happened is catching up to me. The rush of adrenaline that helped me sprint my way here is starting to fade, and I'm suddenly left feeling so fucking exhausted. So scared, and the tears start to fall again before I have a chance to stop them.

"Hey." I'm not surprised Hudson is the one who stands by my side and hands over a hoodie. He has the softest soul of anyone on the team. Kindhearted and always looking out for other people, he's a natural helper. Someone who soothes and protects, and that's what we all need right now. "Are you all right?"

"You know the answer to that." I sniff. "It's *Riley*."

"I know." He tips his head back and glares at the ceiling. "I should've forced him to come back to my place. I shouldn't have let him leave. Fuck. I should've gone with him."

"If you hadn't let him leave, maybe this would've happened to both of you. You have Lucy and Madeline, Huddy. Can you imagine what that would've done to them if something happened to you? You're their safe space now."

"It's not fair."

"It's really fucking not fair."

"I think—"

Hudson is cut off by the doors to the emergency room opening. A doctor walks out, and every player rushes toward him.

"I'm guessing you all are here for Riley Mitchell?" he asks, and Maverick shoves his way to the front of the group.

"We're his teammates. Is he—"

"He's breathing," the doctor tells us, and Hudson squeezes me so tightly I lose feeling in my arm. "That's the good news."

"And the bad news?" Coach asks. He's aged ten years since I saw him on the bench during our game. There are dark circles under his eyes. A red mark on his neck and a shirt that's on inside out. "Please."

"He suffered very serious injuries to his right leg with massive blood loss. Surgery to repair the leg… well, it's impossible. We're going to have to do a transfemoral amputation, and after, he'll—"

"What the fuck does transfemoral mean?" Maverick barks out. "You're going to have to dumb it the fuck down for us."

"He's going to lose his leg above the knee," I blurt.

"Jesus fuck." Ethan kicks a wall, and Grant is quick to wrap his arms around his middle before he can do any damage. "This is the best fucking hospital in the city and you can't fix his fucking leg? What the fuck do they pay you to do?"

"Hey," Hudson snaps. "Knock it off. Getting mad isn't going to fix anything."

"This guy isn't fucking doing anything."

"I understand this is upsetting." The doctor doesn't bat an eye at Ethan's outburst, and I wonder what other kinds of behavior he's seen working in the ER. "However, this is the best outcome given the severity of his injuries."

"When is the surgery?" I ask.

"We're prepping him now. We'll be in the OR for at least a few hours. His residual limb should heal in four to six weeks, but he can be fitted for a prosthetic and start walking with assistance as soon as he's comfortable. He'll need to recondition his muscles and relearn things like balance and coordination. It could take up to a year to feel like his old self."

"Will he be able to skate again?" Maverick asks, voicing what we're all thinking.

The doctor gives us a sad smile that speaks volumes. "I'll update you all when I can."

He leaves us with that, and everyone migrates around the waiting room. A couple of guys sit on a couch. A few others spread out across a handful of chairs. Ethan drops to the floor and Grant sits next to him, putting his head in his lap and softly murmuring to him.

I don't think anyone is going to leave anytime soon. Not until we know Riley is really okay.

"I'm going to get him skating again," I whisper to Piper and Emmy.

"Lex, I don't—"

"Hockey is his whole life." I stare at the doors leading to the patient rooms. "I'll work with him. We'll do it together."

I've always been a determined bitch. Once I put my mind to something, I don't stop until it happens, and I'll be damned if Riley goes down without a fight.

FOUR
RILEY
JULY

ONE MONTH SINCE THE ACCIDENT

PUCK KINGS

MAVVY
Hey, Mitchy. Checking in.

HUDDY BOY
Let us know if you need anything.

G-MONEY
We missed you at team dinner last night.

MAVVY
The docs said your one month checkup went well. You doing okay?

EASY E
Hello from paradise, motherfuckers!!!

Attachment: 1 image

Look at that blue ocean. I live here now. You assholes can find a new center.

ONE MONTH SINCE THE ACCIDENT

SULLY

Fucking hell. Can you all shut up? Maybe Riley doesn't want to be fucking bombarded by 10,000 messages singling him out.

And sending a picture from the Bahamas, Ethan? Really? This isn't about you, you selfish prick.

MAVVY

I'm not going to leave him out of the chat and I don't want to fucking ignore what happened to him.

G-MONEY

It's been a month and he hasn't talked to us.

SULLY

Maybe because he doesn't want to talk to us. Did you ever think of that?

MAVVY

Stop being a dick, Sullivan.

SULLY

Or what? Are you going to put me in my place, pretty boy? Your wife would have a better shot.

MAVVY

Get Emmy's name out of your fucking mouth.

HUDDY BOY

Both of you need to stop. He'll talk to us when he's ready.

SULLY

Here comes Mr. Nice Guy who always does the right thing. Does your head hurt from wearing a crown?

RILEY

MAVVY

What the actual fuck is your problem, 32?

SULLY

My problem is something traumatic happened to our teammate, and when you keep bringing up the same shit, it's not going to help him feel better.

EASY E

We could talk about….

I don't know.

G-MONEY

This fucking sucks.

EASY E

Imagine how it must feel for Mitchy, dude.

ME

Leave me the fuck alone.

You have left the chat

FIVE
RILEY
AUGUST

TWO MONTHS SINCE THE ACCIDENT

PIPER

> Hi, Mitchy. I stopped by your place and handed over some of Liam's chicken parmesan to your mom.

> I'm glad she and your dad are there.

> I know I'm not one of the guys, and I know it probably doesn't mean much coming from me, but I'm here for you too. If you ever need anything.

> Or just a friend who will listen.

SIX
RILEY
AUGUST

TWO AND HALF MONTHS SINCE THE ACCIDENT

COACH

> We have a meeting scheduled with the GM, owner, CEO, president, training staff, and all the coaches two weeks from today.

> I expect you to be there.

> I know what you're going through, Mitchell.

> You can't hide from it forever, and you can't get through it alone.

SEVEN
RILEY
SEPTEMBER

THREE MONTHS SINCE THE ACCIDENT

COACH

I'm done being nice.

Let's try this again.

You're still a member of my fucking team, Mitchell.

When I schedule a meeting, you're expected to attend. I'm sick of coming to your apartment only to be told you're out when I know for damn sure you haven't left your building in fucking months.

Next Thursday. Noon. At the arena.

Do NOT make me track you down again.

EIGHT
RILEY

I STARE at the ceiling tiles.

There are forty-two of them.

Like the hockey number I'll never wear again.

That's fucking ironic.

"How are you feeling today, Riley?"

I blink and glance over at my therapist.

Dr. Ledlow knows exactly how I'm feeling.

It's the same way I felt yesterday, the day before that, and the three months that have passed since the night of the accident and my world flipped upside down.

I'm pissed off.

Helpless.

Like I'm suffocating as my world crashes around me and I can't do anything about it.

It's been like this for twelve weeks. An endless cycle of being angry at everything while also grieving the life I'll never get back.

No more skating with the boys.

No more shooting on an empty net.

No more outdoor rinks and Winter Classics.

No more signing jerseys with my name on the back.

No more hockey, and I don't know who the hell I am without hockey.

I've been playing since I could walk. My first word was puck. My earliest memories are of skating on a frozen pond up the road from our house in Illinois. Learning to lace up my skates and how to hold a stick. Growing up and scoring a goal in the World Junior Hockey Championships. Taking my college team to its first ever Frozen Four appearance and winning, then signing with the Stars after my junior year.

Thousands of people dream of making an NHL team. Few actually do it, and I'm a kid from Chicago who got lucky.

Not lucky enough, I guess, and that's what hurts the fucking most.

Riley Mitchell.

The former NHL star.

Now what am I?

A guy who bets on games?

A guy who sits in the stands and watches his teammates get everything he dreamed of?

The future is bleak as shit.

"Fine," I grit out, then I wonder if I could make the walls cave in. It wouldn't make things worse, and I guess there's some comfort in that. "Just fine."

"How's the pain?" he asks.

I've been on so many medications, I can see how people get addicted. When the first twinge of an ache starts and I feel the phantom limb syndrome my doctors warned me about, I'm wishing I could pop another pill.

Or four.

It feels *good* when you're not hurting, and all I do these days is hurt.

"Fine," I repeat.

Might as well make it my middle name.

"Are you getting used to the crutches?"

I glare at the assistive devices leaning against the arm of

the couch. I hate the fucking things. The skin under my arms is raw. I'm still trying to figure out how to balance on one leg as I move around my apartment because I can't just pop on my temporary prosthetic limb in the middle of the night when I need to pee, but I refuse to be pushed around in a wheelchair.

"What do you think? I got up here, didn't I? Nice job having an office on the third fucking floor, by the way. Real accessible."

Dr. Ledlow blinks. He's unfazed by my outburst and jots down a few words on the notepad resting in his lap. He's probably mentioning that I'm unstable. I can't wait for the team to read his notes and think I need serious help.

Maybe I do.

"You know the more it takes for you to talk to me, the longer we have to do these sessions, right?" he tells me.

I grind my teeth together.

I do know that.

The team and the league mandated therapy sessions for me when I got out of the hospital, but I'm not ready to be psychoanalyzed when I'm still so mad at the universe.

I'll probably always be mad about the deck of cards I've been dealt.

Massive blood loss.

Severed tendons.

Nearly being crushed by the other car.

An amputated leg above my right knee.

Days that should have been spent celebrating with my teammates were spent in the hospital where doctors weren't sure I was going to pull through.

Sometimes, I wish I hadn't.

It would've been easier for everyone than the burden I've gifted them, and that makes me angry all over again.

It's a miracle he's alive, I heard a nurse whisper when I was in and out of consciousness.

Drunk driver, Coach told my mom when I couldn't open my eyes. *Four times over the legal limit.*

Haven't seen a patient so roughed up in years, a doctor said when I woke up from surgery.

"I'm not sure why the league gives a shit." I huff and stare out the window. It looks like it's going to rain. I used to love watching the thunderstorms roll across Lake Michigan when I was a kid. I'd count the lightning strikes. I'd try to gauge how far away the storm was and smile at the first crack of thunder. "I'm never going to play hockey again."

"You don't know that. Plenty of athletes go on to compete in events with prosthetic limbs. Look at the sled hockey team that plays in the Paralympics."

"No thanks."

Dr. Ledlow sighs. I'll give him credit for showing up to our sessions. If I had to deal with me, I'd probably quit.

"Who's downstairs waiting for you today? Is it your mom?"

"Yup. I'm a child getting picked up from school."

"You've met with your prosthetist?"

"Yeah." I sigh. "He's not bad."

An amputee too, I learned when I went to the first of my fittings a month after surgery. I'm lucky my wound is healing as quickly as it is. It's allowed me to get the ball rolling on an artificial limb, which is complex as hell.

There's 3-D imaging. A socket and a metal pylon that's going to act as my calf. A fake foot. A dozen other pieces that go into creating the final product, and I'll be getting mine soon.

And then I have to retrain my body to function with the prosthesis, which is just fucking great, because I've been slacking on my physical therapy. I skipped my session at the outpatient office yesterday, and I don't plan to go tomorrow.

Everything's always come naturally to me. Thinking about

having to relearn how to balance—how to fucking *walk*—makes me want to scream.

I should be used to all of this; my dad lost his leg when I was a teenager. He was a firefighter, picked up a shift from a buddy, and ran into a burning building to save a woman and her child.

He barely made it out.

After I woke up from surgery, he told me he'd help me learn how to adjust to my new life. He was there with me when I decided between a mechanical or microprocessor-controlled leg, but all of this is a burden on him. Another responsibility delegated to someone else because I can't do it myself.

"Riley," Dr. Ledlow says gently. "No one expects you to be okay. You almost died. You lost a part of yourself, and you're never going to get it back."

"I've never had any anger issues on or off the ice. My penalty minutes are some of the lowest in the league. I paint to decompress and read romance books, for fuck's sake. But here I am, thinking about things I want to break and the things I want to yell at the people who piss me off. Spoiler alert: it's every-fucking-body."

"Seven stages of grief," he tells me. "You're on stage three: anger. Rage toward the situation. Rage toward yourself and others and the universe."

"I get to go through four more stages?" I groan and stare at the ceiling again. "Can't wait."

"The good news is you're feeling *something*. And I want you to express those feelings."

"What comes next?" I mumble.

"They're not necessarily linear, but if we're going by textbook definitions, you'll face bargaining after anger. Followed by depression and—"

"Yippee."

"—testing then acceptance. You'll come to terms with this

change eventually. Life will go on. I'm not asking you to give me a mile, Riley. I'm not even asking for a foot."

"I hope not. I only have one now, and it would be pretty fucking rude of you to take that from me."

"Humor is a positive sign. Maybe that will be your coping mechanism." Dr. Ledlow chuckles. "All I'm asking for is an inch. Any forward motion is still progress. Okay?"

"Okay." I reach for my crutches and stand. "Sure."

"I'll see you in a few days. And I've been told to remind you about your meeting with the team next week. Coach Saunders was adamant I get the message to you."

"What's the point?" I look at him. He's not much older than me. Mid-thirties, maybe, if I had to guess, and he came highly recommended according to my mom, who's been driving me to my appointments three times a week. "Why bother when we all know what they're going to say? No skating. My contract is voided. *Thanks for all you've done for the team, but we need to make room for a guy who can actually handle a stick.*"

"Because they're your family, and they love you."

I rub a hand over my chest, thinking about the flowers and balloons that were in my hospital room when I woke up. All the food that's filled my fridge and the low voices I hear when I'm locked in my bedroom.

I thought I was losing my mind at first, but the noises turned out to be my teammates—again, according to my mom. They sit in the living room for five, six hours. Sometimes there are hushed conversations. Sometimes I hear video games being played on my TV. Other times—most times—it's quiet.

They don't try to get me to come out, but I know they're there.

And it makes me cry into my pillow.

"Okay." My fingers curl around the hand grip of my crutches. Dr. Ledlow is nice enough to hold the door open for me. "I'll go."

I make my way out of his office and wait for the elevator, grateful when I get to the ground level and back outside. I can breathe better out here, and I don't care how unbearable the September heat is in my hoodie and sweatpants.

I'm not ready for the world to see my scars yet. The ones on my leg, yeah, but the others that are still healing: my arms. A small spot on my cheek. My left shin and knee.

TMZ got a hold of photos from the crash, and they still pop up on ESPN every now and then. I threw up in a trash can the first time I saw them. Now I can get through a solid forty-five seconds of seeing my face plastered on the TV before I have to change the channel.

"Hi, sweetie." My mom rolls down the passenger side window of my SUV. "How did it go? You stayed in there longer than you did last week. That's encouraging."

"Mmhm." It takes me a second to lower myself into the seat, and I wince at the exertion. "I guess."

"Dad and I have our flight to Chicago in the morning. I've been in touch with the airline and explained our circumstances. They're willing to let us change our return ticket so we can stay—"

"I'll be fine." I stretch out my left leg and drop my head against the seat. "You both have done enough to help me. I'm going to have to figure it out for myself eventually."

"Are you sure?" She reaches over and puts her hand on my thigh. "You might be twenty-six, Riley, but you're still my baby. I—"

"I said I was fine, Mom. Stop fucking coddling me," I snap. I push my glasses up my nose. Hot tears sting my eyes. "I'm sorry. I'm an asshole. That was… I didn't mean—"

"I know you didn't." She moves her hand to my hair. It's gotten long, and it likes to stick up in random directions when I wear a hat. My barber texted me and said he'd come to my apartment to cut it so I wouldn't have to figure out a way downtown, but I haven't answered him. I haven't answered anyone in weeks. "I know you're feeling hopeless, and you might be thinking—"

"I'm not." I swallow. "That's a lie. I have. I was. But I'm not anymore."

"Good. That's good."

She sniffs. When I look over at her, I notice how much she's aged since the time I saw her at an away game in Chicago last season. Her skin is paler. She's lost weight. Her hair—which she usually keeps bright blonde—is fading to brown.

It's like I've sucked the life out of her, and that's reason enough to make sure her and Dad head home tomorrow and get back to their routine.

I don't want to be the reason for anyone's unhappiness.

My own is enough.

"I won't." My voice shakes. It feels like there is sand stuck in my throat. "I promise."

"My sweet boy." Mom pats my cheek and smiles. "Do you look at your father any differently because he lost a limb?"

"No. He's a hero."

"Your kids are going to say the same about you one day."

"Kids." I snort. "That implies someone is going to want to fall in love with this." I gesture up and down my body. All of that—dating, friendships—seems like a far-off dream. "I'm a mangled and messed up piece of a human."

"That's what love is, Riley. No one ever said it was easy."

"Easy." I stare out the window at the people living their lives while I'm over here having an existential crisis. Teetering on the edge of a breakdown. "I don't think anything is going to be easy for me again."

NINE
LEXI

I'M SO FUCKING LATE.

I'm going to blame my alarm I silenced twice this morning.

Goddamn Apple and their nine-minute snooze feature.

Shoving the last bite of bagel in my mouth, I tear into the conference room at the United Airlines Arena where I should've been five minutes ago, out of breath, sweaty, and wishing I wasn't wearing jeans.

"I'm here." I collapse in the first chair I find and dig through my purse for my water bottle. There's a stitch in my side, and my lungs hurt. I do Pilates multiple times a week, and I thought I was in better shape than this. That run from the employee parking lot and two flights of stairs kicked my athleticism to the curb, and I've been humbled. "Sorry. Traffic."

Stuart Klein, the Stars' recently appointed Director of High Performance and my new boss, narrows his eyes.

I don't like that look.

I know what that look suggests.

If you were a man, I'd laugh and say "no worries." Since you're a woman, I'm about to chastise you in front of everyone because no matter how hard you try, it's not going to be good enough.

Fucking prick.

I've worked my ass off for my spot on this team. I've fought from the ground up, graduating with a degree in exercise science and kinesiology, then getting my master's in athletic training.

I've outworked my male counterparts time and time again to claw up the ranks from the ECHL to the AHL and, eventually, the NHL. I've been knocked down, but I've gotten up. I'm proud to be the person in charge after just four years with the Stars. I'm honored to be the one who oversees other titles like Head Physical Therapist, Head Performance Coach, and Manager of Player Rehabilitation.

I deserve to be here, and I'm not going to let some douche who doesn't know my work ethic think he has me figured out.

Thank god I don't interact with him on a day-to-day basis.

I might be smiling sweetly on the outside, but inside, I'm hoping he chokes on his breakfast. I'm trying to figure out how to sneak laxatives into his coffee. I'm eager to show him how *good* I am at my job so I can say *see? Anything boys can do, girls can do better.*

"Now that everyone is where they should be, we can start," Stuart draws out.

Instead of rolling my eyes at his insinuation, I glance around the table to see who's joining us today. This meeting has been canceled and rescheduled so many times, and the fact that it's actually happening is the biggest surprise of the year.

Our owner and governor, Kirk, is here, along with our CEO, Jared, and the Stars general manager, William.

There are so many white men in this room that I'm worried the New Balance, high-waisted khaki shorts, and white socks stocks might drop while they're all here.

Coach Saunders is across from me with his arms folded across his chest. The rest of the training staff fills the other seats, which leaves the last spot to…

Riley.

I haven't seen him since the night of the accident, and my heart skips a beat when his eyes briefly meet mine. I try to give him a smile so he knows I'm here for him, that I'm on his side, but he looks away. He scowls, and the rejection stings.

"This might be a difficult meeting for you, Riley, so we're going to go off your cues," Kirk starts. "We don't need to make any decisions today, but with the season approaching, we want to get the ball rolling."

"Ball rolling on what?" Riley scratches his jaw. His fingers drift over the beard he has now. The stubble is new, but familiarity sinks in when he shoves his glasses up his nose. "We don't need to sit here and pretend like I have a future on this team. I know it. You all know it. The idiots on social media know it. Let's not pretend I'm going to make a miraculous comeback and play on opening night. I'm miserable. I'm not who I used to be, and sitting here with you all is my idea of hell."

Riley's never been rude to the media like Liam is, but he doesn't have the charisma Maverick exudes. He's polite, answers the questions he's asked, and moves on. This attitude and snappiness are new, and I'm not sure what to make of it.

"You're always going to have a spot on this team, even if it means you're permanently on the bench," Coach Saunders says, and the consideration in his voice is something rare. He's usually barking out orders to the guys on the ice. Yelling over whistles and looking like he's going to break a whiteboard, but there's sincerity in his tone. "We're going to honor your contract. Every penny of it."

"*What?*" Riley blinks. "You're not serious."

"I'm serious. It comes with stipulations, though. You're not playing, but you're expected to do everything else that's required of players on my team. Therapy and rehabilitation—both physical and mental—which I know you've been bullshitting up to this point, are mandatory. Showing up to practice and games and traveling with the team is non-negotiable. So is voicing your opinion when I ask for feedback on lines and what isn't working with a shift. If you don't want to put in the work, that's fine. We'll go our separate ways, and you won't be on our payroll."

Riley is quiet. He stares at his hands, and I wonder what's running through his mind.

When I asked the guys if they've talked to him, they said he removed himself from their group chat. He doesn't answer their messages. He doesn't come out of his room when they stop by and visit.

I can't imagine the weight he's carrying.

To have something you love ripped out from under you is heartbreaking, but to lose a physical part of yourself too?

It's unfathomable.

"Fine," Riley finally mumbles. The relief on Coach's face is instantaneous, and I bet he was expecting more of a fight. "Whatever."

"I, um, did some research," I say, and everyone in the room—except for Riley—turns to look at me. The combined wealth around me is pushing two billion dollars, so I'm sure these men must think I'm an absolute fucking joke.

"Research?" Coach asks.

"Yeah." I clear my throat and roll my shoulders back, refusing to be intimidated. I'm a strong, capable woman who deserves her place at this table. "There's another hockey player who lost his leg via amputation after going into cardiac arrest during a game. He's able to skate today. It's not the same level of intensity required of NHL players, but—"

"Thank you, Laura, for your insight," Stuart says. "But it's pointless. You know we shouldn't be worrying about skating right now. We need to focus on a long-term rehabilitation plan, which—"

A noise startles me. I knock my water bottle over, and the sound echoes in the quiet room. When I turn, I notice Riley's palm splayed out on the table.

"She wasn't finished speaking," Riley says, deathly low. The look in his eye is murderous. A shiver races up my spine when he curls his fingers into a fist. My cheeks turn bright red when he stares at my boss and tilts his head to the side. "And her name is Lexi. L-e-x-i. That's not difficult, is it? Treat her with respect and get it right, or I'm leaving."

Holy *shit*.

I think I need to get my head checked, because that outburst was the hottest display of emotion I've ever seen in my goddamn life.

"Of course." Stuart reaches for the papers in front of him. He shuffles them, and he might be close to exploding. Or firing me. "My apologies."

"Better. We'll work on it." Riley leans back in his chair and looks my way. His gaze is soft, but his attention is intense. Overwhelming, like I'm the only one in the room. I don't know why I'm suddenly nervous, but I feel like I can't *not* be. "What were you saying?"

"Right." I reach into my purse and pull out the file I've been working on the last few weeks. The research and interviews I've done have consumed me, and while I'm shocked we're sitting here having this meeting at all, I'm so glad we are. "Like I mentioned, skating again is a real possibility. It's going to take time. The therapy Coach mentioned is one of the components, but there will be additional training as well. Add in relearning how to walk with a new piece of machinery you're not familiar with, and you're going to need to put in hours of work. And I mean *work*, which includes giving your best effort and not stopping when you want to quit."

I pause for a breath, surprised when no one interrupts me.

They're normally eager to throw out ideas they think are better than mine and talk over me, but Riley must've gotten his message across.

The romance books I read are right: having a guy turn a little unhinged and defend your honor is sexy as hell.

"We're going to need a promise from you that you're going to show up. Your performance doesn't have to be great. It just has to be something," I say.

Riley draws in a breath. His bottom lip quivers before he drops his eyes to the table. When he pushes his glasses up his nose again, I see faded cuts on the back of his hands and the marks near his wrist that are turning to scars.

God.

I want to hug him.

We're not best friends but we are *friends*. After spending eight months together year after year, and seeing the reminder of what happened to him while hardly anyone else glances his way, makes me want to burn the world down.

"Do you really think you could do that?" Riley asks.

I nod. "I do. But only if you're willing to meet us halfway."

"What—" He exhales slowly. "Can you give me an idea of what this plan would look like? If it's even obtainable."

"Of course." I open my folder and nudge a stack of papers his way. I skipped a dinner date with the girls two nights ago to put this together, and I'm glad I did. I love my friends to death, but seeing the hope in his eyes makes a version of happiness I've never experienced before race through me. "That's a list of exercises you'd start with, and we'd build from there. I consulted with an occupational therapist as well as your prosthetist, and I think with a dedicated leader who believes in you and has knowledge of your situation, you *will* skate again."

"Max," Stuart clips, and our Manager of Player Rehabilitation sits up. "Take a look at this and see if it makes sense. If it does, I want you to be at the helm of Mitchell's recovery. We'll be the league leaders in rehab. Other teams will try to model their program off of ours. We could probably sell and market this—"

"Do you ever shut the fuck up?" Riley asks, and Stuart gapes at him. I do too, because I've never heard a player be so direct with someone in a position of power. Every person in charge of Riley's future is in this room, and he doesn't seem to care who he's talking to. "Is there a reason why you're planning to delegate this to Max when he had no part in designing the plan?"

"That's what we pay him to do. It's literally in his job description. It's more labor-intensive than stretching quadriceps when a player has a cramp during a game," Stuart answers. "He's who I trust."

I hate the shame that runs through me with his condescending tone.

I'm so used to defending my job to people.

They hear *athletic trainer* and diminish what I do to only handing out Band-Aids. They ask if I've slept with anyone on the team, if I've found a good use for the stretching tables we have in the training room, and they never believe me when I say I wouldn't come within a hundred feet of a relationship with a player.

To hear someone who's supposed to be my *boss* diminish my work so blatantly makes me mad as hell.

So much for that Women in the Workplace celebration we had back in August.

"He's who *you* trust?" Riley grabs his crutches and stands. He's unsteady on one leg—he's not wearing his prosthetic today—but he makes a show of leaning over the table and glancing at Stuart's lower body. "Funny. I don't see you walking around with a missing fucking leg. Until you do, *I'm* the one making decisions about who works with me. The only way I'll agree to this is if Lexi is the one in charge. It's her plan. It's her job, and she outranks everyone on your team. Do I make myself clear?"

"Yes," Kirk interjects. "Very clear, Riley. Going forward, Ms. Armstrong will lead your rehabilitation. She'll give us weekly progress reports to ensure you're sticking to your end of the agreement, and we'll uphold our end."

"Lovely." Riley looks my way again. It's less intense than before, a gentleness in his gaze. A reminder he's still in there. "You're the best of the best, Lexi. You kept our team injury-free for eighty-two games and then some. When Hudson hurt his shoulder, you had him back on the ice in four days, and he hasn't had any pain since. When Grant took a puck to the neck last year, he played again that night because of your treatment. You're qualified, and you know your stuff. I'm not interested in working with someone who isn't familiar with my body."

Familiar with his body sounds entirely too intimate for what I do, but I *am* familiar with his body.

I know he's ticklish on the back of his left leg, just above the bend of his knee. I know he prefers heating pads over ice when he's feeling stiff. I know about the scar he had on his right foot from where he injured himself when he was a kid.

I know so much about him, but looking at him now makes me think I don't know him at all.

Who could ever pretend to know what he's gone through?

"I…" I rub my hands on my jeans. I feel like I'm on fire. "I would be honored to take on this role."

"Great." Riley makes his way to the door. "Thanks for the meeting."

He leaves without saying anything else, and the tension in the room dissipates. Small conversations break out, and I'm surprised when Coach throws a crumpled piece of paper at my shoulder from across the table.

"Do you have a minute to stop by my office?" he asks.

Dread sinks like a brick in my stomach. My hands are clammy, but I give him a feeble nod. "Of course."

It's never good when Coach wants to talk to you, and I think I might be in a shitload of trouble.

TEN
LEXI

BRODY SAUNDERS WAS a phenomenal hockey player.

I've watched tapes of him skating, and I was in awe. I've never seen someone move across the ice like he did. It was like poetry in motion. Athleticism disguised as raw, unfiltered beauty, and a talent I haven't seen from anyone since.

A center and former number one draft pick who left Boston College after his freshman year, he led his team to two Stanley Cup championships in three years. He was the league's point leader for five consecutive seasons and on his way to being one of the greatest of all time before a freak injury sidelined him.

I read about what happened: the way his teammates' blade sliced the skin above his knee and the surgeries that followed. How poorly his rehabilitation was handled. The training staff rushed to get him back on in the lineup to salvage their season, and he wasn't the same player when he returned.

Forced to retire prematurely because of lingering pain and a blow to his ego, he slid into a leadership role with ease. After bouncing around between associate and assistant coaching gigs, he became the head coach for the Stars before I joined the team, and I know he's responsible for a lot of their success.

Coach is rough around the edges. He's sarcastic with a dry sense of humor, blunt, and not afraid to hurt your feelings. The only time I see him smile is when he's talking about his daughter, Olivia, who just turned twelve.

I've always liked the guy and his take-no-shit attitude, but his presence is intimidating. At six-six with dark hair and dark eyes, if someone told me he was a serial killer, I'd believe them.

"Sit." He closes the door and walks around his desk. I comply immediately, dropping into the chair and tapping my foot. "What's wrong?"

"Nothing's wrong."

"You're fidgeting."

"I'm not fidgeting."

"So, you're not wringing your hands together and bouncing your leg?" He lifts his chin at my clasped palms. A smirk curls on his mouth. "My mistake."

"Sorry." I put my hands at my sides and offer him a sheepish smile. "You and I never talk one-on-one, and I'm nervous. Blame my daddy issues."

A surprising noise that sounds like a laugh comes out of him. "I'm, what? Six years older than you?"

"Can't say I spend my days looking at your Wikipedia page, Coach. Do you spend your time looking *me* up?"

A full laugh comes next, and I relax. "You know I don't sugarcoat things."

"You definitely don't."

"I want you to offer me the same courtesy."

"That sounds ominous."

"Do you really think you can get Riley to skate again?"

"Yes," I say without hesitation. "Could he play in hockey competitively again? Maybe, but I don't want to promise anything."

"He hasn't been doing well since the accident."

"Well, obviously. His world has been upended."

"I mean mentally." Coach pauses. "His mom mentioned he expressed numerous times about wanting to…" He trails off and clears his throat. "Not be here anymore."

"Here, like, in DC? He requested a trade?"

"No. Alive."

I grip the arm of the chair and inhale sharply.

Mental health has always been a controversial topic in professional sports, especially with male athletes. In recent years, more and more players have been open about the struggles they face off the ice: depression. OCD. Suicidal thoughts.

Social media doesn't help. I see the comments posted on the Stars' official accounts after a loss. Some of the messages are horrific. They're things I could never imagine saying to anyone, and they make me sick.

I don't want to think about the unread messages the players might have sitting in their inboxes.

I've always known Riley to be one of the happiest guys on the team. He's always smiling. Always joking with everyone. He loves kids, loves to volunteer, and I've *never* seen him get mad at anyone.

Before today, I guess.

To hear he's struggling so deeply breaks my heart. It makes me want to burst into tears, because I want to help. I want to make him laugh. I want to make him smile again, and I'll do anything to help ease the pain he's carrying.

"Thank you for telling me," I finally say.

"You're going to be working with him in a close capacity. I wanted you to be aware. I don't think he's having those thoughts anymore, but it's important to me you have all the information."

"I'm going to do my absolute best to work with him physically, but I don't want there to be any unrealistic expectations.

It's going to be an uphill battle. The odds are going to be stacked against him."

"Lexi, the fact that he showed up to our meeting today blows all my expectations out of the water. If he skates again, great. I just want him—" Coach stops to fix the picture frame on his desk. His phone lights up, and he glances at it briefly before turning it face down. "Here. With us."

"So do I. It's going to be slow at first. We're not going to see a lot of improvements right off the bat. Based on his lack of balance with his crutches while only using his newly dominant leg, it's obvious he hasn't been doing any of his rehabilitation exercises. But we'll get there," I say.

"I know you know this, but don't—"

"Rush him. I won't. We're going to go at his pace, not mine."

Coach tosses me an appreciative glance. "I have a meeting with Kirk in a few. We haven't released an official press statement about Riley's future with the team yet, but the media outlets are hounding us. That's the plan for this afternoon."

"Smart. I'll work on a detailed long-term recovery plan and send it your way."

"I don't trust anyone else with this undertaking, Armstrong."

"You aren't Team Stuart?"

"I want to punch that guy in the fucking face. He went to college with one of the alternate governor's sons, so it's above my pay grade, but I swear to god if any of my players have a single complaint about him, he's gone. That includes you."

I smile, feeling appreciated. "Between us, I also want to punch him in the face."

"Glad we're on the same page." Coach looks at me. "Get our boy back, yeah?"

"I'll do my best," I say, his ask making my soul ache.

We exchange goodbyes and I take a deep breath when I step out of the arena and into the late-morning sun. That meeting was emotionally charged, and I need a second to decompress.

When I look to my left, I spot Riley leaning against the wheelchair ramp leading to a security checkpoint. He's staring at his phone. His shoulders are curling in, and I make a split-second decision.

"Hey," I call out. He jerks his head up. His eyes meet mine, and when he doesn't scowl, I take it as an invitation to walk over. "What's up?"

"Waiting for an Uber," he says. "Hopefully I won't get in another accident and almost die."

"Glad to see you have some humor left in you." I point to my black Audi across the street. "I can drive you."

"I'm fine."

"That wasn't really a suggestion. It'll give us a few minutes to talk about your rehab sessions we're starting on Monday. Do you want to walk, or should I pull the car around?"

"I can walk." Riley glowers at the road, and I'm adding *stubborn* to the list of his new personality traits. "You don't need to baby me."

"I wasn't sure, given the way you acted in the conference room." I hear the click of his metal crutches following me when I start for the car. I slow my stride so I don't get too far ahead of him. "Are you going to team dinner tonight?"

"No."

"Why not?"

"Don't want to."

"Gosh. You're a peach." We reach the crosswalk, and I hit the button for the pedestrian signal. "You lost your leg but picked up a bad attitude? Working together is going to be so fun."

Riley huffs. He shakes his head and lets out a sigh. "Sorry."

"For what? Being a dick?"

"Yeah." He rubs the crutch tip into the pavement and

looks down at me. I've always felt tall standing at five-ten, but he's making me feel short. "None of this is your fault. I don't mean to project. My parents flew back to Chicago the other day, and everything's been an adjustment while I learn to fend for myself."

"It's not my fault. And it's not your fault either."

"If I had gone to Hudson's house like he asked… if I had stayed at the club later and not been such a party pooper, this wouldn't have happened."

"Maybe an asteroid is going to hit Earth tomorrow, and we're all going to die. Do you want to keep playing this game?" I ask, arching my eyebrow.

"Point taken." The crosswalk tells us it's our turn, and we move across the street. "This is the most I've talked to anyone besides my therapist or parents in months."

"Did you already forget your social skills?" I open the passenger door for him when we reach my car. "You're better than that."

"Am I?" A wince crosses his face when he lowers himself into the seat. "Not sure that's true."

"Do you want to keep these in your lap? Or should I put them in the back seat so you have more room?" I ask, gesturing to his crutches.

"The back seat is fine. Thanks."

"There are your manners." I grin and open the door behind the wheel, making sure the crutches fit across the seats. "Let's get out of here, Mitchy."

He tells me his address and I plug it in, turning out of the parking lot and heading for his apartment. Neither of us says anything, and I don't want to push him to make conversation. The last thing I want to do is build a divide between us before we even start working together.

"How's your summer been?" he finally mumbles five minutes into our drive.

"Busy, but good. I teach Pilates every morning during the

week then head to the arena for strategy meetings where we talk about what we're going to focus on for injury prevention this season."

"Those reformers are torture devices. How do people like doing that for exercise?"

"Same could be said about skating."

"You don't like to skate?" Riley turns to face me, looking horrified. "Who doesn't like to skate?"

"Women from Florida who think the idea of balancing on a single blade sounds like hell."

"But you think Pilates is fun? That's not right."

"No one asked for your opinion, Mitchy."

Out of the corner of my eye, I see him start to smile. But then he hangs his head and frowns, like he's not sure he's allowed to be happy.

"I haven't talked to the guys since the accident," he tells me.

"Why not?" I ask, hoping it doesn't come off accusatory.

"I don't know. I don't want them to feel like they have to do something for me. There's nothing they can do."

"They're your friends, Riley. There are plenty of things they can do."

"The last thing I want is for them to start pitying me."

"Maybe if you told them that, they'd understand why you haven't been around lately."

"Too logical."

That makes me laugh, and Riley gives me another small smile.

Progress.

"I've been doing research on exercises tailored to your new body, but I want to make sure we're going down the right path," I tell him. "I've consulted some of the athletic trainers who work with Paralympic athletes, and I think we're going to get a good routine down."

"You did all of that? For me?" Riley stares at me with

wide, dark eyes. "Why would you put in so much effort for something you're not sure is going to work?"

"It's going to work. I won't let it *not* work."

"Have you always been so sure of yourself?"

"I'm a woman in a male-dominated space. I'm the only female head athletic trainer in the league, and I'm the first to hold the title. Even if I don't believe I can do it, I say I can. So, no. I haven't always been this confident, but I'm getting there."

"You should be." He drums his fingers on his thigh. "You're good at what you do."

"I wish everyone thought that way." I merge on the highway and turn on the radio. "What kind of music do you like?"

"No preference. I listen to pop music when I get—" Riley stops mid-sentence. "When I used to get to the arena."

"Pop music, huh? Never would've guessed." I smile and fiddle with the volume dial, turning up some hit that's been playing on the radio for weeks. "I had you figured as a metal fan."

"What?" He laughs loudly, and it makes me warmer than the late summer heat outside the windows. "The fuck gave you that idea?"

"I'm messing with you. I really expected classical music or something stoic. Harps, maybe?"

"It's the glasses, isn't it?"

"You're a big nerd, Mitchy. Don't hide it."

"I like—liked—to play something upbeat before puck drop. Can't really do that with Beethoven." He rubs his jaw, a smirk forming. "I do know how to play piano though."

"Shut up."

"Dead serious. I took lessons when I was younger. Almost pursued it after middle school, but then I learned how good I am—was, *fuck*—at hockey, and there was no going back." He clasps his hands together. His happiness fades away in his dejected tone. "Maybe I'll pick it back up. I'm going to have a lot of free time."

"No, you won't." I put on cruise control and keep to the right lane. I have no idea if he has any PTSD or anxiety following the accident, and the last thing I'm going to do is blaze down the highway and startle him. "We're starting physical therapy in a week, and I need you to give it your all. Every day, sometimes twice a day. Think you can handle that?"

"Do I have a choice?"

"Of course you have a choice."

Heavy silence falls between us. I tap my fingers to the beat of the song and smile at the sunshine. It takes until I exit off the highway for Riley to talk again, and when he does, his words are strained. "I hate living like this, so I want to be able to handle it. But I'm not sure I'm going to be able to."

"Of course you are, Mitchy. You have me in your corner," I say, and his gaze is cautious. Reluctantly optimistic, almost. "If there's one thing I love to do, it's prove everyone who's ever doubted me wrong. That's what you're going to do too."

ELEVEN
RILEY

I'VE WALKED through United Airlines Arena hundreds of times, but it's different today.

I'm not here for a game.

I'm not here for a team meeting.

I'm not here for a morning skate.

I'm here because I'm regaining control of what's left of my lower body, and I'm fucking terrified.

"Morning Mr. Mitchell." Darnell, one of the longtime arena custodians, waves in my direction. "Good to see you."

"Morning, sir," I answer, getting my head out of my ass.

I might be pissed off at the world, but the last thing I'm going to do is give the man who's worked for the team for three decades the cold shoulder.

I wince and maneuver down the hall with my prosthetic leg and walker. The leg isn't the final product, only a preparatory prosthesis used to help my residual limb stabilize in volume and shape, and it's uncomfortable as hell. I'm not used to the weight and the way it alters my gait, so I have to hold out hope it'll get easier to use.

I don't have much of a choice.

I knock on the door to the athletic trainer's office even

though I'm the only one in the hall. The boys are enjoying their last week before training camp starts, so they won't be around. I opened Instagram last night for the first time in months and saw photos of them in different parts of the world.

Ethan and Grant, the youngest guys on the team, rented a yacht and are sailing around the Caribbean. Hudson, Madeline, and Lucy are doing a week down in Florida at the theme parks. Maverick and Emmy are in Michigan to propose a PWHL expansion team.

I stopped scrolling after that. The idea of posting a photo from my couch while everyone else is out living their adventure-filled lives seemed depressing as hell.

"Come in!" Lexi calls out, and I push down on the handle.

"Hey." I move gingerly into her office. "Sorry I'm late."

"No worries. I'm finishing breakfast, so you let me have a few more minutes to eat." She smiles up at me from her desk, the last bite of a bagel in her hand. "Give me two seconds and I'll be ready."

"Take your time. That walk kicked my ass, and I could use a second to catch my breath."

"Wonder why it kicked your ass." Lexi wipes her hands on a napkin and tosses it in a trash can. She twirls her hair into some sort of updo, pinning it in place with a large clip. "Probably because you haven't been doing your exercises, right?"

"Is this how working with you is going to go? You're going to keep calling me out?"

"Yup. Tough love, Mitchy. Do you want me to kiss your ass?"

I blush and dip my chin.

There are a lot of things I'd like Lexi to do to me—with me and for me too—and none of them are appropriate for the workplace.

I've had a crush on her for goddamn years, but I guess I need to start getting over my attraction to her.

We're going to be in close quarters together. She's going to see me when I'm vulnerable and incapable of performing in certain areas of my training, and I've always hated failing.

And failing in front of a beautiful girl?

No fucking thanks.

Plus, from what I've overheard from her conversations with friends, she's not someone who's interested in relationships.

She likes physical intimacy, not emotional attachment, and I still haven't figured out how the hell I'd even navigate that with the current state of my body.

Women in the past have used all sorts of phrases to describe me: *cute*. *Sexy*, but in a nerdy way. *Hot as hell* when I slide a blindfold over their eyes. *The man of their dreams* when I kiss their wrists, untying them from the ropes I like to use to keep them still while I eat them out.

I wonder what they'd say now.

"No. I don't need you to kiss my ass." I shove away every thought I've ever had about Lexi and lock them in a box where I won't be able to find them. Platonic only. I will not dream about the curve of her ass or how much I like her long legs. "But thanks for the offer."

"Good." She pops to her feet with more energy than I'd expect from someone at nine in the morning. "Don't get comfortable. We're going to the training room." Her eyes flick to my sweatpants. "I hope you brought shorts."

"I didn't. I, ah, didn't want people to stare at me."

"I get it, Riley, but it's just me. I'm not going to stare. This is my job. I'm going to look at you like I'd look at any of the other guys in the locker room. You're built a little differently now, and it's no big deal."

"There are a lot of marks on my body." I follow her through the door to the brightly lit space full of treatment tables and exercise equipment like bands and stability balls.

"And I'm not talking about a bruise on my hamstring you've seen after a game."

"Can't wait." She smiles and pats one of the tables. "What are you wearing under your sweatpants?"

"Uh. Briefs?"

"Perfect. Strip, Mitchell."

The room is suddenly a thousand degrees.

She's seen me in less than my briefs before, including a small towel draped over my ass while she worked on a cramp in my calf before game four of the Stanley Cup finals. I know it's my own fault for not wearing what she asked me to—clothing that wouldn't restrict my mobility—but my cheeks still burn when I move my walker to the side and hook my thumbs in the waistband of my pants.

What if there's a huge hole in the crotch? What if I accidentally put on the joke underwear Maverick got me last year that has hot sauce bottles all over the back with the words *smack my ass* across my dick?

Lexi doesn't watch me undress. She turns her attention to a stack of foam rollers and hums softly as she sorts through the various lengths, grabs one, and tucks it under her arm.

I shove the sweatpants down my thighs and exhale a sigh of relief when I find a pair of black briefs without any suggestive innuendos.

Thank fuck.

"Definitely going to wear shorts next time." I grunt and step out of the sweatpants. "You could also make the room cooler."

"It's sixty-seven degrees." Lexi walks over in her black pants and long-sleeved Stars shirt. "It's comfortable, and if I put it any lower, the maintenance staff will be on my ass about electric bills."

"How often are we going to be doing these sessions?"

"Monday through Friday and twice a day. You'll have

weekends off, and we're going to have to alter the schedule when the regular season starts." She gestures at my right leg. "Could you take off your prosthetic for me?"

"Isn't the point of these sessions to figure out how to move with it on?"

"It would be, if you had been following your outpatient exercises for the last two months. Because you haven't, we're starting at square one."

"Right," I grit out as embarrassment races up my spine. I sit on the edge of the table and slowly take off my prosthetic. She watches this time, and when I'm finished, she leans it against the wall for me. "Now what?"

"I'm going to run you through a couple of movements to learn the range of motion in your amputated leg. When is your final prosthetic appointment?"

"In a month."

"Good. That gives us time to catch up. Lie back, please."

I scoot my ass back until I can lie all the way down, sighing when my body relaxes. This is familiar. I've been here, in this exact position, dozens of times. I've spent hours on this table stretching, and I try to tell myself this is just another game day morning.

"What's the most serious injury you've worked on?" I ask.

Small talk was part of our routine before, and I'm trying to get my mind back to that place.

It's how I learned she's an only child who hates mushrooms. Where I discovered she likes to read under three fluffy blankets, and she always has to wear a pair of socks. She'll drink a hot coffee even when it's pushing a hundred degrees outside, and she doesn't like scary movies.

I've shared parts of myself with her, telling her about playing both lacrosse and hockey in high school and the two-hour line I waited in to meet my favorite author when they came to town.

"Besides this? When I was in the ECHL, a guy tore his ACL. That was a hard rehab because he was stubborn as hell. I'm learning you two might have that in common."

"He sounds like a delight."

"He was frustrated. I'm sure you can relate."

"Yeah." I adjust my glasses and stare at the fluorescent lights above me. "Guess I can."

"The first exercise we're going to do focuses on moving your residual limb. Can you bring it off the table and lift it in the air? *Good*," Lexi says. I hope she can't see the way I'm wincing or the sweat on my hairline. "And lower it for me? Perfect, Riley."

"How many times?"

"What's your favorite number?"

"Zero."

"Nice try." She laughs. "Let's do ten reps."

"Goddammit."

"Come on, Mitchy. You can do it."

I'm not used to being on the receiving end of praise that doesn't stem from how I'm playing on the ice or how fast I am with the puck, but I like it. I like the way it dips low in my stomach then moves up and across my shoulders. How it lights me up and makes me feel invincible, if only for a second. It's how I'm able to focus, how I'm able to blow out a breath as I count each rep, and I'm proud I don't yell out while my body screams in pain.

You can do it.

For her, I'm going to try my damn best.

When we finish the first exercise, we go into hip movements and something Lexi calls a pelvic tilt. She works on my hip flexor and bursts out laughing again when I mumble a string of curses as she pushes down on my amputated leg.

It hurts like fucking *hell*, but under the pain, there's something else: thoughts that I may be able to do this.

We stop for a ten-minute break, and I'm grateful when she brings over a bottle of water. I chug the fluids down in three gulps and wipe my forehead with the back of my hand, already utterly fucking exhausted.

I've been lucky not to have any major injuries throughout my career. I'm glad I've kept my body healthy, because I can tell these sessions aren't going to be a walk in the park.

And Lexi?

There's a gleam in her eye. A spark of excitement I'm desperate to hold close to my chest.

It's the first time in a long time I've been anything other than miserable and pissed off, and I don't know how to react.

"This is humbling." I toss the empty bottle in the trash and groan. "I'm getting my ass kicked."

"It's going to take some time for things to not feel difficult. When we're not working on your rehab, you'll be with the conditioning coaches to rebuild your upper body strength. You're going to be a totally different guy by Christmas."

"You're going to turn me into the Hulk, aren't you?"

"I'm going to try my best."

"Can't wait." My phone buzzes on the table. My agent's name scrolls across the screen, and I push myself up on an elbow. "Do you mind if I take this?"

"Of course not." Lexi flashes me a pretty smile. "We'll start back up when you're finished."

"Thanks." I slide my thumb across the screen. "Marcus. You finally tracked me down."

"Only took me fucking weeks," he says on the other end of the line. "Did you block my number?"

"No." I adjust my position so I can lean against the wall behind me. "Okay. Yes, I did. But only because I wasn't ready to talk."

"Are you ready now?"

"I guess."

"Good, because I just had a nice chat with Brody fucking Saunders who told me he's leaving you on the Stars' payroll? That would've been nice to know," Marcus says, and I can't help but smile.

He played years before I came into the league, but he's always been a businessman. After he won the Cup and became the record holder for most points by a Black player in NHL history, surpassing the great Jarome Iginla, Marcus retired. He said he was ready to move on to the next thing in life, which was helping young athletes earn the money they're worth.

He's been a shark, pushing the Stars for a contract extension and making sure I'm getting paid like my veteran teammates. I'm not the best skater or scorer on the team—those titles belong to Maverick—but I'm damn good at what I do. On any other squad, I'd be a top priority. The go-to guy. But I'm happy here.

Or, I guess I was.

I don't know what the hell I am now.

"It's contingent on a few things." I say.

"Like?"

"Physical therapy. Rehabilitation. I'm working with Lexi Armstrong. She's—"

"I know who she is."

"You do?" I frown. "How?"

"I know things, Mitchell. Things that would blow your mind. Is she there with you right now?"

"Yeah."

"Put her on for me."

I look at Lexi. "My agent wants to talk to you."

"*Me?*" She points at her chest. "Why?"

"I'm not sure, but if there's one thing I've learned about Marcus, it's that he doesn't like to be told no."

"We have something in common then. A mutual bond." There's not a lick of apprehension in Lexi's eye when she takes the phone from me and presses it against her ear. She might be a goddamn superhero. "Hello?"

After a few seconds, Lexi is laughing. She's nodding along, humming in agreement about something I can't hear, and looking over at me. When she hangs up, she gives me a wide grin.

"I like him."

"Most people do," I say.

"He wants you to call him tomorrow. He also asked if I was making you suffer, and when I said I was, he told me he didn't want to take up my time."

"Asshole," I mumble. "But I love him."

"And he loves you, which is why you're going to call him." Lexi taps my thigh. "Sit all the way up, please. And put your hands behind you."

"At least buy me dinner first, Lex."

"Oh, Mitchy." She grins. "Don't tell the others, but you're my favorite."

We go through another round of exercises. I cringe at the hip extensions and almost cry at the next set of leg lifts. Lexi doesn't make any comments about my lack of flexibility or how *hard* all of this is for me, and I'm fucking grateful when she calls time an hour and a half later.

"How are you feeling?" she asks.

"You're a hard-ass." I take off my glasses and grab the towel she hands me, wiping my face. "I'm going to be sore for days. I didn't know my hips had so many muscles."

"You're going to be even more sore when I tell you we're doing the same thing tomorrow." She sits on a stool and scoots across the floor so she's close to the table. "Have you always worn glasses?"

"It used to be only at night when I was getting ready for bed. I get so much sweat in my eyes during games, lately I started switching my contacts out for glasses when I'm not on the ice. It's a comfort thing."

"I like them." Lexi smiles, and it's her turn for her phone to chime. She pulls it out of her pocket, reads something, and rolls her eyes. "Sorry."

"Everything okay?"

"Yeah. Just someone on Tinder canceling our meet-up tonight. He said his girlfriend found out about his account, and he can't make it."

She snorts and tosses her phone on the table to my left. The screen lights up with another notification. I sneak a glance at the lock screen and smile at the photo of her and her girlfriends on the ice after our Stanley Cup win, streamers around their shoulders and confetti in their hair.

God.

She's beautiful.

This is going to be harder than I thought.

"We're pieces of work," I offer.

"Amen to that. Let's not talk about my abysmal personal life. Did Coach tell you about the first preseason game and what they're going to do for you?"

I stiffen. I haven't talked to Coach since our meeting last week, and I have no clue what's going on. "No. Why?"

"The team wants to recognize you with a ceremonial puck drop."

"A *puck drop?*" I throw my towel at the wall and scowl. "Like I'm some kind of hero?"

"I told them I didn't think you'd be onboard with it, but no one listened." Lexi moves the foam roller we've been using out from under my hamstring. "I tried."

"What happens if I don't do it?"

"Coach said, and I quote, 'I will drag him by his hair until he's on the ice.' Don't think you have much of a choice."

"Fine." I sigh and stretch my arms above my head. My shoulders hurt. My neck does too. "I'll do it, but I'm not going to be happy about it. I hate attention. And I hate people looking at me differently these days."

"You play in front of twenty thousand fans every night."

"Played."

"Should be a good game," she says, ignoring the correction. "We're going against Emmy's team."

"Is there anything else we need to do today?" I ask. Hearing about the upcoming season isn't bringing me the joy it usually does. I don't want to sit here and talk about the team's schedule. "Or can I go home and soak in the bath for two hours?"

"You can soak." Lexi is careful when she grabs my prosthetic and brings it over to me. "You need to make sure you're changing the position of your hips often. And no sitting in chairs for long periods of time. Prop up your residual limb. Got it?"

"Yes ma'am."

She watches me put on my leg, and I'm aware of her attention. She lobs a handful of questions my way and furiously jots down notes on her clipboard. It makes it hard to focus, but I manage to get through the assembly quicker than I did earlier this morning.

"Are you taking an Uber home?" she asks.

"Yeah. I don't feel comfortable driving."

"Because of the accident?"

"Because I'll have to use my left foot, and the backwardness of it all throws me off."

"If you ever want some company when you try to tackle getting behind the wheel again, I'm happy to be a passenger."

"Thanks, Lex." I pull on my sweatpants and reach for my walker. "This wasn't completely horrible."

"I'm honored. That's a nice compliment from the guy who didn't want to see me when he walked in here."

I huff out a chuckle. "Guess things change. See you tomorrow?"

"And the day after that, and the day after that. You're going to be sick of me soon, Mitchy." Lexi drops her elbow to the table and cradles her chin in her hand. A smirk curls on the edge of her mouth, and her eyes twinkle. "Think you can handle it?"

"Yeah," I say, and for the first time in months, I might actually believe it.

TWELVE
RILEY

COACH
Don't make me kick your ass for not showing up to the game tonight.

I'm counting on you, Mitchell.

ME
I said I'd be there.

COACH
You also said you'd meet up with me and Marcus on Monday, and you didn't. Same with the first day of training camp.

ME
I was tired.

COACH
I'm tired every fucking day of my life.

ME
It must be exhausting to be so annoying.

COACH

> Watch the attitude.

> I'm a persistent motherfucker. Don't test me.

I LOOK up at the sign welcoming everyone to tonight's preseason opener at the arena and pull on the sleeve of the jersey I was asked to wear. Fans are filing inside, some holding homemade signs and others decked out in Stanley Cup champions gear from head to toe. I'm sure the boys are on the ice warming up, and this will be my first time seeing them since the night of the accident.

I'm nervous as hell to be around them.

What if they forgot about me?

Even worse, what if they hate me because I pulled away from them?

I rub a hand over my chest, startled when my phone buzzes in my pocket. I maneuver over to an alcove away from passing people so I can have some privacy and lean my crutches against the brick wall. I still need them to feel comfortable on my feet, and I can't wait to be rid of them.

"Dad?" I answer. "What's up?"

"Hey, son. Are you at the game?"

"Yeah." I drop my head against the bricks and sigh. "I am."

"Are you standing outside the arena and delaying going inside?"

"Do you have a camera on me?"

"No." He laughs on the other end of the line. "I did the same thing the first time I reentered society after my amputation."

"You did?"

I think of the party my mom put together to celebrate his

release from the hospital. Some of his buddies from the station came out, and so did the family he helped save. A couple neighbors stopped by, and from what I remember, we had a good time. There was laughing. Games. Drinks and good food. His friends swapped stories about Dad being an idiot, and he smiled all night.

"It took me forty-five minutes to work up the courage to come out of the kitchen and visit everyone," Dad says. "And that was after I threw up three times."

"Really? I don't remember any of that."

"I didn't let you see it. I put on a brave face on the outside, but inside, I was shitting bricks. The last thing I wanted was to be treated differently, and I was convinced everyone was going to start walking on eggshells around me. I was afraid of the awkward conversations that were bound to happen because how is a moment like that not uncomfortable?"

"What happened?" I ask. "It didn't seem awkward."

"When I walked out of the kitchen, I froze, and everyone stared. You remember Jimmy Jackson, right?"

"Yeah." I smile at the mention of the station's former chief and one of Dad's best friends. "Of course I do."

"He walked up to me, stuck out his hand, told me he'd be pissed as hell if I didn't dress up like that leg lamp from *Christmas Story* for Halloween, and that was it. It was acknowledged, and we all moved on."

"I'm worried I won't have anything in common with the guys anymore. They have skating and hockey, and I don't. Did you ever feel like that?"

"In the beginning. My goal was always to return to my job, and I eventually did, but even if I hadn't, my friends would've stuck around. I had one less limb, but I wasn't different from the guy they used to know. Your friends haven't left you, have they?"

"No. I've been the one to shut them out and do the ignoring."

"Because you're still coping with what happened, and no one is going to fault you for that. If they do, they can fuck off."

I laugh. "Thanks, Dad. I wish you and Mom were here."

"We could've been if you hadn't waited until this morning to send a text about what was happening today."

"I know. That was shitty of me. I'm sorry."

"Don't apologize for your grief, son. It's hard as hell, but you're going to make it to the other side. You know I'm here if you need anything. Questions. Complaints. Halloween costume ideas," he says. "Your mother and I are so proud of you. We've always been proud of you, and we're going to keep being proud of you."

My phone buzzes five times in rapid succession in my hand, and I know it's Coach blowing up my messages to ask where I am. "I gotta run, Dad. Well. Not literally. Can't do that yet. It's more like I'm going to limp inside with my crutches because I'm still unsteady on my feet."

"They suck, don't they? Give it a few more weeks and you'll be done with those things except for when you're not wearing your prosthetic."

"I'm thinking about installing a urinal next to the bed just so I don't have to use them in the night when I need to pee."

Dad laughs. "Shucks, Ri. You've always been damn smart."

"Love you."

"Love you too, kid. Which jersey are you wearing tonight?"

"The retro one from two seasons ago the merchandise team designed for our fifty-year anniversary. I assisted Mav on three goals the game we wore these. First time in my career doing that. Maybe this thing is lucky."

"That one's always been my favorite. Chin up, son. The finish line is closer than you think."

We exchange another round of goodbyes, and I shove my phone in my pocket, feeling less alone.

I'M SHAKING when I open the door to the Stars' locker room, and my crutches aren't helping my steadiness. I've avoided the space when I've been here for my rehab sessions, but there's no way around it tonight.

I guess it's as good a time as any to confront the reality of my future: being a spectator, not a player. Never putting on hockey pants again unless I join a beer league down the road.

I step forward and stare at my cubby.

There's no gear. No sticks, no skates. I can't find the water bottle I forgot to take home at the end of last season, and I wonder if it got tossed in the trash with my jerseys.

My last name and number are still etched across the wood, but it's only a matter of time before someone from arena operations comes in and peels the nameplate away.

With the regular season starting in fifteen days, the team officially put me on the LTIR this week. It means I'm going to be out at least ten games, even though we all know I'll never suit up in a Stars jersey again.

I get it.

It was a strategic business move by management. It lets the Stars exceed the salary cap for a new guy who will take my spot on the roster, and I check ESPN every day to see if any signings have been announced.

Free agency is done. I doubt the team will initiate a trade so early in the season, and I'm betting they'll call up someone from our AHL affiliate, the Virginia Comets. Lexi told me she hasn't heard any names being tossed around, but when it happens, I know they'll give the new guy my old space.

For as nice as everyone's been to me, I don't expect this to go on much longer. They need to move on. They need to figure out a new lineup so they can get back to winning games. Come April when the boys are making a playoff push, I'll be watching from the tunnel.

Alone.

A forgotten has-been.

I trace over the letters in my name and sigh. I'm tempted to rip the sticker off, but before I can, there's a loud noise behind me.

I whip around and find Maverick standing in the entrance to the locker room wearing his full gear. His helmet falls from his gloved hand when his eyes meet mine. He gapes at me, blinks twice, then pops his mouth open.

"Holy shit," he whispers.

"Hey," I say. "What's up?"

"What's up? What's *up*?"

Maverick charges toward me. I'm afraid he's going to yell at me for ignoring everyone and leaving the group chat. For disappearing for months and falling off the face of the earth. When he drops his gloves like he's ready for a fight on the ice, I brace myself for a swing.

No punch comes.

Instead, he's wrapping his arms around me. He's hugging me so tight, my feet come off the ground.

"Fuck," I mumble.

"Jesus Christ, man. I've been so fucking worried about you," he says.

"I'm fine." We both know I'm bullshitting him, but he doesn't call me out on it. He only hugs me harder until a sob works its way from my throat. "I'm sorry."

"I'm so glad to see you." Maverick pulls away and looks me up and down. He doesn't blink twice at my crutches. "You look—"

"Don't lie to me, Miller. I look like shit."

"I was going to say scrawny as hell. Fucking Ethan could kick your ass in arm wrestling, and that Canadian is the weakest one on the team." He grins. "Fuck, dude. The boys are behind me. They're going to—"

"Riley?" Grant yells. He drops his stick and nearly trips over his skates when he runs to me. "Is it really you?"

"It's me, G-Money."

"Thank fuck. I missed the shit out of you, Mitchy."

Familiarity grips me when the rest of the team files into the locker room. They're all there, crowding around and giving me a group hug.

Ethan kisses the top of my head and proudly shows off his new tattoo hiding under his shoulder pads: a motorcycle with a dozen hearts around it. Ryan Seymour digs through his duffle bag and pulls out the card his daughter made when I was still in the hospital, and I smile at the scribbled drawing that looks like it could be flowers.

Or eight stick figures on a stripper pole.

Even Liam gives me a hug, but as soon as he pulls away, he bites his jersey. He starts talking to himself like he does before every game and pretends it never happened.

Hudson is the last one to make his way over. He unclips his helmet and grins. "Hasn't been the same without you around, Ri."

"Took me a while to come back." I shrug. "Still not sure I want to be here, but I'm working on it."

"Don't do that." He levels me with a serious look and a frown. "Don't go dark. You can do that shit with the media and people who don't know you, but don't do it around us, okay?"

"I'm not—"

"You are. Which is fine, Riley, but we're your brothers. We want to see the messy and fucked-up parts of your life, okay? After my mom passed, I was broken. The guys on the team were the only thing that saved me. And I'm not saying you need to be saved. Just… let us be waiting with a life jacket if it starts to feel like you're drowning, okay?"

His mom was diagnosed with breast cancer, and when she died, he slipped into a trance. He didn't eat. Didn't sleep. He went through the motions of playing hockey, but he didn't really *play* hockey.

I don't want to get like that. I don't want to be so far gone I'm not recognizable. Judging by the sympathetic glances being tossed my way, I might be halfway there.

"Yeah," I say, bitterness sitting heavy on my tongue. "Okay."

"Mitchy!" Ethan yells. "I'm adding your ass back to the group chat. You missed a lot of shit."

"You haven't missed anything," Hudson says, and it's another lie. They've all moved on, and I'm sure I've missed hundreds of things like birthdays, important moments… Ethan and Grant finally aging out of their ELCs and not being forced to share a hotel room on road trips anymore. "And you don't have to join the chat again. You know these idiots talk too much. It's annoying as hell."

"Might be nice to get my mind off other things." I gesture at my leg and shrug again. "What's a few text messages?"

Hudson clasps my shoulder and smiles. "I'm really fucking glad you're back, Mitchy."

I HANG out in the tunnel while the PA announcer welcomes the crowd. I can feel the electricity all the way down here, and I know the Stanley Cup ring ceremony before the regular season opener is going to have even more energy.

The guys want a three-peat. The fans want a three-peat. It's expected at this point, and with the depth and talent on the team, they should be able to get it done even without me.

"Hey," a voice calls out, and I stop tossing the puck I'm holding. When I glance up, Lexi smiles at me.

She swapped out the clothes she was wearing earlier today during our session for a game night outfit of stretchy black pants, a polo, white sneakers, and a Stars bomber jacket.

There's a light blue ribbon tied to her long ponytail, and it matches the logo stitched on her shirt.

"Hey," I answer.

"Glad to see you can follow directions."

"Sure."

"What's wrong?"

I look out at the ice and watch my teammates line up. Grant stands next to Hudson, filling the spot where I'd be, and my chest pinches tight. "I don't want to do the puck drop."

"You've done a puck drop before."

"As an athlete smiling for a photo. Not as the one doing the puck dropping. It's usually for important people: kids battling cancer. The people who fundraise a million dollars for charity during the Marine Corps Marathon weekend. Not me, the guy with the bad attitude."

"Riley." Lexi walks over and stops in front of me. I don't like how sad she looks. I hate the wrinkles between her eyebrows. The frown lines around her mouth. "You *are* important."

"I didn't go to war." I pull off my glasses and pinch the bridge of my nose. I'm irritated. Pissed off. Sick of having all this unwanted attention on me that won't stop. "I wish everyone would quit treating me like I did something special. I didn't. I'm alive. That's it."

"Isn't that worth celebrating? People are happy you're okay." She touches my shoulder before letting go and tucking a clipboard under her arm. I see the lineups for tonight listed and narrow my eyes. "Let them have this, then you can disappear for a while."

"Why is McDavidson starting with Hudson? Seymour is the better player."

"Do you think I'm going to question Coach's lineup choices?" She snorts. "I don't want to be on the receiving end of his wrath."

"Not sure who made that decision. It wouldn't be my call."

"Look at you. Maybe you have a future in coaching."

"Doubtful." I can barely make it through a session of the summer camp we do with the local kids in August. It's too chaotic. Made up of too many moving parts, and there's no way in hell I'd survive a full sixty minutes in the pros. "Don't think it would be my jam."

"How are you feeling today?"

"Do you mean mentally or physically?"

"Either."

"That's a loaded question."

Lexi tilts her head to the side and stares at me. "We're friends, right?"

"Yeah." I nod. "We are."

"You can tell me anything. I won't judge."

"Anything, huh?"

"Yup. I mean, if you mention you make molds of your dick with lunch meat, I'll probably be concerned, but I'm sure I've heard much worse."

I burst out laughing. It's the funniest thing I've heard in weeks, and my sides ache because of it. "Fucking hell. *Lunch meat?*"

"Oh, yeah. Salami. Ham. Turkey, occasionally, and—"

It's a shame I don't have a chance to ask about the logistics behind deli meat dick construction, because the PA announcer is saying my name and inviting me to the ice.

I gulp down a deep breath.

"Hey." Lexi touches my elbow. "If you really want to get out of here, I'll sneak you out the back. I'll even find a sketchy van to make your whole experience memorable."

"Let's just get this over with."

"I'll be here when you're finished," she says.

"Could you… I don't want to take my crutches out there. Everyone is already going to be giving me sympathetic looks, and I don't want to add fuel to the fire. Will you hold them for me?"

"Of course. And take your time, Riley. I'm sure you're still getting comfortable with your new machinery, but you're looking much steadier already. Your limp is much less noticeable, and I bet you'll be off your crutches while using your prosthetic in no time."

I nod and trudge down the carpet that's been rolled out of the tunnel for me. Busting my ass in front of thousands of people sounds like my idea of hell, so I take my time. I follow the path onto the ice and past the bench where my teammates are. They give me high fives and pat my head, whooping and hollering loud enough to make me blush when they bang their sticks against the boards.

Maverick and the captain of the Baltimore Sea Crabs, Benny Fowler, smile from the end of the carpet.

"Good to see you back on the ice, Mitchell," Benny says, not letting our college rivalry from playing against each other at Michigan and Ohio State follow us to the NHL, let alone here tonight. "That light blue sweater is a fuck ton better than the ugly ass yellow one you used to wear."

"Like your red was any better." I hold the puck out in front of me. There are tons of cameras surrounding us. Too many bright lights and someone with a microphone I'm going to avoid like the fucking plague. "And I'm not back on the ice, am I? I'm on this side of the puck drop now. Big fucking whoop."

"Wow. No more Mr. Nice Guy, huh?" Maverick crouches and pivots toward the camera. Benny mimics him, and I stand between them feeling short as hell without skates on. "Always wondered what you'd be like if you were an asshole. Smile, Mitchy."

THIRTEEN
RILEY

A CAMERA FLASHES when I drop the puck on the ice. Not flipping anyone off should win me an award, and the smile I plaster on is fake as hell.

At least it gets the job done.

I exchange a handshake with both guys and give the crowd an awkward wave. I'm not used to hearing people chant my name. That kind of attention is normally reserved for players like Maverick and Ethan who enjoying showing off.

Not me, and I don't like it.

"Wow." Lexi laughs when I make it back to the tunnel. "Can't tell if you're at a hockey game or about to get a root canal."

"That was painful."

"People say the same about the dentist."

"I'd prefer the novocaine." I grimace and lean against the wall, popping my hips back so I can adjust my prosthetic. "I never want to do that again."

"No more appearances. Noted. I'll put in a word with the people in charge."

"Appreciate it."

"What are you doing after the game?"

"Going home, sitting on the couch, and being miserable. Might listen to that sad Sarah McLachlan song while I do it. Why?"

"Wow. As fun as that sounds, I have a proposition for you." Lexi fixes the collar of her jacket. "Want to grab some food? There's a diner nearby that I love. They have the best milkshakes in town."

I haven't been social with anyone since the night at the club, and what happened after makes me want to immediately say no.

But a pang of loneliness hits me square in the chest.

I've spent so many days alone. I've spent so many hours wondering how the hell I'd dive back into interacting with my friends. Doing something other than moping around sounds like a nice break from the monotony I've slipped into.

Plus, Lexi is smiling at me. She's looking at me with wide, hopeful eyes, and that damn crush of mine wins out because I like seeing her happy. I'm nodding before I can come up with an excuse and saying, "Sure. Sounds good."

"You just made my day." Her soft smile turns into a grin, and I swear I can feel it behind my ribs. It makes the whole space around us warmer and brighter, and I'm a sad, sad man, because after so many fucking days in the dark, I want to feel like that again. "I'll wait for you outside the locker room."

"Great." I lift my chin. The guys are skating to the bench after player introductions and the national anthem, and I don't want to take up too much of her time. She's important, a woman with responsibilities and people to help. "Do you need to get to your spot?"

"Shit. I do." She laughs. "I'm always antsy for our first game, even if it is the preseason."

"Really? I thought you'd have it down by now, Armstrong."

"Don't worry. I know what I'm doing, Mitchell. But even

pros are allowed to get nervous. I better go. Coach is going to give me an earful."

"Wouldn't be Coach if he's not bitching about something."

"Exactly." Lexi holds my gaze. "Tonight might be hard for you, Riley, but try to have some fun. You love this sport, and there's nothing wrong with loving it from off the ice."

I don't know why the words mean so much to me, but they do.

"I'll do my best," I say.

"That's more than enough." She walks away, only stopping to give me one last smirk over her shoulder that makes me feel less alone than I have in months. "I'll see you later, Mitchy."

THE BOYS ARE PLAYING like shit.

They're down by three, they can't find a rhythm, and the assist Hudson set up for Maverick to try to finally score ricocheted off the goal post. McDavidson, who replaced me in the starting lineup, is fucking atrocious. I'm not making the observation because I'm bitter he's on the ice and I'm not; any hockey fan with an ounce of knowledge on the sport can see he's hurting the team. I don't think the guy did any sort of conditioning during the offseason. He's getting beat across the line on every play and repeatedly asks for shorter shifts.

Coach even went with a last-ditch effort and put in Bruce Livingston, the duster who barely sees any minutes, to try bringing some energy off the bench, but he scored an own goal, and that pretty much sealed our fate with two minutes to go.

It makes me an absolute dickbag to even think it, but part of me is glad they're not having immediate success. It makes me feel like I contribute to the team, like I'm not easily replaceable. I'm sure I'll go back to being pissed off when they find their groove and start a winning streak, so I'm going to enjoy it while it lasts.

When the final horn sounds, the crowd boos. The guys hang their heads and skate off the ice, and Grant groans as he walks down the tunnel.

"We looked fucking awful out there." He unclips his helmet and scowls. "Good thing they didn't give us our rings tonight. That would've been sad."

"We'll figure it out," Hudson says, always the voice of reason. "The loss doesn't mean anything come playoff time."

"We got *smoked*, Huddy." Ethan pulls off his glove with his teeth. "A peewee team could've played better than us."

"What did you think, Mitchy?" Maverick slings an arm over my shoulder. "You probably saw shit we didn't."

"You don't want to know what I thought," I say.

"Yeah, I do. I'm captain of this team, and as much as it's going to suck learning new shifts and different lines, it's what we have to do."

"I want to know too." Coach props the door to the locker room open with his foot. "Especially if it's something we can fix early on."

"I don't know what you were thinking when you started McDavidson. Seymour is the better skater. McDavidson should be on the third line like he was last year, and Brooks should be on second." I pause for a breath. "And Ethan lost sixty percent of the face offs he should've easily won."

"Wow, Mitchy." Ethan stops at his locker and drops his stick at his feet. "That hurts."

"Sorry. Just being honest."

"Seymour's takeaways have been some of the lowest in the league," Coach says, and he motions for me to follow him. "McDavidson was top twenty in the league with blocked shots last year."

"Yeah, and he has the highest percentage of goals scored

against us when he's on the ice." I shut the door to Coach's office behind me and lean against it. I've been in pain all night, and it's a relief to alleviate some of the ache in my limb. "You have offensive weapons who can score—Miller is good for at least two goals a game. Grant is becoming more sure of himself and looked great tonight. But without me out there, you're leaving a lot of defensive work to Hayes, who can't do it all on his own when his pair is getting beaten across the line every time."

Coach sits and steeples his fingers. "You've been doing your research."

"I've been obsessed with statistics since my high school coach said I wouldn't make the first line on a college team. So, I studied the shit out of the best defenders in the league, realized it's not about fancy skating or being the best scorer, and honed in on the areas of my game that would elevate me to the next level."

"You ended up winning the Hobey Baker Award when you were at Michigan. I'd say you turned out okay."

"Yeah. I did. Can't say the same about McDavidson. I think he's used to being one of the best players on the ice at the collegiate level, and that's not translating to the big leagues yet. Offenses blow right by him."

"I'm impressed, Mitchell."

"By what? My hockey IQ? I've been playing over fifteen years, Coach. I know a few things."

"No." He unbuttons his sleeves and rolls them to his elbows, showing off a dozen tattoos. I spy his daughter's initials. A pair of skates and a design that looks like a ribbon. "This is the most you've looked alive in months. Who knew calling out shitty playing was the way to get you out of your funk?"

"Oh." I pull on the sleeve of my jersey. I might've been watching from the outside, and the boys might've lost, but it was fucking *fun* to be back around the sport I love. Seeing the guys in action gave me some motivation. It makes me want to get my ass in gear. To work hard so I can maybe skate with them again one day. "Hockey has that effect on me, I guess. It makes me happy, even when everything else in my life is shit."

"I know what it's like. The amount of times this sport has saved my ass, even after breaking my heart, is astronomical," Coach says. "Maybe this means you'll start showing up to morning skates. I remember that being part of our agreement."

"Sure. Yeah. I will."

"How are your sessions with Lexi going?"

"Don't you get a report from her?"

"I do. But I also like to hear it from you."

"She's kicking my ass," I say.

"Good. I'm proud of you, kid. You're getting there."

"Where is there, exactly?"

"Fuck if I know." Coach laughs. "Living again? Experiencing an emotion other than self-loathing? I went through it too. It's a bitch, but better days are ahead."

"Appreciate the pep talk, Coach." I turn the doorknob. "Do you need anything else from me?"

"Yeah. Speak up more. It's going to take us months to figure out a lineup that clicks. If you see a play on the ice that isn't working, I hope you'll tell me."

"I can do that."

"Glad to hear it, Mitchell. Now get your ass out of here. I have lines to fix."

I don't need to be told twice, and with a nod, I make my way into the locker room. The guys are undressing, tossing their jerseys into a pile and setting their helmets in their cubbies. Someone is blasting Kendrick Lamar, and the music gets turned down when Ethan spots me.

"Mitchy," he calls out, jumping to his feet. "I have an awkward question for you."

"No, I will not get a dick piercing to match yours," I answer, and Grant snickers. "Not my style."

"If you ever change your mind, I'll give you the name of my guy. He does good work."

"Never going to change my mind. What's up?" I ask.

"I've been looking at some photos online but, ah, I was wondering if I could—" He gives me a sheepish glance. "I've never met someone with a prosthetic leg, and I want to learn how it works. In case… I don't know. In case you need anything? In case I meet someone else who has one? Not that you aren't capable," he adds in a rush. "I'd just want to make sure I'm doing the right thing. Being an ally without being a dick, you know? Or like I'm some savior. Could I, um, see what it looks like?"

The room is silent. I'm sure some of my teammates are wondering the same thing, and this might be the best time to tackle the elephant in the room. Hudson said they're my brothers, and he's right. We've all seen each other at our highest highs and lowest lows, and if I can't be myself around them, I'm never going to want to be myself around anyone.

"Yeah." My voice is thick. This seems like an important step, and I grab a chair shoved in the corner. I set my crutches on the ground, sit down and unlace my shoe, pulling it off. "This is my right foot. It doesn't bend and flex the way my left foot does. I can't show you the rest of the leg without stripping, but—" I work the bottom of my joggers up over the metal pylon. "This is what my calf and shin look like now. Further up is my mechanical knee, a valve, and a socket, which is where my limb sits in a liner I use to protect my skin. There's also a pin that goes into the socket."

"Holy shit." Ethan sits in front of me. "That's fucking incredible."

"This isn't the final product, and I'm still learning how to use the prosthetic," I admit. "A few sessions with Lexi though, and I can already see a difference in how I'm walking and standing."

"Lexi, huh?" Maverick grins. "How's that going?"

"Good, yeah." I scratch the back of my neck. I'm not going to tell them seeing her has become the highlight of my day. They'd give me so much shit. "Management almost paired me up with one of the new members of the training staff they brought in, but I shot that shit down."

"Wonder why," Liam mumbles, but it's loud enough for all of us to hear. "Definitely isn't because of your feelings for her, is it?"

"I don't have feelings for her." I flip him off, feeling like I was out there with them for sixty minutes tonight. It's our usual post-game chirping, the locker room shit-talking I've really missed. "It's because she's the most qualified for the job."

"Looking at her ass can't hurt," Ethan says, and I kick him. "*Ow*, you fucker. It was a joke."

"Don't talk about her ass. And don't include her in any of your jokes," I warn him, then I look down at my lower body. "I'll wear shorts to morning skate tomorrow so you can see what the rest of my leg looks like."

"That would be sick. You're like a bionic superhero," Grant says.

"I don't know about that."

"Want to grab a beer with us?" Hudson offers. "We're going to head to Johnny's Place for a round."

"Water for me," Maverick says. "I'm back on my no-drinking plan."

"Because the season is starting?" Ethan scoffs. "Weak. You used to be a party boy, Miller."

"And now I'm in future dad mode. Emmy is trying to get pregnant, and imagining her carrying my baby is the hottest thing in the fucking world. It means giving up alcohol, and

I'm glad to do it." Maverick's attention flicks over to me. "What do you say, Mitchy?"

"Thanks for the invite, but I told Lexi I'd get some food with her." I roll my pant leg down and stand. "I should get going."

"Oooooh, Mitchy and Lexi, sitting in a tree," Grant sings, and I wish I had a glove to throw at him. "First comes food, then comes—"

"I'm leaving. Congrats on the loss," I say. "Glad to know you all suck without me."

"Wow. Way to kick us when we're down, Ri." Ethan clutches his chest. "Thanks for letting me see your leg!"

"Yeah, yeah." My fingers fold around the door handle, and I fight back a grin. "It's good to see you assholes again."

FOURTEEN
LEXI

RILEY and I settle into a booth at the back of the diner after a short drive from the arena. We made small talk on the way over, casual conversation about my Pilates class tomorrow morning and what shows he's been watching.

The restaurant is empty, but Riley still put on a baseball hat before we walked inside in an attempt to not to be recognized. Standing at six-two and wearing a jersey with his name stitched across the back makes it almost impossible to hide, but I didn't put up a fight when he took the side of the table that keeps him from facing the door.

"These food options are going to give me a heart attack." He scans the plastic menu and flips it over, snorting when he finds the sandwich offerings. "A five-cheese grilled cheese? Christ. Hello, high cholesterol."

"Hey. I'm not here for a long time, so I'm going to eat the foods that make me happy. That includes a massive grilled cheese and a side of fries that are better than any orgasm I've ever had. You know what they say: fries over guys."

"You have my attention." Riley looks up at me. "Maybe the wrong people have been trying to make you come."

"Maybe." I bite my bottom lip and smile. This feels a lot

like flirting, and I'm tempted to jokingly ask if he can do better. "And wait until you taste the milkshakes. They're nirvana."

"I've always been a fan of things that are sweet," he says, and I swear his eyes flick down my body. "Why do you think I head for the dessert table first at team dinners? The salad can wait."

"But you're over here complaining about grilled cheese?" I laugh. "Make it make sense, Mitchy."

"It's different, Armstrong." He leans back and stretches out his legs under the table. His knee knocks against mine, and he adjusts his position so we're not touching. I kind of liked it when we were. "The game sucked tonight, huh?"

"It wasn't the best performance, but the wins will come. It's going to take some time." I study him. "How are you doing? I'm sure it wasn't easy to watch the guys play and not be out there with them."

"It sucks, but what can I do? This is my life now. It's not like I'm going to heal up and join them anytime soon. I have to get used to all of this at some point, no matter how badly it's going to hurt to watch them succeed without me."

"Have you been doing the exercises I gave you to do at home? The extra focus is going to help speed up your recovery."

We're late into September, and I've been kicking his ass during our rehabilitation sessions. For two hours a day, five days a week over the last three weeks, I have him on the trainer's table, running through grueling exercise after grueling exercise.

There's been progress in some of his movements; his hip flexors and abductors are more flexible. His balance is better. He doesn't rely on any assistive devices when he's moving around with his prosthetic on anymore, but his residual limb is still weak. His core muscles aren't what they used to be, and

I'm afraid he's skipping the training he's supposed to do when he's alone.

"No." Riley taps the table. "I'm tired when I get home from the arena after working with you and the strength and conditioning coaches, and…" He trails off, lifting his shoulder in a shrug. "Sometimes I wonder what's the point?"

"You're doing a lot right now physically. Being tired is perfectly normal." I clear my throat, switching gears. We don't need to linger on the things he's not doing right. "Let's talk about something else. Tell me about your family. You're an only child, right?"

"Wow. Diving into the personal shit, huh?"

"I don't have a filter and I'm curious."

"Don't be that curious. I'm not special. I grew up outside Chicago and went to Michigan to play hockey."

"I love Chicago. I've done the marathon twice. It's a nice city."

"A marathon and Pilates? Do you only like sports that kick your ass? Have you tried bowling? Table tennis?"

"They make me feel invincible, and I want to be ready to fight the patriarchy if society collapses." I pause to give my order to the server. Riley puts his in too, and I grin when he asks for the grilled cheese with extra fries. "It's also fun to be better than men at things. Running and Pilates put everyone on an even playing field."

"I don't know about that. You'd kick my ass in a marathon. Even pre-injury. I suck at running."

"Isn't skating just running with blades on your feet? Your stamina is through the roof, which would make you good at running."

"I have great stamina," Riley says, and that *has* to be flirting. "Running is higher impact than skating. The blades absorb some of the momentum and force we're putting on our bodies, and there's not as much stress on your joints. I glide with my skates. Can't do that while running. You have to take each step."

"Skating takes a lot of skill. Balance, stability. I look like a giraffe learning to walk when I put on skates."

"You want to talk about balance and stability? Your Pilates classes are hell. Actual hell. I think my soul leaves my body when you make us get in some of those positions. Who knew women in athleisure wear were strong enough to take over the world?"

"So, you don't want to come to the group class I'm doing with the team the first week of November?" I tease.

"I didn't say that." Riley rubs a palm over his jaw. "It's humbling. I'd like to be included even if I complain."

"You're welcome anytime. Even if you want to sit and watch."

"Have you always been athletic?"

"Yeah. They've always been my happy place. I was a cheerleader and also played on the high school basketball team. When I went to college, I fell in love with hockey. There's something poetic about a sport so brutal being so beautiful."

"Where did you go to school?" he asks. "I'm guessing nowhere in Florida. Do they even have hockey down there?"

"Besides the intramural team Grant started at FSU? No. I went to the University of Minnesota." I laugh. "It's far from where I grew up, and I wanted to spread my wings. I wanted to see what else was out there, and I ended up in the hockey capital of America. Turns out, it changed my life."

"It's a fun sport, isn't it? It's cool you like to watch it, that it's not only a job for you. And I'm glad more women are coming to games. I know Emmy is helping with that rise in viewership. A woman playing in the NHL? It's unheard of but fucking incredible."

"She definitely is," I say, proud of my best friend for breaking every glass ceiling that's tried to cage her in. "And you can't forget Amelia Green out in Denver. She's an associate coach."

"She'll be a head coach in no time."

"I hope so. It also helps that so many men are supportive. You have Maverick wearing Emmy's jersey to games and incurring a fine every night for breaking the league's dress code. Other players are repping inaugural PWHL teams." I laugh. "I can't tell you how many times I've been out somewhere and made a comment about a game that's on, only for the dude I'm with to roll his eyes and accuse me of not being a *real* fan. It's annoying."

Riley frowns. "Let me guess: they're the same ones giving you horrible orgasms."

"What gave it away?"

"It's not hard to spot toxic masculinity."

"They lose their minds when I tell them I work for a professional sports team. It's like I don't belong in your realm. Dicks only, you know? Fuck all of us who have a vagina and like to watch people get rammed into plexiglass. Guess I need to get back to the kitchen."

"You belong," he says, and the edge of fierceness nudging its way into his tone makes me smile. "Do you remember what I said in the team meeting we had? You're the best of the best at your job, and dudes who think otherwise suck. Instead of complaining about women liking things, they could open an anatomy book and figure out how to get you off."

"Thanks for the enthusiastic support and for joining the feminist cause. We're happy to have you." I reach across the table and bump my knuckles with his. "Tell me something else about you, Mitchy."

His chuckle is deep, rich, and he tosses a straw wrapper at me. "Is this a date, Armstrong?"

"God, no." I wrinkle my nose. "No offense, but I don't date."

"You don't?"

"No. It takes up too much time. There's too much effort without any return." I fold then unfold my napkin. "Consider this a light interrogation. I've spent days memorizing the shape of the mole you have on your left calf—it looks like a spade, by the way. It's only fair you tell me something scandalous about yourself."

There's a moment where his cheeks turn pink. Where he opens his mouth and closes it, shaking his head once. "I don't have anything scandalous to share."

"Darn. I was really hoping for bodies in your closet."

"Nope. No bodies," Riley says around a rush of air, and my interest is piqued. Whatever he's hiding, it's good. Some secret I'm not sure I'll ever get out of him but desperately want to. "I like to read on the couch. I've been getting into painting. I don't go out and party. I'm boring as hell, Lex."

"That's a shame."

"If you want someone cool, you'll have to hang out with Ethan. I think he has eight different pieces of jewelry he swaps out on his dick piercing."

I choke on a sip of water. "*Eight?*"

"That was back in May. He's probably reached double digits at this point. I bet he's keeping stores open with his business."

"Wow. Okay, dick piercings aside, we're not finished talking about you. Unless…" I arch an eyebrow. "Anything you want to share on that topic?"

"Nope. Sorry to disappoint."

"That's fine. I guess I'll settle on learning what superpower you wish you could have."

"Shit. Going for the jugular." He murmurs his thanks to the server when she delivers our food, reaches for a napkin, and sets it in his lap. "Being able to fly would be cool. Pausing time would also be handy. I could get so much shit done without losing any sleep. What about you?"

"Mind reading. But that could be a curse." I take a bite of

my grilled cheese and moan around the crunch of bread. *So much better than faking an orgasm.* "I have this flaw where I want to make everyone happy. If I could read their minds, I'd figure out how to do that. On the flip side, I'd probably learn things about them I don't want to know."

"It's impossible to make everyone happy."

"I know. Doesn't mean I can't try."

Riley hums and pulls his sandwich apart. "You have a good heart."

"What makes you say that?" I ask, my skin warming from the compliment. I'm used to being told I have nice boobs. A smackable ass and legs that fit around a guy's head perfectly. It's rare to hear a nice thing about something other than my body, and it's downright confusing. "My heart is just like everyone else's."

"No, it's not. I see the way you interact with guys on the team and with fans. You're patient." Deep lines bracket his mouth when he frowns. "You're patient with me, even when you shouldn't be."

"I'm patient with you because it's my job." I wince when I hear how that sounds. "What I mean is you deserve to have someone who is patient with you. As for the fans, I love kids. It makes me happy to see these young boys and girls with their families at games and having a good time. My mom and I used to go to football games together when I was growing up, and those experiences with her made me who I am today."

"Do you want kids?"

"Oh." The question surprises me. I guess it's only fair after asking him to tell me personal details about himself. "No. I don't. I like other people's children, and I'll hang out with them all day. I love to babysit Maven's kids and spend time with Lucy. I know I'll feel the same when Maverick and Emmy have a baby, but I don't want any of my own. Which goes against everything I've ever been told as a woman. I guess I'm just selfish."

"You don't strike me as someone who does what people tell her to do. That's a good thing, by the way." Riley pops a fry in his mouth. "And the last thing you are is selfish."

"What do I strike you as?"

He downs a long sip of water before answering. I'm embarrassed to admit I'm on the edge of my seat, waiting to hear what he has to say.

"Self-aware, unique, and interesting," he finally tells me.

"Interesting?" I laugh. "That's the most neutral adjective in the world. Fish are interesting. Weather is interesting. Restaurant décor is interesting. I'm not sure I want to be interesting."

"Okay. You're special. Is that better?"

"You think I'm special?"

"Of course I do," he says, and it feels like there's a fist wrapped around my lungs. It's squeezing tight, making it difficult to breathe. "You're very special, Lex."

"Well." I pick up my sandwich, taking a big bite so I can avoid replying. One nice thing from him, and I'm giddy, like I'm attention-starved. Maybe it's because it sounds more real coming from Riley. It's something authentic, something honest, and not because he wants me to get him off which is what I'm so used to hearing. "Thank you."

We continue to talk while we eat, sharing stories about our parents and our childhoods. When he mentions the time he accidentally swallowed a marble, I laugh so hard the Oreo milkshake I ordered comes out of my nose.

It's his turn to cackle when I tell him about my spring break trip to Panama City at twenty-two that ended with me drunkenly getting a seashell inked on my hip bone because I love the beach.

It's fun and it's easy and it's so *different* from the other times I've gone out with a guy recently. With them, there's always an end goal of sex. Intimacy and bedroom compatibility are at the forefront of my mind, so it's nice to just laugh. It's nice to stuff my face with delicious food and not care when Riley points at the string of cheese hanging from the corner of my mouth.

"Hang on." He leans across the table and licks his thumb. He drags his finger down my cheek then shakes his head, glee sparking behind his eyes. "There was ketchup buried under it. You have layers to your mess."

"I'm saving it for later." My tongue sneaks out and I lick away the trace of food. It's not lost on me that Riley watches me the whole time. "Thanks for being a part of the cleanup crew."

"Happy to help. This is the most fun I've had in a while," he admits, his leg knocking against mine again. I feel the jut of the metal from his prosthetic, the hard shell of the socket where his residual limb sits, but I don't make a move to pull away. "It's been… cathartic. As cathartic as good food and good company can be. Between this and hanging out with the boys… I needed it, if that makes sense."

"You've been spending a lot of time rehabbing your injury and not doing things *you* want to do. Balance is good."

"I'm still trying to figure out the things I want to do."

"Let's brainstorm." I dig in my bag and pull out a pen. I grab an unused napkin off the table and straighten the corners. "We'll call it Riley's Life List." I doodle the title at the top, adding a heart after the last word. "We can put anything on here."

"Anything?"

"Yeah. Like skinny dipping in the Potomac or having a picnic under the cherry blossoms."

He's quiet for several seconds, and I'm afraid I've overstepped. That I've read this whole situation wrong, but then he puts his hands behind his head and offers me a tentative smile.

"I want to ride on the back of Ethan's motorcycle," he starts, and I hurry to jot it down. "I want to go on a roller coaster and scream until my throat is sore. Skinny dipping in the Potomac sounds like a death sentence with the river current, but skinny dipping in general sounds like a fucking blast. I want to… eat food that's so spicy, it'll make me cry. I want to get another tattoo and… fuck. I don't know. What else? Don't make fun of me, but I'd like to have a kiss with someone that's so mind-blowing I can't think straight."

"I always knew you were a romantic. Must be all those book club meetings you guys have." I write down everything he mentions and smile. "Anything else?"

"I want to overpay for one of those carnival games at a fair. The stupid ones where you have to toss a ring on a bottle, you know? I always thought they were so gimmicky, but now, I want to give them a shot. Guess the second chance at life thing makes me want to drop money on rigged entertainment." Riley adjusts his glasses. "And I… I want to skate again. Not just a lap around the rink. I want to skate until my legs—leg—gives out. I want to feel the burn I used to feel when I pushed my body to the brink of exhaustion in a game."

"These are great." I leave space at the bottom of the napkin for him to add more if another idea comes to him. "There better be pictures of the skinny dipping when it happens."

"When you get a random picture of my ass, you'll know what it's for."

I laugh and cap the pen. "I can't wait."

"Are you going to tell me what would be on your list? Seems only fair since I just revealed some of my deepest, darkest secrets."

"Riding on a motorcycle is *not* a secret. I want to do it too, but, fine. Let's see." I tap my cheek, deep in thought about my dreams and wishes. "I'd like to open my own Pilates studio. I like where I am now, but I'd love to have full creative control to design classes for athletes and people with disabilities.

Skinny dipping sounds fun. I want to drive out to the middle of nowhere and watch a shooting star go by."

"Now who's the romantic?" Riley smirks. "I'm surprised, Ms. Independent."

"I didn't say I needed a man there with me. My best friends are better than any dude." I move my nearly empty plate away and put my elbow on the table. "I don't know. Being kissed until I can't think straight sounds nice. I've never been kissed like that before."

"I feel like you need to add *good orgasms* to your list. You're missing out on a world of fun, Lex."

"Thanks for rubbing it in my face, Mr. Satisfied." It's my turn to throw something, and he dodges out of the way from the rogue fry I lob at him. "What's it like to have never been disappointed?"

"Pretty great, actually." Riley laughs. "Fuck. My therapist is going to be proud of me. This is the most I've talked to someone in ages."

"It's because I'm so interesting, isn't it?"

There's a flash of something dark behind his gaze. His eyes turn a shade I haven't seen before, but he blinks it away before I have a chance to characterize it.

"You're a smart-ass is what you are," he says.

"Oh, I definitely am. A proud one at that."

"Thanks for the company tonight, Lexi. I wasn't in the best mood when I got to the arena, but I'm better now."

"I'm happy to help. It's a long road, Mitchy, but you're not on it alone."

"I know." Riley pulls out his wallet and drops four twenties on the table. He bats my hand away when I try to put my credit card on top of the cash. "You're a good friend."

"We're just getting started, pal." I grin at him, afraid to admit this might be the most fun I've ever had with a guy. "I'm going to be the best friend you've ever had."

FIFTEEN
LEXI

> **ME**
> Hey. Missed you at our session today.

> **RILEY**
> Got caught up with something.

> **ME**
> No worries! See you tomorrow?

> **ME**
> Missed you at our session. Again.

> **RILEY**
> Got caught up with something. Again.

> **ME**
> Now who's being the smart-ass?

> **ME**
>
> Okay, really? Three times in a row?
>
> Once, I get. Twice, shit happens. But three times? This feels intentional.
>
> I hope you're okay.

GIRLS JUST WANT TO HAVE FUN(DAMENTAL RIGHTS) AND GOOD SEX

PIPER

Are we all free for dinner tonight?

EMMY

I'm in. It'll let me gloat some more about my victory against the Stars.

ME

It was the preseason, babe. Wins and losses don't mean anything.

PIPER

Hasn't your team lost their first 5 regular season games?

MAVEN

We all know the Stars are going to kick the Sea Crabs' asses at the next matchup in December.

EMMY

Wow. What happened to hoes before bros?

ME

Loyalty to our team goes much deeper, Em. But we still love you!

MADELINE

I know Hudson plays on the Stars, but other than that, I have no emotional attachment to hockey. I'm proud of your win, Emmy, and I hope you do it again!

EMMY

That's what I'm talking about. Thank you, Mads.

MADELINE

As for dinner, I'm free tonight, but I can't stay out too late. Lucy has a field trip tomorrow, and I volunteered as a chaperone.

MAVEN

Count me in!

ME

I'm free, but I'm coming from the arena. I also can't stay out late. I'm grabbing a nightcap with a comedian whose show finishes around eleven.

PIPER

A comedian? That's new.

ME

Desperate times call for desperate measures. I'm horny, and I've hooked up with him before. I know he can deliver.

EMMY

I support it. Everyone deserves the chance to get off.

ME

I knew you were my girl, Hartwell.

"HAPPY SIX WEEKS OF INJURY REHABILITATION," I say when Riley stalks into the athletic trainer's room for our afternoon session with hunched shoulders. "I brought you something to celebrate the occasion."

His eyes drop to the doughnut I'm offering him, and he scowls. "No thanks."

"Are you sure? You mentioned how much you love desserts, and I thought it might be a nice pick-me-up."

"Positive."

"Wow. I hope you don't have a costume picked out for Halloween. You'd make a great Oscar the Grouch." I take a bite of the glazed doughnut. I didn't have time to grab a bite to eat after the lunchtime Pilates class I taught downtown, and I sigh around the pastry. "That's fine. More for me."

"Can we skip the small talk? I got my ass handed to me in the weight room, and the last place I want to be is here."

I pull back at his sharp words and try to tell myself they're not directed at me, but rather the situation. I plaster on a smile and pat the table, relieved when he sits on the edge of the leather and unties his shoes.

He might have an attitude, but I'm glad to see him after he no-showed our last three sessions. I had to come up with excuses to explain his absence to Coach, and I was afraid I wouldn't be able to pull another justification out of my ass if he skipped again.

"We're going to do static gluteals and side hip flexions today," I say. "Then we'll finish with hip extensions on your stomach. You made good progress with that exercise the last time we were together, and I want to see if you've increased your range of motion."

Riley grunts, and I'm not going to let that mean anything except reluctant acceptance. He pops off his prosthetic leg and passes it over to me, a routine starting to settle into place after weeks of working together.

"Are you experiencing any pain today?" I ask, filling the silence in the room.

"Yes."

"Do you want me to massage your residual limb?"

"No. I don't care."

"Clearly. Can you lie on your back, please?"

I get another grunt in response, and if he keeps this up, he'll have his own irritable asshole language soon. He positions himself flat on the table, arms folded across his chest with his eyes closed, and I consider it a small win.

"What do I do?" he grumbles.

"You're going to keep both legs straight, squeeze your buttocks as tightly as possible, then hold for five seconds."

"And why am I doing this?"

"Because I said so," I answer flippantly. I'm not in the mood to be challenged today, and I refuse to buy into the bitterness he's throwing my way. "We're going to do ten reps."

Riley uncurls his arms and rests them by his sides. His fingers dig into the leather, and a labored breath escapes him when he tightens his glutes.

"This fucking hurts," he grits out, and I move so I'm standing by his shoulders.

"Is it okay if I touch you?" I ask, and he gives me a curt nod. I put a hand right below his collarbone, applying the slightest bit of pressure so he can't move his upper body. "Keep your spine on the table. You're lifting your shoulders, and that's going to cause pain in your lower back."

"I don't fucking understand."

"Squeeze here." I slip my other hand under his leg, a palm flat on the hem of his gym shorts as I tap his glutes. "And don't lift this," I add, drumming my fingers against his chest.

I've worked around men throughout my career, and I'm used to athlete's bodies. I've become desensitized to the masculine parts of them when they step into the training room, noticing muscles and ligaments rather than a figure I could be attracted to.

The last thing I need is someone assuming there are sexual undertones to my job. I don't want people to think I get pleasure out of touching a nearly naked man when he's under my care, and it's a very thin line women in my field have to toe at risk of allegations about ulterior motives running rampant.

But when Riley opens his eyes and locks his gaze with mine, I realize how *intimate* this position is. It's not injury prevention stretching. I'm not diagnosing a knee or calf wound sustained on the ice that involves a quick, sterile check. I'm touching him. I'm guiding him, lifting his glutes off the table, holding him there, and easing him back into the recovery position while he lets out a soft groan.

"Feel the difference?" I ask. The skin under his gym shorts is warm, and I clear my throat in hopes it also clears the fog in my head. "There should be less pain."

"I guess. It doesn't feel like this exercise is doing anything."

"It might not be right now, but these movements are building blocks. They're necessary if you want to regain your stability and prevent any further injuries."

"Too late for that." Riley finishes his ten reps, and I pull my hands away. "What now?"

"We're going to take a minute to let your body recover in between sets."

"Don't want to do that. I want to get this over with."

He's usually tense during our sessions, but his anxiousness is next level today. Something must be bothering him, and I take a deep breath. "Okay. We'll move to hip flexions. Do you want to start with your right or left?"

Riley turns onto his left side and bends his left leg, a decision made. "Now what?"

"I want you to lift your right thigh slightly, then bring it as close to your chest as you can. After, you're going to push your leg backward as far as you can. Think of it as a pendulum."

His eyes screw shut as his right thigh lifts an inch off his left leg. When he tries to swing his residual limb forward, he falls onto his back.

"Goddammit." He yanks off his glasses and pushes the heel of his palm into his eye. "I can't fucking do it."

"Riley. It was one time. We'll try again and—"

"I don't want to try again. I'm not good at any of this. I'm tired. My entire fucking body hurts. My brain fucking hurts."

"Failing is part of the process, and—"

"I don't want to go through a process." He shoves his glasses back up his nose and rolls his hips until he's sitting up. "I don't want to do anything."

"We could—"

"No," he says, cutting me off. He reaches for his prosthetic, and I sigh, passing it over to him. "I'm done for today."

"Okay. Do you want me to get you a water?"

"I want you to give me my right leg back so I don't have to be humiliated day after day after fucking day."

I wish I fucking could, because seeing you so mad at the world hurts, I almost shout.

Anger simmers off of him when he rolls the gel liner into place and positions his limb in the socket. My heart breaks when he can't get the pieces lined up the first time, but I don't volunteer to help. What the hell kind of assistance can I offer someone who doesn't want my help? Who doesn't want to be around me?

I keep my mouth closed, disappointed when he stands and rocks his hips from side to side. He fixes his shorts and ties his shoes, heading for the door in a cloud of irritation. Starting my mornings with him have been the highlight of the last month, and I that quiet joy slips away with every step he takes.

"Have a good rest of your day," I say, not wanting to leave things like this, and he hesitates for half a second.

I wonder if he'll turn around and give me another shot, but he doesn't. He jerks down on the handle and storms out of the training room, and everything feels darker when he disappears.

I DROP into a chair at the table where my girlfriends are waiting for me and let out a groan after walking to the restaurant in the crisp October air. "I need a drink."

"What happened to starting a conversation with hello?" Emmy closes her menu and grabs the pitcher of beer in the center of the table so she can pour me a glass. "Are you afraid your comedian won't be as funny the second time around? You poor thing."

"Please don't tell me he makes jokes about the sex you have at his shows," Piper deadpans.

"That's slimy. I'll kick his ass," Maven adds.

"I haven't been to any shows, so I couldn't tell you if he did. And I'm a knockout in bed. I'm not worried about him having anything negative to say." I take a long sip of the alcohol and drop my head back. "It's been a rough day, and I feel like a complete bitch for saying that."

"This is a safe space." Madeline Galloway, Hudson's girlfriend and recent addition to our group, squeezes my arm. "You're allowed to vent and talk to us about what's going on in your life."

"Riley and I have been working together on his recovery for over a month now and…" I bite my lip. Frustration threatens to break in my voice, but I swallow it down. "It's more difficult than I thought it would be."

"Is it because you're working with an injury you're not familiar with?" Piper asks. "I'm sure that must be challenging."

"Kind of? This is the first time I've worked with an amputee, but I've done extensive research to make sure I'm handling his recovery gracefully and in the correct way. I just don't want to fail. Not because of how it'll reflect on me, but because of how much Riley wants everything to work out." I take another sip of beer and set the glass down. "I'm used to working with people who want to be there so they can get stronger, and Riley would rather be anywhere else. He's still mad at the world—and rightfully so—but he's not giving me anything to work with. He's started skipping our sessions, and an hour ago, he stormed out of the training room because he failed one exercise one time."

"Poor guy," Emmy says. "He must really be going through it."

"Have you talked to him?" Piper asks. She's always so levelheaded and pragmatic when I start to feel emotional or worked up. "Maybe he doesn't know he's acting that way."

"He knows, and he's being a dick about it. He's allowed to have a chip on his shoulder, but I thought we were getting somewhere. When we went to dinner together after the preseason opener, it seemed like he was turning over a new leaf." I rub a hand over my chest, an ache that stings like a bruise settling beneath my shirt when I think about the frustration on his face a short while ago. "Guess that's not the case."

"That must be hard," Piper says. "And I see it from both sides. You're totally valid in your frustration. This is a job you were given, and it's hard to perform your job correctly when the other person doesn't meet you halfway. I can also understand why he's reluctant to show up. Grief isn't linear. Some days are good. Some days he has the energy to give his full effort, and other days he probably struggles to get out of bed. Sounds like he's been having a string of those struggle days lately."

"We help people because it's the right thing to do," Maven says. "Even if they don't want to be helped, we have to keep showing up for them."

"He knows he's never getting back to the guy, let alone the

player, he was before his accident, so I bet he's hesitant to move forward. He's clinging to the past. If hockey was taken away from me, I don't know who the hell I'd be," Emmy says. "It's my whole identity, and I'd be lost without it."

"Some days when we're together, he'll have a good session where I'll see improvements not only in his physical capabilities, but in his morale too. He'll laugh and joke and give every ounce of effort he has. The next day, though, he's scowling and acting like he hates everything in the world," I say.

"Give him time," Emmy explains. "I've played with guys who have had their livelihood snatched out from under them because of a serious injury, and the aftermath is almost always more brutal than the original accident. Riley has to find himself again, and until he does, you're going to be in the line of fire."

"You're right." I pick up a menu and sigh. "I shouldn't be talking about this with you all. I need to respect his privacy like I would with anyone else. It was nice to vent, but can we pretend like I didn't say anything? I want him to feel comfortable around me, and gossiping behind his back was shitty and unprofessional."

"That was in no way crossing a line," Piper assures me, then pats my hand. "But it's forgotten."

We order our dinner, and conversation shifts away from me. Piper fills us in on how her offseason promotion from rinkside reporter to color commentator is going. Emmy shows off the bruise from her game last night, a mark just below her collarbone. Maven hands over her phone so we can gush over photos of her son, and Madeline, award-winning chef she is, shyly mentions the website she's going to start that will feature her favorite recipes.

The food is good. The alcohol tastes better than the glass of wine I had alone in my apartment last night, and I'm so glad to have the chance to catch up with them.

We're all busy with life and work and a hundred other

things with a higher priority like relationships and kids, and I never want to take the time I get with them for granted.

I didn't have a lot of girlfriends growing up. When I started working with my ECHL team, there were a couple wives of the players I got along with, but it never felt like a permanent thing. It was surface-level friendship, a night out here and there, but not people I could spill my guts to. The same happened in the AHL, but when I ended up in DC, lightning struck. I met Piper, and that was it.

I've gone from one best friend to four, finding the kind of support system I've always wanted. We're each other's cheerleaders. There's no competition, no jealousy. We celebrate our wins and mourn our losses together without any sort of resentment when things go right for someone else.

Men come and go. Love is fleeting, and I don't believe in romantic soulmates.

I believe in platonic ones though, and these girls are mine.

"Are you excited for your date?" Madeline asks me. "What's his name?"

"It's not technically a date. Just a hookup." I smile and switch my beer out for water. I don't want to be tipsy when I leave. "And his name is Dan. I think he lives in Boston? I can't remember. It's not important for what we're doing."

"Can I ask a personal question? I've been friends with you all for almost a year now, but I want to make sure I haven't missed something," she says.

"I'm an open book. You can ask me anything."

"You mention hooking up with guys, but nothing about relationships. Not that there's anything wrong with that," Madeline hurries to add. "I didn't date anyone for years before Hudson and I got together, so I don't mean for it to sound like I'm accusing you of missing out on something great. I'm curious *why* you don't date."

"In my twenties, I was in a relationship that didn't work out," I answer with a shrug. "It boils down to not wanting to be disappointed, and I've found that men constantly disappoint me. I've always been happier on my own, and I don't want to rely on someone else to make me happy. I like sex though. I like being able to express myself in the bedroom, and I'm a firm believer that you don't need to be in love with someone to be physically attracted to them. Maybe one day I'll settle down, but for right now, I'm having fun. And there's nothing wrong with that."

"Our girl is a free spirit." Piper loops her arm around my waist and puts her head on my shoulder. "It's going to take a special guy to tie you down."

"Men have one-night stands all the time, and they're considered kings of the world," Maven chimes in. "When women have sex with multiple people, we're considered sluts. Why? Why is there such a double standard?"

"I could write a thesis on that question," I say. "I'm convinced it comes down to the power dynamic. A lot of men have a problem with powerful women, and women who are in touch with their sexuality are powerful. It's all bullshit if you ask me."

"I love that you do what you want," Madeline says. "I respect your extracurricular activities, and I hope you're getting the best dick of your life."

That makes me giggle, and soon, we're all laughing. Emmy wipes under her eyes, and we eventually stop when a nearby table glances over at us like we've lost our minds.

"I needed this," she says. "The season is underway. Maverick and I are getting ready to spend seven and a half months apart while also trying to have a baby. Laughter is very necessary."

"Anything to report there?" Maven asks gently, and Emmy shakes her head.

"Not yet. I've never been patient a day in my life, so this is *really* testing me. I'm trusting everything will work out in the end, no matter what that looks like."

"We're here," I say. "If you ever need anything."

"I know you are, and I love you all for it."

"We need a toast before everyone gets on with their night." Piper lifts her glass, and we all follow suit. "To incredible women. To friendships. To a special love no man will ever give us."

"Cheers," I say, knocking my drink against theirs, my heart full and eternally grateful for the path my life has taken.

The guy I'm supposed to be working with doesn't want to see me, but my girls do, and that's all that matters.

SIXTEEN
RILEY

PUCK KINGS

EASY E

I can't believe we have a four-game road trip next month. Doesn't the NHL know we're the reigning champs?

SULLY

We're not the same team we were when we won the Cup.

ME

That's my fault.

MAVVY

It's not your fault. The drunk asshole who hit you is at fault.

G-MONEY

Do you have to go to trial like on SVU???? And testify????? Too bad Olivia Benson won't be there. She's hot as hell lol.

HUDDY BOY

I think you might be a little out of her age range, kid.

G-MONEY

Says who? I like older women. Maybe she likes younger guys.

SULLY

You're barely legal to drink.

G-MONEY

Okay, grandpa who is retiring in two years.

SULLY

Can we not? I haven't announced that yet. I don't need my phone getting hacked and that news leaking to the media.

MAVVY

THAT'S what you're worried about if your phone is hacked?

The photos on mine would get me in so much trouble lol. And Emmy.

HUDDY BOY

Stop. You're going to make my ears bleed.

EASY E

I'm with you, Cap. I have some nice photos of Tella on there.

SULLY

Who the fuck is Tella?

EASY E

...Donatella?

Do you all not listen to me when I talk?

SULLY

Never.

HUDDY BOY

Please don't tell me you have a file on your phone full of photos from women, Ethan.

EASY E

Uh, no, and rude of you to assume so. Donatella is my motorcycle, fuck you very much.

G-MONEY

You named your bike DONATELLA? WTF?

EASY E

One of them, yeah.

It's a Kawasaki Ninja H2R.

Ninja.

Teenage Mutant Ninja Turtles?

Leonardo, Donatello, Raphael and Michelangelo?

Except Tella is a lady <3

SULLY

I'm leaving this chat.

G-MONEY

You can't leave yet! Mitchy hasn't told us if he's going to testify and meet Olivia Benson!!!!!!!

ME

I'm meeting with my agent to talk about all of that.

MAVVY

Keep us posted.

G-MONEY

Yeah. We'll totally show up to court like Elle Woods's friends do in Legally Blonde and cheer for you!

HUDDY BOY

Do you need anything from us, Ri?

ME

A time machine would be nice so I can go back six months and not have any of this happen.

EASY E

I'd build one for you if I could.

ME

Thanks, Ethan.

MAVVY

Let us know if you need anything, Mitchy. We're here for you.

ME

I appreciate you guys.

G-MONEY

That's what friends do!

Quick. Someone make the DUN DUN sound lol.

Sully has left the chat
Easy E has added Sully to the chat

EASY E

> Leaving the chat while I'm talking about Tella? The nerve.

"I'M glad to see you back in action after your self-imposed isolation from social gatherings," Marcus says to me. "Aren't you excited to deal with the bullshit that comes with having to communicate with people?"

"Can't fucking wait," I draw out, sitting across from him in the conference room of his office building.

Marcus lives in New York full time, but he has offices in DC, Orlando, and Los Angeles. He's the busiest man in sports right now, representing players from every professional sports league in America as well as a handful of college kids, and he likes to be available when we need him.

He also hasn't dropped my ass after dodging him for months, and when he asked for this meeting, I knew I'd be a goddamn idiot to skip it.

"I'm going to keep this quick because I know you're headed to see Coach next, but I wanted you to know the District of Columbia set a trial date for the driver that hit you in June. It's scheduled to start next summer, and the DA is asking if you'll testify."

"We have to wait that long to put that scumbag away?"

"Yup. They're pursuing criminal charges because the fucker was driving without a license. It was also his third DUI."

"Jesus fucking Christ." The taste of vomit climbs up my throat, and I swallow it down. "And he was still on the fucking road?"

"He won't be after all of this is said and done." Marcus sighs. "I'm sorry, Riley. I can't imagine this is easy to hear, but I wanted you to know."

"It makes me want to visit whatever jail cell he's sitting in and beat the shit out of him. He could've killed someone."

"It's a miracle he didn't. The universe isn't finished with you, Mitchy."

I rub a hand over my chest. "We'll see about that. Thanks for telling me. Do I have to testify?"

"No. But it'll help the case if you do."

"I'll think about it." I shift in my chair, the idea of having attention on me making me uneasy. "What's this surprise you have for me? You mentioned you'd end our meeting with something good, and I hope *that* wasn't what you consider good."

"Oh." Marcus grins and taps his phone. A second later, the door to the conference room opens. I spin, and I nearly fall out of my seat when I see who's in the entryway. "It was important to me that you two reconnected, and I thought you'd feel the same."

"Lamar?" I croak, standing on shaky legs. "Holy shit."

"Riley." He smiles, and I beeline it for him, grabbing his shirt and pulling him into a hug before I can think twice. My cheeks are wet with tears, and a laugh shakes my shoulders. "I'm so glad to see you."

I've laid awake every night since the accident thinking about him. The police wouldn't give me his last name because of the ongoing investigation, and I didn't have a lot of information to go off of to track him down. The media reports didn't mention any casualties from the accident, and I've been holding out hope he's okay.

I pull away and look him up and down, relieved to see him put together, *healthy*, and without a scar in sight. I wipe my eyes with the back of my hand and hug him again, really fucking overwhelmed by the swell of emotion rattling inside my head.

"The feeling is really fucking mutual. Come sit," I say, pointing to the open chairs at the table. "You look great."

"So do you. I waited at the hospital that night to make sure you were okay." He sits next to me, and I scoot closer to him. "Your whole team was there. I've never been so scared in my life."

"Will you tell me what you remember?"

"We were driving, and you gave me money. The light turned green, and I started accelerating. Out of the corner of my eye, I saw bright headlights, and then we were airborne. We landed upside down, and I started yelling for you. You didn't answer and—" Lamar closes his eyes and takes a deep breath. "You looked dead. I got out of the car and tried to pull you out. A couple cars stopped and helped me, then I called 911 while someone did CPR."

"How did the team know to go to the hospital?" I ask. "I was the only one in the car with you."

"I found your phone. The screen was cracked, but I hit the first name at the top of your call log. Maverick was the one who answered, and I guess he told everyone else." Lamar sighs. "I would say it was the scariest night of my life, but that's selfish. It pales in comparison to what you experienced."

"I remember us flipping. I remember pain, but that's it. There's nothing there until I woke up after my surgery."

"Your surgery," he repeats, and he glances at my legs for the first time. "The doctor mentioned an amputation."

"My right leg above the knee." I drum my fingers against my prosthetic. "I guess there wasn't much of a choice."

"Are you healing okay?"

"As well as I can." I wince when I remember the way I stormed out of the training room two weeks ago. I've been back since, knocking out the exercises Lexi gives me the best I can, but our small talk has been almost nonexistent. I'm pissed at myself for taking my frustration out on her, and I know she's pissed at me too. "I'm a work in progress."

"I really thought that was it for you, man." Lamar's voice

cracks, and Marcus slides a water bottle across the table to him. "And it was all my fault."

"No. Don't fucking do that. The only person at fault was the piece of shit who hit us. You saved me. I don't think I'd be here without your help. Are *you* healing up okay?"

"I've been going to therapy. Talking to a professional helps," Lamar says.

"I don't want you to carry any of the weight from that night. I don't blame you. I've *never* blamed you. I don't know if that helps with closure or anything, but I need you to hear it."

"That means a lot, Riley."

"Did your wife have the baby?" I ask. "You said she was expecting and—"

"A girl." Lamar beams, and I'm not sure I've ever seen someone so happy. He pulls out his phone and opens his photo roll. "We named her Destiny."

"Shit." I have to wipe under my eyes again when I see him holding a newborn close to his chest. "She's beautiful."

"Looks just like her mama."

"I'd love to meet them one day," I say. "Your family."

"They'd love that. Aliyah kept telling me to reach out to you on social media but I saw you hadn't posted anything since—" He pauses. "It didn't feel right to pester you when you didn't want to be bothered."

"It wouldn't be pestering. Never. I'm so fucking glad Marcus arranged this." I look at my agent, hoping he can feel the gratefulness I'm trying to convey. "We'll have to do it again soon."

Lamar shows me some more photos of his family, and I tell him about my teammates. He asks about my parents, and when I mention my dad and I have matching prosthetics, he laughs.

"Sorry. That's not funny," he says.

"What are the odds?" I grin. "I'd love to stay and chat

more, but I need to get to the arena. Can I give you my number so we can plan to get together soon?"

"I'd love that," Lamar says, and I plug my contact information into his phone. "Take care of yourself, Riley. There's a reason you pulled through that night. Your purpose is so much bigger than you think it is."

"It's hard to remember that sometimes, but I'm trying." I stand, and we exchange another hug. "Don't be a stranger, man."

After he leaves, Marcus puts a hand on my shoulder. "You doing okay?"

"Yeah." I nod, feeling like I'm on the verge of bursting into tears again. Three times in an hour would be a new fucking record. "I can't tell you how much it means to me that you did that."

"Happy to do it. You want a ride to the arena?" he asks. "You're going to be late if you wait for an Uber."

"That would be great. I don't need Coach chewing me out. I'm sure he's going to yell at me for something else."

Marcus and I take the elevator downstairs, and I climb into his Range Rover. He turns down the radio and pulls out of the parking garage, heading for the arena.

"I want to apologize for being distant the past four months," I say. "It's taken me a long time to process what happened to me. It's selfish and shitty, and I didn't mean for you to get stuck in the crosshairs of the aftermath—especially because of how much you do for me professionally and personally. I haven't been appreciative."

"I get it, Riley. I haven't taken anything to heart, and I know you've been quiet for a reason." He glances over at me. "How are you doing?"

I stretch out my right leg, adjusting my prosthetic. "Fine."

"Let's try this again. How are you *really* doing? And don't give me that bullshit answer you think I want to hear."

"Today? I'm fine. Yesterday? I ate a pint of ice cream and didn't leave the couch."

"Not every day can be sunshine and rainbows. A lot of days suck, but you got out of bed today. That's a win," he says.

"Time to throw a fucking party."

"You're doing your rehab? And going to your therapy appointments?"

"Um." I stare out the window and shrug. "Occasionally."

"You'll work on bumping that up to frequently?" Marcus asks.

"I'll do my best."

We spend the rest of the drive talking about the first month of the season. I share my thoughts on the teams that are surprising me and the ones who have been underwhelming. Marcus doesn't mention the Stars and the rough start they've had so far in October, and I'm glad.

"We're here." Marcus pulls up in front of the players' security entrance at the arena and unlocks the doors. "Good luck. You're going to need it."

"Thanks." I laugh and lean over and shake his hand. "And thanks for having my back."

"Always. Tell Brody he's an asshole."

"With pleasure."

I climb out of the car and give Marcus a salute as he drives away. The guys had morning skate earlier today, and with no game this evening, the hallways are empty. I make a detour on my way to Coach's office, stopping at the edge of the tunnel leading out to the rink and taking a deep breath.

I stare at the surface, hating how beautiful it looks. My favorite time to skate is when the barn's just been cleaned. The ice is smooth. Glassy. There's not a single shaving to be found, and what I would fucking give to lace up and get out there.

"Pretty, isn't it?" Coach says from behind me. I hear his

heavy footsteps, and when I turn to my right, he's following my gaze. "Want to know a secret?"

"You're part robot?"

"Close. Sometimes after a game, I wait until everyone leaves. Then I'll climb up into the stands and look at the ice for an hour."

"Why?" I ask.

"Why not?" He points to the path leading to the penalty box and walks that way. "It calms me in a way nothing else does. I don't even need to be out there and it offers me comfort years of therapy can't bring me."

That's how I've felt lately, and it's why I follow him without asking another question.

The plexiglass usually up during games is down, giving us an unobstructed view. I sit next to Coach on the bench and lean forward, inhaling deeply.

"Is it crazy to say it smells like home?" I ask. "If home had a smell."

"No." Coach snorts. "That's what I think too."

We're quiet for a while. Sitting here without cheering fans, a PA announcer or thumping music is eerie, but also soothing. I can feel my mind shutting off. My breathing evens out, and I smile.

"What kind of trouble am I in?"

"None."

"I've been skipping my rehab sessions."

"I know you have. It's hysterical hearing the excuses Lexi come up with to cover for your ass."

"She's been doing that?" I ask.

"Yeah. My personal favorite is when she mentioned you were awaiting a very important package."

I bark out a laugh. "You aren't going to yell at me?"

"Nah." Coach uses his thumb to peel off a piece of stick tape from the wall. "I thought I'd try a different approach."

"I can't wait to hear what you have in mind."

"I've been where you are, Riley. I've been the guy on the bench who can't play. I've been the one to give everything I have to this sport, only to be let down. And I'll tell you what: it fucking sucks. It's the worst feeling in the world to see your teammates achieve shit without you, but then you feel like a dick for wanting them to fail. I've gone through the jealousy. The anger. The self-loathing. It never turns out well."

"What do you suggest I do instead?"

"The longer you let what happened consume you, the longer everything else in your life is going to suck. You have to mourn it. Loathe it. But then you have to learn you're so much more than this injury. So you're not 'Riley Mitchell, hockey superstar' anymore. Who gives a fuck? You're still Riley fucking Mitchell. You just happen to be injured, and that's okay." He pauses for a beat. "What would you tell your younger self if you found out you got a second chance at life?"

I blink and focus on the Stars logo at center ice.

I haven't thought of that. I've been so worried about what I can't do that I haven't bothered to consider what I *can* do, which is fucking *live*. Enjoying everything I was seconds away from losing. And *holy fuck*—I've been such a selfish bastard treating other people like shit.

"I'd tell myself to get the fuck over it. Respectfully," I finally mumble after a stretch of silence that feels like years. "The only way I can go is forward, so I might as well enjoy what I have."

"There were so many days I almost threw in the towel," Coach says. "I cut off my friends. My teammates. My family. I didn't talk to anyone for weeks."

"How did you climb out of the hole?"

"I didn't have much choice. Fate intervened. The night I finally left my apartment, I went to a bar. I got drunk, hooked up with a woman who made me feel something other than sad, then became a dad. I didn't have time to stew on what I didn't have, because I was holding a tiny, perfect human who looked at me with blue eyes, and I realized it wasn't just about me anymore. I couldn't play, but I could coach. And coaching meant stability. A paycheck to support my family and still being around the sport I loved. Why would I go back to the moments everything was so shitty for me when I had a miracle waking me up at three in the morning to give my newborn a bottle?" He smiles. "If it weren't for Olivia, I'm not sure how my life would've turned out. It's not always easy. You can't magically become undepressed, but you have to find something that makes you feel *good*."

"Wow." I glance over at him. "Are you saying I need to chug some liquor and find a pretty girl to sleep with?"

Coach snorts. "I don't care what you do, but you need to do something. You can't live like this forever, Riley."

"I know." I blow out a ragged exhale. "It's exhausting."

"And you can't let it define you. Not when you're so much more than what's under your clothes." He pinches the bridge of his nose. "That sounded stupid as hell. Pretend like I never said it."

"Nah. I think I want to make it into a shirt: *It's not what's under your clothes but what's inside that counts.*"

"Watch it," he warns.

"Thanks for this, Coach. The guys all mean well, but they don't get it."

"Of course they don't. No one does unless they've had the most important thing in their life stripped from them. Guess that means it's time for you to find a new most important thing."

"I don't know what that could be, but I'll keep that in mind."

"Good." Coach clasps my shoulder. "No one is rooting for you more than me, kid."

"I'm still going to make a shirt with your inspirational quote on it."

"I dare you. And the minute you're back to skating, I'm going to make you do laps until you hate me."

"Yeah?" I grin. "Looking forward to it."

SEVENTEEN
LEXI

I'M GOING to murder Riley Mitchell, and I won't have any remorse for my crime.

He skipped our rehab session—again—and he's not answering my texts. If this were the first time he no-showed, I'd be concerned.

Since it's the sixth time in two weeks, I'm *pissed*.

Instead of lingering in my office and trying to explain his absence to Coach, I grab my keys and phone, heading for my car in the employee lot. I pull up his address from the time I took him home and make the quick drive to his apartment, not thinking twice as I ride the elevator to the sixteenth floor and bang on his door.

"Open up, Riley." I rub my fist and stretch out my fingers after an aggressive three minutes of knocking. "Don't make me cause a scene in front of your neighbors."

There's a moment where I think he might not be home, but then I hear the click of a lock. The door slowly opens and Riley stands on the other side...

Shirtless.

The gray sweatpants he's wearing sit low on his hips. His

glasses slide down his nose, and he pushes them up with his index finger before crossing his arms over his chest.

Jesus Christ.

Riley Mitchell is *hot.*

Maybe it's because I haven't allowed myself to look at him as anything other than an injured hockey player I'm working with so I can keep my firm boundaries in place, but being here, seeing his body outside the confines of the fluorescent lights in the training room and away from the arena where we have very specific roles is like seeing him for the first time, and, *oh.*

Hell.

He's a *man.*

I'm noticing physical features I've never picked up on when we've worked together. Details I shouldn't be categorizing and appreciating like sculpted biceps and defined lines across his chest. Dark hair trailing down his stomach and disappearing inside his pants and abdominal muscles that could be cut from glass. A faded scar or two near his hips and a certainty to his posture he didn't have a month ago.

He's goddamn beautiful, so much so it feels like I've stopped breathing the longer I stare at him, and I can't believe the fucking audacity of him to hide a body like that under clothes.

"What do you want?" he asks, and my eyes snap up to meet his.

"Glad to see you're alive," I say, doing my best to swallow down the flash of lust I'm experiencing from seeing a bare-chested man. "It would've been nice of you to send a text. Or answer the sixteen I sent you this morning."

"Sorry. Overslept," he says, not appearing very sorry at all. "Do you need something?"

"Yeah, I do." I push my way into his apartment, determined. He doesn't put up a fight and closes the door behind me while letting out a heavy sigh that sounds like he's been carrying a weight on his shoulders for years. "What the hell, dude? I try to be respectful of your time, but you've been nothing but inconsiderate of my schedule."

"I'm sorry," Riley mumbles again, and when I turn to look at him, he's hanging his head. His hands come up to land on his hips, and I watch his throat bob around a swallow. "I was getting ready to head your way, but I got distracted."

"By?"

"ESPN. They did a whole segment on whether or not they think I'll be able to skate again. They brought in a doctor who broke down my injury and talked about the challenges I'm going to face if I ever want to get back on the ice. It felt like a huge invasion of my fucking privacy." He lifts his chin and runs a hand through his hair. "Then my prosthetist called and confirmed the appointment for my final leg fitting next week, and I kind of spiraled."

"Fuck ESPN."

The corner of his mouth twitches. "That's what I said."

"Why did the call with your prosthetist send you spiraling? Isn't that a good thing? You're moving in the right direction. You won't have something temporary anymore. It'll be permanent."

"Yeah." Riley leads me to the living room and sits on the couch, motioning for me to join him. I drop on the cushions and relax. "It also makes all of this a reality. I'm not delusional. I know what happened. I know my leg isn't going to grow back. I know I've been in a prosthetic for a while now, but the second I put that final leg on, that's it. It'll be my new life until the day I die, and… that's hard to grapple with."

"Oh." I play with the ends of my hair. Heaviness fills the space between us and I take a deep breath, trying to find the right words. I'm not sure there are any. *I'm sorry* sounds insensitive. *I understand* sounds disingenuous, because I *don't* understand. I'll never understand. "I never thought of it that way."

"Please don't throw me a pity party. I'm doing that enough

on my own, and I really don't want you to start. Not when I'm used to you kicking my ass."

"It's a good thing I didn't bring up the streamers and balloons I keep in my car."

I get a half smile, and it makes me feel like the luckiest girl in the world. I take the break in conversation to look around his living room, noticing the bright blue paint and a wall of windows. There's a bookshelf full of romance novels in the corner and some LEGO designs on the middle shelves. I spot an easel with a half-finished canvas propped up on it, and it looks like he's trying to paint Starry Night.

"Snooping?" Riley asks.

"Is it considered snooping if I do it without trying to be sneaky? This is my first time in your apartment."

"It's nothing special, but it's home." Riley grabs a decorative pillow and sets it in his lap. "I'm sorry for ditching today. And the other days. I met Lamar, the guy who was driving me the night of the accident last week, and then Coach and I had a really good heart-to-heart. My therapy sessions are going well. I was ready to change my shitty behavior and get back on track with my rehabilitation and with you. I got up this morning and got dressed. I was even looking forward to seeing—" He stops abruptly. "To trying new exercises and pushing my body, and that's the first time that's happened. But then I just... I couldn't."

"Thank you for telling me, and I'm sorry I didn't consider things from your perspective. It won't happen again." I scoot closer to him, and his fingers graze my shoulder as he adjusts the cushions to make room for me. I shiver at the surprising contact. "Maybe we can make an effort to be more honest with each other? If you need a day off, you'll tell me. And I'll listen."

"Yeah." He smiles. "I'd like that."

"You said you meet up with Lamar? How did that go?"

"I cried three times," he says, and my smile matches his. "It was really fucking good to see him."

"I met him the night in the hospital. He stayed there with us. He was so distraught, and I know he wanted to make sure you were okay. Oh, Riley." I put my palm on his knee without hesitation, and he rests his hand on mine. "It's such a sensitive situation to be happy about, but I'm so happy for you."

"Me too. He told me he stuck around with you all and… *fuck*. I needed to see him to know he was okay. To put an end to all of this resentment I've been carrying." Riley squeezes my hand, and I like it so much. "Marcus told me they set a trial date for the guy who hit us. It feels like everything is finally moving in the right direction."

"It's about time, isn't it?" I knock my knee against his, and I'm met with soft laughter. "The universe needs to give you a break for a change."

"You're telling me. For a while there, it seemed like I had a streak of serious bad karma."

"I'd never wish for you to have to go through that kind of turmoil again," I say, and I swear he drags his thumb across my knuckles. "But watching how you're prevailing even on the days where you think you aren't? It's so cool to see, Riley."

"I told Lamar I'm a work in progress."

"You are. We all are. You're not alone."

"I know I'm not." He gives my hand another squeeze and pulls away. "Thank you for being patient with me."

"Patience is something I'm working on," I say.

"And showing up is something I'm working on."

"I'm really proud of you." I can tell he's ready to move on to something else, and I smile, pointing to one of his bookshelves. It's practically overflowing, and I spot some of my favorite titles organized by the color of their spines. "What are you reading right now?"

The boys on the team have a book club, a monthly meeting where they talk about the stories they read. I've never been to one, but I hear they're passionate about their choices. There have been heated debates. Arguments and even a food fight. Grant didn't talk to anyone for a week because they made fun of his obsession with a fictional character.

I'm glad they have a hobby away from the ice. Something that entertains them when they're not playing one of their eighty-two games, and that keeps them out of trouble.

"I'd rather not say," Riley answers.

"Why not?"

"It's, ah, kind of dark?"

I grin. "Now you have to tell me."

"You can read it yourself. I finished it last night." He stands and walks to the bookshelf, grabbing a paperback with a black cover and handing it to me. "Check the trigger warnings. They're there for a reason."

I flip to the first page and my eyes widen. "Oh, shit. 'Exhibitionism'? 'Gruesome murder'? Two of my favorite things. Can I really borrow it?"

"Of course." Riley clears his throat. His cheeks are redder than they were before he gave me the book, and I wonder if he has to skip certain scenes when he reads. I wonder if the explicit descriptions of sex embarrass him, because judging from his blush, he'd rather be talking about anything else. "Do you want something to drink?"

"I have a better idea." I tuck the book under my arm. "I'm taking you to lunch."

"Lunch? Why?"

"Because you need to eat, and even though you skipped our session this morning, you're not getting out of your weight training session this afternoon. You're going to need carbohydrates, and the only way to do that is to consume food."

"Fine, but I'm buying. It's my apology for being a dick."

"Good answer." I pop to my feet. "Any suggestions on where to go?"

"How do you feel about sandwiches?"

"I've been known to be a fan."

"Then I have the perfect place." He looks down at his naked torso. "Let me, ah, put on some different clothes."

"Really? But the view is so good," I tease, and his blush deepens.

"You're a goddamn flirt, Armstrong," he calls out over his shoulder as he makes his way down the hall.

"You like it," I call back, and I swear I hear him say *yeah, I do* before he disappears, and a strange sensation flutters in my chest.

THIRTY MINUTES LATER, we're sitting at a table in the back of a sub shop. It's tucked away from the main streets of DC, hidden around a corner and situated next to a thrift store, but it smells delicious. The serving sizes are bigger than my head, and when Riley asked if he could order for me, I trusted him to make a good choice.

"Holy shit." I take a bite of my steak and cheese. Tears almost spring to my eyes. Angels rejoice. I suddenly believe in heaven. "This is the best sandwich I've ever had in my entire life. Bury me with this, please. How the hell did you find this place?"

"I wasn't making a lot of money my rookie year on my ELC. I couldn't afford to go with the veterans to the steakhouses they liked to visit, but I needed to eat. I made a wrong turn one afternoon when I was looking for the drugstore, wound up here, and I've come every week since." Riley wipes his mouth and points at the wall. "That's me with the owner."

"Oh my god." I laugh at the photo of him behind the counter, an apron tied around his waist and a wide grin on his mouth. There are wrinkles around his eyes. His head is tipped back like the photo was captured mid-laugh, and he hasn't looked that happy in *weeks*. Maybe ever. "You look so young. And cute. What happened?"

"Watch your mouth, Lexi," he says, and the deep timbre sends a shiver down my spine. He's used that voice before, and it always elicits the same response: a swoop in my belly and my thighs squeezing together. "I'm still plenty young. And cute."

"Much younger than me. You're, what? Twenty-seven?"

"Twenty-six, but thanks for the extra year." He takes a bite of his ham and cheese and smiles. There's a drop of mustard on the corner of his mouth, and he licks it away. "And I'm not that much younger than you."

"I remember when I was twenty-six. I was freezing my ass off in Ohio at a job where I was under-appreciated."

"Was that your first athletic trainer gig? How many teams did you work for before you got to DC?"

"Yeah. I got my bachelor's degree then my master's. After I graduated, I found a job with an ECHL team where I spent a few years. Next was the AHL, and finally DC. It's funny. Before I landed in Ohio, I almost took a job with a G League basketball team. I wonder how different my life would be if I'd gone down that path instead."

"Basketball makes sense because you played in high school."

"You remember that?"

"Of course I do. We talked about it a few weeks ago, and my memory isn't that shitty. It's an important part of your life, and it's worth remembering."

"Damn. I guess my bar for men and remembering details is that low."

"Understandable. We don't have a good track record."

"When I went to college, I made a list of careers that would allow me to work with my hands and help people rather than sit behind a desk and stare at a screen all day. It's been a journey, but I wouldn't change it for the world," I say.

"You're a much better trainer than the person we had before you."

"Really? Tell me more. I love talking shit."

Riley laughs and pops a chip in his mouth. "It was my rookie year. He was a dick. Never listened to any of the players' concerns or bothered to ask what we thought about an injury. I'm all for tough love, but his methods bordered on sadistic."

"I'm a woman."

"Are you?" He tilts his head and stares at me through his glasses. The lens on the right has a smudge on it, and I have the inexplicable urge to pull them off his face, wipe them clean, and hand them back over. "I had no idea."

"I mean I don't have the luxury of acting like that. If I make one wrong move, I'm out of a job. That's why I rely on a player's input when asking about methods of treatment."

I leave out the other parts: how I'm careful not to get too close to any of the players out of fear I'll lose my job over fraternization. Acknowledging I'm probably getting paid less than my colleagues but not making a fuss about the pay discrepancies because I don't want to be labeled as a bitch.

"I know Emmy experienced some of that behavior when she came into the NHL. I didn't know it extended to other parts of the league too."

"It does, but we don't need to talk about it. I'm... honored, I guess, that you believe in me enough to ask me to be the one to lead your rehabilitation."

"I didn't have to think twice. I feel safe in your care." Riley stares out the window to his right. "I really am sorry about not showing up today, Lex. I have good days, but I also have a lot of bad days. I'm trying not to let the bad days overshadow the good ones. It's hell sometimes. I'm working on it. I promise."

I remember what the girls said when we had dinner together, how I need to show up for him even when he doesn't want to show up for himself, and guilt wraps around me. I set my sandwich down. I wipe my hands and reach across the table, pressing my fingers into his forearm.

"My behavior earlier was uncalled for. Showing up to your apartment? Demanding you get your act together? That's… it's shitty," I say.

"I like that you're holding me accountable." Riley grins, and it's fucking *beautiful*. Carefree, light. Brilliantly bright. I'd love to make him smile like that again. "Everyone else is tiptoeing around me like I'm going to break. And, yeah, I guess I might, given the whole one-leg thing, but I also need a reality check from time to time."

I pull my hand back and cover my mouth to stifle a laugh. "Sorry. I'm not laughing at you."

"You can laugh." A dimple carved deep on his cheek shows up. "My therapist thinks humor is my coping mechanism."

"We all have our things. Are you going to come with the guys to Pilates the week after next?"

"I'll try. If I show up, how about we call that our clean slate? After you kick my ass on the reformer, I promise I won't skip another rehab session."

"Really?" Hope springs in my chest. "I'm game for a new way of life if you are."

"Oh, I'm game, Lexi." Riley pushes his plate out of the way and leans forward. He smells like soap and coffee beans, and I refuse to inhale his scent. "I'm going to be the best damn patient you've ever had."

"Good luck, Mitchell. It takes a lot to impress me."

"Guess I have my work cut out for me." A cocky smirk is tossed my way. "It's a good thing being the best has always come naturally."

"We'll see about that."

"Yeah." His foot nudges mine under the table. I don't pull away. "We will."

EIGHTEEN
RILEY

PUCK KINGS

G-MONEY
I need an excuse to get out of Pilates on Friday.

Maybe I can say I have foot-mouth disease?

That's contagious, right?

HUDDY BOY
You're not skipping, Grant. Lexi and Coach added this to our training schedule for a reason.

G-MONEY
I almost tore my hamstring last time, Huddy. Don't make me go!!!

EASY E
Better than tearing your shorts.

MAVVY

If you're not wearing underwear this time, Ethan, I'm going to make you skate laps for fucking days.

I don't want to see your balls.

EASY E

Some people do.

SULLY

I can assure you that no one on this earth wants to see your balls.

EASY E

Ouch, Goalie Daddy. That wasn't very nice.

HUDDY BOY

Lexi said you're coming today, Ri. That's exciting, man.

ME

Not sure how many moves I'll be able to do. I'll probably fall on my face. But I'll give it a try.

G-MONEY

You're going to be better than me.

HUDDY BOY

You don't have to be good at everything, Grant.

G-MONEY

It's like you don't even know me!!!!

MAVVY

Dinner after Pilates? You can all come to my place and I'll order pizza.

HAT TRICK

G-MONEY
Pizza??? During the season??? Cap has lost his mind.

SULLY
No dinner.

EASY E
We'll drag you there, Sully.

ME
I guess I can do dinner.

G-MONEY
We're getting the band back together, boys!!!!!!!!!!!!!!!!!!!!!!!!!!!!!!!!!!

HUDDY BOY
You're going to have to kidnap Goalie Daddy if you want him to show up.

G-MONEY
Don't underestimate my abilities, Huddy Boy.

ME
I have my last fitting for my permanent prosthetic today.

DAD
Already? Wow. Time flies, doesn't it?

ME
The temporary one kind of sucks, doesn't it?

DAD

It really sucks. And think of how far technology has come!

My old ass had to use something that felt like it was made of plastic!

ME

I'm going to notice a difference, right?

DAD

Without a doubt.

You're going to be so impressed with how much more complex it is. It'll be functional and lightweight too. It's also tailored to you, so it should be more comfortable.

ME

I can't wait. Now I understand why you were constantly moving your hips and trying to adjust your leg when you first got your prosthetic. I can't do anything if the limb feels even a little bit off where it's sitting in the socket.

DAD

The adjustments will be start to become more and more minor. I'm not even aware I'm doing it anymore.

Send me a picture when you get yours. I want to compare it with mine.

ME

You can ask for an upgrade. Maybe they have a BOGO deal.

DAD

Ha. Glad to hear you getting your humor back, son.

THE LAST FITTING for my permanent prosthetic is easier than I thought it would be. My doctor lets me know he'll send the final product to my apartment in a few days, and that's it.

One chapter closed, another opened.

I feel light on my way to Pilates. The November weather is tolerable. There's a pep in my step that wasn't there two weeks ago, and I'm not experiencing any phantom limb pain. Turns out, following the exercises I'm supposed to do makes everything easier, and I'm finally figuring out my balance and gait.

When I pull open the door to the studio downtown, I'm immediately hugged by Piper.

"Riley Mitchell," she says, face buried in my shirt. "It's about time you showed up to a team event."

"Piper Mitchell. I saw you two nights ago at our home game."

"I know. But this is different. I missed you. I missed hanging out with you outside the barn."

"I missed you too, Piper," I say, giving her a hug.

She steps back and holds my hands, surveying me. Her attention doesn't linger on my legs even though it's the first time I'm wearing shorts out in public with my prosthetic, and when her gaze moves back to my face, she lets out a heavy breath.

"How are you feeling?" she asks. "You look good."

"I'm getting there." I squeeze her palms. "You look good too."

"Watch yourself, Mitchell," Liam says, appearing behind Piper and pulling her to him so her back is flush against his chest.

"Which Mitchell?" Piper teases.

"That one." Liam lifts his chin my way. "I don't like when people play with things that are mine."

"Wow." Piper elbows his ribs, and a smile works its way onto his mouth. All this fresh air away from my apartment is making me hallucinate. "Don't call me your *thing*."

"Sorry, sunshine. You know I didn't mean it like that." Liam glances my way. "You do look good, Mitchy."

"I didn't know this was going to turn into a compliment train," I say. "Flirt with me a little more, Sully."

"Don't expect anything else," he tosses back.

I point over my shoulder to the reformer device in the corner that's calling my name. "I'm going to grab the machine away from the front before someone can steal it. I'll see you all after."

I stop to say hello to the other guys, doling out high fives and hugs before I make it to the back of the studio. It's darker over here. Quieter too, and I'm glad I have a space where I can try the exercises and, inevitably, fail privately.

"Hey," a sweet voice says, and I relax at the sound of it.

I glance up and find Lexi in front of me, hands on her hips and a wide smile on her mouth. She looks like a fucking knockout in tight leggings and a shirt that shows off the bottom half of her stomach. Her dark hair is up in a ponytail, but some pieces fall out and frame her face.

Fucking hell.

I'm never going to get over this crush.

"Hi," I answer, hoping my voice doesn't crack. "What's up?"

"I'm sorry it's cramped in here. I had to rearrange the room so I could fit an extra reformer. I wanted you to have an area to try the exercises you feel comfortable with, and I thought it might be better than putting you front and center." Her posture straightens and she smiles again. "There's no pressure to do any of the workout, and I'll be showing modified moves if you want to try those instead."

"Thanks," I say. "I'm going to try my best. I, ah, did some

research earlier. I read a couple articles that said Pilates helps to align the body, which is important for people who—"

"Experience postural imbalances due to the loss of a limb." Lexi nods, eyes bright. "I read that article too, and I immediately thought of you."

I know it's part of her job, but the idea of Lexi spending her free time researching ways to help me sends a rush of exhilaration up my spine. It makes me imagine there's a world in which she's doing it because she wants to, not because she has to. Because she likes spending time with me, not because she's *required* to spend time with me.

The thought makes me puff out my chest and stand taller. It gives me some of the confidence I haven't been able to find since the accident.

She told me it takes a lot to impress her, and I'm going to do everything in my power to make sure I have her attention.

"Thinking about me in your free time, Lex?" I ask, testing the waters.

Lexi smirks and takes a step closer to me. Her finger touches the center of my chest, and the press of her nail into my thin shirt is enough to send my brain reeling.

"Sounds like you might be thinking about me," she says. "Looking up the exercise I teach? Keeping your word about showing up? I'm going to pretend it's because you missed me."

I did miss her.

I haven't skipped a single rehab session since the morning she barged into my apartment like a tornado and we had that good conversation. I'm at the arena every day, putting in the work like I'm supposed to, but with the season underway, she's had to adjust our schedule to accommodate the other guys who are starting to get aches and pains.

I didn't travel with the team for their first extended set of away games of the season last week, sitting at home while they played back-to-back games in Oakland, Dallas, Denver, and

Toronto, and I've been looking forward to spending time with her again.

"I'm only here to watch Grant cry," I say, and that makes her laugh.

"I made sure the class was going to be hard as hell just for him," she says.

Lexi pulls her hand away from my shirt and spins on her heel, heading for the front of the room. I do my goddamn best not to drop my eyes to her ass, but I fail miserably. I only blink out of the trance I've fallen into when Hudson drops his towel on the machine next to mine and snaps his fingers in my face.

"You're staring," he tells me.

"No, I'm not." I pull off my hoodie and slide out of my shoes. "And mind your fucking business, Hayes."

"Deny it all you want, Mitchy. But I see everything, and your subtlety is shit."

LEXI WASN'T KIDDING.

Her class is hell on earth. I know I'm weaker than I used to be and still trying to figure out how to move this new body of mine, but even Hudson, who's normally a fucking rockstar at Pilates, is struggling next to me.

"What the hell?" He wipes his face with his damp towel and chugs half his water bottle. "I don't remember her being this cruel last season."

"Last season you were busy flirting with your personal chef." I put my hands on top of my head and try to control my breathing. "You didn't pay attention for half the class."

"And I'd do it again," Hudson says smugly. "You're moving really well, dude. Looks like you're getting some of your flexibility back."

"Really? Because it feels like I can barely touch my toes. This prosthetic is heavy as fuck." I haven't really been participating today, but it's nice to get my heart rate back up and do some of the upper body moves.

"How's everyone feeling?" Lexi asks through her microphone, and Grant wails.

"Like I'm going to die," he whines from two rows in front of me. His thighs shake, and he digs his fingers into his muscles. "This is torture. Hell. The worst thirty minutes of my life. What did we do to deserve this?"

"I talked to the Oakland athletic trainer when we were out in California, and he told me some of the cross-training his players do to prevent injuries," Lexi says.

"They had the worst record in the league last season," Connor calls out. "Who cares what they're doing?"

"They're a team on the rise and going to be one to watch over the next five years. The only way you all are going to be Stanley Cup champions for the third time in a row is if you work harder than everyone else and do things they aren't doing. You have to be the best on and off the ice, and that includes training underused muscles."

"Goddammit." Ethan rips off his shirt and throws it on the floor. "Now I want to run through a brick wall. Let's fucking go."

Lexi grins. A new song starts over the speakers. "Everyone up. We're going into Warrior two lunges."

My teammates and Piper get into position and I watch them. I don't trust myself enough to balance, so I take the opportunity to sip on my water and decide who I think is going to topple over first.

Grant.

It has to be Grant.

"Want a modification?" Lexi asks, appearing in front of me and turning off her microphone. "The guys might look like they're dying, but I can't find a drop of sweat on her body. She could probably go for another hour and a half at this intensity and not bat an eye. "You can do it on the ground instead of on the platform. It'll give you more stability."

"I'm not sure I'll be good at it."

"Who said anything about being good?"

"Okay." I stand and look at my legs. "What do I do?"

"The same thing you'd do on the machine. Do you remember this move?"

"Vaguely. Can you give me a refresher?"

"Sure." She smiles and moves to my side. "Is it okay if I touch you?"

Screaming out *fuck, yes, anywhere you want* is probably too aggressive, so I nod. I try not to blush when she rests her palm on my hip, and I'm glad the lighting is shitty back here. The last thing I need is for Hudson to glance over and point out how red my cheeks are, even if I would blame it on my lack of athleticism rather than the hot girl I'm crushing on giving me a lick of her attention.

"Tell me what to do, teach," I say.

"Put your right leg forward and your left one behind you. Lunge into your right leg—don't worry about getting too deep—and make sure your knee points the same direction as your toes. You're really going to feel this in your core, quads, and hamstrings. You should also notice your hip abductors being engaged. We've worked on those in our sessions, remember?"

"How could I forget? They hurt like hell."

Lexi flips her microphone back on. "Let's go two more, then we'll switch sides, everyone," she says.

I grit my teeth. Sweat rolls down my forehead, but I stay focused. I take a deep breath, trying to center myself, and Lexi gently pushes down on my shoulders.

"Relax. There you go," she murmurs, her touch warm and soft. I bet the rest of her is warm and soft too. Her thumb presses into the muscles around my neck, and I almost whimper. "That's so good, Riley."

Fuck me.

Up to this point, my attraction to her hasn't been a physical thing.

It's been something manageable. Something I can pretend only exists because we've been around each other for years and she's one of the few women I interact with, not because I think she's smart, talented, gorgeous, and incredible.

But now it feels like her hand is lingering on my body longer than it needs to, and my mind can't help but wander. I'm dreaming about what her palms would feel like skimming across my stomach. Dipping under the waistband of my shorts and wrapping around my cock. How she would taste if I was given the chance to take her to bed and worship her like she deserves.

I squeeze my eyes shut and try to get rid of the images of her on her knees, mouth open and tongue out while she tells me she can take *more*, but then she exhales a breath that tickles my skin. She gets me to stretch an inch lower, and I'm a helpless mess of thoughts that would get me in serious fucking trouble.

Jock straps.

Sweaty jerseys.

Two-year-old skates that smell like death.

I try to think of anything but her, because I refuse to get fucking hard in front of my teammates.

"Jesus," I mumble. Any pain I might be close to experiencing disappears when she moves her hands to my hips, her grip settling there.

"Are you okay?" Lexi asks, and the question makes me want to laugh.

No, I'm in hell. I'm picturing you naked, and I want to die. Do you have any other secret tattoos besides the one on your hip I want to see? What about piercings? Would you like it if I tied your wrists together, or would that freak you out?

"Great," I say instead. I focus my attention on the guys in

front of me. On Grant falling off his machine and Maverick shaking out his sweaty hair. "I'm great."

"I've been working on a strength-building program for you. It's similar to what I give guys to work on to prevent injuries, and we're going to start that next week."

"Does it involve any other torture methods?"

"Nope. Just a mat and the ground."

"I can get behind that."

"One minute break," Lexi calls out, turning her microphone on. "Then we only have two more exercises."

"Are you going to Maverick's after this?" I ask when she clicks her microphone back off.

"Maybe. I don't want to intrude on a guys' afternoon out. It's important for you all to bond, and I'd be in the way."

"I've seen more of Hudson's ass over the last five years than I've seen women naked. I've probably seen it more than my own ass, if we're being honest. I think we're all set on bonding."

"You don't look at your ass in the mirror?" she asks.

"No. Do you?"

"Regularly. I have a spectacular ass." Lexi fixes her microphone over her ear. "I want you to try the last two sets of exercises. They're core exercises, and they're going to help with your altered center of gravity and the balance challenges you've been experiencing."

I'm still caught on her spectacular ass comment, but I nod. "Want to make a deal? You say you'll come to Mav's, and I'll try the exercises."

"Riley Mitchell." She pops a hip out. I'm a fucking champion for not looking at her curves. "I didn't know you were the bartering type."

"What do I have to lose?"

"Fine." She grins and flips her hair over her shoulder. "You've got yourself a deal, but don't expect me to go easy on you."

"I'd never expect that." I lift the hem of my shirt to wipe my cheek, smirking when her eyes dip to my stomach. I'm going to pretend she likes what she sees. "Stop staring at me, Armstrong."

"Just for that, I'm adding in a third exercise." She flips me off and walks to the front of the room. "You all can blame Riley for these next moves," she tells the guys and Piper. Everyone groans except me, and I don't care.

I'm having way too much fucking fun.

NINETEEN
LEXI

THERE'S nothing I love more than kicking men's asses and watching them cry.

Especially when they think they're the superior species.

None of the DC Stars guys have the toxic masculinity that sometimes finds its way to my classes when a group of dudes who have never tried Pilates think they can outlast the women who I've been working with for years, but it's still fun to make professional athletes hurt for an hour during a good workout.

An invitation to Maverick and Emmy's place for pizza means they're not too mad at me, and I kick off my shoes in their foyer next to a ridiculous pair of bright yellow sneakers that have to belong to Ethan.

"I'm getting pepperoni and cheese," Maverick announces over the sound of video games being played on the big-screen television in the living room. "Anyone want something different?"

"Sounds good, Cap," Grant yells.

"Put some food in me, Mavvy," Connor adds.

"I wish the rest of the girls were here," Piper says after pulling me into the kitchen away from all the boys and handing me a bottle of water from the fridge. "It's always more fun when we're together."

"Same. But Emmy is traveling. Maven and Madeline have kids. We'll always come second to them," I say.

"I'm okay with that, because they're cute as hell, and I love being an aunt." Piper stands on her toes and peeks over my shoulder. "Speaking of cute as hell, I saw Riley eyeing you during our class."

"That wasn't a subtle segue at all." I snort and twist the cap off my water, kicking myself for leaving my reusable bottle at the studio. "And I'm sure he was eyeing me. It's part of the routine when I give directions on the moves we're doing."

"He was eye fucking you."

"Stop." I laugh and throw the cap at her. "He was not."

"Guess I must've imagined him looking at your ass then."

"He was in the back of the room. How the hell would you have even seen that?"

"I see everything," she says slyly. "Even Liam picked up on it, and that's saying something. You know he never wants to get involved in people's personal business. He'd rather gouge his eyes out than talk about someone's relationship."

"Such a charmer, that goalie."

As much as I want to deny Piper's claim, I'm not oblivious.

I could feel attention on me this afternoon. It went beyond the usual awareness I experience while teaching a class. It was intentional. Like I was being watched for a reason, and I'm not surprised it was Riley.

It seems like he's always watching me these days. I'll glance across the tunnel where we're standing during the game and see his gaze flick away from me and back to the ice. In our rehab sessions, he looks my way between stretches. There's a small smile. The dip of his chin to his chest, as if he's embarrassed he got caught, but then he does it again.

I don't mind.

It's nice to be looked at, especially by him, and it's not

because I can't get the image of him shirtless with those damn sweatpants out of my head.

His attitude shift is encouraging. Minus the four-game trip we just wrapped up that took us away from DC for a week, Riley and I have been spending time together. We've been texting here and there—mostly progress reports about his exercises while I was out of town—and it's fun to know I finally have his attention after trying for weeks to get it.

"Riley and I are friends." I move to the cabinets and grab a stack of plates to use for the pizza. "And working together. That's all that's happening between us."

"That was a very neutral answer." Piper hands me a mountain of napkins. "Did his crush magically disappear?"

Crush.

That word makes me want to blush because when was the last time someone had a crush on me?

And when did it start to make me feel giddy?

I bite on my bottom lip to stop a smile from forming, feigning nonchalance. "I have no clue what you're talking about."

"Are you two gossiping in here? I love a good gab session with the girls." Grant strolls into the kitchen and grins. "I want to know what you're talking about. Unless it's who has the biggest dick on the team. I can tell you the answer is—"

"Unprofessional. And not in front of ladies." I flick his ear. "I'll tell you what we're gossiping about if you tell *us* what's in that notebook you carry around. You've been holding onto it for a year."

"It's not important," Grant rushes to say. "Only women's numbers. I got hoes in every area code, you know?"

He can't lie to save his life.

I haven't seen Grant with a woman in months. He's not sneaking anyone back to his room at away games. I'm not sure he's thrown a puck to a female fan since the season started, and he's so protective of the black leather notepad he pulls out now and then, I'm starting to wonder if he's keeping nuclear codes in there.

Whatever he's hiding, it must be important. He doesn't let it out of his sight.

"Not a good enough answer to hear our gossip." I stick out my tongue and head back to the living room with the plates.

The guys are spread out throughout Maverick and Emmy's house. Some are playing video games. Others are sitting on the couch and talking. Ethan is shirtless—again—and asking Connor to count his abs, and I shake my head. When I spot Riley outside on the terrace, I slip away from everyone and the conversations they're having.

Some fresh air sounds nice.

So does his company.

I pull open the large glass door that leads to the paved patio and shut it behind me. He turns at the noise, his chin on his shoulder as he looks at me.

"Hey," he says.

"Hi." I shiver at the early evening breeze, wishing now I brought my jacket with me. The sweat from class has dried, and I'm suddenly missing the warm fall weather. "What are you doing out here alone?"

"Just needed a minute. You know how the guys get. My social tolerance is less than what it used to be, and I don't want to snap at someone for being loud because I'm pissed off at everything these days."

"Do you want to be alone?" I walk over and stand next to him. "I understand wanting some space."

"No. You don't piss me off."

"What a relief." I smile up at him. "You did great in class today. How are you feeling? Any pain I should be aware of?"

"Better than I thought I'd feel. I know we've been meeting every day, but it was nice to push my body in a different way. It almost made me feel like I was part of the team again, and I haven't experienced that since our Cup win."

"Nothing like some torture exercises to bring people closer together."

"And me getting my head out of my ass. I've been pushing the guys away, but today was a reminder that they're my brothers." Riley leans back from his hips and reaches for his leg, seemingly adjusting something with his prosthetic. "I can push them all I want. They're not going anywhere."

"They really aren't, Riley." I put my hand on the sleeve of his sweatshirt. "None of us are."

"It's taken me a while to understand that, but I finally do."

"I'm glad." I shiver and pull my hand away so I can wrap my arms around my body. "Hell. I didn't know the nice afternoon was going to turn into a frigid night. The temperature must've dropped, like, twenty degrees."

"Hang on." Riley takes off his glasses and tugs his sweatshirt over his head. His shirt gets stuck in the unclothing process, the thin cotton material crawling up his stomach and showing off bare skin. "I'm not cold."

"Oh, that's okay. I don't want to—"

"I wasn't asking, Lexi. Arms up, please," he says, and the hint of authority behind his voice has me nodding. It has my slowly lifting my arms above my head and exhaling in relief as he guides the fleece over my shoulders and down my torso. His fingers graze across my stomach when he fixes the pocket in the front, and I'm instantly warmer. I don't know if it's from the added layer or his touch. "There we go."

"Thank you," I murmur, laughing when he tugs on the drawstrings near my neck to tighten the hood. The move makes me step closer to him, but I don't mind. Not when he moves his touch to my elbow to keep me upright. "I'm only accepting this because I like hoodies. The ones that don't belong to me in particular."

"You're stubborn, aren't you?"

"No." I bury my nose in the fabric. The scent of coffee

and soap tickles my nose, and I do my best to hide my inhale. "I like to do things for myself. Accepting help is hard for me."

"And watching you freeze to death is hard for me. We both can't be winners tonight, and I don't like to lose. Keep it for as long as you'd like," Riley tells me.

"I'll get you back one of these days," I huff, my words all bark, no bite. "Are you excited to join the team at our away game next week?" Riley pivots his body so he's facing me, and I mirror his pose. Our eyes lock, and there's hesitation behind his gaze. "What's wrong, Mitchy?"

"Can I tell you something that might make me an absolute asshole?"

"You could never be an asshole. Your secrets are safe with me."

"There's still resentment when I watch the guys play," he says. "It's not the same anger I had at the beginning of the season, but I'm not fully happy for them."

"I think that's a normal psychological reaction. They're doing something you can't do—*yet*—and it dredges up jealousy that they're out there and you're not."

"That's exactly what my therapist told me. He says traveling will be good for me. I've moved onto the testing stage of grief, apparently. Go me."

"Yeah? What does the testing stage include?" I ask.

"Experimenting with new ways to cope and adjusting to what happened to me. Finding a new normal. A bunch of other zen bullshit I don't buy into."

Riley shrugs. He reaches my way, and for half a second, I think he's about to touch my cheek. *Oh, god.* Is he going to kiss me? Do I want him to? That's not something I've ever considered before but now I am. What is happening? Why is—he changes direction at the last minute, dusting something off my shoulder instead, and the twinge of disappointment that flashes through me almost makes me pause.

"But fuck it," Riley continues. "He's getting paid. I'm

getting a checkmark in the box next to the things I'm supposed to do. Everyone wins."

"There are going to be lots of exciting things on the trip. You have the Florida sunshine. The guys on ELCs complaining about having a roommate even though they're twenty-one. *Oh.* You can't forget the food on the charter plane."

"You have to be joking."

"I'm serious!" I swat at him. I expect him to pull away, but he doesn't. "Those cookies the flight attendants hand out are *heavenly*. I mentioned how much I liked them, and the new girl working our flights this season gave me a box to take home with me. I've been eating them for days."

"I'll give you the Florida sunshine, but it's going to be awkward as hell to watch a game in an arena that's not ours. At home, I know everyone. I can stand in the tunnel and not feel like some creep who's lurking and staring at the athletes. In Miami, people aren't going to know who the hell I am."

"You could put on gear and sit on the bench," I suggest. "As long as you're fully dressed, you're allowed to be there."

"A skate that fits my prosthetic foot? I'm not sure that exists," he says.

"We'll figure something out." I look him up and down, trying to see if I can spot any goosebumps after his chivalrous act of undressing benefited me, but probably didn't benefit him. My eyes home in on his pocket, an odd shape pressing against the fabric of his gym shorts. "What the hell is that?"

"What's what?" Riley glances down. He snorts and reaches into his left pocket. "A lime."

"Do you regularly carry fruit around with you?"

"No." He tosses it in the air, catches it, and switches it to his other hand. "I wasn't sure Maverick had any. I stopped at the store on the way over."

"You—" I blink. It feels like I'm missing the punchline of a joke. "I'm confused."

"You mentioned you liked limes in your drink. Didn't know if that only applied to cocktails or all forms of fluid."

"When did I mention that?"

"June," he says simply, and he leaves it at that.

I stare at him. For a second, it feels like the world tilts on its axis, because *what the fuck* do you mean he brought me a lime because he remembered an offhanded comment I made months ago? And—*god*. Come to think of it, it was the night we were all out celebrating The Cup. The night he lost his leg. The night his entire life changed.

What is he doing remembering my drink preferences?

"Oh." I swallow, not sure what else to say. My heart is somewhere near my throat because it's trying to escape my body. My skin is prickly with awareness. What the actual fuck is this unknown feeling coursing through me? "Right."

Gratitude, I think.

Awareness of a man doing something nice for me because he wants to, not because he wants to sleep with me.

Friendship that differs from what I have with the girls.

Riley wraps his fingers around my wrist and slowly turns my hand face up. His thumb brushes along the vein on the inside of my wrist before he lets go and sets the lime in the center of my palm.

"Which is it?" he asks.

"Which is what?"

"The lime preference. Is it in all drinks? Cocktails only?"

"You really want to know?"

"Mhm." Riley leans in, invading my space, and I don't do anything to make him leave. "I really do. Won't be able to sleep tonight until you tell me, actually."

"We wouldn't want that." I grip the lime and bring it to my chest, my eyes on his. "I like it in all my drinks. I have a bottle of lime juice I keep in my fridge, but it's not as good as the real thing. Always slips my mind when I'm at the store."

"I can be your lime guy." He tosses me a coy smile. "If you want."

"I like the sound of that." I smile and slip the lime in my pocket. "Thank you, Mitchy."

"You're welcome." Riley tugs on the drawstrings again, and I inhale sharply. "Are you warm enough?"

I'm way past warm.

My body is a goddamn inferno.

"Yeah," I say. Piper waves at me through the doors, and I hold up a hand to tell her I'll be right there. "I'm great. Fine. Dandy."

"You told me you were hard to impress. How am I doing?" he asks, and a laugh rattles out of me.

"I'm on my way to being impressed."

"Good." He looks up at the moon. His dimple pops, and gosh is he pretty. "Patience is a virtue. I'll get there one day."

"I can't wait to see you try," I say, and I sure as hell mean it.

TWENTY
LEXI

"I LIKE road games more than I like home games." Piper sits next to me on the charter plane and drops her purse on the floor. "It's so exciting to play in enemy territory and see new cities."

"Hearing away crowds boo me is one of my favorite things in the world," Maverick says as he shuffles past us, a duffle bag slung over his shoulder. "I fucking love chirping with guys who think they're better than us."

He talks a big game, but the Florida Ospreys have a good chance at beating us tonight.

We're nowhere near the team we were at this point last season. Our record is sitting around .500 as we head into the middle of November, while a year ago, we were on top of the league standings and riding a six-game win streak. The good news is the boys have started to adjust to Riley being out of the lineup. Coach changes his first line every game, and I can tell he's close to figuring out the missing piece that will turn things around.

I'm a loyal gal, a proud Stars employee who hopes to finish out her career with the same club because she loves DC and everyone on the team, but there's a secret part of me that is so damn happy the boys have been blown out three out of their last five matchups.

It's for Riley's sake. I know how much he wishes he was out there with them, and every loss shows him he's not just a number. He's someone the boys have chemistry with, someone they trust, and you can't replicate that kind of compatibility easily in this sport.

"They're probably booing you because you're a show-off." Liam drops a kiss on Piper's head and makes his way to the back to sit with the guys. "And a pain in my ass."

"Love you too, Goalie Daddy," Maverick sings.

"Do you all want to get dinner tonight?" Maven files into the row behind us and yawns. "I could use a glass of wine. Or five."

"Everything okay?" Piper asks, turning around to look at her. "Do I need to talk to Dallas? He might kick footballs for a living, but I'll kick his ass."

"No, my husband is wonderful, though I love how feisty you are for being all of five feet tall," Maven says. "Coordinating kids' schedules with school and extracurricular activities and careers in two professional sports leagues is exhausting. And I have help! My dad jumps in when he can, and everyone else in my family is willing to drop what they're doing and lend a hand if need be. I don't know how the single mothers do it. Remind me to buy Madeline a really nice Christmas present. She's a damn superhero for solo parenting for as long as she did."

"Mothers are incredible. I could never do what you all do," I say, digging through my bag and pulling out my iPad so I can do some work on the flight. "I'm in for dinner, by the way. How about we buy a bottle of wine, order room service, and have a movie night in one of our rooms?"

"Music to my ears. What about you, Piper. Want to join, or do you and *your husband* have plans?" Maven asks.

"Please." Piper snorts. "Liam is too superstitious for me to get more than five minutes with him before a game. He has a very strict pregame ritual."

"Tell us more." I grin at her. "Does he bite his shirt in the bedroom too?"

"I am not answering that." She grabs her eye mask and tugs it down her forehead. "But I'll say I haven't been unsatisfied in years."

"Well deserved after years with a shitty ex-husband." I wave to the rest of the boys making their way on the plane. Ethan and Grant bring up the rear, stragglers like always, and I crane my neck. I haven't seen Riley yet, and when I can't find him, I frown. "Where's Mitchy?"

"Did you miss me, Armstrong?" his deep voice says, and I jerk my chin to look up at him.

"Eavesdropping, Mitchell?" I toss back, and he grins.

"Hard not to when you're practically shouting my name to the whole airplane."

Oh, I like this version of him.

It's the cocky, sarcastic side he doesn't show too often, but when he does, it's a sight. Fun, and definitely flirty. Light and carefree. I'm seeing more and more glimpses of this Riley, the guy he was before that night in June, shining through his personality recently, and it makes me match his grin.

"You'd know if I was shouting your name, Riley," I say, and I'm glad when he drops his head back and laughs.

It's fun to meet him toe-to-toe and give it back to him. Watching the blush crawl up his cheeks is an added bonus, and lately, I'm noticing more and more how goddamn *cute* he is.

"You know I shout yours when you give me those horrible exercises," he says.

"And I love every minute of it."

"Glad it makes you happy." His eyes cut over to Piper and Maven, and he smiles. "Have a good flight, ladies. Don't let Lex get you in too much trouble."

"Don't even say it," I tell the girls when Riley takes the seat next to Ryan Seymour eight rows back.

"I knew about Riley's crush, but yours is a new development," Piper says.

"I do not have a crush on him. We tease each other. That's what friends do."

"Ah. I remember when Dallas and I were just friends," Maven chimes in. "And all those times I thought about climbing him like a tree while claiming it was *platonic*."

"Same with me and Liam," Piper adds. "Those are famous last words."

"Unlike you two, I can control myself." I pop in a wireless headphone so I can block out whatever else they want to say. "And now you're drinking alone."

THE GUYS PLAY an unbelievable game the next night. They win by three goals, Liam has a shutout, and we celebrate by taking over the hotel bar and restaurant.

Everyone is rowdy and hungry, and I'm delegated to be on nacho duty. I finally get to the front of the line to order at the bar, and I'm cut off by a guy who towers over me.

"Um. Excuse me. I was next," I say.

"Shit. I'm sorry." He scoots to the side and motions me forward. I'm thrown off by the British accent, but I take the spot next to him and rest my elbows on the bar counter. "I was so determined to get a basket of chips, I didn't notice you, and I apologize for jumping ahead in the queue."

"Ah. See, in America, we call them fries. And lines."

"Which is arse backward."

I laugh. "Apology accepted, but I'm sorry too. I'm starving, and I can get snappy if I'm not fed every few hours. We're coming up on six now, so the danger zone is near."

"Oh, shit. Sounds like a matter of national security for you to order your food first." He wipes his hand on his jeans and thrusts it my way. "I'm James."

"Lexi," I tell him, smiling at the warmth of his palm against mine. "What brings you to the Miami Marriott on a Wednesday night?"

"The *french fries*, obviously." James pauses and gives me a shy smile. "And the beautiful women."

"At least you have your priorities right." I put in three orders of nachos and spin so I can lean against the bar ledge. "But, really. Why Miami?"

"I'm a pilot. I'm on a layover, and the company thinks thirty hours near a Buffalo Wild Wings is exactly what we want to do with our free time."

"It's not?"

"Nah. I prefer The Cheesecake Factory."

I laugh. "Who doesn't love a thirty-page menu?"

"You get me, Lexi."

"Where are you based?"

"London. Heathrow Airport is my second home," James says.

"I'm jealous. You have the good Cadbury chocolate in the UK." I spot Riley approaching us, and I wave. He lights up and waves back, the grin he's wearing falling slightly when he sees the man next to me. "The best you can find in our airports is overpriced Skittles."

"Works for me. I love tasting the rainbow." His attention bounces to Riley, then back to me. "Why does this bloke look like he wants to punch me?"

"He's probably also very hungry, and I'm spending too much time talking to you and not enough time delivering nachos to needy athletes."

"I can help," James offers.

"I can also help," Riley interjects, glancing down at me. "You good, Lex?"

"Wow. Two men willing to help me? There's a joke somewhere in there. I appreciate both of you offering, but I have the nachos covered. Single, independent woman reporting for duty." I smile at Riley. "You didn't have to come over here. The guys have been so excited to hang out with you, and they are way more interesting than me."

"I wouldn't say that." He puts his hands in his pockets and shrugs. "You're more fun."

"I'm flattered." I touch the curve of his elbow, and he looks down at where my fingers sit on his bare skin. "But I'm fine. Really. Go have fun, and I'll see you on the bus in the morning."

"Right." Riley gives me a single nod. "I think I'm going to head upstairs. I'm not in a socializing mood. And I'm not very hungry."

"Are you sure? I can bring up some food for when—"

"I'm okay. Have a good night, Lex," he says.

Riley pushes his way through the group of players congregating around tables. I watch him leave, and I don't know if I should chase after him. The last thing I want to be is a bother when he wants some peace and quiet, and when he disappears around the corner toward the elevators, I sigh.

"Wow," James says, and I jump. I forgot he was there. "Poor guy. I didn't mean to cockblock him."

"What are you talking about?" I ask.

"Nacho Man. He was clearly hoping you'd kick me to the curb so he could have some time with you. Offering to carry the nachos was a bold move."

"*You* offered to carry the nachos," I say.

"Yeah, but he *offered to carry the nachos*." James smirks. "If you know what I mean."

"No way. Riley is my friend," I say, and I feel like a broken record. I need to tattoo it across my forehead so people *stop fucking assuming* the two of us are together because we spend five seconds interacting. "He would've come up if any of the other guys were talking to me at the bar."

"They aren't though, are they? They're keeping their distance."

"We're friends," I repeat, and James shrugs.

"Friends or not, that bloke wanted you all for himself."

The bartender puts three large trays down on the bar, and I balance them on my arms. "I should go," I say. "I have an important job."

"I'll say. Nice to meet you, Lexi." James pretends to tip a hat in my direction. "Be good to your friend. He seems like a good one."

I drop off one of the trays of nachos to the girls and the other to Grant's table, keeping one for myself. I'm suddenly not in the mood to socialize either, and before anyone has a chance to ask where I'm going, I hightail it for the elevators.

I check my phone with the list of room numbers for the guys and find Riley's, riding up to the fourth floor and knocking softly on his door.

He doesn't answer at first, and I'm afraid I've made a mistake by coming here. Then the lock clicks. The handle turns, and Riley is there, shirtless with messy hair and glasses sliding down his nose, a pair of crutches in his hand.

"Hi," I whisper, and he blinks at me.

"What are you doing here?" he asks.

"Can I come in?"

He hesitates, fingers wrapping around the door jamb before he nods once and steps back. I nudge my way into his room, and he closes the door behind me.

"Did you need something?"

"Are you in pain?" I point to the crutches. "You haven't used those in a while."

"I have to use them at night when I take my prosthetic off, which is what I was about to do."

"Oh." I clear my throat and hold out the tray of food to him. He looks down at it, but doesn't take it. "I brought you nachos."

"No thanks," he mumbles.

"What the hell was that, Riley?"

"What was what?"

"Downstairs. You said you weren't hungry when I know you haven't eaten anything since the team lunch earlier today. And then you just left."

"It's nothing," he mumbles again.

"I'm a good listener," I offer.

"You wouldn't understand."

"Then tell me so I can try."

"Why do you care?" Riley sets down his crutches and closes the distance between us. I take a step back, caught off guard by his close proximity. My shoulders press into the door behind me, and I inhale sharply when he puts his palm flat on the door, next to my head. "Why did you bother coming up here?"

"Because I care about you." I lift my chin, defiant. "I would check on any of the guys if they left abruptly, but it's *you*. I've spent enough time with you over the last two and a half months to know something is bothering you. And I want to help."

Riley stares at me, his chest heaving. I wait for him to yell at me. I wait for him to kick me out or tell me I'm overstepping, but he doesn't.

He brings his left hand close to my face, just like he did that night on Maverick and Emmy's terrace, and this time, he rests his palm against my cheek. His touch is shaky, gentle, and I inhale a sharp breath.

"That guy you were talking to downstairs was a waste of your fucking time," he rasps. "I hate him."

Understanding dawns, and my spine straightens. I wet my lips, and his eyes follow the path of my tongue. "You were jealous," I whisper.

"Of course I was fucking jealous. He had your attention. And I'm fucking desperate for it."

"I'm not down there with him. I'm up here with you. What are you going to do about it?"

"What do you want me to do about it?" Riley challenges, and my mouth parts.

His question hangs in the air, the ball in my court, and it's like time stands still. I can think of a dozen things I want him to do about it, all of which I've never considered before.

This is a dangerous line I'm toeing. I've never stepped this close to the boundary with a player before. I've never even *considered* it, but it's like I'm being physically pulled to him. I'm working against a force outside of my control, and when he moves his hand from my cheek to the back of my head, I realize I want *him*.

Maybe I've wanted him for a while now.

"I want you to kiss me," I say, growing more confident in my decision with every word. Riley's eyes widen, and I shove the tray of nachos onto the small table to my right. "And then I'd like you to make me come."

I don't have time to justify my ask.

One minute, we're staring each other down.

The next, his mouth is on mine. His tongue is swiping across my bottom lip and I'm letting out a moan as my arms wrap around his neck.

Riley moves closer so his chest presses against mine. He's warm and his lips are soft, but his kisses are rough. They're hot and heavy and bordering on the point of aggressive, like he's been waiting for this moment for *years*.

"*Fuck*," he murmurs. The word is sinful. Both steady and unhinged. His mouth moves to my neck, kissing below my ear, and my back arches off the wall. "Are you—"

"I'm fully aware of what I'm asking." I put my hand on his chest. His heart is racing. His pulse is jumping. *I did that.* "And it's not a mistake."

"Tell me to stop," he practically begs. "You have to tell me to stop, Lex, because otherwise, I'm not—"

"I don't want you to stop." It rushes out of me, a tangle in my chest. "I want you to do everything *but* stop. Kissing. Coming. Both at the same time. Preferably sooner rather than later. Or I'll go ask James if he can help instead."

"Don't you fucking dare," Riley growls. He surprises me when he wraps my hair around his wrist and gives it a tug. I gasp when my chin tilts up, our eyes meeting. "You're so fucking bossy. Is this how I get you to shut up? By giving your mouth something to do?"

Holy fuck.

None of this was on my bingo card for tonight.

I figured I'd eat some food with the team. I'd have a drink or two with the girls then head upstairs to get off with my vibrator after a long shower, but this is *so much better*.

Because Riley is looking at me like he's a man starved, like he needs to kiss me again *right this very second*, and I've never been good at denying someone what they want.

"Come on." I run my fingers through his hair. "Doesn't it sound fun? It's only one night," I say.

"One night," he repeats, weighing the words. "And then we—"

"Pretend like it never happened."

"Would that make things awkward between us?"

"I won't be awkward if you won't be awkward. We're both adults, right?"

He stares at me again, and his attention is unnerving. It makes my nipples hard and my underwear wet. I wait with bated breath for his answer, and it comes in the form of a smile. With his thumb tracing down the curve of my jaw and his mouth against my ear.

"Fuck it," he whispers, kissing me again. "One night. Let's play, Lexi."

TWENTY-ONE
RILEY

I DIDN'T MEAN to start kissing Lexi when she got to my room, but now that I am, I can't bring myself to stop.

She's too distracting. Too fucking sexy when I guide her over to the couch and she moves across the cushions to straddle me, a leg on either side of my thighs. She grins when she runs her fingers through my hair, and I'm harder than I've been in months—fucking years, probably.

I'm in so much trouble. She's barely touching me, and I'm thoroughly wrecked. God help me when she takes off her clothes.

"Should we talk about this some more?" I ask.

"We could." She drags her nails down my chest and leaves a trail of red marks in her wake. "Or we could keep going and not talk. What else is there to say?"

"Okay, yes. *Yes*. I want to keep going, Lex, *obviously*. But..." I curl my fingers around her chin then tilt her head down to look at me. Her lipstick is smudged. Her eyes are wide, and she is so goddamn beautiful. "Are you... do we..." I trail off, not knowing what the hell I want to ask. "*Fuck*."

"That should definitely be on the list. Kissing and coming, remember?"

I laugh and rub my hand up her arm. She shivers and leans forward, and I reach out to pinch her nipple. She drops her head back and whines, and I'm six seconds away from ripping every piece of clothing off her body.

"Moment of honesty?" I ask, my brain finally catching up to my dick after having the woman of my dreams on top of me.

"Please," she says.

"I haven't been with anyone since…" I gesture at my lower body. "I haven't touched myself either. This is ah, embarrassing, but it needs to be said. I don't know if things will work how they're supposed to work. I didn't… I should've looked this stuff up online. Do I leave my leg on? Do I take it off?"

I feel vulnerable sharing this with her, but I need her to know what's going on in my head. I don't want to set her up for disappointment, and considering the logistics of how sex would work for me now hasn't been on my radar. It hasn't been in the realm of possibilities of things that might happen to me, but Lexi is looking at me with hooded eyes. She's touching my face and stroking her thumb along my cheek, and maybe, *maybe*, we can figure this out together.

Trial and error and all that shit.

The heat between us cools. I'm afraid she's going to politely rescind her offer. I'll have to ask for a trade, because it's going to be embarrassing as hell to walk out of here with my tail between my legs after her rejection and see her tomorrow.

"Riley," she says, voice pitched low. "I want you to do whatever you're comfortable with. If that means starting in one position and stopping halfway through to adjust, we'll do that."

"Are you sure?" I ask.

"Positive. I'm not turned off by your body. I don't care about scars or prosthetics. I'd like to see you. And I want you to see me." Lexi's fingers curl around the hem of her shirt. She pulls it over her head, revealing a thin black bra strap that shows off her cleavage, and I whine. "If you want."

"Christ." My hands skate up and over her ribs. She's smooth and warm under my palm, and my thumbs trace along the underside of her bra. "I want that so fucking bad."

"I know I was the one who initiated this, but I need to tell you something."

"Anything."

"I've never been with any of the guys on the team. Ever," she adds. "I've never been attracted to any of them. I've never used sex to get ahead. I don't want you to think I run around—"

"I'd never think that," I say fiercely. "You work so hard, and you're damn good at your job. Besides"—I hook my fingers in the strap of her bra and snap it against her skin, electrified when she lets out a sharp hiss—"I don't have a lot of pull on the team. I'm bottom of the barrel right now. I'm not even technically on the roster, for fuck's sake."

"Okay. Good. You're the only one I've ever…" She laughs. "Wow. The only one I've ever straddled in a hotel room."

"Any regrets?"

"None so far."

"What are your other rules, Lex? You're in charge here. Tell me what you want and how you want it, and I'll make it so fucking good for you."

I'm not going to argue about the one-night stipulation. If it's that or nothing, my choice is going to be her. Always. Because she's moving her body and wiggling in my lap until the jut of my cock rubs against the seam of her leggings. Because she's groaning. Rocking forward, her mouth inches from mine, and I'm not in the mood to argue.

I grab her hair again. I wrap the strands around my fist and kiss the corner of her mouth.

"I asked you a question, Lexi. Stop being needy and answer me."

Her inhale is sharp enough to cut glass. She pulls back and I study her, searching for any sign I've gone too far. That I've pushed too hard, too soon, but when our eyes meet, I find a flush on her cheeks and on the top of her chest. Both her bra straps fall down her arms, and I wait for her to make the next move.

Lexi slowly takes her hands off me. She reaches behind her and I blink, watching her breasts spill free as her bra falls off.

Fuck.

Her tits are the perfect size, full and round, and I'd give just about anything to fuck her there. To cover her chest with my cum and write out my name so the lucky bastard who gets to have her after me knows who was there first.

"I'm going to be honest with you," she says, and I blink again, everything around me blurry.

"About what?" I rasp.

It's a wonder I haven't combusted yet, and I'm terrified what it's going to be like when I'm inside her, because this alone could do it for me. A couple thrusts, and I'd be finishing in my pants like I'm a prick with no self-control, and I wouldn't give a shit.

"Men rarely make me come. I fake a lot of my orgasms. Almost all of them. After, I go home, and I finish the job with my vibrator." She wraps her fingers around my wrist. She guides my hand to her neck and rests my palm there. "It's okay if you can't get me off. I'll let you watch me fuck myself with the toy I keep in my suitcase."

I'm going to hell.

I don't stand a chance at redemption, and that's fine by me.

I squeeze her neck, applying the faintest bit of pressure around her windpipe until her smile grows. "Get on the fucking bed, Lexi. And leave your leggings on. I bet I can find your clit without even getting you naked."

She grins and jumps off me, heading for the bed on the far side of the room. She sits on the end of the mattress and I run my hand through my hair, needing a second. Needing a hundred fucking seconds, because I have to do this right.

I stand and slowly walk toward her. Lexi tracks my movements. Her eyes roam down my bare chest and to the front of my sweatpants. She reaches for me when I get close, and I cup her cheek.

"I don't have any other rules. And no hard limits. One night. We keep this to ourselves after. We have fun. That's it. I trust you," she says, turning her head to kiss the center of my palm. "I meant what I said earlier, Riley. If something doesn't feel right or you're uncomfortable and you need a second, we'll stop. I want you. So badly. And that means wanting *all* of you."

I'm going to be obsessed with her after tonight, I just know it. A fucking goner, but that's a problem for later. I'm too hard right now. I'm too fucking worked up from looking down at her swollen lips and her hair scattered everywhere.

"I want you too." I climb on the mattress and hold myself above her. "Can I touch you?"

"Anywhere. Everywhere." She arches her back and wraps her ankles around my waist. Her heels press into my spine, and I rest a hand on her hip. "Please."

That's all I need. I tease her, running my hand up her thigh then down her other leg. Her eyes close. She grips the sheets, twisting the comforter until it's a tangled mess. When her mouth parts and I can tell she's close to begging me, I press my thumb on her clit and rub a slow, lazy circle.

"Did I find it?" I nudge her thighs wider with my hips, crowding her space. I want to see her. I want to hear her and smell her. I want to be fucking *consumed* by her. "Or should I keep trying?"

"That—" She stutters out a breath and squeezes her eyes shut in a way that tells me she's so damn stubborn. "You're close."

"Lying isn't cute, Lexi." I repeat the movement, shocked by how easy it feels to move my body around hers. "Did I find it?" I ask again, thumb pressing harder.

She's wet. I can feel her through her leggings, and I'm tempted to rip the damn things off. I'm close to asking her to fuck my palm.

"Yes." Her voice cracks. Her hold on the sheet wavers, and she lifts her hips. "Riley. *Please.*"

"Those other guys you were with don't know the first thing about taking care of a woman, but me?" I drag my knuckles across her entrance. She cries out, and I smile. "But not me. I know exactly what you need."

I don't know where the hell my confidence is coming from, but I'm going to keep rolling with it. I circle her clit again and reach up, pinching a nipple between my thumb and forefinger. Her legs tip open wider and I lean over her, my teeth sinking into her bottom lip. She's whispering something I'm going to pretend is my name, and I kiss her, just because I fucking can.

"You are—" Lexi stops. She swallows and opens her eyes. Her gaze is hazy, lustful. "An asshole."

"An asshole?" I slow the circles I'm making and grin. "How?"

"You know you're good at this."

"You seem to be benefiting from it."

"So are you." Her palm settles on the front of my sweatpants, and she gives my hard length a gentle stroke. "You like this, don't you?"

So fucking much. I'm in heaven. I could stay here forever. The only thing that would be better is having my head between her thighs, and I'm done drawing this out. I take a second to scoot down the mattress, eyes level with the seam of her leggings, and she tugs on my hair.

"I think I'm going to like everything with you," I say, licking a hot swipe over the black nylon.

Lexi moans, a raspy sound that splits in half when I use my fingers too, finding the rhythm she likes—faster circles. Slower when I yank her leggings down and leave her underwear on, fucking her with my tongue over the lace and fogging up my glasses. I'm going to savor her when I taste her for real, naked and without anything between us.

She pulls on my hair again, and that makes me want to tie her hands up. If this was something longer than just tonight, I'd take my time. I'd slip a handcuff knot up her wrists to keep her in place and see how much I could push her. Maybe I'd attach her ankles to the end of the bed so she was spread open wide for me to enjoy whenever I wanted.

Fuck.

"I'm close," she whispers, and she sounds mad about it. It makes me smile. "Can you—a little more—*shit*. Yeah. Right there."

I press down on her stomach with my free hand. I want to watch her come. I want to watch while I pluck her apart, piece by piece, and when I tease my fingers against where I'm going to bury myself later, pressing against the lace of her underwear so I'm almost inside her, she detonates.

And I've never seen a more beautiful sight.

There's a sheen of sweat on her brow. Her chest is heaving, and my name is falling from her mouth. It's a chant of *Riley* and *please*, and it's hot enough to make pre-cum leak from the tip of my cock.

"That's it," I murmur, her entire body reacting to the sensation of the orgasm. "That's so good, Lexi. Look at you."

It takes a minute for her to come down from the high. When she does, her limbs relax, and she settles against the mattress. I kiss the spot above her knee. Her thigh. Her hip bone and the tattoo she told me about, a small seashell no bigger than my thumb that's sexy as hell.

I work my way up to her mouth, bumping my nose against hers and kissing her softly until her eyes flutter open and she touches my cheek with a smile.

"Wow." She draws out the syllable like she wants to keep it to herself. "That was hot."

"How'd I do?"

"I didn't have to fake too much."

"Brat." I kiss her neck and run my tongue along the line of her throat. "You didn't fake a second of that."

"I can be very convincing." Lexi drapes her arms around my neck and massages her thumb into my nape. I close my eyes and sigh. "That also wasn't what I was expecting."

"What were you expecting?"

"Something sweeter. Softer." She brings her mouth to mine and kisses me, her tongue running along the path of my bottom lip. "Not so mind-blowing."

"I'm happy I could deliver." I splay my palm across her ribs and touch along the underside of her breast. They're the perfect fucking size. Everything about her is perfect. "Are you doing okay?"

"I'm on top of the world." Lexi kisses me again, and I can feel the truth behind the words. "Can I touch you now?"

"You don't have to. I'm, uh… it's going to be quick," I admit. "Like, mocking-me worthy because of how short I'm going to last. If I can finish at all. We'll see."

"I don't care about that." She drops her hands to her chest and pushes her tits together. I wonder if that's what she does when she's alone. When she's using her toy and thinking about something—or someone—specific while she gets off. "It means you're enjoying being here with me."

"Okay. Yeah. Um. That would… you can touch me."

"Here." Lexi sits up and scoots out from under me, patting the spot on the mattress she just occupied. "Lie down. Your legs must be killing you. I'm sure these are new positions you haven't put your body in in a while."

My quads are screaming at me, but I wasn't going to ask her to hold off on her orgasm so I could stretch out my hip flexors. I'm not a selfish asshole.

"I'm okay," I grit out, hoping she can't see me wince as I get on my back. "Like I mentioned earlier, I haven't been with anyone since my last test. Everything would come back negative."

"For me too." She watches me while I maneuver my hips and get comfortable, propping my head up on the pillows. "I've been too busy working with the stubborn hockey player who's apparently an expert in female anatomy."

"Science was always a favorite subject."

When I'm settled, Lexi rubs her hands across my bare chest. She tugs on my sweatpants with a deliberate yank, pulling them halfway down my legs so she can take out my cock. Her fingers curl around my shaft and I groan, my left foot flexing and my right hand forming a fist when she strokes me up and down.

"Wow," she whispers. "You're so big."

I smirk. "Think you can take all of me?"

"Easily. And everywhere you want to try."

"Care to test that theory?"

Lexi brushes her hair out of her face. She bends from her hips and keeps her eyes locked on me as she lowers her head and sucks me into her mouth without blinking.

TWENTY-TWO
LEXI

I'VE BEEN with men who couldn't get me off even after I walked them through the process step by step, and here comes Riley Mitchell, the quiet NHL player who wears glasses and reads romance novels, who just gave me the best orgasm of my fucking life.

That has to be why he knows what he's doing. I bet he's the type of guy who uses the books as reference tools. He probably studies them with a highlighter in his mouth so he can pick out the parts he wants to try, the parts he thinks he'd be good at.

Unbelievable.

Other men should take notes.

I didn't know what was happening. One minute he was kissing me, and the next he was making me come while I was still wearing my underwear and had my leggings halfway down my thighs.

A thousand gold stars for the blushing boy.

His cock is heavy and salty on my tongue, and I angle my head so I can take him deeper. He's big—easily the biggest I've ever had—and I hollow out my cheeks while I get used to his length.

Riley massages my scalp, and when I add my palm to the base of his shaft and twist, his hips lift off the bed. His hand tightens in my hair, tugging on the strands just to the edge of painful before easing off and rubbing the base of my neck.

"Fuck," he slurs, and I think that might be his favorite word. "You're a fucking goddess. I can't believe—" He stops mid-sentence and I blink up at him, a tear caught in my eye. He's watching me with an expression I can't read. It looks like he's stuck somewhere between lust and absurd happiness, and he wipes my cheek with his thumb. "I'm so glad I get to have you like this, Lexi."

I pull off him with a pop, drool hanging from my mouth and my jaw tight. I swap out my mouth with my hand, spitting on my palm before stroking him up and down.

"Could you come like this?" I ask, and his nod is vigorous. I don't know how he doesn't give himself whiplash. "I want to see it."

"If I only get you for one night—*shit*—I want to fuck you."

"You can fuck me. Come first, then we'll go again."

"Seems like you're changing the rules on me, Lex. What happened to *just once*?"

Riley reaches out, his palm landing on my breast. He pinches my nipple then turns the pebbled peak between his fingers—hard—and moisture pools in my underwear. I'm not used to being turned on while giving a blowjob, but watching Riley unravel is doing something to me. His restraint is slipping; his movements get jerkier. His words are more slurred, inaudible. He's lifting his hips to thrust into my hand, and while I'm glad he's going to get off, I'm also glad to see how much mobility he has in his lower half.

A web of emotions burrows its way into my chest, taking root, but I shove them away when I swirl my tongue over the head of his cock and swallow down the pre-cum I find there.

"Just one night. We can do a lot of things in the same night," I clarify, and his laugh is soft. It turns into a groan when I put my mouth on him again and his shaft hits the back of my throat. "If you want."

"I've told you." His hand squeezes my shoulder so hard I'm going to have fingerprints all over my body tomorrow. I can't wait to look at them in the mirror. "I do want that."

I smile around him and don't say anything else, learning exactly what he likes and exactly what it takes to get him close to the edge: my hands working up and down then cupping his balls and my tongue lapping over his slit then licking him from base to tip.

I enjoy every fucking second.

Riley was right. It doesn't take long for the muscles in his left leg to strain. For his grunts to turn louder and fill the room and his hand to tug my hair in warning.

"Lex, I'm going to—"

"I love to swallow," I say, a quick rush of air, and his groan is the last thing I hear before he fills my mouth with warm and sticky cum.

"God. *Fuck*. You are…" Each word is punctuated with a stroke of his thumb. A gentle touch and a soothing graze while the rest of his body spasms. "Wonderful."

I smile at the compliment and take my time to swallow his release and work my mouth off him. When he's finished, I sit back on my heels. I lick my lips and glance down at him. He's staring up at me, wonder in his eye, and he opens his arms, an invitation there. I make quick work of shoving my leggings off but leaving my underwear on, and I curl up next to him with my head on his chest.

"How are you doing?" I ask.

"That's an unfair question." He's winded, practically gasping for air. "Because you rocked my fucking world, so I can't tell if things feel great or if I'm losing my mind."

I laugh. "Maybe both, if I had to guess."

"Yeah." He brushes the hair away from the back of my neck and drops a kiss to my forehead. It's the most romantic thing a guy has ever done for me, and that's alarmingly sad. "Definitely both."

"How does everything feel?" His sweatpants are halfway down his body, and I reach out a hesitant hand, resting it on the socket of his prosthetic leg. "Your leg?"

"Different. It doesn't hurt, but the sensation is... new." Riley shrugs and buries his face in my hair. "Something I'll have to get used to after engaging in clandestine affairs."

"Whoa. Big words there, Mitchy."

"Watch it, Armstrong. I might be close to sedated, but I can still make you pay for those smart-ass comments." He presses a finger into my ribs, and I squeal. "And I read books. I know plenty of big words."

"What are you reading right now?"

"A cowboy romance. Grant bought us all hats to wear at our next book club meeting. He's trying to talk the social media team into doing a western night at an upcoming game, but he's not having a lot of success."

"Yeehaw. Please send me a photo after. Who needs a horse when you can ride a cowboy?" I say around a yawn. "It's been a long day, hasn't it?"

"Morning skate for the guys. A game. Hanging out at a bar. Watching some other guy flirt with you only to be the one to make you come." Riley matches my yawn and pulls me tighter to his chest. "I could sleep for hours."

"Want me to leave? We have an early flight tomorrow."

"Nope. I'm not letting you out of my sight until I get this underwear off." He snaps the elastic band against my skin, smoothing over the sting with his thumb. "It's pretty. Do you always wear stuff like this?"

"I like to spoil myself," I admit. "I'm in an industry with barely any women, and I don't want to appear too girly out of fear the men in power won't take me seriously." I roll my eyes. "Even though what I wear and how I do my hair has no impact on how well I do my job."

"You know what we say to that? Fuck 'em."

"There you go with that feminism of yours. It's very attractive."

"Shucks, Lex. You're going to make me blush."

I tilt my chin and gaze up at him. His eyes are closed, glasses sliding down his nose. He looks relaxed, blissed out with the hint of a smile on his mouth and stubble on his jaw. I reach up and put my hand on his cheek, stroking over the rough hair.

I can't believe he made me come like that. The girls and I have joked before about who we thought would be the best in bed, but I've never given the debate a lot of serious thought. After tonight though, I know the answer to that question.

None of them could compare to Riley.

A shred of regret races through me after remembering the conditions of our time together. It would be *so easy* to see him again, and that's the problem. Easy never stays easy for long, and I value Riley's friendship. I like our time together on the treatment table and all the moments in between. Anything more than a few hours together could ruin that, and I don't want to push him away.

"You're thinking hard." He runs his fingers through my hair, careful when he gets to a knotted section. "Everything okay?"

"Yeah. Yes." I kiss his pectoral muscles and drop my chin to his chest. His eyes open, and I bite back a smile. "I'm fine."

"Anything you want to share with the class?"

"No. Only that you look tired. And you're half asleep," I say.

"You gave me the best blowjob I've ever had."

"*Ever?* Careful, Mitchy. You're going to give me a complex."

"You know you're good at that. You know you're sexy." His hand skims up my leg and stops on my hip. My breath catches when he teases his fingers along the lace of my underwear. "Right?" he rasps. "Or do I need to show you?"

"You can show me," I whisper. "I've always been a good learner."

"I need another minute. Athlete, recovery, out of practice, all of that. But I want to make you come again." He yanks on my underwear, pulling them down just far enough so he can almost see my pussy. "Can I take these off?"

When he's teasing me like this, whispering in that low tone with heavy-lidded eyes that look like he's about to pounce, I'm helpless. A proud patriarchy supporting woman, because who am I to deny him what he wants?

Especially when what he wants is *me*.

"Please," I tell him, not embarrassed by the way it comes out like a beg.

"I'm going to fuck you after." Riley pulls away and pushes his palm into my shoulder to get me to lie flat on my back. I'm not sure anyone's ever been so gentle with me while also having fire behind their eyes, and the juxtaposition makes me shiver. "Sound good to you?"

"I'm so glad I didn't stay downstairs."

He laughs and switches positions, finding his way back between my legs. I see the wince flash across his face when he gets settled on his stomach, the way he reaches down and does something with his prosthetic, and I want to tell him he can take it off if it'll make him more comfortable because I don't like to see him in pain.

"Me too," he agrees.

Riley drags my underwear down in a torturous pull. When he gets them off, he keeps his eyes on me when he shoves the pair in his pocket with a sheepish grin.

"Saving those for later?" I ask.

"I need something to prove I slept with the hottest woman in the world. No one would believe me."

"You don't seem like the bragging type."

"I'm not. You said this stays between us. And it will."

His cheeks turn pink. I don't know how this is the same man who just bossed me around. He's not shy when his attention roams down my body, taking in my breasts and my stomach then stopping between my legs.

He groans, and it might be the hottest sound I've ever heard. There's fierceness behind the noise, and I can't find it in me to be embarrassed by how thoroughly he's looking at me.

"See something you like?" I ask, the words splintering when he blows a puff of air against my clit.

"Gonna fucking worship you," he grunts, thrusting his hips into the bed, and I know he will.

He's purposeful when he pushes a finger inside me, another groan firing from his throat when I open my thighs wider to give him more space. Riley fucks me slowly, carefully, watching my every move to figure out what I like without having to tell him.

When he adds a second finger, I shut my eyes. I try to steady myself, the overwhelming wave of satisfaction starting to roll through me, because he curls his fingers. He presses on my clit with his thumb, then his tongue, and there's no way in hell I should already be so close, so soon.

"God," he whispers. "If this is what you look like taking my fingers, how are you going to look when you take my cock?"

"Like I'm being impaled, probably." I gasp, squirming when he drapes his arm firmly across my stomach so I can't move. I'm desperate for more of him, the sensation too much but also not nearly fucking enough. "On account of how big you are."

Riley laughs. He licks a long swipe over my pussy and the mattress dips when he thrusts his hips again. There's too much happening around me. His hands are *everywhere*; moving from the inside of my thighs to my ankles so I rest my feet on his shoulders. Back up and sliding under me so he can grab a handful of my ass in a tight squeeze.

It's exquisite. I feel boneless when he goes from two fingers inside me to three, the stretch a delicious ache as my entire body starts to respond to him.

"Say something," I blurt, mortified by the outburst.

"What?" He kisses my knee then sucks on the skin, a spot I didn't know I liked being touched but absolutely love. "What do you want me to say?"

"I like being talked to. Being—"

"Praised. You like being told you're good, don't you, Lexi?" His touch turns rougher, possessive. "You might be strong and independent, but at the end of the day, you want to know you're taking me so fucking well."

TWENTY-THREE
LEXI

I WHINE. Heat washes over me, and the high I'm chasing is within reach. I scramble for it, sinking into the awareness of being with someone who pays attention. Who watches me, *reads* me, and when Riley shoves his glasses up his nose and puts his tongue on me one more time, I lose it.

It's the hottest, nerdiest thing I've ever seen, and a million stars explode in my vision. I cry out, reaching for the back of his head and pressing his face into my pussy because it's *so fucking good*, I want it to last as long as possible.

"I want you to make a mess, Lexi," he mumbles against me, his stubble scratching against my skin. "Drench my hand. Let that be another souvenir. I'll never wash it again."

A second orgasm sneaks up on me, less intense but just as wonderful, and my toes scrunch. I whimper, caught off guard by his ask. A sob escapes my mouth, and I feel Riley moving. His fingers slow, his touch relents back to soft and easy. Fresh tears spring in my eyes, and I'm exhausted. So weary that more tears fall, and I try to cover my face with my hands.

"Hey. *Hey.*" Riley sits next to me and pulls me into his lap. He strokes my back and kisses my wet cheek. "What's wrong? Talk to me, Lexi."

"That was—" My body shakes, the lingering pleasure undeniable. Maybe it's going to stay with me forever. "So—"

"You did so well," he murmurs, and he's hard under me. The tip of his cock presses into my ass, and *gosh*, I want that too. "So good. Twice? I've never—"

"Me either." I kiss his neck and the space below his ear, smiling when he hums. "You're magic."

"*You're* magic." His mouth is on my shoulder, and I'd love to find a way to tattoo his touch on my body. "We can stop there for the night. I don't need—the first time was beyond my wildest dreams."

"I want you." I lift myself off him. "How…should you—"

"I'm going to, ah, keep my leg on." Riley swallows. "Tonight. I'm… I don't want—"

"I've seen you without your prosthetic before." I rest my hand on his right thigh, the metal of his leg hard against my palm. "And you're beautiful. I want you to know that."

"*Fuck*." He shakes his head, disbelieving. "We're going to have to get creative here. I didn't have a chance to look up the best sex positions for people who are missing limbs."

I stifle a giggle, but he laughs too. This all feels so normal, something we've done a hundred times, and the realization makes my stomach swoop low.

"Do you think there's a website for that?" I ask.

"There's definitely a Reddit thread somewhere."

"People on the internet are very knowledgeable."

"I'm thinking—" He stops to lick his lips and look at my body again. He takes my nipple between his fingers, twisting it and smiling when I hiss. "You on top. Riding me. That doesn't involve the muscles in my lower body."

"I like that idea. Do you want help taking your pants all the way off or—"

"I can do it."

Riley squeezes my waist and we adjust our positions so he can swing his legs over the side of the bed. He grunts when he shimmies his sweatpants off and I crawl over so I can kiss his shoulders. So I can wrap my arms around him and skate my hands down his body, my fingers aching to feel him.

I've never been one for physical touch or cuddling after sex, but it's different with Riley. It's like I can't get enough of him, and when he's finally naked and looks back at me, I want him in every way I can have him.

"Get on the bed," I say, and his smile hitches wide.

"I like when you're bossy." It takes him a beat to stretch out on the mattress, but when he does, his hand slips into mine. He strokes his thumb over my knuckles and tugs me toward him. "C'mere."

"I want to look first."

"You've seen my body."

"I haven't seen you like *this*. It's different when we're not at the arena. Can I?"

"Yeah." He nods. "You can."

I look at his tattoo and the hair on his stomach. At the faint scars and muscles that are weaker on the right side of his body. I travel lower to his cock standing tall, then to his legs. I study the prosthetic I've seen before and his foot, mesmerized by every inch of him.

He's perfect.

"You said you wanted me on top?" I ask, and he nods again, quicker this time.

"I would've picked that position even if I could move around however I wanted. I know I finished the first time, but I don't know what my body is capable of during round two. I might not—"

"That's okay. We'll try together and figure it out."

"There's, um, a condom in my wallet. On the dresser under the television."

"Were you planning to get lucky tonight, Mitchy?"

"God, no. This is a fever dream. Ethan brought a box to the arena a week ago and threw them around the locker room.

I didn't want the custodians to have to clean them up, so I found one the guys forgot to grab and shoved it in my wallet. I forgot about it until now."

"Look at that divine intervention." I hop off the bed and hurry to the dresser, opening his wallet. A small photo falls out, and I pick it up. "What's this?"

"The team picture from last year. I like to remember the good days."

"Is today not a good day?" I ask over my shoulder.

"Today is the best day I've had in months," he says. "By a longshot."

"We should make a point to say which days are good." I tuck the photo back in its place and pluck the foil packet from behind a twenty-dollar bill. "So you don't forget."

"I like that idea," he says, and when I turn to walk back to him, he holds up a hand. "Stop there for a second."

I freeze in my tracks. "Is everything okay?"

"Just wanted to watch you. You're so beautiful."

I smile and slow my steps toward him. I climb on the bed and crawl between his legs, bringing my mouth close to his.

"Do you like watching, Riley?" I whisper.

"Yes," he says, voice thick. "I do."

"It's a shame you got me off earlier. I would've let you watch me play with myself."

He moans and snatches the condom out of my hand, tearing it open with one rip. "You aren't fair."

"Sorry, Riley baby." I straddle him, hovering myself over his length. Before I have a chance to spit on the latex for lubrication—I'm actually afraid he might hurt me—he's sliding three fingers back in me. Making me writhe above him and roll my hips, and everything in me pulls tight. "Now who's not playing fair?"

"Sorry, *Lexi baby*," he murmurs, mimicking me, and I hate how much I love it. "Looks like I don't need to do too much work to get you ready. You're still wet."

I groan when he pulls out of me, left aching and needy. He guides me down, lowering me until the head of his cock pushes against my entrance, and my groan turns into a gasp.

"That's it." Riley wraps his pinky and thumb around my throat, his middle three fingers at my mouth. "Open up and suck."

My lips pop open and I groan again when he puts his fingers on my tongue. I taste myself on him, and I lick away the moisture I left behind. I don't have a chance to ask what happens next because he's lifting his hips. He's sinking deeper inside me, and everything gets hazy.

"*Fuck.*" It's my turn to curse, and the world spins around me. "You—"

"Are only halfway in," he grunts, and I don't know if I want to laugh or cry. "Can I—"

"I will kill you if you don't move right this second, Riley."

He listens, guiding me down and muttering his encouragement along the way. Cautious until he's fully buried, then he stops moving.

"Holy shit. Look how well we fit together," he says, and I glance down at where we're joined. "Fucking perfect."

It *is* perfect, and when our gazes lock, something snaps in both of us.

I lean forward and crash my mouth into his at the same time his hands find their way back on me; at my throat, the small of my back, kneading my ass.

I lift off him then slam back down, our groans in sync when I ride him like my life depends on it.

"Good?" I ask, checking to make sure he's doing okay.

"No." A head shake, and I almost freeze before he touches my clit. "Better than good. So goddamn incredible."

Our movements match, both of us wanting to help the other finish. He's thick inside me, and every time I roll my hips, he answers me with a thrust of his own. The rhythm is easy, effortless. He touches my neck again, a squeeze that tightens around my throat when I nod to show my consent. I watch him, mouth parted, eyes closed, while I rock forward, then up, then down his shaft until there's no space between us, not wanting to miss out on a single inch.

"Riley. I think I'm going to come from—"

"Thank fuck. I'm waiting for you to go first."

"Why am I not surprised you're so chivalrous in the bedroom?" I drop my head back, hair swishing against my back. "Why am I not surprised you're going to be the first guy to get me to finish from sex?"

"It's"—a thrust—"A fucking"—Another thrust that makes me cry out. His fingers are back on my clit, circling and teasing—"Honor."

I give in, not questioning the reasons why he's capable of doing things no one else has ever done. It doesn't matter, because everything is a mess of limbs and sweat and a mumbled, *can I finish inside you?* and an emphatic *god. Yes, please* before we're both tumbling. Falling headfirst into nirvana that takes over my entire being, but Riley holds me steady.

I feel him pulse inside me, finishing, and a vague thought races through my head: what would it feel like with nothing between us? No protection, just him?

Somewhere in the back of my mind I know it would be ecstasy.

"Well," Riley finally says after our breathing returns to normal. After my skin starts to cool and the sweat on my chest starts to dry. "I think my therapist will be happy to know I'm out of the depression stage of my grief. A condom full of cum has to mean I'm on the upside of things."

I burst out laughing and fall forward, my chest pressing against his. He holds me there, secure and safe while he pulls out of me. We both hiss at the break in our contact, and a void settles over me as my shoulders shake and he laughs too.

"You could also be donating to a sperm bank," I suggest, smiling when he arranges me next to him on the bed.

"True." He carefully slides the condom off his length and ties it off, tossing it toward the trash can in the bathroom. He misses then huffs out a chuckle. "Oof. Fucking ugly shot there. There's a reason I play hockey."

"A swing and a miss." I kiss his cheek. "Thanks for the great fuck, Mitchy."

"You're not leaving yet, are you?"

"That was the point of this. We get off, then I go."

"My dick is still half hard. You'll hurt my ego if you leave now. And you should shower. Sex ed and all of that."

"You make a convincing argument." I sigh and grab the sheets, draping them around us. "Fifteen minutes and one shower, then I'm hitting the road."

"Forty-five, I'll order us room service, then I'll do recon in the hall to make sure none of the guys are getting back at the same time."

"What kind of room service?"

"What's your favorite food?"

"Grilled cheese," I say. "With a big ass pickle."

"Ah, yes. You and your love of heart attack-inducing sandwiches." Riley grabs the hotel phone, adjusts his crooked and smudged glasses, and looks down at me. "Fries?"

"Yeah." I swallow. "And a shit ton of ketchup, please. Oh! And a milkshake."

"Oreo, right?"

"Yeah," I repeat, the word stuck. "That's right."

"Get comfortable, Armstrong. You're not free from me yet."

Forty-five minutes turns into a shower where Riley sits on the lid of the toilet and talks to me while I wash my hair. A heaping pile of food and an old western movie we barely watch because we're too busy making out. Chatting about his teammates and my friends. And when I finally slip out of his room two hours before we need to be downstairs to catch the team bus to the airport, I'm so exhausted, but I can't locate a smidge of regret.

My phone chimes when I press my keycard against my door, and I wait until I'm safely in my room before I open it.

> RILEY
>
> Dude. I just hooked up with the HOTTEST woman.
>
> And I stole her underwear.
>
> *Attachment: 1 image*

It's a picture of him with my thong between his teeth, the flash of the camera reflecting in his glasses. His hair is a mess. There are marks all over his chest and neck from my mouth and fingernails, and something unexplainable stirs in my soul when a fourth message comes through.

> RILEY
>
> Today was a good day.

> ME
>
> It was, wasn't it?

> RILEY
>
> See you soon, Lexi baby.

TWENTY-FOUR
LEXI

GIRLS JUST WANT TO HAVE FUN(DAMENTAL RIGHTS) AND GOOD SEX

PIPER
Where did you disappear to the other night, Lex?

ME
When?

MAVEN
After our game in Miami! You dropped off food for us, then we didn't see you again.

ME
Oh! I was tired and wanted to head back to my room early.

PIPER
Did you take the cute guy you were talking to at the bar with you? ;)

> **ME**
> The pilot? He was British and nice, but nope.

> **EMMY**
> Don't ever get involved with a pilot. They're all slimy.

> **MADELINE**
> Is this from firsthand experience, Em?

> **EMMY**
> I will not confirm or deny my experience with shitty men.

> **MAVEN**
> That's a yes!

> **PIPER**
> Are you feeling better now, Lex?

> **ME**
> Like a new woman.

> **EMMY**
> Amazing what some rest can do.

> **ME**
> Rest. Yeah.

A WEEK LATER, and I'm still thinking about the filthy things Riley and I did.

I'm thinking about his mouth and his hands, and when I wonder about how many people he must have been with before me if he's *that good* at knowing exactly what to do, a flicker of jealousy creeps up my spine.

I'd probably burst into flames if I stepped inside a church, but I can't bring myself to care. Not when I'm seeing him for the first time today since he got me off and stole my underwear.

We've sent a few text messages back and forth, but it hasn't been anything substantial. Neither one of us have brought up *that night*, and something like nerves have been sitting in my stomach since I woke up this morning.

I almost canceled our session, but I don't want him to think I'm hiding from him.

Or worse.

Developing feelings for him and wanting to do it again.

I snort and toss the towels some of the guys used after an earlier ice bath into the hamper. The door to the training room clicks open behind me, and my heart jumps to my throat. I slow my breathing and turn around with a grin, only to be disappointed when I find Coach in the doorway.

"Oh. Hey," I say, and the scowl he's wearing deepens.

"Something wrong?" he asks.

"Nope. I thought you were someone else."

"I'm adding you to the list of people disappointed to see me."

"Not sure what you're talking about. You're at the top of the list of my favorites."

"Sarcasm isn't a good look on you, Armstrong," Coach draws out.

"What's up? You never come in here," I say.

"Because I hate when people come into my workspace without an invitation. I like to extend that same courtesy to other people when I can."

"Wow. You're such a Good Samaritan."

"Doing my civic duty. Is Mitchell here yet?"

"Nope. Should be any minute." I grab a spray bottle and wipe down the treatment table Liam was on thirty minutes ago while I tended to his sore ankle. "Why?"

"Just wanted to check in and see how things were going."

"Stick around. I think you'll be impressed when you see his progress. I know I'm not an occupational therapist, but I hope I've done a good job."

"She's done a great job," Riley says, stepping into the room. "Don't let her sell herself short."

"Hi. Hey. What's up?" I ask.

Our eyes meet, and the air is tense. There's a pause, a throat clearing, my gaze bouncing to the front of his shorts and knowing what's hiding underneath. A cocky smirk he tosses my way before he adjusts his glasses and strolls over to the table, and I hope Coach can't pick up on the awkwardness between us.

"Your gait looks great, Mitchell." Coach unfolds his arms from across his chest. "And I'm glad to hear Lexi hasn't had to make any excuses for you lately. Not a single absence listed in her progress reports since October."

"I'm a good student," Riley says, and I swear I hear the undertones behind his statement.

"He's doing well, isn't he?" I beam and grab a rolled-up towel. "We're increasing the intensity of the physiotherapy exercises today. Do you want to stick around?"

"No. I don't want to overstep," Coach says. "And my daughter has figure skating lessons this afternoon."

"No hockey for her?" Riley asks, sitting on the edge of the table and swinging his legs to the front. "She could be the next Emmy. I'm sure she has some of your skills in her blood."

"Trust me, I've tried. She wants to wear figure skating dresses, not pads." He glances at me. "You good?"

"Why wouldn't I be?" I grab the clipboard I use to track Riley's progress and sit on a rolling stool. "All is well here."

He turns his attention to Riley. "I'm proud of you."

"Thanks, Coach." Riley smiles and gets to work on his prosthetic. "And thanks for believing in me."

With a grunt, Coach disappears out the door, and the room gets quiet.

"So," I say brightly after flipping through my stack of notes. "We're going to try some new things today."

"New things? Like what?" Riley asks.

"Bridges and similar things. Your core is getting stronger, and I want to see how you fare with some different movements. My hope is in the new year we'll start working on the exercises you're used to doing as a hockey player like single-leg squats and RDLs."

"Sounds good to me. I was at my prosthetist's office yesterday. I've had some trouble walking the last couple of days, and he had to adjust my socket. It's nice to have a break from lugging this thing around."

Riley pops off his leg and I take it from him, leaning it against the wall like I always do. We have a routine in here, but that routine hasn't included wondering if he still has a hickey on his neck from our night together. A quick glance while he scoots back on the table shows the mark below his ear has faded, and I'm a little sad about it.

"Did his adjustments help?"

"Yeah. It's amazing how things can be out of whack by half a millimeter and throw everything else off." He fixes his shorts and stretches out his left leg. "I've been very good at doing my solo exercises this week. I, uh, wanted to make you proud."

"Yeah?" I stand and set my clipboard on the stool, moving so I'm next to him. "I'm sure you will."

"What are we doing first?"

"Bridges. I need you on your back, please."

"No laughing at me." Riley maneuvers his body, and I wait patiently until he's flat on the table with his arms folded behind his head. "God. I can't believe people sleep like this."

"Back sleepers have something seriously wrong with them."

"How do you sleep?"

"On my side. What about you?"

"Side sleepers unite." He turns his chin so he's looking my way. There's something else on the tip of his tongue, but he closes his mouth. He takes a deep breath, bringing his legs together. "What do you want me to do?"

Make me come again.
Put your hand around my throat.
Tell me how good I am.
A million other things that should not *still be lingering in my brain.*

"With your left foot on the table, you're going to lift your hips in the air," I say, worried it sounds too breathy, like his presence is affecting me when it absolutely shouldn't be. "Then you'll bring your hips back down, and we'll repeat."

"Whenever I think the exercises are going to be easy, they end up kicking my ass." He grimaces when he moves his body, and his fingers dig into the leather of the table. "How do you come up with these things?"

"I spend a lot of time researching. I study documents from hospitals and outpatient facilities. I consult with people knowledgeable in limb loss. I'm learning a lot, but I'm used to treating hockey injuries. I want to make sure I'm giving you the right exercises to work on the right parts of your body."

"I'd say it's working. Moving is easier than it was in September. I hope it's because I'm actually getting stronger, not the weather getting cooler. November is great, isn't it?"

"Really great."

I put my hand on his shoulders to keep his chest from lifting off the table. I can't believe we're talking about the *weather*. It's like we're both actively avoiding mentioning the elephant in the room, and I hate it.

I'm never sleeping with someone I work with ever again.

"How was your week?" I find myself asking, desperate to break the silence between us.

It's not like us, and every second that passes where he doesn't say anything, I'm transported back to his hotel room and the slick glide of his fingers. The sounds of his heavy breathing and the feel of his hands everywhere on my body.

My poor vibrator has been working overtime, and I only thought about him once when I got off last night.

Okay, twice, but only because I can't get those words—*I know exactly what you need*—out of my goddamn head.

Fuck him and his dirty mouth to high heaven.

"Fine." Riley grunts when I touch his residual limb to test his range of motion. "I FaceTimed my parents so they could see I'm surviving. Went to a therapy appointment. Hung out with Hudson, Madeline, and Lucy at the library."

"Sounds like a busy week."

"Yeah. It's nice to be busy. Better than sitting on my couch and moping. What about you?"

"Nothing special. I started a new book. Taught four Pilates classes. Went on a run down by the Potomac."

"What book did you start?"

"A romance book."

"Vague. Which one?"

I forget Riley isn't going to mock me for my literary choices. He—and the other guys on the team—are enthusiastic supporters of romance novels and the women who read them. I don't have to brace myself for the teasing "romance books have no substance, so they don't count as a *real* book" that normally follows.

God forbid someone likes to pretend they're in a fictional world where women are treated right and orgasms are plentiful, because no way in hell does that happens in the reality where I'm currently living.

Except for Riley.

"Lex?"

"Hm? Sorry," I say.

"Is everything okay?"

"Everything is fine. I got distracted there for a minute."

"I knew it." Riley sighs and pushes up on his elbows. He

positions his legs over the table and stares at me. "You regret last week."

"*What?* No. I don't. At all."

"You don't have to lie to protect my feelings, Lex, and if I'm making you uncomfortable, I can take my rehab back to an outpatient facility so you don't have to deal with me."

"Riley." I step closer to him. "That's not what's going on here. I'm… confused how we're supposed to act around each other because I've never seen the person I've hooked up with out in the real world after the fact, and I'm going to be seeing a lot of you."

"You're the one who said it was only one time." His smile hitches. He leans back on his palms and watches me. "If I had it my way, we would be going back to your place after this and having round two."

"That wouldn't be very friendly of us, would it?"

"I don't know. I've never slept with a friend before."

The offer is tempting, and for half a second, I consider it.

But then I remember there are at least five more months left in the season, and I don't want to spend them awkwardly dancing around him while our friends watch and wonder why we can't be in the same room.

It was sex.

Great sex.

That's it.

And I need to get my head out of my ass and stop thinking about him.

"I'm sorry. I'm being weird. Can we start the day over?" I ask.

"Too late. I'm already sweating my ass off from your training plan. There's no going back now." He kicks his left leg out, foot nudging my knee. "Tell me what book you're reading or I'm going to be pissed."

I relax, laughing when he blinks at me with big, wide eyes. "There are motorcycles involved."

"Ethan would be so proud."

"It's good. I'll bring it for you to read when I'm finished."

"It's like our own library system."

"Yeah, and you're distracting me from getting your exercises done. Get on your stomach, Mitchell. I'm onto your games."

"Guess I need to find a new distraction tactic." He lifts his shirt to wipe his forehead then his glasses, and I know he's testing me. I pointedly stare at the floor. "I'll figure you out, Armstrong."

"We're doing hip extensions next. Same position you would get in for hamstring curls."

"Love when you're bossy." Riley swings his lower half around and lays on his stomach. "What am I doing for this one?"

"You're going to lift your residual limb off the table."

"Ah. Okay. How many times?"

"Twelve."

"Fuck. You're mean."

He starts the movement with his right leg. I place both of my hands gently on his lower back, right on the start of his backside, to make sure he's working the correct muscles.

"Keep your stomach on the table," I explain, getting a grunt in response. "There you go. That was a great adjustment, Riley. Feel the difference?"

"Unfortunately," he grits out, and his next rep is slower. "Like this?"

"Perfect."

I keep my hands on him, my grip slackening with each rep he completes. I want him to do it on his own, and when he finishes number twelve, he groans.

"That was hard as hell."

"You did great." I grab a towel and a water, bringing them over to him while he sits up. "Does anything hurt?"

"There's some throbbing and tingling on the right side of

my body. My leg hurts even though it's not there. It's weird. It doesn't happen all the time. Sometimes it's like static."

He runs a hand over his right thigh, thumbs pressing into his muscles. He works lower, massaging his residual limb, and I watch him so I can try to learn what helps.

I read about phantom pain when I started researching limb loss and what happens after an amputation. It's a physiological experience with a few root causes like nerve damage and central sensitization, and besides medication and some therapies that may or may not be effective, there's only so much you can do.

"Is there anything I can do to help?" I ask.

"Nah. I don't want to take any pain meds. I started to rely on them too much after my surgery, and I don't want to go down that road again. I've also looked into things like mirror therapy, but I think I need to get a year of healing under my belt before I try anything new."

"I know I'm not qualified for anything beyond athletic training and some physical therapy, but if there's something I can do to make the pain less, I'm happy to try."

"Weirdly enough, these exercises are helping. I'm feeling less of the phantom sensations than I was in September and October."

"You're strengthening the muscles and nerves in your right leg. That helps with the pain, according to my research."

Riley gives me a long look, and I don't know what he's trying to convey. His eyebrows are pulled together, but there's a softness in his gaze. Gratitude, almost, in the tilt of his head and his heavy exhale. "It means so much to me that you've spent your free time looking things up on my behalf."

"I've never worked with an amputee before, and I want to make sure we're doing this right and in a way that could get you back on the ice one day."

"Do you… still think that's possible?" Riley asks, and I nod.

"I do. You're making a lot of improvements, and as we start to shift to the exercises your body remembers from years of playing hockey, we can talk about approaching the ice again."

He swallows and glances at me. "I can't thank you enough for all you're doing, Lex. I wouldn't be this far along in my recovery if it weren't for you."

"Yes, you would." I hand over his water bottle, and when he takes it from me, his fingers brush against mine. An electric current runs through me with the contact, and I have to control my breathing. "You'd be just fine."

There's a pause, but it's not as awkward as before. Riley sips the water and stares at the wall. I set the towel next to him and sit back on my stool.

"It was good, wasn't it? Our night together," he says.

"No." I can't help but smile, remembering his words. "It was goddamn incredible."

"That's a good answer. I won't bring it up again."

"Moment of honesty?"

"Please," he says.

"I'm glad you did. It was one time. I had a lot of fun. We've acknowledged it happened, and now we can go on with our lives."

"Friends?" Riley holds out his hand, and I wrap my fingers around his.

"Friends," I repeat. "Now get on your back, Mitchell, so I can torture you some more."

"There she is." He laughs, light and loud. "Glad to see you again, Armstrong."

This friend thing is going to be so goddamn easy.

TWENTY-FIVE
RILEY

PUCK KINGS

EASY E

What do you think, baby? Do you like it?

Attachment: 1 image

SULLY

Why the fuck are you sending us pictures of you shirtless in a motorcycle helmet?

And who the fuck are you calling baby?

Is that a washcloth on your dick?

Fucking Christ. I hate this chat.

G-MONEY

He's calling me baby, obviously.

MAVVY

It would definitely be me.

EASY E

LMAO whoops. Wrong chat.

HUDDY BOY

... You send photos of yourself naked in a motorcycle helmet to other chats?

EASY E

Uh, yeah. I'm not out here getting NBA money, so I need to do something to make some extra cash.

Kidding!!! I have a social media account where I post videos of me wearing my motorcycle helmet. The ladies love it, and I've been texting one.

MAVVY

Jesus. This sounds like a recipe for disaster. When your dick pics are leaked, I can't help you.

ME

Be careful, E.

EASY E

Awww. You guys love me.

The world would be lucky if they got to see my dick pics.

And this girl doesn't know who I am. No faces, no names. She's cool.

ME

You like her?

EASY E

I mean, I like the photos she sends me.

HUDDY BOY

I can't wait for the day you grow up.

G-MONEY

Okay, but who WOULD you call baby out of all of us? Me, right?

ME

Oh, boy. Here we go.

Sully has left the chat
Easy E has added Sully to the chat

EASY E

I'd call Sully baby, obviously.

And I'd follow it up with a Daddy too ;)

Wait. Does Piper call you that in bed?

SULLY

If you say her name one more time, I'm going to fucking murder you.

G-Money has left the chat
Mavvy has added G-Money to the chat

G-MONEY

I can see I'm not wanted here.

ME

I'd pick you, Grant.

G-MONEY

Shucks. Thanks, Mitchy. I love you too.

MAVVY

What about me?

HUDDY BOY

We should really talk to someone about our co-dependence.

EASY E

Attachment: 1 image

Whoops, did it again!

MAVVY

At this point, I think you're trying to show us your dick.

HUDDY BOY

Ethan. Your jersey is behind you in that picture. And so is the team photo from the Stanley Cup last year.

EASY E

I'll say I'm a dedicated fan boy. She'll never know.

SULLY

It's a shame I didn't get drafted by Utah. Life would be much better.

MAVVY

You don't mean that, Goalie Daddy.

SULLY

No, he doesn't and this is Piper responding and letting you all know he secretly smiles when he reads the group chat but now I have to hide because he's throwing me over his shoulder for telling you that and hfsdfuew798ytfu89ji14

G-MONEY

Goalie Daddy really loves us.

This is the best day of my life.

NOVEMBER TURNS TO DECEMBER, and the boys have put together a 15-17 record during the first two months of the season. I'm feeling better both mentally and physically, and I've successfully gone four weeks without getting on my hands and knees and begging Lexi to let me fuck her again.

Boy, am I proud of myself.

After the initial awkwardness wore off, things got back to normal. She keeps kicking my ass in the training room, I keep showing up, and we talk like the sex didn't happen.

It's for the best: the longer I think about the night we were together, the more tempted I am to pull her underwear out of my drawer and jerk off to it.

Last I checked, that's not very *friendly* behavior, and I like how things are going. I don't want to fuck anything up by acting like a goddamn creep.

"Mitchell," Coach calls out, and I glance his way from where I'm sitting on the bench watching morning skate.

"What's up?" I ask.

"Come by my office when we're finished here. I want to talk to you about something."

"Ooooh, Mitchy is in trouble," Ethan sings out from the stickhandling station he and a few other guys are in, and Coach glares at him from center ice.

"We were going to wrap up today with some easy skating and a light half-ice game, but since Richardson wants to run his mouth, we're going to run a corner to half wall two v one drill where he's the single player. Again and again and again without a break. The first pair who connects on four consecutive passes in a row without Ethan stealing the puck gets to sit out of morning skate tomorrow," Coach says, and everyone groans.

"My quads are fucking smoked," Grant whines, skating

toward the bench to grab a sip of Bodyarmor from his bottle. "Ethan never shuts the fuck up."

"Be the first to not let him steal the puck." I stand and lean over the boards so I can have a good viewpoint of the drill. They're going to be confined to a small area on the ice, and I don't want to miss everyone trying to kick Ethan's ass. "You can do it."

"My passes have been shit this year. I have two assists—that's almost last in the league. And I'm notorious for turnovers after missing a pass. Any pointers?" Grant asks.

"You know I'm a defense guy, but you need to expand the area where you can receive the puck. You're not going to get a tape to tape pass every time, so you can't be afraid to adjust your grip to try to keep your blade on the ice. Here. Let me see your stick."

"All yours, Mitchy."

Grant tosses me his CCM stick, and I flip it in my hands. I inhale sharply as I run my palms down the length of the carbon. It's the first time I've held one since the night of the accident, and I squeeze my eyes shut to hold back a sob.

After so much time away, it's like coming home.

My thumb rubs over the tape on the handle, and I grip it tight.

"Okay." My voice shakes. "Let me get on the ice."

"Right this way, sir." Grant skates backward to the bench gate and opens it for me. He holds out his arm so I can steady myself, and I grip his practice jersey. "Show me your mastery, Mitchy."

"Don't let me fall on my ass," I warn him, and Maverick skates up behind us.

"I'm here for reinforcements," he says, and I swallow down the ball of emotion sitting in the center of my chest. "Ready to catch if necessary."

"I weigh a hundred eighty-five pounds," I say, and Maverick scoffs.

"Please. I squat double that, Mitchy, and lifting people is one of my favorite hobbies. Just ask Emmy," he says, and I laugh.

"I'd prefer not to." I turn to Grant. "Watch my hands. If I keep the same grip on the stick when I reach out for a far pass as I would for a tape to tape pass, I'm only going to be able to catch it with the heel of the stick, which could cause a turnover. If I keep my bottom hand loose, I can slide the stick through my bottom hand in whatever direction I need to go—either closer to the blade when the puck is coming to your feet, or up to the handle if the puck is far out. The blade will stay on the ice, and you can control the pass more efficiently."

"That makes so much sense. Can I try?" he asks, and I nod, handing him the stick.

He taps the blade on the ice and Maverick skates to the blue line, firing off a pass that's headed to Grant's left. He follows my instructions, sliding his hand down toward the blade, and stops the puck from soaring straight past him.

"There you go," I say, and Grant leaps in the air.

"Holy shit. You're a genius, Riley. Pass me another one, Cap," he yells to Maverick, and a second one is shot his way. This time, he brings his hand up the stick, whooping when he stops the puck again. "Oh, this is a fucking game changer."

"That's a great drill, Mitchy." Maverick skates up next to me, spraying ice on my sneakers. "Where'd you learn it?"

"My college coach. It goes against our instincts as players to keep our gloves glued to the stick, but it works," I say.

"I'm gonna be the league leader in assists, baby," Grant yells, taking off for the pairs of players lining up for the drill.

"Don't forget, Mitchell. My office after this," Coach says, and I nod.

"It's good to have you back out here, Mitchy," Maverick says, tapping my calf with his stick. "We've missed you."

I smile, taking in the feel of the ice under my foot. The

bright lights and the smell of sweat clinging to his jersey. "It's good to be back."

I SLIDE into the chair across from Coach thirty minutes later and look at him. "What's up?"

"How do you feel about coaching?" he asks, cutting right to the point.

"Uh, in general?"

"How do you feel about being a coach?"

"It's not something I ever considered because I don't think it's for me."

"Why not?"

"I'm not sure. I don't know if I'm patient enough."

Coach lifts an eyebrow. "And I am?"

"You know what I mean." I pull on the sleeves of my hoodie and shrug. "I don't think I have enough hockey smarts to guide other players on what they're doing wrong."

"I've been working with Grant for months to get his passes under control, and you fixed it in five minutes."

"I don't know if I would call it *fixed*. I gave him a suggestion and it worked one time."

"It was a good suggestion." Coach leans back in his chair and stares at me. "I want you to have more of a role at practice and during games. I know you can't be on the ice in your skates, but I want you out there running drills with the guys. Giving them a different perspective than what I can provide and offering fixes for problems I'm not seeing."

"Really?" I sit up straight. "What's the catch?"

"No catch. I'm waiting on approval from the league to add you as a non-uniformed player allowed on the bench in a coaching capacity."

"Are you serious?"

"Dead serious, Mitchell. You took this team to back-to-back Stanley Cups. You should be out there with us chasing a three-peat, but life isn't fucking fair. I'm doing what I can to balance the scales."

"Wow. Okay. Yeah. I'm… that would be awesome. I'd be honored."

"When I get the go-ahead from headquarters, you'll have to follow the rules we do: suit and tie. Conducting yourself in a professional manner which means no chirping. That kind of thing."

"Yes, sir," I say, and he nods.

"Good. I'll let you know what they say."

"Thanks for thinking of me. If given the chance, I won't let you down." I stand and smile. "See you at the game tonight."

He doesn't say anything else and I slip out of his office, surprised when I find Maverick waiting in the hall.

"What are you still doing here, Cap? You should be resting up for tonight," I say.

"Wanted to make sure everything was okay. Getting pulled into Coach's office is fucking terrifying."

"It usually is. He, um, invited me to be on the bench during games as a non-uniformed team official. I think I'm going to take him up on it."

"What?" Maverick launches himself into my arms, and I laugh when we almost tumble over. "That's fucking cool, man. Congratulations."

"Beats standing in the tunnel with my hands in my pockets," I say. "Not sure I'm worthy enough to stand behind you all, but we'll see."

"Nah. You're worthy as hell." He pulls away and clasps my shoulder. "It's going to be a privilege to play with you again, Riley. The rest of the guys will feel the same."

"It's been a rough half a year. The worst days of my fucking life, honestly, but you all have been there with me every step of the way. Thanks for sticking around even when I didn't want anything to do with you."

"We're brothers. Family." He slings his arm around me, and we head for the locker room. He's careful to slow his steps so I can keep up, and it makes me smile. "We're always going to show up."

I could get used to things going well. Used to feeling genuinely *happy*.

I can only hope it lasts a long fucking time.

TWENTY-SIX
LEXI

GIRLS JUST WANT TO HAVE FUN(DAMENTAL RIGHTS) AND GOOD SEX

PIPER

I wish they made underwear for specific occasions.

Example: my dress is very tight and I don't want to have any visible lines.

ME

It's called going commando, Piper.

MAVEN

You walk around without underwear on a regular basis?

MADELINE

My post-baby body could never.

MAVEN

Same.

EMMY

I'm with Lex. I do it all the time. Makes it fun to tease Maverick with photos when I'm on the road.

ME

He's unbearable when you're not around. That man is obsessed with you.

EMMY

As every man should be. I love it.

PIPER

Any suggestions on the underwear dilemma?

ME

Try going without any. Trust me. You're going to feel so free.

PIPER

Until my vagina ends up on the internet because I didn't know my dress was see-through thanks to a camera flash.

ME

I bet you have a nice vagina.

PIPER

That's so sweet! I think I do.

ME

Commando or bust, Piper!

PIPER

Fine. But I'm bringing a spare pair and putting it in my bag.

MAVEN

A purse panty. You might be onto something, Piper.

MADELINE
I hate that word.

EMMY
Same. I just gagged.

ME
Make Liam keep them in his pocket. That could be a fun game.

PIPER
Oh. Now YOU are onto something, Lex.

ME
Just want to make sure my friends are getting the attention they deserve.

MAVEN
Such a girl's girl.

ALWAYS HELD in a swanky hotel with a hired band, delicious food, and top shelf alcohol, the team's annual holiday gala is one of my favorite events of the year.

The guys are all proud hockey players who won't hesitate to get in a fight on the ice, but at their core, they're philanthropists—good men with soft hearts. Members of the community who show up for those who have less than them. And it's always so inspiring to see how much money they raise for charity at the end of the night.

I shiver as I walk up the steps to the Four Seasons Hotel, grateful when the warm air of the lobby wraps around me. I hand over my shawl to a young guy at coat check and accept a flute of champagne from a passing server, smiling when I see Piper bounding toward me in a form-fitting pink dress.

"Holy shit, Lex." She grabs my hands, making me do a slow spin on the marble floor. "You're a *knockout*."

"Do you like it?"

I run my palm down the gold gown. With the spaghetti straps, a plunging V-neckline that dips below my breasts, and a floor-length skirt with a train, I was worried it was too over the top, but Piper's whistling makes me confident in my choice.

"Your ass is actually insane. You look like a Greek goddess. That dress was made for you."

"Thank you." I tuck a piece of hair behind my ear. The messy high ponytail I pulled it into an hour ago is starting to come loose, but I don't trust myself to take it down and try to replicate it a second time. "And look at *you*. Pink is so your color."

"I'd wear it every day of my life if I could." She loops her arm through mine and leads me to the ballroom. Music rings down the hall, and half a dozen people stop to say hello to us. "I went with your no underwear suggestion, by the way."

"And? What do you think?"

"I could get used to this. It's freeing. Plus, I feel *sexy*. No one knows I'm not wearing underwear—besides you, of course—but I do, and that's kind of hot."

"It's *so* hot. I'm proud of you, Piper." I kiss the top of her head and grin when I spot the rest of my friends circled around a high-top table draped in a white linen. "Everyone looks so good."

"There you two are." Emmy pops out a hip and looks us up and down. "Damn. Everyone cleans up well, don't they?"

"You win that award, Emmy." Madeline smiles and takes a sip of her champagne. "Your ability to go from sporty to hyperfeminine should be studied."

"When I was younger, I had a coach tell me no one was going to want me to be a part of their team if I wore ribbons in my hair. It took away from my *toughness*, he said, so I decided to wear more ribbons and more makeup and more heels when I wasn't on the ice. He's choking on his words now," she says. "Who says women can't do hard things just because of how we dress?"

"Amen, sister." I lift my glass her way. "It's so good to see all of you. I hate that we're all so busy during the season, but I'm glad we get to spend tonight together."

"You probably only get me for two hours. Liam won't last much longer than that." She waves across the room to the goalie sitting at a table, looking miserable while Grant chats his ear off about something. I hold back a laugh when he picks up a knife and spins it between his fingers. "Maybe an hour and a half if we're lucky."

"I'm going to grab a drink from the open bar. If the organization is paying for it, I'm going to order the nicest alcohol they have. Does anyone want anything?" I ask.

"I'll take a red wine," Piper says, and Madeline nods.

"Make that two, please."

"I'll take a Chardonnay if you can carry it," Maven adds, and I glance at Emmy.

"Nothing for me. I'm fine."

A secret smile curls on her mouth when she taps her water glass, but I don't ask any questions. She and Maverick have been trying to get pregnant for months now, and she doesn't owe anyone an explanation or story of what might be happening behind the scenes.

I give her hand a squeeze and tuck my clutch under my arm, making my way over to the open bar. The line moves quick, and when I place my order for the four drinks, I turn and survey the ballroom to see how the night is going.

"Are you here with someone?"

"Pardon?" I glance to the right and spy a man in a tuxedo.

"I didn't know if you were one of the player's girlfriends or wives," he slurs, and I eye the two drinks he's holding. This is a classy event, and from the smell of alcohol rolling off of him, he should probably be cut off. "Or a sister. I like sisters."

"I work for the Stars."

"You do?" He perks up and sways on his feet. It's going to be bad news if he topples into the champagne flute display. "Are you in marketing?"

"Head athletic trainer, actually," I say.

"What's that like?"

"I spend my days focusing on injury prevention. I'm the first responder for any medical emergency that occurs on the ice, and I can identify musculoskeletal injuries the way other people can identify cars," I say, giving the rehearsed answer I'm used to tossing out. He's too drunk to remember anything else. "I like it."

"Huh. Sounds boring."

"I get to be around a sport I love and make money from it." I shrug. "Not sure we can call it boring."

"You're feisty, huh? I've always liked that in a woman."

"And easily annoyed." I spin and thank the bartender for the drinks by dropping a ten in the tip jar with the wads of twenties and fifties. "If you'll excuse me."

"Do you need some help?" the man asks. "I have a hand."

"Do you? It looks like your hands are full."

"Shit. I'll hold one with my teeth. I don't mind. I can—"

"She said she was fine," a new voice interrupts, and I smile on instinct.

Riley.

I look his way, breath catching when I see his thick-framed glasses and stubble on his jaw. His tuxedo fits him like a glove, showing off curves of the muscles he's been hard at work rebuilding. A pair of silver cufflinks flash under the chandelier lights, and his shoes are so shiny I can see my reflection in them.

I'd happily take two of him.

He's so damn pretty.

"Hi," I say.

"Hi," Riley answers, eyes sliding over to the guy beside me. "I can take it from here."

"I was already—"

"I really don't want to have to get security involved, but I will if you don't leave her alone." He flexes his hand at his side, and *yup*. Just as hot as the movies. "Am I clear?"

"Sorry," the man apologizes, clutching both drinks to his chest. "Enjoy your night."

When he disappears, Riley's focus snaps back to me. "I'm impressed."

"With what?"

"Constantly having to ward off men? Having to explain *no* to someone multiple times? Life must be exhausting for you, but you make it look so easy."

"It's a plight, I'll tell ya." I laugh and toss my ponytail over my shoulder. "It's nice to see you in something other than your sweaty gym clothes, Mitchy. You clean up well."

His eyes wander down my body, clearly in no hurry as he takes in my dress and the black heels I paired it with. He whimpers and brings his fist to his mouth, biting his knuckles. "Hell. You look gorgeous, Lexi."

"Thank you." The compliment nestles its way into my chest, right next to my heart, and I don't know when I became such a fucking sap. "It's nice to be out of my leggings."

"I'll say. Are you having a good night?"

"I was until Drunky McDrunkerson told me my job was boring."

"Do you think it's boring?" Riley asks.

"No. I love my job."

"Then fuck what he has to say."

"Wise words, Mitchy." I smile. "What about you? There are a lot of people around. How's your social battery?"

"Liam and I have an escape plan ready to go the second the auction ends. The drinks should be flowing by then, and I think I'll be able to sneak out of here before people start trying to ask me about my leg."

"An escape plan, huh? What does that involve?"

"Walking out the door and leaving. I'd like to see someone try and stop us," he says confidently.

I laugh again. "You've clearly thought this out."

"Oh yeah. It's not my first time ditching a social gathering I don't want to be at."

"Between the two of you, I think you'll be actively avoided." I pop a shoulder in a shrug. "It's a bummer you were planning to leave early though."

"Yeah? Why's that?"

"I was hoping you'd save me a dance," I say, grabbing the bar tray of drinks off the counter and starting back to the girls. "If you want."

His hand rests on my elbow, and I stop. "Do you want me to save you a dance, Lexi baby?"

I'm immediately thrown back to that night—the heat of his mouth, his shuttered moans and the way *fuck* rolled off his tongue. My skin warms instantly, a response to the nickname used in the privacy of our secret rendezvous.

It sounds wicked out in the open, a sinful, *lustful* plea that makes my nipples harden and my thighs squeeze together. I look at him, not surprised to find his cheeks pink and his chest rising and falling like he's been sprinting for miles, and every logical reason I ever had for staying away dares to fly out the window.

It's not him.

It can't be *him*.

It's the orgasms he gave me. The mind-blowing, earth-shattering, organ-rearranging pleasure brought on by his tongue and his fingers, and that's why I whisper, "Yes." My voice is thick before tacking on a softer, "Please."

"You have to know I love when you beg."

I swallow. He's not even trying to conceal what he wants,

but I guess I'm not either. Not when I take a step toward him and tip my chin, mouth inches away from his ear, and say, "I'm not wearing any underwear."

"You are so unfair," he murmurs.

"Maybe you should do something about it," I say, pulling away. "You know where I'll be."

The walk back to the girls is a blur, and I know I'm a badass bitch when I don't try to look over my shoulder to see if Riley is watching me. I slide the tray of drinks onto the table, grab my gin and tonic, and take a long sip.

"Are you okay?" Piper frowns and touches my cheek. "You're burning up."

"Please tell me you put that asshole in his place. And please tell us what he said," Emmy says. "I could *see* the steam coming out of your ears."

"Something about my job. The usual." I swirl my straw around and swallow down another gulp. I should've asked for straight gin, no tonic. The whole fucking handle, really. What the *fuck* is wrong with me? "And yes, I put him in his place."

"I knew you would." Maven smiles and reaches for her glass, lifting it in the air. "Fuck the patriarchy."

"Hear, hear." Madeline clinks her drink against Maven's. "And was that Riley you were talking to? Don't tell Hudson, but I always thought he was cute."

"Yup. That's Riley."

"Are your sessions going well?" Piper asks. "He seems so much happier after being behind the bench for a game or two."

"It looks like he's living again," Emmy adds. "Coach offering that role to him probably changed his life."

"They're much better." I let my attention drift across the room again and find Riley talking to a blonde woman in a black gown. He nods along with whatever she says and smiles at some parts. There's a twist in my chest when he throws his head back and laughs, and I down the rest of my drink. "I'm so proud of him. If he keeps progressing like this over the next two months, we're going to be able to try skating with his prosthetic. I hope the guys will come out and help him around the rink when it's time."

"Oh my god. They'd be there in a second," Piper says.

"They wouldn't miss it," Emmy adds.

"I'm going to put a plan together." I set my empty drink down and smile at the women around me. "All of you are dating or married to *very* rich athletes, most of whom will be in this auction starting soon. Should we go spend some of their money?"

"I'm bidding on Grant," Emmy says with a wicked grin. "Maverick is always more fun when he gets jealous."

"Funny. I was going to bid on Ethan." Piper giggles. "Liam will absolutely storm out."

"I can't bring myself to bid on anyone but Hudson," Madeline admits.

"Because he's too sweet and no one wants to see him sad." I motion to the center of the ballroom where people are lining up for the auction. Each winning bid on the DC Stars players goes to the charity of their choosing, and in return, the bidder gets an afternoon with them. "Let's have some fun."

TWENTY-SEVEN
RILEY

IT'S a good thing I didn't die the night of the accident.

If I did, I wouldn't have gotten the chance to see the real heaven that is Lexi in her gold dress.

My tongue's been hanging out of my mouth for the better part of two hours, and every time she sways her hips, I'm close to bolting out of the hotel ballroom for some fresh air.

I knew I was attracted to her, but after tonight?

I'm fucking *ruined*.

A stronger man would try to put some distance between themselves and her. They'd do everything they could to get her out of their head because they know nothing will ever happen between them—she said so herself—but I'm the weakest, most pathetic motherfucker in existence.

I'm not going anywhere.

"I can't believe Emmy bid on fucking *Grant*," Maverick grumbles, pulling me from my daydreams of dark hair wrapped around my fist and the soft moans she lets out right before she comes. He glares at our second line right winger and scowls. "I'm her *husband*."

"Who is clearly not jealous at all," I say. "This is totally normal behavior."

"This is nothing. Cap leveled that guy who plays for Toronto last season after he found out he liked one of Emmy's Instagram photos." Hudson laughs. "Obsessed is an understatement."

"Maybe she's asking Grant to put on a mask and chase her through the woods," I offer, and Maverick gasps. "You know he likes dark romances, and that's a pretty common scene."

"She *wouldn't*. He wasn't included on her orgy list!"

"I'm missing something," Hudson says.

"You and I are on Emmy's orgy list. There was something about a dream," I tell him. "I didn't get any details."

"Don't ever tell me them if you do. Em is like my sister—I don't need to be thinking about her like that." Hudson grimaces. "No offense, Mav."

"Same," I add. "I also don't need Mavvy kicking my ass. I'm not as fast as I used to be, and there's no way in hell I can outrun him."

"The only one who needs to run is Grant fucking Everett." Maverick stands and shoves his chair back. "I'm going to kill him if he touches her."

Hudson and I watch him storm away, and my former defense partner laughs.

"How has he not figured out Emmy does this on purpose?" he asks. "It's so funny to watch."

"He'll learn one day." I scan the room and my eyes immediately fall on Lexi. She's like a goddamn magnet for my attention. She's standing in the middle of the dance floor, arms above her head while she moves to the rhythm of an upbeat song playing from the DJ's speakers. "I might go grab a drink. You want anything?"

"I'm good." Hudson's eyes follow mine, and he hums. "Maybe you'll find your way to the dance floor. Rumor has it the DJ is easily persuaded to put on a slow song if you slip him some money. At least, that's what Liam and Maverick told me."

"Why would I want to do that?"

"I don't know, Mitchy. Why would you?"

I watch Lexi spin, that goddamn dress a flurry of tempting gold and sparkles and weakening self-restraint, and I leap out of my chair as fast as my leg will let me.

"I'll be back," I say.

"No, you won't," he answers with a smirk. "Have fun."

I dodge a group of our top-tier season ticket holders who look like they want to ask me a dozen questions. I autograph a team photo for someone who tells me they're going to auction it off to raise money for the Boston Marathon and bump my knuckles against Ethan's. I only stop to slip the DJ a wad of cash—it could be a hundred dollars or a thousand, I'm not paying a lick of fucking attention—and make my way onto the dance floor just as the beat slows and the lights dim.

"Hey," I say, and Lexi spins to face me, a smile pulling on her lips.

"Hi," she says. "I thought you might've left."

"Not yet. I figured I needed to cash in on that dance you wanted me to save you."

"Perfect timing. You didn't have anything to do with the song choice, did you?"

"Me?" I touch my glasses frames and shrug. "No. I've been with Hudson and Maverick this whole time."

"Interesting. Guess it's fate then."

"Guess so." I offer her my hand. "My leg is killing me from standing all night so I can't promise any good moves, but I'm going to do my best."

"We can just stand here." Lexi's fingers fold around mine. Her other palm rests on my shoulder and I drop my left hand to her waist, my fingers bunching in the soft material of her gown. "I'm not picky when it comes to ballroom dancing."

"Good to know." Shooting pain races up my right thigh, but it's easy to ignore when she closes the distance between us and smiles from ear to ear. "Have any other drunk finance bros bothered you?"

"Why is it always finance bros?" She laughs, her head dropping back and her shoulders shaking. "Why can't it be a… a scientist? Or a meteorologist? Someone interesting."

"Do you know a lot of meteorologists?"

"I follow this woman down in Florida who has a weather show. She's been in tornadoes and hailstorms, and she's a total badass."

"I didn't know you had an affinity for weather, Lex."

"I don't. Just women who are breaking glass ceilings."

I stroke my thumb over the curve of her hip and her breathing stutters. "I meant what I said earlier. You look fucking gorgeous."

"Thank you," she says softly. "I've always liked dressing up. I try to find ways to make what I'm wearing cute—even if it's team-issued gear—and I love that more and more clothing companies are designing sports jackets and game day outfits for women that go beyond a simple T-shirt."

"You pull off team-issued gear well. Meanwhile I'm over here in a long-sleeved Stars shirt looking silly."

"You do not look silly."

"I kind of do." I smile. "I didn't mind dressing up for games, but now, it's a pain. Pants are difficult to wear these days because my prosthetic makes my right leg a different size from my left. And don't get me started on shoes."

"What do you mean?"

"It's a whole thing with my feet."

"I like feet," she says.

"I didn't know that was a fetish of yours," I tease, and she smacks my shoulder. "Kidding. My right foot is smaller than my left."

"It is?"

"Yup. And it doesn't bend and flex like my left foot does.

I've had to rebuy the shoes I love in a half size down so my foot doesn't slip out."

"What do you do with the shoe you don't wear?" Lexi asks.

"Nothing. I can't bring myself to throw them away, and donation centers won't take a single shoe. It would be cool if there was a foundation for amputees that let you find the sizes you need without wasting the other half of the pair."

"Maybe you can start one," she suggests.

"I don't have a ton of free time." I laugh. "My plate is kind of full right now."

"True." Lexi's hand moves from my shoulder to my back, and she rubs her palm down my spine. "You just grimaced. Are you hurting right now?"

"A little. I don't want to lose out on my dance though."

"We could've danced in the chairs." She pauses and giggles. "Okay. That makes it sound like we're at a strip club."

"Wouldn't know. I've never been."

"Really?"

"Yup. Not my thing."

"What is your thing?"

You.

Naked and on top of me.

"Somewhere that's not so, ah, public?" I clear my throat. The tips of my ears are on fire, and I shrug again. "I'm selfish, I guess. I want things that are just for me. I want to know I'm special."

"Such a romantic. You are special, Riley. I hope you know that."

"So are you," I say.

Comfortable silence nudges its way between us. We keep dancing, and at some point, she rests her head on my chest. I wrap my arm around her when she shivers, trying to warm her up, and her sigh is content and on the cusp of happy.

"I'm glad you didn't leave," she whispers.

"So am I. You would've had to dance with Ethan, and that'd be a travesty." I press my thumb into her nape, rubbing the tension I find there, and Lexi sighs again. "Are you staying in DC for Christmas?"

"Yeah. My mom has a cruise booked with some of her girlfriends, so I'll be ordering Chinese and watching *It's a Wonderful Life* all day. What about you?"

"I'll be in town. I'm nervous to fly commercial for the first time during the holidays to Chicago to visit my parents. I'm going to set off all sorts of alarms, but my dad says that's the best part. The look in people's eyes when he tells them he has to be pat down because of a metal leg is always priceless."

"Wait. Your dad has a prosthetic leg too? What happened?"

"What are the odds, right? He used to be a firefighter, and he was severely burned after rescuing a family from their home. That was, hell, fifteen years ago? Maybe twelve? Being an amputee is second nature to him now, but I'm still learning."

"And you're doing a damn good job." Lexi pulls away and puts both hands on the center of my chest. "He's going to be so proud of you when you see him next. How could he not be?"

Compliments from her mean more than they do from anyone else. It might be because she doesn't give them out freely; she's not Piper, who is a constant a ray of sunshine and loves to be nice to everyone.

Lexi is tougher to crack. She's a little jaded, sharper around the edges, and it's becoming more and more clear she has walls up to protect herself because of a situation that's happened in the past. There's something holding her back, and I doubt I'll ever figure out what it is.

"Thanks," I murmur. "I thought about not coming tonight. Lots of people, lots of physical activity. But I'm glad I did."

"Why's that?" she asks.

"Because I got to see you," I say, and her eyes meet mine. "I'm always glad when I get to see you."

"Has today been a good day?"

"Yes," I say without thinking. The word comes naturally when she's around. "It has."

"I'm glad. You deserve all the good days, Riley."

We dance together for another song, only pulling away when the pain in my leg becomes distracting. After, we sit at a table and laugh at my teammates, trying to gauge who's had the most to drink and who will be the one to shut the party down. When Piper invites her over for a sleepover, Lexi squeezes my shoulder and tells me she'll see me on Monday for another one of our sessions.

I watch her go, a single thought echoing in my brain.

Funny how all my good days include her.

TWENTY-EIGHT
RILEY

LEXI
Merry Christmas Eve Eve!

I have a gift for you.

ME
You do?

LEXI
Yeah. It's nothing big, so don't get your hopes up.

But I wanted to get you something.

ME
I have a gift for you too.

LEXI
You do?

ME
Yup.

I'll bring it with me to our session today.

LEXI

> Speaking of our session, do you mind if we push our time back by thirty minutes? Hudson is having soreness in his ankle, so I'm going to tape up his foot to see if that helps. The rest of the AT staff is off for the holiday, so I'm working overtime on everyone's aches and pain.

ME

> Of course. If you're too busy, we can push our session to after the holiday.

LEXI

> Nice try, Mitchy. I'll see you at 10:30.

I GROAN when I finish my last set of bridges on the treatment table. An hour of Lexi's rigorous exercises, and my whole body is screaming at me. She didn't show me any mercy, and when I sit up to stretch my back, the leather is covered in sweat.

"How is it these movements kick my ass more than the drills Coach used to make us do?" I take off my glasses and wipe my face with a towel, grateful when she hands me a bottle of water. "I never thought I'd take an hour of edge work drills over lifting my ass off a table ten times."

"You're building back the strength you lost, and I'm working parts of your body you didn't work before. I'm not rehabbing you to just be a hockey player; I want you to be able to walk and move and jump and crawl and stand on one leg." She tosses a towel in the hamper. "How is your lower half feeling today?"

"Fine. That quad set was hell on earth, but nothing is causing me pain."

"That's great to hear. Like I mentioned in one of our

other sessions, as we head into the new year, I really want to focus on the exercises you're familiar with and relate our activities to the hockey movements you would do on the ice. That's going to give us a good baseline for your capabilities," she says, and excitement runs through me.

I trust Lexi completely. I know the timeline she's giving me is what's best for me long-term, but I'm fucking *stoked* to hopefully get back on the ice soon. I'm not sure how it's going to go, and I bet I'll take a spill or two, but knowing all the time and energy I've put in won't be for nothing makes me giddy.

"I can't wait for that," I say, and she smiles.

"We're almost there. I'm proud of you for sticking with our routine, and I promise it's going to pay off in the long run."

"I trust you." I swing my legs to the edge of the table and slide my glasses back on. "Are we finished for today?"

"Yup. You're officially free from me until after the three-day break. How are you going to spend your time?"

"By giving you a present." I point at my backpack shoved against the wall next to my prosthetic. "It's in my bag."

"You really didn't have to get me anything," she says, standing from her stool and walking to my bag. "It's wildly unnecessary."

"The same can be said for you. Besides, we're friends. I like to get my friends gifts."

Lexi digs through my backpack and pulls out a wrapped gift with a red bow on it. I spent too many hours wondering how I should sign the card, finally settling on a lame as fuck salutation of *best, Riley*.

"We are friends." She grabs a bag that's been hiding under one of the tables before she plops back down on the stool. "Which is why this is for you."

"Holy shit, Lex. Whatever is in here is way too big."

"There's a joke somewhere in that comment."

"Get your head out of the gutter," I say, and she laughs.

"It's not that big, I promise." Lexi waves her hand in front of her face and lifts her chin. "You first."

"No way. You open yours first."

"If you insist." With a smile, she reads the note on the front and tucks it in the pocket of her jacket. She rips open the wrapping paper, no rhyme or reason to her process, and my eye twitches when she rolls it into a ball and chucks it at the trash can. "You look like you're going to be sick."

"I didn't know you were a goddamn savage when it came to opening gifts."

"You're one of those people who folds up the wrapping paper, aren't you?"

"*No*," I huff, offended. "But I'm more careful than *that*. Jesus. You're like a goddamn windstorm."

"That's why you have your own bag to open. You can do whatever you want with it." She grins and looks down at the book on her lap. "*Business Building 101: How to go from Nothing to Something*."

"You, um, mentioned you thought about starting your own Pilates studio one day. I don't know the first thing about creating a business, but according to the internet this book does. I know it's stupid, but I—"

"How do you remember all the things I say?" Lexi's gaze meets mine. "The limes. My dreams for a studio. That I played basketball when I was younger?"

"I listen," I say.

"Most people—" She stops herself mid-sentence and hangs her head. "No one ever listens."

"Because they suck. You shouldn't..." I trail off, not wanting to sound like an asshole who is telling her what to do. "Don't spend your time with people like that."

"This is really thoughtful, Riley." She traces over the letters in the title and curls her fingers around the spine as she brings it tight to her chest. "Thank you. I can't wait to read it."

"You could also use it as a doorstop. No pressure. I'm not sure how useful it'll even be, so—"

"Just say you're welcome, Mitchy." Lexi laughs. "It's perfect. I don't want to use it as a doorstop."

"You're welcome," I mumble, embarrassed she actually likes the gift.

"It's your turn." She jumps on the table next to me, sets the book down, and scootches the bag my way. "There are two things in there."

"Wait a second. We didn't say anything about the number of gifts," I argue.

"Exactly. We didn't set a limit." Her grin is sly, and it's a shot to the chest. "Reach to the left first. It's the smaller present."

I follow her orders and reach into the bag. Lexi boos when I pluck the tissue paper out and neatly set it aside, and I burst out laughing. My fingers brush the corner of something sharp, and I pull out a glass picture frame.

"What is it?" I ask.

"It's your Life List from our meal at the diner. I saved the napkin and framed it so you could have something to look at when you get out of bed in the morning. Good days and lots of memories to be had." She shrugs, color creeping up her neck, and her dark hair curtains her face. "I figured when you accomplished something on the list, you could take it out, cross it off, and add something new."

"Wow." I rub a hand over my shirt and touch the glass, smiling at her swoopy handwriting and the ketchup stain in the corner. Everything I mentioned is there, forever immortalized on the unfolded piece of paper. "This is perfect."

"It could also be used as a doorstop if you—"

"Shut up." I reach over and poke her side. She squeals and bats my hand away, almost falling off the table in the process. She grips my left thigh to steady herself, slow to remove her hand when she's back upright. "I'm serious. This is really thoughtful. Thanks, Lex. I'm going to hang it in my bedroom."

"I'm glad you like it. Open the next one."

I put the frame on top of her book and yank out a big box out of the bag. I flip the top open and blink down at a pair of brand-new Bauer skates.

"What—" I swallow, throat unbelievably dry. "Skates?"

I shoved all of mine in the hall closet after I got home from the hospital. I haven't looked at them since, too afraid the ghosts from my professional athlete past might come out and haunt me if I stare at them for too long.

"I've been working with their skate rep," she starts, and I hear the tint of nerves in her voice. "I mentioned who the skates were for and how you need two different sizes now, and after talking with your prosthetist about your foot measurements, I ordered a pair. They're, um, custom. The left is the size you used to wear, and the right is slightly smaller to fit your prosthetic foot. I lied the night of the gala. I know your feet aren't the same size anymore, but I didn't want to let on about your gift." Her smile turns sheepish, shy. "I also like to hear you talk."

"Shit." A tear escapes from my eye, and I wipe it away with my thumb. "Lexi. This is the nicest thing anyone's ever done for me."

"It's nothing."

"It's a whole lot of fucking something."

"I-I want you to be comfortable when you get back out there, and you won't be comfortable in what you were skating in before. I also thought new skates, new journey? Maybe."

I squeeze my eyes closed and drop my head back. The fluorescent lights above me don't help, and before I know it, my shoulders are shaking. A sob works out of me, and Lexi's arms wrap around my middle. She lets me cry, holding me until I'm out of breath and the tears stop falling.

"When I woke up after the accident and saw I lost my leg,

I wanted to die," I whisper, and Lexi holds me tighter. "I thought about it. I wondered what I could use in the hospital room to make it happen. Bed sheets were my plan. Or lying to the nurses about how much pain medication I had taken until I overdosed. It's… it's fucking *stupid* to say this, and maybe the people who have never been an athlete wouldn't understand, but the minute I realized I couldn't play hockey anymore, I didn't see the point in existing. That's all I knew. That's all I had. That's all I *was*."

I stop to take a breath. I didn't realize I was shaking, and I rest my cheek on top of her head. It feels fucking *good* to admit this to someone besides my therapist. I'm letting it out in the open, and with every word I say, I'm lighter, buoyant, so I keep talking.

"And then you and I started working together. I didn't believe you when you said you could get me to skate again, because I couldn't even fucking *walk*. On the hard days when my head is cloudy and that anger I felt in the beginning creeps up, I think it's all a lie. I won't be able to do it. I'm going to fail, so why even try? But now I'm looking at a pair of skates and—" I press the heel of my palm against my left eye. "I think I really can."

"Oh, Riley." Lexi pulls away from me and cups my face with both of her hands. Her palms are warm, smooth, and I relax under her touch. "You can. I know you can. It's not going to be easy, but look at everything you've accomplished the last six months. This time next year, you're not going to recognize yourself."

"I'm sorry. The last time I cried over skates was when I was seven and my parents got me a new pair." I snort out a laugh and run my fingers over the synthetic boot. "I begged for them for months."

"I'm glad you like them. I was afraid I was overstepping, and I'd never want to make you uncomfortable."

"You could never make me uncomfortable." I wipe my eyes again. "This is the best gift I've ever gotten."

"I, um, added something after they were delivered. On the blade holder there." She taps the white piece of plastic connecting the blade to the skate. "It's silly."

"*For all the good days*," I read. "I fucking love it, Lex. Thank you. So much. I can't tell you how much this means to me."

"I'm glad you like it." Lexi squeezes me one more time and untangles our limbs. "We'll try them out soon. I promise."

"I can be patient. I'm willing to wait as long as I have to. Even knowing this is a possibility is beyond anything I could've ever imagined."

"Riley?"

"Yeah?"

She takes my hand in hers. "I'm really glad you're still here."

"So am I. And I'm really glad we're friends." I drape an arm around her shoulder. "Merry Christmas Eve Eve, Lex."

"Merry Christmas Eve Eve, Riley," she whispers back, and this might be the best Christmas I've ever had.

TWENTY-NINE
RILEY

PUCK KINGS

> **MAVVY**
> Can someone host team dinner this week? We're getting the guest bathroom remodeled and there's shit everywhere.

> **G-MONEY**
> Like... actual shit? That's disgusting.

> **MAVVY**
> No, idiot. Like tools and materials and tiles.

> **G-MONEY**
> OH. That makes more sense lol.

> **SULLY**
> I can't wait until I retire. No more social gatherings. No more group chats. No more going places I don't want to. I can sit in my house all day and not have to talk to anyone.

G-MONEY

You're still stuck with us for now, Goalie Daddy!!!

EASY E

Yeah, and when you retire, we're going to track you down and knock on your window every single day!!!

G-MONEY

Ooooh, stalker behavior. You know how much I love that.

MAVVY

Speaking of, who's hosting book club this month?

HUDDY BOY

I think it's my turn? Fair warning: Lucy is going to ask to paint everyone's nails before she and Madeline go out for the night.

If you tell her no and make her cry, I will not be happy with you.

G-MONEY

Don't let Sully near her lol. He makes everyone cry.

HUDDY BOY

Believe it or not, she loves him.

MAVVY

Huh. Weird.

Did everyone have a good NYE?

ME

Uneventful for me.

EASY E

We gotta get you back out there, Mitchy. I'm sure you have TONS of DMs from girls who would love to spend time with you... if you know what I mean ;)

HUDDY BOY

Everyone knows what you mean, Ethan.

ME

I'm all set. And I haven't opened Instagram in months.

EASY E

Could you send them my way then, plz?

I'm getting tired of using my hand.

MAVVY

Probably because no one else wants to touch you with a ten-foot pole.

EASY E

Ouch, Cap.

G-MONEY

Someone bring GTA 5 to dinner, please. I can't find my copy anywhere.

HUDDY BOY

It's at my house, Grant.

G-MONEY

Thank god!!!

Sully has left the chat
Mavvy has added Sully to the chat

SULLY
I haven't known peace in years.

G-MONEY
And you're never going to with us around!!

ME
I can host dinner this week. I haven't had anyone over in ages. My doorman is starting to think I don't have any friends.

MAVVY
He's going to be in for a rude awakening when we all show up.

G-MONEY
I'm going to make a shirt. RILEY AND GRANT 4EVER

ME
That's unnecessary.

G-MONEY
Is it though????

I TOSS a lime in my hand and set it on a cutting board. Grabbing a knife, I slice it into small wedges and drop them in a glass bowl on the counter.

"Are you a chef now?" Grant steals a crouton off the top of the Caesar salad I made and pops it in his mouth. "Why are you in here with a knife?"

"I'm making garnishes." I drop the knife in the sink and wash my hands. "In case someone wants to add something extra to their drink."

"Wow. I'm barely able to get a paper towel to wipe my hands when Maverick and Emmy host dinner and you're out here distributing *garnishes*? You should be in charge more often."

"Thanks, G." I crane my neck, looking toward the front door. "Are we missing anyone?"

"I'm pretty sure everyone is here. Oh. Lexi hasn't shown up, but I heard Piper tell Emmy she was running late."

"Cool. I guess we can get started."

"Can I ring the bell?" He practically jumps up and down and reaches for the bell we started using last year to get everyone's attention when the food is ready. It's an ugly brass thing, and I groan when he lifts it off the table and shakes it multiple times. "Okay. I don't want a noise complaint from my neighbor."

"Please. Like anyone could ever hate you."

"I'm sure plenty of people hate me."

"Nah. You're a good dude. Now, Ethan? He's bound to have some enemies." Grant dives for a plate and starts loading up on green beans and mashed potatoes. "The two times we've played against New York this season, he's had his highest penalty minutes. Won't fucking stop chirping their center on face offs."

"Does he even know their center? Or is he being an idiot and starting shit to start shit?"

"Guess they were rivals at BC and BU. I think there's bad blood there."

I hum and step out of the way so everyone can load up their plates. Piper gives me a hug and tells me everything looks great. Madeline adds a tray of brownies to the long line of food, and Hudson doesn't bother waiting for her to finish unwrapping the dish before grabbing one and shoving it in his mouth. There's pushing and shoving, and Emmy waits patiently next to me while Maverick gets her plate ready.

"Wow. Look at that service." I lift my chin to Maverick balancing the food on his forearms. "You've got a winner there, Hartwell."

"I do, don't I?" She smiles and nudges my shoulder with hers. "You doing okay?"

"Fine, yeah."

"Don't bullshit me, Mitchell."

I bark out a laugh. "I forgot how much of a hard-ass you are. Today has sucked. My leg hurt during morning skate because I was standing for too long. Everything's pissed me off up until you all getting here, and I'm tired as hell."

"That's more like it. If you want to escape, I can handle everyone."

"Nah. I'm good. Being around my people helps." I scan the room again, disappointed. "Do you know when—"

"Sorry I'm late." Right on cue, Lexi bursts into the kitchen with a box tucked under her arm. "I had a meeting at the arena that ran long and I've been going nonstop for hours."

Everyone stops to say hello to her, and it takes a few minutes before she makes her way around the kitchen and stands in front of me.

"Hey," I say, and the syllable cracks. "You made it."

"And I brought chocolates." She hands over the box, and I smile at the assortment of treats secured in neat little rows. "Please accept my apology for my tardiness."

"Nothing to apologize for." I take the desserts and set them on the counter out of sight from the heathens causing mayhem in the kitchen. The cleanup is going to take me hours. "You must be hungry. Grab a plate. Do you want a drink?"

"Sure. I'll take a gin and tonic, if you have it."

"I can make that happen." I grab a glass from the cabinet, not mentioning I went out and bought a handle of gin to add to my liquor cabinet in case she asked for some. "I got some limes for you too."

"My lime guy." Lexi grins, accepting the drink and taking a sip. "This is my first time at your place besides helping you up to your door and storming into your living room. Do I get a tour of your apartment before dinner? I want to learn all your secrets."

"Secrets." I laugh and gesture for her to follow me out of the kitchen packed with bodies and down the hall. "I don't have a lot of those."

"Come on. You have to be hiding something. An ex-girlfriend in your closet? A box of pictures of people's feet?"

"That's what you really think of me? I'm a murderer with a phalange fetish? I'm honored, Lex."

"Which toe is your favorite? It's the pinky, isn't it?"

"God, please stop." I gag and point out the bathroom and spare bedroom. "You're going to make me sick."

"The big toe. I *knew* it."

"You're a goddamn smart-ass." I push open the door to our left so she can make her way inside. "Welcome to my incredibly boring bedroom."

Lexi puts a hand on her hip and surveys the space, nodding as she goes. "Curtains? A headboard? A *laundry hamper*? Oh, my god, Riley. You're a fully functioning adult male."

"You sound surprised."

"I am. The bar is low, and I'm impressed."

"Please tell me some of your horror stories so I can feel better about myself. What's the worst apartment you've ever been in?"

"Worst apartment?" Lexi bends to survey the bookshelf shoved against the wall that houses my favorite novels. She touches each book, smiling when she gets to certain titles and pulling out her phone to take pictures of others. "There was the guy who shared a room with his sister."

"I hope it was a studio apartment."

"Nope. A three bedroom. They were *really close* and didn't like to sleep in separate rooms."

"I just threw up a little."

"So did I when he said we had to be quick because him and his sister had a movie to watch together. In his *bed*."

"Damn. My curtains make me look like I have my shit together, don't they? I might be missing a limb, but at least I'm not into incest." I grin and sit on the edge of the bed. "Tell me more."

"There was the guy with the army of stuffed animals, which I don't mind. I know people have items that are sentimental or bring them comfort. I wrote a paper on that for a psych class during my undergrad, and I'd never make fun of someone for what brings them joy. What bothered me was when he turned them all around when we had sex because he didn't want them *watching us*." Lexi sets her drink on my dresser and opens the top drawer. "And then he apologized to them after we finished because we took too long."

"Fucking Christ." I shake my head and lean back on my elbow. Down the hall, I hear an argument over a slice of pizza, and I throw a pillow at the door so it shuts. "You need to find new people to sleep with."

"You didn't have anything weird about you. We got along just fine, didn't we?"

I dredge up the memory of her with her head tipped back and her thighs open wide. The underwear of hers I still have shoved in a drawer and how it felt to have her nails dig into my shoulders when I had my head between her legs.

Just fine sounds like an understatement.

"We did get along just fine," I say slowly, and from the way she grins, I wonder if she's thinking about that night too.

"What about you? Are you going to tell me some of your—" Her mouth drops open when she gets to the bottom drawer of my dresser. I didn't even see her open the middle ones. "Oh my *god*."

"What?" I sit up and frown. "If you find any feet pictures in there, someone planted them."

"Are these *ropes*?"

Oh, fuck.

I haven't used them in so long I forgot they were in there.

I could deny they're mine. She'd believe me if I said they were a gag gift from one of the guys on the team. We do stupid shit like that all the time with each other, and a collection of ropes wouldn't be the weirdest thing one of them has given me.

But a loud, annoying part of me wants to be honest with her.

She's seen me when I'm weak and vulnerable and pissed off at the world. Why would I hide it from her?

"Yeah," I finally say. "They are."

"What the hell are they for?"

"I sail sometimes?"

"*Riley.*"

"Okay, fine. They're, uh, for sex. I have certain… interests in the bedroom."

The room is so quiet, I swear I can hear my heart racing.

"You didn't… when we…" She holds up a rope and glances at me. "In the hotel room—"

"It's a preference, not a requirement. I can get off just fine without it. Clearly."

"What is *it* exactly?"

"Being in control." I stand and walk to the dresser so I'm next to her. Being this close feels like I'm about to get into some trouble, and I can't bring myself to care. "With consent of course."

"Of course," she echoes. "How do you… is this something you advertise?"

"No. The last thing I need is someone from the media branding me as a guy who likes to hurt women when that's not what I do at all."

"What do you do?"

"Anything. Everything." I take the rope from her hold and lift my chin in the direction of her hands. "May I?"

"Yes," she breathes out. "Please."

The word almost short-circuits my brain when I gently push her palms together. "I said I like control. That means being the one to dictate when a partner touches me. When I touch a partner. When they come." I use the rope to secure her wrists with a single column knot. It's a simple knot, one that can be easily released by pulling on the free end of the rope, because I don't want her to think she can't escape. "It includes bondage. Eliminating senses like sight and sound. Punishment like spanking if they don't listen and rewards when they do." I bend the rope so she has to hold the excess in her grip, and her inhale is sharp. "Everything is with consent, like I said. And safe words."

"Do you do this your first time with a woman?" Lexi whispers. She turns her wrists to look at the ropes. "How do you know their boundaries?"

"Never the first time, and only after a long conversation. Like I said, I can get off just fine without it. I've had a few relationships where I didn't use any of this because the woman wasn't comfortable with it, and that's fine by me."

"How do you even find out you like this?"

"I'm an athlete. Or, I was. I can't speak for all guys who play sports, but I think a part of the control factor is written in our DNA. As for learning how I knew I liked it, I, um, did some experimenting."

"You don't strike me as someone who..." She trails off, still staring at the rope. "Do the guys know?"

"No. I told you I like to keep private things private. There's nothing to tell."

"This is a lot to process."

"Let me take these off of you." I reach for the rope, but she yanks her hand back to her chest before I have the chance to release the knot. "Are you okay?"

"I-I..." Lexi bites her bottom lip. "It's embarrassing."

"You found my secret stash of sex toys, Lex. I could crawl in a hole and never come out. We're well past embarrassing."

"Moment of honesty?"

"Anything. It doesn't leave this room."

"I-I've always wanted to try something like this."

"You're going to have to be more specific."

"A hookup where I give over control. It feels like I'm *always* in control with my job and my personal life. The guys I've been with in the past always made me lead the way in the bedroom. They took my independence and sexual forwardness as someone who likes to be in charge, when I—"

"Didn't want to be the one with the power?" I finish for her, and the dip of her chin tells me I'm right. "Have you ever used ropes in the bedroom?"

"No," she whispers.

"Have you ever been restrained with anything? Someone's tie? The belt of a robe?"

"No."

"And that's something you want to try?"

"Yes. I might hate it, but… it's one of my biggest fantasies. I've never felt safe enough with someone to explore it and find out."

This is very dangerous territory. My teammates are fifteen feet away and could come in here any minute. We said *just once*. I've spent weeks trying to get Lexi out of my head, and seeing her wrists turn a pretty shade of pink from where the ropes press against her skin is making forming coherent thoughts *really fucking difficult.*

Especially when it sounds like she's implying she feels safe with me.

"I want to respect your rules," I croak. "We agreed we would sleep together one time. Doing this—" I gesture at the knot and will myself not to get hard. "Goes well past that."

"You're right. I'm sorry," she whispers.

"You have nothing to apologize for, Lex."

"This is—" Lexi tries to release the knot but can't. "Forget I asked. Can you—"

"I've got you. Stop moving for me? Thank you."

I pull the loop on the excess part of the rope until it loosens, and when I untuck the rope from where it's pressing against the inside of her wrist, it falls to the floor. I curl my fingers around her wrist, inspecting her to make sure she's okay, and smooth my thumb over the tiny mark that was left behind.

"I should…" She shifts and licks her lips. "The girls. The team. Dinner."

"Right. Yeah." I drop the discarded rope back in the bottom drawer and shove it closed. "Don't forget your drink."

"Thanks. I'll see you later?"

"My house. Nowhere really for me to go."

"Right." She laughs, but it's forced. "Thanks for giving me a tour."

"Sure." I shove my glasses up my nose to give my hands something to do. "No problem."

Without saying anything else, she turns for the door and disappears down the hall. I watch her leave, feeling like I definitely fucked up.

THIRTY
LEXI

I'M IN A DAZE.

Ever since I walked out of Riley's room, I can't focus on anything but the red mark on my skin, the confidence in his eyes when he unknotted the rope from around my wrist, and how *sure* of himself he was when he talked about the things he liked.

I wasn't lying when I said bondage is something I've never tried in the bedroom but always wanted to. I can't explain *why*; I'm not in the least bit submissive. If a man tried to tell me what I could and couldn't do, I'd probably punch him in the face.

There's something about knowing I can't escape, knowing I can't get away and I'm just a vessel of pleasure for someone else that's hot as hell.

And I shared that fantasy with *Riley*, the guy who blushed when he saw me naked.

I need to move and find a new job immediately, because *what the fuck is wrong with me?*

"Earth to Lexi." Piper snaps her fingers in front of my face, and I blink. "Are you okay?"

"Hm? Yeah. I'm great. I think I drank that last gin and tonic too quickly. I should eat something."

"Here." Emmy hands over a plate of olives and puts a hand on her stomach. "I'm stuffed, and I don't want those to go to waste."

"Why do you have a plate of only olives?" I ask. "Do we not care about the other food groups?"

"Years ago, I mentioned to Maverick I liked them in my drink, and he started carrying around a jar so I can have them whenever I want," she explains. "It's probably the reason why I fell in love with him."

"Maverick did that for you?" I frown and glance toward the kitchen where a bowl of limes sits on the counter. I added two to my last drink, smiling at the citrus flavor when I took a sip. "I didn't know that."

"Oh, yeah. Before I even gave him the time of day, he was handing over olives he'd ordered from Greece." She rolls her eyes, but I see the smile she's fighting to hide. "He's so extra, but knowing he remembered that… it made me feel good. Important, you know?"

There's been a collection of limes at every event Riley's attended this season, and that can't be a coincidence. I knew he had a crush on me, but that… that seems special. *Important*, like Emmy said, and when my eyes meet Riley's from across the room, I turn my attention back to the girls, afraid to look at him for too long.

"Have you all ever used any, um, accessories in the bedroom?" I ask, dropping my voice low so none of the boys can overhear us. The last thing I need is someone being nosy and announcing my question to the entire team. "Ropes or things of the sort?"

"Okay. Talk about a topic change," Piper says.

"Maverick uses hockey tape." Emmy grins. "It's fun, and who doesn't love a product that can be multi-functional?"

"Wow. You could be a spokesperson," Madeline says, and she glances at me. "Are you seeing someone who is into that?"

"Wait. You haven't mentioned hooking up with anyone in a while." Piper leans forward. "Are you becoming celibate?"

"God no." I laugh. "I could never. Men might be dicks, but some of them have good dicks, and it would be a shame for those to go to waste."

"So why the questions about bondage?" Maven asks.

"I don't know. Just curious. I've never tried it."

"Most important thing is trusting your partner," Emmy says, and I nod. "You have to know if you say stop, they're going to stop. You also have to be okay giving up your control. It's not as easy as it sounds, and it's uncomfortable at first. You realize you have nowhere to go, but when you relax and understand you're safe, it's *good*. I can send you some websites Mav and I looked at if you want."

"What websites?" Maverick asks, appearing by her side.

"None of your business." She swats at his stomach and he lifts her off the couch in a single swoop, throwing her over his shoulder. "Oh my god. Put me the fuck down, Miller."

"Nope. I'm taking you home, Hartwell. We play against each other tomorrow night, and when I kick your ass on the ice, I don't want to hear any excuses about how you're tired and sore."

"I should head out, too." Madeline checks her phone. "Lucy's babysitter is in high school, and I don't want her to have to stay at the apartment too late."

"I'm pretty sure Liam is already in the car." Piper yawns and jumps to her feet. "Want a ride home, Lex?"

"I'm okay. I drove, and I'm going to help clean up because I didn't help set up." I smile at my friends. "I'll see you all tomorrow at the game."

"Let us know when you get home." Maven gives me a hug and I wave as the team starts filing out of Riley's apartment.

"I can take care of this," Riley says when we're the only

two left in the living room. He holds up a trash bag and smiles. "Everything is going to get thrown in here."

"They're all savages. It's going to take you forever if you do it by yourself." I stack up eight paper plates and walk toward him, dropping the trash in the bag. "I can start on the dishes."

"Nope. I'm not going to let you. I offered to host, and cleaning up comes with the territory."

"Good thing I'm not asking for permission." I push past him for the kitchen, staring at the pile of silverware and glasses in the sink. I roll up my sleeves and grab a sponge. "I think we need to start doing all drinks in Solo cups. This is too much work for one person."

"I forgot to run out and get some this afternoon." He drops the trash bag and stands next to me, turning on the faucet. His hip bumps against mine, and I scoot to the right to give him more room. "I'll wash, you dry?"

"Teamwork. I like it. Gosh. More men belong in the kitchen."

Riley laughs and starts on the lowball glasses the guys used for their liquor. We find a rhythm and work quickly as the pile starts to dwindle. In between washing and drying, we make casual conversation, and it takes all of my restraint to *not* bring up what I learned about him in the bedroom.

I ask him how he's liked being behind the bench at games and if he's given coaching more thought. He tells me he's been sharpening the skates I got him for Christmas and even tried the right one on with his prosthetic to see how it feels. I'm happy to hear it fits, and I need to send a thank-you note to the people at Bauer for all their help in the process.

Forty-five minutes later, the kitchen is spotless. You wouldn't know twenty hockey players stormed through here an hour ago, and I yawn when I fold up the used dish towel and set it on the counter.

"Much easier with help, right?" I ask, and Riley nods.

"Yeah. Thanks for not letting me be too stubborn." He dries his hands and sighs. "Lex. I want to apologize for earlier."

"What happened earlier?"

"Back in my bedroom. I crossed a line by letting our conversation get that far, and I'm sorry for not putting a stop to it. I understand if you want me to work with a different athletic trainer going forward."

"What are you talking about? I've seen your dick, Riley. We spent an intimate night together, and you think learning you like to tie people up is what's going to make me not want to work with you anymore? Please." I snort and jump onto the counter. "I'm not scandalized. I'm *intrigued*. There's a difference."

"Were you serious about what you said?" He closes the distance between us, positioning himself between my thighs. His hands land on either side of my hips, and he stares me down. "About what you want to try?"

"I wouldn't lie about that."

I've never been ashamed of my sexual preferences. I've been open about what I want in the bedroom and haven't cared if someone judges me, but this conversation feels deeper. More personal. It's not a man I'm never going to see again or someone I matched with having one goal in mind: getting off.

It's a man I know well, who seems to enjoy the things I enjoy, and that propels me forward.

"We agreed on one night," Riley says slowly. "We agreed to be friends."

I gnaw on my bottom lip, wanting to get this next part right. "The first time was fun."

"It was phenomenal."

"We had a good time, and yeah, it was a little awkward after, but we got through it. What if we do it again? You can't deny there's chemistry between us, and we worked really well together. I've never… sex wise, that was the best night of my life."

"What are you asking me for? To be your boyfriend?"

"Absolutely not." My laughter dies in my throat when he inches closer. I drop my head against the cabinet behind me and watch the heat behind his eyes. "Not that."

"Is the idea of me being your boyfriend funny, Lexi?"

"No. *No*. Of course not. You're a nice guy, and I'm sure you'd be a wonderful boyfriend. I just… I don't want that. I don't want a relationship. I want… no emotions. No messy feelings. That's not my style."

"You want to be fucked," he says, and the detachment in his voice makes my skin warm. He makes it sound dirty, *filthy*, and I can feel my underwear getting wet. "Why me?"

"Because I know you can deliver? Because I trust you? Because I… I told you what I wanted to try and you didn't make a joke out of it?"

Riley takes a step back, and the air around me deflates. I can think more clearly when he's not in my space.

"Fuck buddies. Friends with benefits. Am I getting this right?" he asks. "You call me when you want me to get you off, and I make you come until you can't think straight?"

"Yup. Yeah. Mhm. Sounds about right."

He rolls his lips together and blinks at me. "No feelings?"

"None. It's sex. That's it."

"Are you going to be sleeping with anyone else?"

"Are *you* going to be sleeping with anyone else?" I ask.

"No," he says without a second thought. "I told you, you're the only woman I've slept with in god knows how long."

"I haven't been with anyone since you," I practically blurt, and he lifts an eyebrow. "What? Is the idea of me keeping my legs closed that shocking to you?"

"No," he repeats. He puts his hands on my thighs and

runs his fingers up the denim of my jeans. "Guess I'm just proud I'm enough to satisfy Ms. Independent."

"One time together and you're this cocky?" I grab his shirt and tug him toward me. I brush my mouth along the corner of his lips, shaking my head when he whimpers. "I'm not kissing you until you tell me yes or no."

"You know what my answer is. I'll be your fuck buddy, Lex. I'll take care of you."

"No feelings."

"None."

"The second one of us starts to—"

"Stop talking." Riley lifts me off the counter, careful to put a hand behind my head so I don't knock my skull against the cabinet. "You don't want me to fall in love with you. No lovey dovey shit. We'll fuck, and you'll leave. I got it."

He walks down the hall, his pace slow. I don't know what I'm supposed to say, only that we're doing this.

Again.

And I'm really fucking excited about it.

"I know you told me to stop talking, but should you be carrying me?" I ask. "I don't want you to hurt yourself."

"I'm fine. It's a short walk, and throwing you over my shoulder is way more dramatic than making you do it by yourself."

I laugh. Riley pushes the door to his room open. He walks me to the bed and sets me on the mattress. As soon as he does, unexpected nerves hit me square in the chest. The last time we did this, we were in a hotel room. An unfamiliar place where we could pretend like we didn't have an attachment to one another.

Now I glance around and see pieces of him everywhere I look: a jersey over the back of the chair at his desk by the window, a second pair of glasses on his nightstand, his phone plugged into a charger.

"Are you okay?" he asks, and I nod.

"Yeah." I point to the bottom of the dresser, heart thundering. "I want you to use those ropes on me."

"Are you sure?"

"Positive."

"You said you've never used them before?" He opens the drawer and pulls out the long ropes I held earlier. "Have you ever researched Shibari?"

"Once or twice," I admit.

"It focuses on friction and wraps instead of knots. The rope is made of jute." Riley holds out the rope for me to touch, and I run my fingers along the natural fiber. "The middle point is called the bight."

"Can I ask a question?"

"Anything."

"With this… are you into the BDSM lifestyle?"

"No. Not my thing. I like being in control, but I don't like dominating or denying. I like for things in the bedroom to be, ah, collaborative? And I like being told what to do too."

"Okay." I nod, and he takes the ropes back. "Can I get out of it if I don't like it?"

"Absolutely. And I have safety shears."

"I don't want my whole body tied up. Only my wrists. Is that okay?"

"Lexi." Riley grimaces when he lowers himself to the floor and kneels between my legs. "None of this is a requirement. I don't want to use bondage every time, if we're being honest. Occasionally is more than enough for me. Not even frequently. Like I mentioned before, I get off great without it. Better than. You made me finish with your *mouth*, and I've been thinking about it every day since. Ropes are a bonus. Something fun to add every now and then."

"You've been thinking about it?"

"More than I'm allowed to admit." He cups my cheek, thumb stroking along the curve of my jaw. "Don't worry. I'm not in love with you. I'm playing by the rules."

"Shut up," I murmur, tugging on his hair and bending my neck so I can kiss him. "Speaking of mouths, I don't like when my friends with benefits use their mouths to talk."

"What do you want me to use it for?"

I grab the hem of my shirt and tug it over my head. I unhook my bra, smiling when Riley groans and rests his forehead against my collarbone, a mumbled *fuck* tumbling out of him. I've always been proud of my body, but hearing his reaction strikes a match inside me.

"This," I whisper, guiding his mouth to my nipple. When he closes his lips and *sucks*, I stutter out a breath. "Perfect."

"Move back on the bed," he says against my skin, and I hate to pull away from him. "Now, Lexi."

The firmness in his demand has me scooting across the sheets, pulse jumping as I lean back on the pillows and watch him. He stands, another grimace dancing across his face, before he climbs on the mattress and taps my foot.

"Shoes off. Jeans off. Underwear off."

I nod, delirious as I kick off my boots, slide the jeans down my legs, and add my underwear to the pile of discarded clothing on his floor. He's still fully dressed, cheeks bright red and his eyes on me, and the power imbalance sends a shiver racing up my spine.

This is what I want.

Someone who knows what they're doing, not a mediocre attempt by a guy who read one Reddit thread and thinks he has everything figured out. Riley's hand rests on my thigh and teases his touch across my stomach, dipping lower so his knuckles brush against my entrance before he moves up, fingers at my throat.

"You liked this," he says, applying the hint of pressure to my neck. "Is it still okay?"

I close my eyes and sink into the gentle way his grip tightens. "Yes."

"Last time we did this, we moved fast. Orgasms. Fucking.

That was it. It's going to be slower tonight, and I'm going to check in with you. You have to communicate with me, Lexi. I can't change anything after we finish, but I can change it in the moment."

"Right. Yeah. Communication. That's very important," I say, but it feels like my head is in the clouds.

"And we're going to have a system. Green means you like what's happening. Yellow means you need to take a second before we keep going. Red is a firm stop. The second you tell me red, whatever we're doing ends. Do you understand?" Riley asks, and when I nod, he pinches my nipple. My eyes fly open and my back arches off the bed. "I need you to *say* it."

"Yes," I stammer, and he smiles.

"Good. Now give me your hands. Please."

THIRTY-ONE
RILEY

MONTHS AGO, I thought the universe was trying to fuck me over.

A car accident, losing my leg, and not being able to play hockey again all in one night.

Now it's like I'm being rewarded for being so *fucking patient* with everything that's happened in my life, because Lexi Armstrong is naked on my bed. She's holding out her hands, blinking up at me with dark lashes and wide eyes, and it's a goddamn wonder I haven't already finished in my pants.

Her body is fucking unreal. Soft curves at her hips. A toned stomach from years of exercise. Strong, long legs that would look best wrapped around my head.

She's the most beautiful woman I've ever seen.

"I'm going to do a double column tie," I say, proud of myself for being able to get actual words out. "It's the same thing I did earlier, but with both of your wrists."

"I didn't mind that," she tells me.

"You were wearing clothes and not tied to the headboard. This is going to be different."

I get started on the knots, making sure to watch Lexi's face every second. She's busy watching my fingers, and after a few seconds, I pull the rope tight to lock the knots in place, satisfied with how it looks.

"Finished?" Lexi asks, and I nod.

"That's it." I slip my fingers between the ropes and her wrists, checking to make sure nothing is too tight. "How does that feel?"

"Weird, but…" She trails off and lifts her hands in front of her, examining them. "Good."

"Any pain? Too much pressure? Hands are the first thing to lose circulation, so if it's uncomfortable, I need to know."

"No." Lexi smiles. "I like it."

"Okay. Good. Yeah." I run a hand through my hair. "It looks good."

"Are you always this nervous?"

"I'm not nervous."

"Yes, you are."

"I'm fine. Just want to make sure you're okay," I say, and I double check the tie knot again.

"I'm more than okay. What happens now?"

"The benefits part of all of this." I lift her hands above her head. "Me doing whatever you ask. Making sure you get off. That's what you want, right?"

Lexi squirms and exhales a puff of hot air that tickles my face. "When you say it like that, it makes it seem like you're not enjoying yourself. It makes it seem like this is only about me."

"Right now it is." I draw a straight line down her body, from her neck to her stomach. "Relax, Lexi baby. You know I'm going to take care of you."

When her shoulders drop away from her ears and she closes her eyes, I tie her wrists to the headboard. I give the ropes a pull, making sure she can release herself if she wants to get out of the ties, as every thought I've ever had about her comes rushing to the surface.

I cup both of her breasts and drag my thumbs over her

nipples, grinning when she squirms again and finds she can't move her upper body.

"*Fuck*," she whispers, eyes flying open.

"Impressed yet?"

"You're a goddamn tease."

"Says the girl who waltzed in here, told me she wanted to be tied up, then made me sit through dinner with my friends while I imagined what she'd look like spread out on my bed."

"And? Is it what you pictured?"

"Better," I say, pressing my palm on her stomach. "Last time I took your underwear. This time, I might need to take a photo of you so I can look at it when I'm sad and lonely in my hotel room during our away games. And I'm sad a lot, Lexi."

"That's the best part about being friends with benefits." She moans when I push a finger inside her and find her pussy tight and wet. "You could knock on my door, have the real thing, and not stick around to find out if I snore."

"Tempting. What would I tell my teammates?" I add a second finger, stretching her out, and her legs tip open wider. She lifts her hips, and I push her back against the mattress so she can't move. "*Sorry. I can't make dinner. I have a needy woman in my room who is demanding my attention?*"

"Throw in the word hot too."

"You're so damn confident."

"Am I wrong?"

"No." I bend to kiss her stomach. My tongue leaves a trail of wet marks behind as I position myself between her legs. "You're not wrong at all. You doing okay up there?"

"Yeah," she says. I glance up at her and watch her tug on the ropes. "This is... I like this a lot."

"I like *this*, a lot." I lick her pussy, tongue pressing down on her clit. "Fuck. I've missed you."

"You've missed my cunt."

I haven't been with a lot of women. The number is small compared to some of my teammates who like sleeping around. But I can say without a doubt in my fucking mind Lexi is the hottest person I've ever slept with.

There aren't any games. I don't have to ask for guidance. She tells me exactly what she wants and exactly how she wants it, blunt as hell when she wraps her thighs around my head and urges my face deeper between her legs.

"No, you brat." I pinch the inside of her knee and she squeals. "I've missed *you*."

"Less talking. More—*shit, Riley*," she whines when I push a third finger inside her. She tightens around me, and it's alarming how much that turns me on. "Right there."

"Wrists okay?" I ask, the words coming out muffled when she squeezes her legs against my cheeks.

"Yes. I just wish—" She stops talking, and I look up at her. When she doesn't continue, I rub a slow circle over her clit until she cries out, arms twisting above her. "I wish I could touch you," she finishes in a rush of a breath.

"You can't have it all, Lexi. I'll take the ropes off after you come."

"That's not fair." She huffs. "I want to leave them on *and* touch you."

"And I want you to come on my tongue so I can taste you. Given our current position, I think I'm going to be the one who wins."

Lexi moans again, and I take my time with her. I do everything she likes, including curling my fingers and burying my tongue inside her and almost passing out from how hard I am, all because I'm touching her.

"Riley. I think I'm going to come." She yanks on the ropes and twists her hips, but I keep her pinned in place. "It's too much. I-I can't—" She gulps down a breath when the rope digs into her wrists, and a sob works its way up her throat. "*Please.*"

"Please what?" I ask, watching her for any signs of discomfort. Her eyes are squeezed shut. Her chest is flushed red and her nipples are hard, and her hair is halfway out of her ponytail. "Do you want me to stop?"

"*No.* It feels too good. It's never—"

"This is how it's supposed to feel when someone is doing it right. As long as you're my *friend*, you're not going to have to fake anything, Lexi."

That earns me another squeeze of her thighs around my neck as she falls apart, a mess of shaking legs and whispered pleas. I coax her through it, tongue still on her clit while I slow my fingers inside her until she's trembling on the sheets.

"Please," she whispers again. "I want to get out."

I'm off her in a second, moving up the bed as fast as I can. I release the knot so her hands fall away from the metal headboard. I tug the rope, breaking her wrists free, and pull her into my lap, cradling her close to my chest.

I kiss her forehead and the top of her head. I stroke her hair, blowing out a breath when she buries her face in my shirt. "You did so well, sweetheart."

"That was—" Lexi sniffs and tilts her head back, gaze meeting mine. There's mascara under her right eye, and I wipe it away with my thumb. "The most intense experience of my life."

"Did I hurt you?" I carefully check her hands, kissing the inside of her wrists and the marks I find there. Blood pounds in my head, fearful she hated every minute of that until her lips turn up in a smile. "Talk to me, Lex."

"No. No, you didn't," she says. The roar around me settles when her palms slip out of my grip, move up my chest, and drape around my shoulders. "I'm fine. I'm so much better than fine. That felt so… *natural.* I loved every minute of it. I have so much adrenaline, it feels like I could go run ten miles."

"That's the orgasm talking. Or you have way too much energy." I put my finger under her chin, kissing her softly. Lexi melts into me, mouth opening and tongue brushing against mine. "Knowing you, both are possible."

"What can I say? One quickie from your fingers, and I'm practically a superhero. Thanks, friend."

"You really did do well. How are you feeling? Do you want some water?"

"Such hospitality." She tosses me a cocky smirk and throws a leg on either side of my waist. It's my turn to blow out an exhale when she slowly brings my shirt over my head, and I hold my breath until she pulls it off and tosses it aside. "I want you, Riley. More benefits. More fun."

"Yeah. Yes. Yup. Let's—" I lick my lips and grip her waist, fingers pressing into the curve of her ass. "There's a condom in the drawer over there."

Lexi leans to her right, stretching for the bedside table and almost knocking the lamp off in the process. My laugh turns to a cackle when she yanks on the drawer too hard, the whole piece flying out and landing on the floor in a wooden heap.

"You need new furniture," she murmurs, plucking a condom from the box I impulsively bought after our first night together. Wishful thinking and all that bullshit. "I'm going to get a splinter."

"I'll buy something new tomorrow. Whatever color you want. Better yet, send me a link of one you like. I'll overnight it."

She grins and spins the foil packet between her fingers. "Do you want to try something new? A different position? How... how can I make this good for you?"

The pre-cum in my briefs would argue that everything we've done up to this point tonight has been fan-fucking-tastic, and she's barely touched me. But I'm calm. I'm fucking easygoing, her *friend* and newly appointed orgasm provider for the foreseeable future, and I'm not going to blow my cover by being a pathetic, yearning mess of a man who will have her any way I can get her.

"Maybe you on top again? If you liked it," I add, and her

smile softens. "Next time we can try something different. I'll… I'll fuck you."

"I like being on top." She kneels next to me and puts her hand on my left thigh. "Are you going to take your pants off? Or do you prefer—"

"I'm going to take them off and leave my prosthetic on again. Was it okay last time? I know the socket isn't—"

"It was perfect. Take off your clothes, Riley," Lexi says softly, and of course I fucking listen. I unbutton my jeans and untie my shoes. She helps me pull the denim over my prosthetic then works on my briefs, making quick work of the black underwear. When I'm naked in front of her, she wraps her hand around my cock and smiles. "Look at you. Getting me off turns you on, doesn't it?"

"Yes, and—" I groan when she opens the condom and rolls it down my length. "We can't spend too much time on foreplay. I want to fuck you, and if you jerk me off, I'm going to come in twenty seconds."

"I bet we could make it eighteen," she says, a challenge in her eyes. She straddles me again, hovering over the head of my cock and leaning forward so she can whisper in my ear. "But, fine. We'll play your way. Fuck me, Riley. You know I like it rough."

I touch her everywhere I can reach; her tits when I squeeze them together, her clit when she drops her head back and moans, her hips when she lowers herself on me, and a light smack on her ass when the first half of my cock sinks into her.

Fucking hell.

Her pussy is glorious. Absolutely divine when she rolls her hips and puts her hands on my chest, using me as leverage so she can get another inch deeper. I lift off the bed, snapping my hips to meet her halfway and thrusting into her as hard as I can.

It's messy and sloppy. The bed shakes and rattles the

window above us. Sweat rolls down our bodies. I hook my thumb in the corner of her mouth then press on her tongue, smiling when I drag her drool down her cheek. When I grab her throat, watching her to make sure I'm not being too unhinged with her—I've about lost my goddamn mind—her pussy squeezes my cock tight.

"Listen, sweetheart," I pant, my nails digging into the swell of her ass. "I'm a selfless man. I want you to finish first. Always. But, um, watching you come undone with your hands bound together really did a number on me. Can we still be friends if I come before you? I promise it won't happen again."

"You are *infuriating.*" Lexi kisses me and I move my hand to the back of her head, holding her there while I claw at the cusp of an orgasm. "Too goddamn nice and—"

"Answer the fucking question," I grit out. "*Please,* Lexi baby."

"At the risk of sounding cliché"—she gasps when I spit on my thumb and rub a slow circle over her clit.—"I'm about to come too."

"Race you there?" I ask, and when she giggles, arms above her head and hair spilling down her back, I lose it.

My entire body tenses, muscles spasming while I fill the condom with my release. My glasses fog up, and everything around me is a hazy blur of colors and sounds. Lexi collapses on top of me, her breath heavy and my name whispering out of her like a slurred incantation when I keep my fingers between her legs.

"I think"—She pauses to swallow, and I feel the bob of her throat against my cheek—"you're the best friend I've ever had."

An exhausted laugh rattles out of me. I'm pretty sure I'm seeing stars. Visions of her falling apart are playing on repeat in my head. "I aim to please."

"You do it really fucking well."

"I'm glad you think so. You're a tough critic." I yawn and drop my head against the pillows. "Did two orgasms impress you?"

"We're getting there."

We both wince when she lifts off my cock and flops on her stomach next to me. She drapes an arm over my stomach and I get rid of the used condom, feeling winded like I'm heading for the bench after being on the ice after a long shift.

"You gonna stay?" I ask, yawning again. "Or are you bolting?"

"I'll stay for a minute. I need to pee. My legs hurt. So do my hands."

I grab her hands and massage the inside of her wrists, thumbs gentle when I pass over the pink marks that haven't faded. "Are you allergic to anything?"

"That's a random question to ask after rearranging my insides. I figured you'd ask about birth control first."

"Sorry. This is my first friends with benefits arrangement. I haven't figured out the rules yet, and I want to make sure you don't go into anaphylactic shock when you're on top of me. Or while your hands are tied up." I pinch her side and she lets out a squeak. "But yeah, that too. Are you on birth control?"

She pushes her hair out of her face and smiles up at me. "I am. And I'm allergic to bees."

"Bees, got it. Won't introduce any of those in the bedroom."

"What about you? Any allergies I should be aware of, buddy?" she asks.

"No. My limb gets red and irritated from the gel liner it sits in sometimes, but I'm not allergic to anything. And if you don't want to use a condom, we can go that route."

"You'd be okay with that?"

"Yeah. But only if we're exclusive. Sex ed and all of that."

"I've never had a friend with benefits either," Lexi admits.

She scoots across the wrinkled sheets and rests her cheek on my shoulder. "It's mostly been one and done for me."

"Personal preference? Or is it because my gender is a constant disappointment?"

"Both." I feel the curve of her smile, and it makes me smile too. "I read romance books. I've seen my friends fall in love and get married and have everything they've ever wanted. I know it happens, I just... it's hard for me to believe it's real and true. Why waste my time and energy on something that might turn around and hurt me six months later? Or, even worse, six years later? I don't *want* to be tied to someone else. I want to make my own happiness. My own rules."

"I guess I could ask the same question about other things. Why get in a car when it could end with me losing my other leg? Just because something could happen doesn't mean it will," I say. "But I get it. Your independence is important to you. Letting another person in offers up the chance for you to lose that part of yourself."

"Exactly." Lexi props herself up on an elbow. "But I still have needs, you know? I may not want a ring on my finger, but I do want a couple of orgasms."

"That's my job." I close my eyes. "I'll be a good friend to you, Lex."

"Speaking of friends, can we agree to keep this between us again? I know if I tell the girls, they'll start coming up with couples names for us and asking how we're *defining our relationship*. I'm not ready for an interrogation."

"My lips are sealed."

"Thanks." She kisses my forehead, and the mattress dips when she rolls toward the edge of the bed. I crack an eye open and watch her scoop up her clothes. "I'm going to head out. I have some guys scheduled for taping before the game tomorrow night, and I need to be at the arena early."

"If you give me a second, I'll walk you out."

"That's okay." Lexi smiles at me over her shoulder,

clasping her bra and putting on her shirt. "I can find the door. It's in the same place it was earlier."

"Will you let me know when you're home?" When she lifts an eyebrow, I roll my eyes. "It's not a marriage proposal. I'd ask the same thing from the guys."

"Yeah, yeah." She pops to her feet and redresses with her underwear and jeans. "If you insist."

"I do insist. Thank you."

"You're welcome." She blows me a kiss, and I laugh. "Sweet dreams, friend."

"See you tomorrow, Lexi baby."

With another smile, she slips out of my bedroom. I hear the toilet flush in the bathroom down the hall, then the click of the front door closing behind her. I count to one hundred, and when I know she's gone, I grab a pillow. I put it over my face and groan, knowing I'm teetering on the edge of a very dangerous slope.

THIRTY-TWO
RILEY

PUCK KINGS

MAVVY
Don't forget about book club tonight, kids.

ME
Might be late. I have a therapy session. I'll head over after.

HUDDY BOY
Madeline made cookies. I'll make sure to save you one.

G-MONEY
What kind of cookies?

HUDDY BOY
Chocolate chip.

G-MONEY
Damn. Peanut butter is my favorite.

EASY E

The world doesn't revolve around you, Everett.

G-MONEY

What's with the attitude problem, Richardson?

EASY E

I've been having some issues with Tella. The engine is acting up, and seems like there's a problem with the chain and drive systems. I'm worried she's not going to make it!!

SULLY

It's an inanimate object.

EASY E

She's the LOML!

MAVVY

Wow. Over all of us?

EASY E

Obviously. I can replace you all.

G-MONEY

That's not nice. No sleepover during our away game next week. I'm revoking your privileges.

EASY E

Lot of big words coming from the guy from the Florida education system!!

G-MONEY

You know what?

Never mind. Canada sounds like a dream.

HUDDY BOY

Ethan, be nice. I hope Tella is okay.

EASY E

> Thank you, Huddy. At least someone cares about me.
>
> The rest of you can fuck off!

"RILEY." Dr. Ledlow beams at me and points at the couch across from the chair he's sitting in. "It's good to see you. Have a seat."

"Thanks." I drop onto the leather and stretch out my legs, massaging my right thigh. "What's up?"

"How's you've been?"

"Busy. I, ah, am working with the Stars in a sort of coaching capacity now. Coach got approval from the league for me to be a team official instead of the roster for the time being, so I don't get to hide out in the tunnel anymore. I'm behind the bench now."

"Are you enjoying that role?"

"More than I thought I would," I admit. "It's nice to feel like I have a purpose, and it's even nicer to feel like I have a purpose that involves hockey. I go to practice. I talk about lineups and help my teammates run drills. I know it's not going to be a long-term thing, but I'm falling back in love with the sport I spent weeks grieving because I thought I lost it. There's a little bit of whiplash."

"That's understandable. You're nervous it's a Band-Aid that will get pulled off and wondering what happens if and when the wound is open again."

"How the fuck are you so good at this?"

"My student loans don't let me be *not* good at this." He rests his foot on his knee and makes a note in his folder. "Let's talk about your physical health. No more assistive devices. No more limping. When you walked in here, if I didn't know you had a prosthetic, I never would've guessed you were using an artificial leg. I take it you've been going to your rehabilitation sessions like the team asked?"

"Yeah. I know I was stubborn in the beginning, but turns out, if you do something you're supposed to do, you get better at it."

"Wow." Dr. Ledlow smiles. "Funny how that works."

"Sucks, honestly." I snort. "I'm learning to be comfortable. I'm adapting to this new body of mine. I still struggle occasionally when I don't have my prosthesis on. Seeing myself in a mirror is... hard. Especially as someone who's constantly seeing pictures and videos of what they looked like before." I reach for the glass of water he set out for me and take a sip. "I'm not sure it will ever be normal."

"It might not be, but that doesn't take away from the progress you've made. You can be comfortable but not content. The two aren't mutually exclusive." He underlines something on the document in his lap and looks up at me. "We've gone a couple months without talking about the heavier stuff because our conversation hasn't led to it, but given our interactions when you first started meeting with me, I'd be remiss if we didn't spend a minute or two talking about—"

"My mental health," I say, and he nods. "It's up and down. In the last few months, it's been more up than down, but the downs hit me out of nowhere."

I rub my jaw, thinking about last night and how I couldn't get my sneaker on my prosthetic foot. It took me twenty minutes and a shoehorn before I finally chucked it at the wall and gave up. There's the mood I was in last week, a beautiful January day where *everything* pissed me off: the sandwich I had for lunch, how scratchy my sheets felt against my leg, the pillow that didn't help with the crick in my neck.

There's no rhyme or reason for any of it. Some days the irritation and depression last for twenty minutes. I'll take a bath, and it'll disappear. Other times it stretches for hours, and I turn off my phone, lie in bed, and stare at the wall. The only good thing during those rough stretches is Lexi. I can always count on her to send me a funny text. I'll get a meme that compliments my dick or a selfie of her in the athletic trainer's room, Liam flipping off the camera behind her.

She's a good friend.

"Some people think of recovery as a straight, flat line. A direct route from point A, which is the onset of grief, and B, which is a new normal. That's not true. It's more like rolling hills and valleys. There will be highs and lows, but they lead to the same place. And sometimes, you'll have a flat line for months before a bump in the road shows up and you have to climb up another hill."

"I have seventy more years of going uphill? I can't wait."

"It can always be worse. You could have eighty."

I bark out a laugh. "Touché, Doc."

"We have to address the elephant in the room." Dr. Ledlow caps his pen and steeples his fingers under his chin. "Before, your depression was bringing on suicidal thoughts. After one of our first sessions, your mother pulled me aside to tell me she found a bottle of medication in your bathroom with a substantial amount of pills missing. I've been doing this long enough to know it's easy to mask the pain by smiling and pretending like everything is fine on the surface when you're battling an army of demons internally. Hell, I've done it myself. Do me a favor for a second. Forget I'm your doctor. Forget I'm a medical professional. Right now, I'm a man asking another man how he's *really* doing, because we don't get asked it enough."

I clear my throat and lean forward in my chair. I can't remember the last time someone asked me that. Has anyone asked my teammates that? Like, *really* asked them? I probably should. It seems pretty important.

"I'm not going to lie. I was having those thoughts," I say

quietly. "Frequently. That pain—physically and mentally—was... I can't even describe it." I turn my head and stare out at the window. "Every day I was in that hospital, I thought how *easy* it would be to just end it all. It'd free up a bed for someone who would actually recover. My parents wouldn't have to give up weeks of their life to help me move around my apartment because I couldn't fucking walk. Would I have gone through with it? We'll never know. I'm not... that's not something I want to do anymore. I'm not kidding when I say the hard days are still *so fucking hard* no matter how much I smile around my friends, but I'm hanging in there. I'm reading again. I picked up a paintbrush for the first time in forever. I'm finally starting to see who I could be without hockey, and I'm trying to find something new to live for after the greatest thing in my life was ripped away from me. I realize there are people who would miss me, and I'd miss them."

"Your parents? Your teammates?"

"And other people."

"Ah." Dr. Ledlow smiles. "A girl or a guy."

"Yeah." I sigh. "A girl."

"Want to tell me about her?"

"We're friends. All we're ever going to be is friends, and I'd rather have her in my life as that than not have her in my life at all."

"You care about her," he says.

"I care about a lot of people."

"You really care about her."

"I guess I do." I drum my fingers on my thigh. Lexi and I got together last week, a quick meetup at my place on her way home from a Pilates class. She was sweaty. I was horny. And I'm slowly but surely getting the hang of this friends with benefits thing. "She's done a lot for me. Everyone has."

"How are you really doing, Riley?" he presses, but nothing about it feels forceful.

"I'm…" I trail off and blink back tears. I pull off my glasses and hurry to wipe my eyes, but Dr. Ledlow doesn't say anything. "I'm okay. I'm closer to good than not, and that's lightyears better than where I was before. A work in fucking progress, I'd say, but also someone who knows they have a bigger role here and is no longer in a hurry to leave." I pause to swallow the lump in my throat. "Thank you for asking."

"We'll stop there for today. You've made some big steps over the last six months, and I'm really proud of you."

"Thank you for being patient with me," I mumble. "I know I haven't been easy to work with."

"I'm always going to be patient with you, Riley. Not because it's my job, but because it's the right thing to do as a human being."

"You're way too good at this, Doc. Your ability to analyze me even when I don't think I'm being analyzed is scary."

"All in a day's work," he says.

I stand and hold out my hand, smiling when he clasps it. "I'll see you next month?"

"You have my number if you need me before then."

"Thanks, man. I appreciate your time."

"My pleasure." He shakes my palm. "And Riley? If something makes you happy, I think you should go for it."

"Would *you* go for it knowing there was no shot at something coming out of it?"

"Your doctors said you shouldn't have survived, but here you are. Aren't you glad they went for it even though the odds were stacked against them?"

"Bastard." I tip my head back and look up at the ceiling. "We'll see."

"Can't wait for an update. Be well, Riley."

I wave and take the elevator down to the ground floor, his words ringing in my ears in the backseat of an Uber all the way to Hudson's place.

"ORDER, ORDER!" Maverick yells. He knocks a rubber mallet on the living room coffee table. "Can everyone please shut the fuck up so book club can commence?"

"I've been waiting for this one." Grant rubs his hands together and grins. "A dark romance where she falls in love with the stalker but only after she makes him crawl on his knees and beg for forgiveness? It's like the author wrote this shit just for me."

"I'm sure she had you in mind the whole time." Hudson offers me a beer, and I shake my head. "I thought this one was just okay."

"Okay? *Okay?* He buys her whatever she wants. He threatens the guy at the bar who harasses her. He's a nice dude who makes sure she's safe when she rides on the back of his motorcycle—"

"There were motorcycles in there?" Ethan asks, looking up.

"Did you even read the book?" I ask.

"Nah. I got busy." He smirks and flips through the pages of the paperback. "I'm a popular guy, Mitchy."

"I did not need to know that."

"If I have to see pictures of the jewelry on his dick, you all get to know how popular he is," Grant says. "Imagine being in line at the grocery store and Ethan's penis pops up on your phone."

"I just gagged." Liam scrunches up his nose and takes a sip of his water. "Please refrain from any further conversation on phallic tendencies. It's cold as shit outside, and Piper has the car tonight. I don't want to walk home, but I will."

"Such a prude." Ethan throws a pretzel at Liam's head, and he catches it without even looking up. "Someone else convince me to read this book."

"She also crawls to *him*." Maverick grins. "That's an underrated microtrope if you ask me."

"Remember that other book where the guy tells her to lose her ring and crawl? Hell." Grant fans his face. "I wish I had the balls to say that to a woman. I wouldn't be able to get the words out."

I wonder if I could get Lexi to crawl to me. She'd probably put up a fight and flat-out refuse in the name of feminism, but I bet I could convince her by crawling to her first. I'm all for an equal power dynamic if it means watching her temporarily hand over control again.

Fuck.

"Mitchy?" Hudson taps my shoulder, and I blink. "You good?"

"Huh? Oh, yeah. Sorry. Distracted." I flash them a smile. "I liked the book more than I thought I would. He's a nice stalker; he makes breakfast for her before sneaking out of her house, and does her laundry when she's at work."

"A respectful king," Maverick agrees.

"And short. We need some excitement for the shorter guys out there," Grant adds. "We deserve love too."

"You're five eleven," he deadpans.

"Compared to you fuckers I'm a goddamn shrimp."

"Your posture is horrible," Ethan says around a cookie he shoves in his mouth. "You need to stand up taller."

"I never thought I'd be taking notes on how to be a good partner from a stalker romance, but here we are." Hudson smiles. "I did Madeline and Lucy's laundry the other day while they were on a field trip because of that scene in the book, and she burst into tears when she got home."

"Women." Grant sighs. "So complex. So brilliant. We're so undeserving."

"Do you think Coach dates?" Ethan asks from out of nowhere. "I could see him being stalker-adjacent."

"I don't want to imagine Coach doing anything with anyone. The same way I don't need to hear about all of your personal business." I tap the title. "We should read book three next month."

"All in favor?" Maverick asks, and everyone's hands go up in the air. "Done. Motion for book three to be February's pick approved."

"I'm going to be pissed if it sucks," Ethan says.

"You're not even going to read it," I answer. "So you don't get an opinion."

"Ooh, Mitchy is *feisty* today. And smiling from ear to ear." Ethan pinches my cheek. "Did you get laid, Ri? The only time I look like this is after I get some good—"

"No," I say, smacking him in the chest with a pillow. "I had a therapy appointment and it went really well."

"I'm proud of you." Hudson nudges my foot with his. "I know you have someone to talk to, but if you need another outlet for your grief, I've been there. I'm always here with a set of ears if you need to vent."

"Thanks, man." I pat his thigh. "I appreciate that."

"Bonding over their past traumas and coming back stronger on the other side," Grant whispers to Ethan. "Doesn't make them any less manly."

"We can hear you, Grant," Hudson says.

"That was the point, Huddy."

Maverick looks at me from across the room. "I know we've said it before, but it should be said again. We're really glad you're here, Mitchy."

"Otherwise, we'd be stuck reading some book where a guy fucks his motorcycle because that's apparently what Ethan is into," Grant says.

"Okay, fuck all of you assholes." Ethan stands and flips us off. "See if I pass you the puck at our next game."

The room descends into chaos. There's an argument about paperbacks and hardcovers. Ethan and Grant try to make a castle out of all the paperbacks we brought and Maverick and Hudson argue about his bookshelf needing to be rearranged. A video game controller gets tossed in my hand and someone pulls up NBA 2K on the big television, and I really can't stop smiling.

This is my home, exactly where I'm supposed to be.

THIRTY-THREE
LEXI

ME
Hey, Mav

MAVERICK
What's up, Lex?

ME
Tomorrow is a big day for Riley. We're going to try getting back on the ice for the first time since his accident, and I was hoping some of you guys could be there.

I'm not a great skater and shouldn't be trusted with guiding someone.

And it would mean a lot to him to have your support.

MAVERICK
Oh, fuck yeah. I'll rally the troops and we'll be there.

ME

No cameras. No reporters. No cell phones. I don't want this to be a media stunt, and I don't want footage of him getting leaked anywhere.

MAVERICK

You have my word. What time were you thinking?

ME

Our sessions start around ten. I know you all have morning skate, so I was thinking we could hop on after the Zamboni cleans the ice?

MAVERICK

I'll shoot Merv a message. He normally waits to resurface until later in the afternoon, but I bet he's willing to make an exception.

ME

Who the hell is Merv?

MAVERICK

The Zamboni driver, obviously.

ME

You know his name?

MAVERICK

I'm captain of this team, Lex. I've made it a point to know the name of every single person in this organization. They know mine. Why shouldn't I know theirs?

ME

Huh. You're something else, Miller.

MAVERICK
Emmy girl likes to say I'm special.

ME
You sure are.

ME
Hiya.

RILEY
Hey, Lex. What's up?

ME
Something exciting is happening tomorrow!

RILEY
Should I know what it is?

ME
Bring your skates to our session. And wear comfortable pants.

RILEY
Are you serious?

ME
Dead serious. We're conquering the ice, Mitchy!

Wanna fuck after?

RILEY
Skating and sex? You know how to get a man excited.

> **ME**
> I wonder if anyone's ever fucked while ice skating.

> **RILEY**
> I don't trust my one leg to walk on solid ground, let alone have sex with someone while on the ice.
>
> Back at my place sounds safer.

> **ME**
> I'm really glad we lied to ourselves when we said we were only going to sleep together once.
>
> Look how much fun we're having!

> **RILEY**
> No self-control, whatsoever.

> **ME**
> I'll work on it.

> **RILEY**
> No, you won't.

> **ME**
> No. I definitely won't!

MERV DRIVES the Zamboni off the ice, and I give him a wave.

To my right, Riley sits on the players' bench and works on his skates. I catch his fingers shaking from here as he ties the laces, and every few seconds he mutters something to himself under his breath.

"Hey," I call out, and he glances up at me. "How are you feeling?"

"Like I want to throw up." He grips the board in front of him and slowly stands. "I don't know what to expect."

"Having no expectations might be a good thing." I shuffle over to him and check my own skates. The laces aren't as tight as I'd like them to be, but I don't want to waste any time. "No matter what happens, you're always going to be a better skater than me."

"The two of us are going to try and make it around the rink?" Riley lifts a wary eyebrow. "I should've worn my helmet."

"Me? Hell no. I'm here for emotional support. There are people better suited for that job," I say, grinning when all the Stars players skate out of the tunnel. "You're precious cargo, Mitchy. I need to make sure you're taken care of."

Maverick leads the line with Hudson, Liam, and Grant behind him. They all do a lap, crouching low to the ice until they stop in front of us.

"Heard we're doing some skating lessons today," Maverick says, and Riley sucks in a sharp breath.

"You all want to be here for this?" he asks.

"There's nowhere we'd rather be," Hudson says.

Liam opens the gate on the end of the bench and lifts his chin in Riley's direction. "C'mon Mitchy," he says, and my heart almost cracks in two when he holds out his hand.

Riley eyes his offered palm for a beat before his fingers curl around the goalie's. Moving carefully on his blades for the first time since last June, he steps onto the ice, legs shaking under his weight.

"I've got left," Maverick says, looping an arm around his waist.

"Right," Hudson adds, his arm resting on top of Maverick's.

"I've always been a fan of behind," Liam grumbles, and Riley's laugh is rough as the trio arranges themselves.

"Do I get to be in front?" Grant asks, practically jumping up and down. He takes both of Riley's hands in his, holding his arms out straight. "This is the best day of my life."

"Snail speed," I yell, and all the boys nod solemnly. I've never seen them look so serious, so focused, and the second Riley pushes off the ice, I'm close to bursting into tears. "Nothing faster."

He's worked so hard for this, and for as much as I know I've played a part in his recovery, these guys are his brothers. He's gone to battle with them, clawed his way out of hell with them, and I want them to have this moment without interrupting. It's special, a once-in-a-lifetime chasm in his timeline, and I lean over the boards, watching them as I fight back proud tears.

"Look at him go," Coach says from my left, surprising me. The rest of the team cheers as the group of five makes their way down the first straightaway, and Ethan starts chanting Riley's name. "Never in a million years did I think he'd get here."

"I did," I say. "I knew it all along."

I smile when the group creeps around the first bend. Maverick and Hudson are doing most of the work, the ones dictating the direction and increasing their momentum while Riley glides along with them, but he carefully lifts his right foot. He wobbles for a half a second before he sets his skate back on the ice and drops his head back as his shoulders shake with either a laugh or an onslaught of tears.

When they make it back to me, they come to a stop. He grips Maverick and Hudson's sides, flailing slightly when Grant lets go of his hands and drops to his knees to fix his laces. Riley's gaze meets mine, eyes bloodshot and misty behind his glasses. A tear tracks down his cheek and catches in the hollow his throat. His lips part and the silent *thank you* he mouths makes me light up. I give him a thumbs-up in return, feeling like I just won the damn lottery.

AN HOUR LATER, things aren't going well.

Riley's fallen three times.

He stops to adjust his prosthetic, grimacing when he takes his right skate off then slips it back on. Frustration is etched on his face in scrunched eyebrows and a line of wrinkles across his forehead, and after another failed attempt around the rink, he climbs into the penalty box and buries his face in his hands.

"Should we—" Maverick looks at him and scratches his jaw. "I don't want to be pushy. But I don't want to be unsupportive."

"He might need a minute. I'm going to get the other guys out of here," Hudson says, glancing at me. "Do you want to talk to him, Lex?"

"Me? I'm not a hockey player. I don't know what to say that would make him feel better."

"You don't need to say anything." Liam gives me a gentle shove, and I hop onto the ice. "Being there is going to be enough."

I grumble at their insistence and skate to the penalty box. I drop on the bench next to Riley, the lack of space apparent when our knees press together, but I don't mind. I like the feel of his body against mine.

"Hey," I say, and his shoulders sag. "What's going on?"

"I'm fucking awful out there. I can't even stand up."

"Yeah, because it's your first time back on the ice in months."

"This was a stupid idea." Riley starts to untie his laces and yanks off his left skate. "I'm tapping out."

"Riley." I scoot closer and put a hand on his forearm. He relaxes under my touch, and I drag my thumb up to his elbow then down to his hand. "I'm a shitty skater. I'm not going to pretend to know what it feels like for you to be out there trying something you used to excel at."

"You can't be that bad."

"Oh, I'm atrocious. We'd be like bowling pins if the two of us went out there." He huffs out a disgruntled laugh, and that encourages me to keep talking. "I'm so proud of you."

"What is there to be proud of?" His voice cracks, and I can't help but hug him. I can't help but squeeze him tight, trying to send all of my encouragement and excitement for him through the embrace. "I tried. It didn't work out. I'm done."

"Tell me about the first time you put on a pair of skates." I bend and unlace his right skate, wiggling it off his foot and smiling at the socks he's wearing that are covered in tiny printed pizzas. "How old were you?"

"Four? Five? Might've been younger than that. My dad is a big hockey guy, and the second I was comfortable walking around the house, he was corralling me onto the ice." Riley stops and lifts his chin, staring out at the rink. Maverick, Hudson, and Liam are playing an easy game of keep away, passing the puck with the inside of their skates and chasing it down when it goes too far. "I remember holding his hand and gliding across the frozen pond. My mom was a nervous wreck."

"Was it fun? Scary?"

"I was so terrified. I was afraid I was going to hurt myself if I fell, and the first time I wiped out, my dad picked me up from under my arms. He put me back on two feet. And the world kept moving. Haven't been scared since."

"How long did it take you to become a good skater?"

"Years. I was shitty at first. There's a video of me as a kid at practice and I'm crawling across the ice because I couldn't balance." Riley pauses. "Probably looked similar to today."

"What did you do to improve? To get to where you are now?"

"I practiced every day. I would skate before school. I'd come home and skate until it was dark. I skated until everything hurt and I couldn't lift my legs, then I skated even harder. One day, it all clicked. I can't really describe it. I got on the ice, pushed off, and that was that. Haven't looked back since. Until now."

"It took time. Effort. Energy. Trying and failing over and over again, right?"

"Right." He sniffs and presses the heels of his palms into his eyes. I hear his choked sob. The agony pulled from his chest when he whispers, "I'd give fucking anything to go back to those days. I didn't know how good I had it."

I'd give anything to let him go back to those days too. To patch him up and make the broken boy smile again, because with every heave of his chest, with every muffled cry and the wall he's trying to keep up, I ache more than I did before.

"None of us ever know how good we have it until it's too late. And it fucking sucks," I say gently. "So today wasn't a good day. Big whoop. Do you know what we do now?"

"What?"

"We forge ahead. We pivot and adjust. We find a new plan, and we try again. And if you don't want to try again, that's fine too. When you're ready, I'm going to be here, okay?"

"Why?" Riley turns and looks at me. "Why are you willing to do this for me? What do you get out of it?"

How do I tell him the time I spend with him is the best part of my day?

I look forward to seeing him walk through the athletic trainer's office door. I'm at ease when he pulls me close to his chest in bed after sex, his face buried in my hair and his mouth warm on my neck. I smile when his name pops up on my phone, a text message that has me laughing and turning my screen brightness down so that no one can see I'm giggling over something silly and stupid.

Those tiny pockets of time are slowly becoming my favorite moments, and my head is a jumbled mess because of it. My happiness has never been tied to another person. I haven't given two shits about what the men in my life do, but I'm finding I'm dependent on making him smile. Determined he has a good day every day, and it hurts me to know he's hurting.

"I get *you* out of it. I care about you, Riley," I say. "You're my friend. And friends show up for each other even when the other wants to push them away."

"I might never be good at skating again," he says, dejection lacing the statement.

"You might not be."

"I don't know if I want to try again. I hate failing."

"You don't have to try again."

Riley stares out at the rink. He watches Maverick, Hudson, and Liam, snorting when Maverick slides across the ice on his stomach.

"But if and when you do, I'll be here." I squeeze his knee. "And I can be very patient, Mitchy."

His attention moves to my hand, and he traces over the bump of my knuckles with his thumb. "I'm lucky to have a friend like you, Lexi. We'll try again another day."

His touch is an inferno. Heat races up my arm and crawls to the base of my spine. I swallow, suddenly dizzy. When he pulls away, it's like a bucket of ice is getting dumped over me. I'm cold down to my bones, and alarms ring in my head.

Come back, I want to shout, and when he scoops his skates off the ground and tosses a tentative smile my way, I'm hit with the overwhelming realization that I might've found myself walking down a path I've never been down before.

Friends, I tell myself.

Bullshit, my brain whispers back.

THIRTY-FOUR
LEXI

RILEY

Hey. Coach canceled practice. I guess half the team has norovirus after our away game last weekend.

Ethan is convinced someone from the hotel staff purposely served us contaminated food because the guys are finally racking up some wins.

The photo he sent of himself puking has made me afraid to ever open a text message again.

I feel fine. It's probably the universe giving me a karmic break after losing my leg, you know? Why make me barf for hours on end when it already took my limb?

Do you still want to meet for our session?

Lex?

> **RILEY**
>
> Haven't heard from you in a day, which isn't like you.
>
> If you need anything, I'm free.

> **RILEY**
>
> Okay. Two days. I'm officially worried.
>
> If I don't hear from you by this afternoon, I'm taking a page out of Maverick's playbook and breaking down your apartment door.
>
> C'mon, Lexi baby. Let me know you're okay.

IT HURTS to open my eyes.

I groan and try to sit up in bed, but my head is pounding. My entire body aches, and it feels like the contents of my stomach are sitting somewhere in my throat.

"Fuck." I fumble for my phone and check the time. It's past nine, and if I want to make it to Riley's session and avoid heavy traffic, I need to get my ass out of my apartment right now.

Except... the thought of moving farther than the confines of my bed makes me want to cry.

I cover my mouth and swallow down the taste of vomit. There's no way I can drag myself to the arena, and whatever I'm battling might be contagious. Squinting at my bright phone screen, I wince as I open my text thread with Riley. There are half a dozen blue boxes that make it seem like he's having a conversation with himself, and I type out a shaky message to him.

ME

> Hey. Going to have to reschedule. Sick. Dying. Cannot function.

I don't bother to wait for a response. I click off my phone and toss it somewhere on the mattress, groaning when I pull the covers over my head. My eyes are heavy, and I try to will myself to go back to sleep.

I doze in increments, but it's fitful. One minute, I'm burning up from the inside out. The next, I'm freezing cold. I'm shivering and reaching over the edge of the bed to grab the sweatshirt that's in a ball on the floor, desperate for another layer to burrow into. I exhale when I pull it over my head, the relief instantaneous. The warmth moves from my shoulders down to my toes, and for the first time in hours, my body starts to relax.

Until the remnants of what I last ate rumble in my stomach and end up all over my sheets.

"Shit," I whisper.

My eyes prick with tears. The smell is revolting, the sight of it even worse, and I throw up a second time.

This is a new low in my life. It's worse than all the times I've been hungover from drinking or done the walk of shame after a mediocre night at someone's house, because I'm all alone. There's no one around to help me clean up the mess I've made, and I feel so fucking pathetic.

Mustering all the strength I have—which is teetering toward nonexistent peppered with the delirious sense of exhaustion—I climb out of my bed and look at my mattress. Taking a breath that feels like I'm at mile twenty-two of a marathon, I pull off the sheets. I throw them in a pile in the corner, utterly ashamed.

I'll sleep on the mattress. Or against the wall. I don't care. I'm so tired, so fucking worn out that the knock on my apartment door makes me burst into tears.

It's too far away, and I don't know who could be here. The girls wouldn't stop by without calling, and when a second knock comes, I drag myself through my bedroom and down the hall, ready to scream at the person on the other side.

"I'm not interested," I manage to get out. "Please go away."

"It's me, Lex," a muffled voice responds. "Can you please open the door?"

I stand on my toes and peer through the peephole, confused when I see Riley on the other side. I fumble with the lock and turn the knob, having to lean against the doorframe so I don't topple over.

"What are you doing here?" I whisper.

"I've been texting you for two days."

"Two days? What are you talking about?"

His eyes roam over my sweatshirt and I glance down, blushing when I realize I'm wearing the hoodie he gave me that night on Maverick and Emmy's terrace at team dinner. His gaze tracks downward to my bare legs and the one sock I have on my left foot, the matching one somewhere else in my apartment.

"It's Friday," he says gently, and I shake my head.

"It's Wednesday."

"No, sweetheart." He steps into the foyer and I shuffle back, the term of endearment sparking a swarm of butterflies low in my stomach. "It's Friday."

"But I…" I turn and look out the living room window. Sunlight floods across the hardwood floor, and I frown. "I've been asleep for two days?"

"Apparently. What's going on?"

"I feel like I've been put through a blender." I motion for him to come all the way inside then shut the door, locking it behind him. I'm lightheaded all of a sudden. Weak on my feet, and I'm afraid I'm going to collapse. "I might be contagious. You shouldn't be here."

"I'm here now. And I'm staying." He puts a hand on my forehead. "You're burning up."

"I puked all over my bed." I try to reach for the wall, but Riley is there. Putting my hands on his shoulders and wrapping his arm around my waist. "It might be in my hair. I need to pee. I slept for two days?"

"Norovirus is going around the team, and it sounds like you have the same symptoms. Coach canceled practice, and half the guys have been puking their brains out for days."

"They can join the club. It's horrific. Wouldn't wish it on anyone." I pause and swallow down another taste of vomit. "Except the person who started this outbreak."

"Let's get you feeling better, and that starts with peeing. I'll help you to the bathroom."

"That goes wildly out of the scope of things you need to do for me. In fact, watching me pee will for sure make me unattractive to you, so maybe you should leave. I like your dick."

"I didn't say I was going to let you use my hands to pee in." He laughs. "I'm just helping you get from point A to point B."

"Riley. I'm—"

"Fully capable of handling things by yourself. I know that. But guess what? Accepting help doesn't make you weak, okay? It just means for a few minutes, someone else can help carry the load. And you've been carrying the load for me for months. Share the burden with me just this once."

"Okay," I whisper, because he's right. I'm so *tired* from doing everything on my own, and a helping hand sounds nice for once. "But only if you don't judge me."

"I've been in locker rooms with disgusting men for years. I can guarantee I've seen and heard a lot worse than you engaging in normal bodily functions."

He doesn't give me another chance to argue, instead leading me to the bathroom, helping me sit on the toilet, then waiting outside the door. I finish and shuffle over to the sink to wash my hands, blinking at my reflection in the mirror and hardly recognizing myself.

I look like I belong in a horror movie. My skin is pale. My hair is a knotted mess and there's dried vomit in the corner of my mouth. I sniff, utterly disgusted.

"How are we doing?" Riley asks through the cracked door.

"Better," I rasp out.

"Good." He nudges his way back inside and glances at me. "What's wrong?"

"I look like a troll who lives under a bridge."

"Have you seen a lot of trolls?"

"No." I sniff again, but I also want to laugh. "Never."

"I have, and you're way cuter."

"You think so?"

"Ah, Lexi baby. I know so." Riley points at the vanity to my left. "Where do you keep your hairbrushes? A secret closet with all your other womanly products?"

"I don't have that many products." My hand shakes as I pull open a drawer and grab a brush. "Here."

"Close the lid and sit on the toilet for me. I'm going to brush your hair, get you cleaned up in the shower, switch your sheets, then make you some soup. You're dehydrated, and you need to get some nutrients in your body."

"I can—"

"Do it yourself? I know you can. But here's the thing, Lexi. I'm not going to be able to sleep. I'm not going to be able to eat. I'm not going to be able to do *anything* except wonder if you're okay and taken care of. Put me out of my misery and *let me do it for you.*"

His words are sharp, punctuated. I sit on the toilet, my back to him. It's my acceptance of his offer, a hesitant transfer of power I so rarely relinquish. I can feel his relief through his exhale, and the second the bristles of the brush run through my hair, the tears fall again.

"Do you have a lot of experience brushing a woman's hair?" I ask.

"You're the first. How am I doing?"

"Really well. You're a natural."

Riley is gentle. He doesn't yank on the knots but takes his time, working in sections until he can run his fingers through the dirty strands without causing me any pain. When he finishes, he turns on the shower, his hand under the water until he's satisfied with the temperature.

"I'll give you some privacy," he says, and I scramble to reach for him. Now that he's here, I don't want him out of my sight. "You okay?"

"Can you stay?" I croak. "Please?"

I've never relied on a man before for anything. Every part of me wants to scream at him to leave. The push for separation and creating emotional distance is embedded in my DNA, so why am I so determined to keep him around?

"Of course. I can't get in there with you. My prosthetic isn't waterproof, but I'll be right here, okay?"

"It's not?" I frown, never considering the logistics. "How do you shower?"

"I take baths. I have a shower stool. They make other prosthetics that can get wet, but mine's too high-tech to submerge," Riley explains.

"Ah. That makes sense." I take off the sweatshirt and the T-shirt underneath it. I shimmy out of my underwear and get rid of the single sock. When I'm naked, I look up at him and find him watching me. "What's wrong?"

"You wear my sweatshirt around the house."

"Oh." My toes nudge the discarded hoodie. It still smells like him, the trace of his soap and cologne clinging to the cotton like it doesn't want to leave. "It's comfortable. And it was the first thing I could find to put on so I could warm up."

"Have you worn it before today?"

Almost every night, because the fabric is soft and well-loved through years of wear, and it always feels like he's hugging me when I put it on. But I shrug at his question, too embarrassed to tell the truth.

Here's Lexi Armstrong, the former queen of independence who is turning into a damn sap.

How the hell do I make it stop?

"Once or twice," I say, and I'm certain he can see right through me.

Riley hums but doesn't say anything else. He holds my hand while he helps me into the shower and stays close like he promised. After I'm clean and my skin is almost raw from the hot water, he wraps me in a fluffy towel and deposits me on the living room sofa. He adds a blanket around my shoulders and another over my legs, and the last thing I remember before I fall asleep is his lips pressing a kiss to my forehead and feeling so unbelievably content.

THIRTY-FIVE
RILEY

ME
Can you do me a favor?

HUDDY BOY
What's up?

ME
Can you ask Madeline what ingredients I should put into a soup for someone who's not feeling well?

HUDDY BOY
Oh, shit. Did you get the bug too?

ME
No. It's for Lexi.

HUDDY BOY
Interesting.

ME
Shut up.

HUDDY BOY

> Maddie says chicken noodle is always good. You get nutrients with the chicken and veggies.
>
> Lentil soup has protein.
>
> But apparently clear broth-based soups are best? Something about easy digestion and hydration.

ME

> Thanks, dude.

HUDDY BOY

> Happy to help ;)

I MANAGED to get Lexi to eat a bowl of the soup I threw together, and after forcing her to drink a whole cup of water, color is starting to return to her face. She looks more alive, and when she stretches out on the couch and tosses the remote my way, I finally let myself take a deep breath.

"I might fall asleep," she says around a yawn, her eyes heavy-lidded and her head resting on an uncomfortable-looking decorative pillow. "Fingers crossed I can keep this soup down."

"Apparently symptoms typically run from one to three days. If you can get through the next couple of hours without puking, I think you're going to be in the clear."

"I don't remember the last time I felt this shitty. Probably the time I went to my first frat party in college and had *way* too many tequila shots. I still can't smell the liquor without having a reaction."

"Damn. That's what I was going to give you when you finished your next glass of water."

"Sorry to burst your bubble. You're going to have to stick with vodka."

"Oof," I say. "That's my downfall. Guess we're moving on to bourbon. A good compromise."

Lexi gives me a smile, and I open up my arms. Her smile stretches to a tired grin and she pivots her body, crawling across the cushions until she settles against my chest.

God.

She feels so fucking *right* in my arms. The last piece of a puzzle and a key slotting perfectly into a lock. Fresh air on your face and coming home after a long day. I maneuver her shoulders so I can touch her hair, and I start to braid the long pieces that hang down her back.

"How is your first visit to my apartment?" she asks, letting out a sigh when I massage her scalp. "Sorry it's under the guise of taking care of my sick ass."

We've done all our hooking up at my place or in her hotel room on the road. A dozen times together, and we've figured out a routine. The invitation via text. The make-out session then the quick orgasm I get out of her. The easy way she climbs on top of me and rides me like there's no tomorrow and the quiet moments after when we clean up before going our separate ways.

I didn't want to push her to see her place, afraid it might seem like I was trying to take a step she didn't want to take. I'm desperate for a crumb of her attention, and if that means turning my bedroom into a sex cave, so be it.

"It is my first time. My self-guided tour was short, but I can tell it's nice," I say with a smile.

There are pieces of her personality woven throughout the entire apartment. There's the old photos and sports jerseys in glass frames on the walls. Her collection of romance books and the dish towels hanging from her oven, one that says *fuck the cook* and the other that has *if it involves fake smiling, I'm not going* stitched on it. A stack of blankets on the arm of the couch and way too many throw pillows.

It's bright and bold and so perfectly *her*, and I'm glad she invited me to stay, even if I had to force my way in.

"Are you immune to this awful sickness?" she asks. "It's impressive half the team is ill and you're walking around like it's just another day in the park."

"Pretty sure my bionic leg can stop any virus. I cheated death once, and now I'm invincible." I finish the braid and secure it in place with the hair tie on Lexi's wrist. "And apparently *not* good at doing hair."

Lexi touches the back of her head and laughs. "You missed a chunk over here."

"Don't question it, Armstrong. Some appreciation would be nice."

"I'm sorry." She tilts her chin and looks up at me. She's fighting a smile, but it doesn't stop her eyes from crinkling in the corners or from her nose scrunching, and she's the cutest thing in the whole fucking world. "Thank you *very much* for being my personal stylist. I'm going to wear it like this to our next game. When I get compliments—and I know I will—I'll make sure to let everyone know you're the one who did it."

"Your sarcasm is top-notch." I touch her forehead, relieved to find her cooler than she was when I first got here. "If the athletic trainer gig doesn't work out, you should think about a career in comedy."

"I'd kill at standup."

"Only if you don't talk about my dick."

"Believe it or not, my life doesn't revolve around your penis, Riley."

I laugh and stretch out my leg. My prosthetic has been acting up today. There's a twinge of phantom pain in my residual limb, and doing laundry, changing sheets, and walking five laps around a grocery store I wasn't familiar with to find soup ingredients hasn't helped the ache.

"Mind if I adjust our positions?" I ask, and she frowns.

"You're not comfortable."

"That's not your doing. That's a drunk driver's doing."

"We could go to my bedroom," she suggests, and when I level her with a serious look that tells her *absolutely the fuck not*, she rolls her eyes. "To spread out and get comfortable. Calm down. I wasn't going to jerk you off. The lingering smell of vomit doesn't really do it for me."

"Bummer. That's the only thing that gets me going. This friendship might not work out long-term."

I stand and bend to pick her up. She tries to protest when I scoop her in my arms, but I'm already heading down the hall. I'm kicking open her bedroom door and setting her on the clean sheets I put on the bed a couple of hours ago.

"Wait." Lexi frowns and unravels herself from the horde of blankets she brought with her. "Why does it smell so good in here?"

"I lit a candle." I point to the burned-out jar on her nightstand next to the glass of water I brought in earlier. "I got everything set up in case you wanted to nap."

"You did that for me?"

"Of course I did." I run a hand through my hair, unsure of what happens next now that she's settled. "I can head out. I'm sure you want to get some rest and I—"

"Will you stay and sleep with me?" she whispers. "Just for a few hours?"

That's not something we've done.

Four orgasms in a row? Check. Slipping a blindfold over her eyes then eating her out? Another check.

But sleeping together without any sex involved? That's new, but she's blinking at me with wide eyes, a hopeful expression on her face, and I'm sitting on the edge of the bed before I can think twice.

"Do you mind if I take off my leg?" I ask. "It's heavy and clunky and I can only sleep on my back when I'm wearing it."

"Oh, god. Yes. Please. Take off whatever you want," she hurries to say.

"When I do, I'm not going to be able to get you anything else unless I put it back on. I use my crutches at home to get around at night, and I don't have that capability here. Is that okay?"

"I can get things for myself. And I can get things for you, if you need them."

"Just a pillow to rest my weary head." I yawn, hit with a sudden burst of exhaustion. "All those hours of worrying about you are catching up to me."

She swats me playfully with her hand. "You didn't have to worry about me."

"Yes, I did." I sigh and give her a long look. "We're friends. Friends worry about each other."

I take off my joggers and press the button on my socket, waiting for the air to release. When it's ready, I let go of the button and the leg pops right off my residual limb. Working the gel liner down and off, I reach forward and rest all the pieces against Lexi's dresser.

"Sorry. It's a whole process," I say.

"Don't apologize. I've seen you take it off at our sessions, but it…" She trails off, and I look back at her. She's watching me like she's taking mental notes, and I wonder what she's thinking. "It feels different when you're doing it in my room."

She's right. It feels intimate, heavy. Something she would see if we got ready for bed together and fell asleep next to each other every night, and *fuck* do I wish that could be a reality.

"It's not nice to stare, Lex," I tease, and she smooths her hand over the sheets next to her.

"I see you and touch you on the treatment table, but I've never gotten to have you like this." Lexi swallows, a bob of her throat that has me moving closer so we're side by side. "Can I touch you?"

"Please," I murmur, eyes closing when she traces the scars on the right side of my body. "I know it's ugly and—"

"You're beautiful."

She guides me onto the pillows. The rest of the blankets she's been using fall from her shoulders. She kisses my cheek then my neck, mouth moving down the front of my shirt and over my briefs. When she gets to the top of my right leg, just at the apex where my body starts to change from Before to After, she kisses there too. A breath rattles out of me and I start to pant as her hands work over my flappy skin where I had a hundred stitches.

Lexi massages my residual limb, and the pain I've been holding on to seeps away with every press and push of her touch along the shape of my new body. I groan, not because I'm turned on, but because even *I* haven't explored myself this personally. It's different from the donning and doffing I do when I prep the limb, more thorough with her gentle grazes and the heat of her mouth right on the spot where I lost the leg.

"Thank you for letting me have you like this," she whispers, and I can't imagine anyone else having me like this.

Would there be the same care and consideration? The same grace she's showing me when she fixes my briefs and draws what feels like a heart on my upper thigh?

I doubt it.

"You can have me however you want," I whisper back to her.

Take my whole fucking heart while you're at it.

With a final press of her lips, Lexi climbs back up my body. She takes my hands in hers and sighs.

"Thank you for all your help today, Riley. For not only taking care of me, but also making me feel like I could do it by myself if I wanted to."

"Of course you could." I cup her face, thumb stroking her cheek. "But thank you for letting me in."

"This sleeping we're about to do is an addendum to our agreement." She yawns and lies next to me. I'm quick to mirror her pose and wrap her in my arms. "A one-time thing."

"I've heard that before."

"I'm serious. It's a nap. That's it."

"Mhm. Just leave a fucking toothbrush at my place next time, Lex."

"We'll see," she says, and knowing it's not a flat-out no makes it impossible for me to fall asleep.

THIRTY-SIX
LEXI

RILEY
Are you doing anything tonight?

ME
Hoping you'll come over and rail me.

RILEY
You're so charming.

ME
That's why you keep coming back for more.

RILEY
I guess it is.

RILEY
California was fun.

ME
It was, wasn't it?

HAT TRICK

> Having to keep quiet because Grant was on the other side of the wall was something new, but I liked it.

RILEY
You did so well, Lexi.

ME
Thank you :)
Same time next week in Dallas?

RILEY
I'll wear my cowboy hat.

ME
Who needs a horse when I can ride you?

ME
Hi. How was your day after you left our session? You seemed a little quiet.

RILEY
Not the best, but it's almost over now.

ME
Anything I can do to help?

RILEY
No. I want to be alone tonight.

ME
You know where I'll be if that changes.

RILEY
Thanks for the space the other day.

I appreciate it.

ME
How are you feeling tonight?

RILEY
Like I want to rail you.

ME
Ew. Yeah. I see what you mean. Let's never use that again.

RILEY
Thank god.

ME
Come over? I made pasta, and I have an extra plate.

RILEY
Calling a rideshare right this second.

ME
See you soon, Mitchy.

I OPEN the door before Riley has a chance to knock. His hand hovers in midair, and I smile when he looks from his fist to me.

"Expecting someone?" he asks, and I tug on his shirt to drag him into my foyer.

"You, you idiot," I murmur, kissing him and wrapping my arms around his neck.

I saw him a few days ago, but a jolt of electricity still rips through me when he palms my ass with his large hand and shuffles me backward until my shoulder blades press against the wall. I hiss and drop my head back, eyes fluttering closed when he curls his fingers around my wrists and lifts them above my head.

"Did you miss me?" Riley dips his chin and kisses my neck, his laughter warm when I squirm under his touch. "You did, didn't you? Tell me how much, Lexi baby."

"Yes. Fuck dinner," I breathe out, lifting my hips and draping a leg around his waist. His hand slides up my thigh, fingers dancing under my skirt and snapping my underwear against my skin. "A whole fucking lot." Two months ago, I would've been afraid to admit it. It's too earnest, too *messy*, but now I know how it drives him wild, how much he likes hearing it. So I smile and wiggle a hand free, pulling on the ends of his hair so his eyes are forced to meet mine. "Want me to show you?"

"I do. And we're going to play while you do it."

"Play? You know I love games."

"Good." Riley plants a kiss on my forehead and sets my leg down. He taps the bag I'm realizing is slung over his shoulder, and when I lift my eyebrow, he puts a hand over my mouth before I can protest. "It's pajamas and a toothbrush, not a mortgage agreement. Ropes, too. I'm going to bind your wrists together, you're going to suck my dick, then I'm going to get you off."

I smile and hold out my hands, adrenaline coursing through me when he drops the bag on the floor and pulls out the set of ropes he used on me before. He's quick to tie my wrists together, this time behind my body instead of in front, and I relax when he gives the ropes a yank to make sure they're tight.

"Do you want to do this here?" I ask, the outline of his cock thick and hard against his jeans as he changes our positions so he's against the wall. "Or do you need the ambience of my bedroom?"

"I need you to stop talking." He pops open the button on his pants and runs his fingers through my hair. With a gentle push on my shoulders, he guides me to my knees and hooks his fingers under my chin. "Take out my cock, Lexi, and get to work."

Oh.

I've seen so many sides of Riley; the calm and patient side when I was sick and he waited for me to scrub my body clean while he talked to me about the game they had just won. The frustrated side when the exercises I give him are difficult and hard to achieve. The happy side when he does something right, pride nearly bursting out of him with the hook of a grin.

But this side?

This side is *dangerous*.

It makes me want to ask him to try some of my other fantasies, knowing full well he'd indulge me because he's weak when it comes to me, and every time we're together, I myself become weaker.

The authority in his voice is welcomed, *wanted*. When I glance up at him, the discomfort from the ropes settles to pleasure, and his eyes are wide.

"How do you expect me to do that when my hands are like this?" I hold up my wrists, and I swear he gets even harder as the movement bows my back. "Have any suggestions?"

"You're a smart girl. Figure it out."

He's not treating me like I'm some breakable, precious thing, and fire stirs low in my belly. I'm always doing the right things at work. I keep meticulous notes about the players' health and am the utmost professional in the meetings I attend, but right now? I exist only for his pleasure, and fuck if that's not the hottest thing in the world.

I stare at his jeans, an idea forming when I sit up on my

knees and lean forward. I tilt my head and grab the zipper with my teeth, dragging it down to the tune of Riley's rough exhale. His hand is back on my head, not forcing me but encouraging me, and it spurs me on.

"That's it," he murmurs. "Such a good problem solver, Lexi."

My entire body flushes with the compliment, and it makes me want to be even better. To do more good things, and I move my mouth to the left side of his jeans, using my teeth to try to yank his jeans down to his ankles.

It's awkward and uncoordinated. The denim is stiff and difficult to move. I have to scoot back with my ass almost in the air to make any progress, but when I finish and find his black briefs tight against his thighs, I grin.

"Look how well you did." Riley grabs my chin and forces me to glance up at him. "I'm proud of you."

I squirm at the praise, testing the limits of the knots wrapped around my wrists. My nipples pebble when I feel he's made the rope tighter than our first time, and I like that I'm at his mercy.

"Thank you," I say, and his smile matches mine.

"You're blushing. You never blush. What's going through your head, sweetheart?"

That *word*. The affection makes me turn another shade of pink, and I bite my bottom lip.

"I like when you say things like that. Men think chanting *good girl* over and over gets the job done, but I-I like to hear different varieties. I know I'm good. I want to know *how* I'm good."

"I like telling you how you're being good." He strokes along my cheek, and then he presses three fingers down on my tongue. He pushes them deeper in my mouth and I gag. Tears flood my eyes, but he doesn't pull back. "Relax. There you go," he murmurs when I hollow out my cheeks. "Do you think you're ready for my cock?"

I nod, more than ready. Blowjobs aren't my favorite thing in the world—I hate being on my knees for a man and not getting anything in return—but with Riley, I *crave* them. My mouth opens wider in anticipation and he smirks in understanding, his fingers leaving a trail of drool on my face when he puts his hand on his hip.

"You did so well before, I'm going to do this part for you," he says, tugging on the waistband of his briefs. They fall to his ankles with his jeans, leaving him naked from the waist down. "How do your wrists feel?"

"Perfect," I whisper, and he nods.

"Good. Now get me off, Lexi."

I've always been good at following directions, so I open my mouth and suck his cock halfway down my throat like my life fucking depends on it. Riley groans, his hand yanking on my hair and wrapping the strands around his wrist. The other reaches down and wraps around my neck, and I'd like to walk around with his palm there every day, a pretty necklace to show off I'm having the best sex of my life.

"*Fuck*. You're too fucking good at this."

I drag my tongue up his length, swirling over the head of his cock and licking up the pre-cum I find there. Instead of taking him back in my mouth, I move to the root of his shaft, then to his balls. He hisses when I lick them and jerks his hips, the hand around my neck tightening.

"Do you like that, Riley?" I ask, and he practically buries my face in his sac. I grin, another swipe of my tongue, and his moan comes out rattled and hoarse.

I go back to his cock and angle my head until I can take him all the way to the back of my throat. When my nose presses against his stomach, he holds me there, fucking my mouth the way he fucks me in his bed: rough, unrelenting. I let him, and my cheeks hollow out as the noise of his snapping hips fills my foyer.

"Going to come," he grits out, and I work even harder, determined to get him there faster.

Tears stream down my cheeks. My arms start to throb, but *god*, it's all amazing. He's barely touching me and I'm turned on, wet and ready for him to finish so he can take care of *me*. I squeeze my thighs together, the sound of him falling apart with every bob of my head erotic, *hot*, and downright filthy.

"Lexi," he whispers, and it's the last warning I get before his release.

He's salty and warm in my mouth. I stay in place, tongue lapping at him as his movements slow and his heavy breathing starts to subside. I'm greedy, desperate to taste him, to not waste a single drop, and before I can swallow down his cum, his hand is back on my throat.

"Not today," he says, eyes on me and pupils blown wide. His glasses are crooked. There's sweat on his forehead. He's so fucking pretty, even when he's thoroughly wrecked. "Open up. I want to see what you did to me."

I'm even wetter with his ask. I pop him out of my mouth and part my lips. My jaw unhinges, and when I stick out my tongue, I swear his growl could move mountains.

"So fucking pretty. So fucking *mine*." He squeezes my cheeks, and it wouldn't take much for me to finish right now. My senses are heightened, my body is aching for him. My eyes almost bug out of my head when he swipes his finger across my tongue then pops the digit in his mouth, a remarkable grin splitting across his face. "You can swallow now, Lexi baby. But if you lose any of it, you're going to be in trouble."

That makes me want to fuck around and find out, because what the hell kind of trouble could I be in? I imagine a handprint on my ass. Watching him press into my throat until my vision goes blurry, and despite my resolve to learn how much I can push Riley Mitchell to the brink of losing his self-control, I swallow down every bit of his cum and show him my empty mouth.

He slumps against the wall but holds out his arms, reaching for me. I stand on shaky legs and move toward him, melting when he kisses my forehead and the tip of my nose, the rope around my wrists releasing with a *thump* to the floor.

"You were wonderful," he whispers, kissing my wrists and rubbing his thumbs along my veins. "You did everything perfectly, and I loved watching you."

"Thank you." I bury my face in his shirt and smile. "I tried really hard."

"I know you did, and I'm so proud of you for taking everything I gave you." His fingers brush through my hair. "Are your hands doing okay?"

"More than okay." I kiss his cheek and step back. "Bedroom. Now."

"Yeah. *Yes.*" He shoves his glasses up his nose and puts his briefs and jeans back on. "Please."

"I'll be there in a minute. You go ahead."

"You sure?"

"I'm going to grab some water." I pat his chest and gesture to the kitchen. "Do you want anything?"

"Just to be inside you. Hurry up, please."

I toss him a grin and make my way to the kitchen. I hear him walk down the hall, and when I know he's safely out of sight, I start taking off my clothes to show off the lingerie I bought the other day.

I have dozens of lace outfits in every type of style you can imagine folded in my dresser, but I wanted something new for Riley. Something I haven't worn for someone else, something I haven't worn for him, and when I look down at the red set, confidence rolls through me.

In only a lacy thong and a bra that doesn't try to hide my nipples, I strut toward my bedroom, horny and ready to be satisfied.

I nudge the door open with my hip, and Riley glances up from where he's sitting on the edge of the bed. His eyes widen when he sees me, and he brings a shaky fist to his mouth so he can bite down on his knuckles.

"Holy shit," he whispers. "Holy fucking shit."

"What do you think?" I spin in a slow circle and rest my hands on my ass cheeks, letting him see how well the lace accentuates the curves I work damn hard for. "Do you like what you see?"

"You're so fucking gorgeous." I face him and slowly tease my hands up my body. I push my breasts together and he whimpers, agony in his eyes when I shake my head. "What? I can't touch you?"

"Have you been good, Riley? Do you think you deserve to touch me?"

"I've been very good," he rasps. "But I can be better. How can I be better?"

I remember the conversation we had in his bedroom when I found his ropes. He mentioned he liked being told what to do from time to time, and I wonder how far he'd go to get what he wants.

"Crawl," I say, and he gets on the floor without a second thought.

A wince flashes across his mouth, but before I can stop him and tell him to ignore what I just said because it might be painful, he's moving toward me on his hands and knees, a determined gleam in his eye I've never seen from him before.

When he's right in front of me, he stays there, looking up and waiting for my next ask. I smile, smug and bold, and lift his chin with the curve of my finger.

"That's a very good boy, Riley."

He blushes a furious shade of red. He opens his mouth to try to stammer out a response, but nothing comes except another whimper, louder, more desperate, and it's fuel to the fire.

"You're going to watch," I tell him. "When I'm close, I want you to eat me out. Can you do that?"

"It would be an honor." He sits up and runs his thumb along my calf, lifting my ankle so my foot rests on his shoulder. "I've always wanted a front seat at the show."

I pull my underwear to the side, not surprised to find myself wet. I've been turned on from the second he got here, worked up from our very first kiss, and I'm not in the mood to draw this out. I want to get off, and I want to get off *now*.

Not wasting any time, I push two fingers inside my pussy and groan at the stretch. Riley inches closer, his exhale hot on my skin, and I balance by resting a palm on top of his head. He doesn't move. He doesn't speak, but his breathing is heavy. With every curl of my fingers and every touch to my clit, his whines get more frequent, and I might need to put him out of his misery early.

"You're so sweet. So perfect. *God.* Look at you," he says. "I love that you can take care of yourself. I love that you want to use me just so you can come. You have to know I'm willing, Lexi. You can have whatever you want from me."

My hand shakes with every one of his words, and I close my eyes. I bring myself to the edge of pleasure, imagining what it's going to feel like when he fucks me in the perfect way he does, and I tighten around my fingers at the thought.

"Riley." I reach for the back of his head and his mouth is on me in a second. He licks me, tongue on my clit and hand bumping against mine so he can replace my fingers with his. "*Please.*"

"Hearing you beg is one of my favorite things in the world," he says, voice muffled from between my thighs. "You're so wet. You love to touch yourself while I watch, don't you? You love teasing me with what I can't have."

"You can have whatever the fuck you want," I pant, keeping my underwear to the side so he can continue to eat me out. "Just make me come. Please," I say again, and his laugh is wicked.

"So desperate for me. I can't wait to hear you say my name when you come, Lexi. I could always use the ego boost."

I writhe against his fingers and mouth, my orgasm within reach. When he gives my clit a light slap, my hips rock forward. I see stars behind my eyes and I cry out, nirvana gathering deep in my belly.

I wait for it with bated breath, but when it doesn't manifest, when the feeling disappears, I jerk my chin down and glare at him.

"What the hell?" I ask, frustrated. "I was almost there."

"I didn't hear my name," Riley says, lips wet and cheeks stamped with my arousal. I have no clue where his glasses are, and his hair is sticking up by his ear. "No name. No orgasm."

"Come on. I've already said your name."

"Yeah, but I want you to scream it this time."

"You're so bossy."

"I can be when it comes to you." He kisses the top of my thigh. "Because I think you like it."

I do like it, and it's why I huff. It's why I tip my head back and sink into the bliss he brings me. When I'm close again, I moan. I claw at his shoulders, and his name comes out as a rushed breath.

"*Riley*. That's so—"

"Am I the best you've ever had?" His tongue flicks against my clit and he pushes four thick fingers in me. "Tell me, Lexi."

"*Yes*," I almost shout, and I can tell he's smiling. "Of course you are."

"I'm so glad. Say my name again, please. It might get me off again."

"*God*," I say, not caring how much power I give him. Fuck my feminism, because he's making me ride his hand. He's making me forget my own name and only remember his. "*Riley*. I'm going to—"

"I can't wait to see," he says, and that's all it takes for me to careen to mind-blowing ecstasy.

321

It's a full-body experience, and I don't know how I stay upright. I don't know how my legs don't give out, the intensity making me grip his biceps so I don't topple over. I moan while Riley works me through it, coaxing a second, shorter orgasm out of me before he kisses my hip and licks my tattoo. Before he gently puts my foot on the floor and stands, an arm around my waist as he hauls me to the bed.

"I think I'm dreaming." I sigh when he sets me on the mattress then takes off his shirt. "Life is so good."

"Any faking?" he asks, and I laugh.

"With you? Never."

"That's what I thought." His eyes roam down my body. "Can I fuck you, Lexi?"

"You know the answer to that," I whisper, and his smile is so goddamn beautiful it hurts.

"I want you to say it."

"Yes." I lick my lips, a fresh wave of heat inundating my body. "Yes, you can fuck me."

THIRTY-SEVEN
RILEY

EVERY TIME I'm with Lexi, it's like a fever dream. Something I know is happening but can't believe, because how am I the bastard lucky enough to see her with her dark hair scattered across her pillows and her hands lifting above her head? How am I the one she asks to come over and take care of her because no one else makes her feel as good as I do?

I like her.

I like her so fucking much.

I like her even more when she reaches for me and I intertwine our fingers, giving her palm a squeeze.

What would it be like if we did this forever?

If I woke up next to her every morning and fell asleep beside her every night?

That would be a thing of dreams and miracles and everything I've ever wanted because it's *her*. The woman I haven't been able to get out of my head from the moment I first saw her. The day she was wearing dark jeans and a bright blue Stars polo, her hair up in a ponytail and a wide smile on her face.

"Are you okay?" she asks, and I hear the worry behind the question.

"Better than okay."

I squeeze her hand one more time and sit on the edge of the bed. I take off my shoes and my clothes until I'm left naked. She's still in her pretty lace set, and I wonder if she has one in every color. A different style for every day of the week. I'd like her to model them all for me, to try them on so I can get my fill of the ways the fabric shows off her curves and how good her tits look when they're pressed together.

I stretch out on her mattress next to her, my head on the pillows and a hand around my cock. That blowjob she gave me was earth-shattering and took almost everything out of me, but I got hard again the minute she told me to crawl to her. And watching her touch herself in the ways she likes? Saying my name like I was the key to her salvation? I almost came in my pants.

"Can I get on top?" Lexi strokes my arm, her hand folding around mine and helping me jerk off. "I don't normally like that position, but with you..." She trails off with a laugh. "Everything is better with you."

"Yeah." I nod, the grip on my shaft slackening when she shifts to her right and puts a leg on either side of my hips. I hold onto her waist, fingers pressing into her fair skin, and she sighs when my thumbs tangle in the waistband of her underwear. "With you too."

She hovers above me, a hand on my chest. She uses her other hand to hold my cock and drags the head through the lace of her underwear, across her entrance. I groan when she teases me by sinking down on my length and pulling herself back up before I can thrust into her. It's maddening, *electric*, and in a sudden burst of strength I didn't know I had these days, I flip her off of me so I'm the one on top and she's on her back.

Lexi gasps and I grin, fisting my shaft and dragging it against the rough material of her underwear again.

"Fucking tease," I murmur, and she wraps her legs around my middle.

"What are you going to do about it?" she challenges.

"You know exactly what I'm going to do about it." I lift my chin. "The ropes are too far away, so I want you to hold on to the headboard."

"Anything else you want me to do?"

"Yeah." I yank her underwear to the side and touch her clit, smirking when she lifts her hips and moans. "Take every inch of my cock and say thank you when I make you come."

"Condom?" Lexi asks, the second syllable cracking when I rub my thumb in a slow circle.

We've talked about not using one, and I know she's comfortable with it, but up to this point, I've worn protection every time. I'm not sleeping with anyone else, and I know she's not either. I've been afraid to remove that barrier out of fear she'll think this is turning into something other than sex and bolt.

I've dreamed about fucking her raw, though. I think about it every time I'm inside her and all the places I'd finish and mark her; across her chest where I'd write my name and add my old hockey number, just because I can. In her pussy so I can see how pretty she is when she's full of my cum. Along the curve of her ass so I can press my thumb into the tight hole she's only teased me with.

Fuck.

I'd put it on my own forehead, spelling out *Lexi Armstrong is going to be the death of me* so the entire world knows who is making me a useless, idiotic mess of a man.

"What do you want?" I ask, deferring to her.

"I-I..." She sinks her teeth into her bottom lip, deep in thought. "I want you to fuck me without one."

Hell.

Forget using my cum.

I want those eight words tattooed across my chest.

Branded on my skin, right above my heart, so I can remember my time of death.

"Okay." I nod. My head is swimming. "We're going to do a little rearranging."

"What can I do?"

"Can you put a pillow under your hips? I'm going to, ah, keep my right foot on the bed and my leg bent so it doesn't start to hurt. I don't want... I'm afraid the lip of the socket is going to rub against your thighs, so if it does, will you—"

"I'm going to be fine." Lexi puts a pillow under her ass, cups my face with her hands, and I relax. "And if it doesn't work, we'll go back to what we know does work. I have no complaints about anything we've done so far, Riley. Five stars. A ten out of ten Yelp rating for your dick. I want to feel you, and I don't care if that happens when you're on top or I am."

"Okay," I say again. "I want you to keep your underwear on. You look so pretty in them, and I like knowing I'm going to make a mess of you."

"Riley Mitchell." Her hands fall from my cheeks and to her underwear, pulling it to the side and giving me access to what I've been dreaming about since I walked through her front door. Wet, pink. So fucking mine. "You are so far from the sweet boy I thought you were."

"Five stars, remember? And don't pretend like you want sweet." I bend my knee and scoot closer to her. I drag the head of my cock against her entrance and she whines. I push inside, the feel of her without a barrier between us goddamn exquisite. "You want everything but sweet."

"I want *you*," she says, her whine turning into a moan when I sink the first half of my shaft inside her. "You, Riley."

That unlocks some possessive, jealous part of my brain I've never tapped into before, and I dive headfirst into the feeling. I don't wait for her to get used to the stretch before I pull out of her and thrust deep into her pussy, not stopping until I'm buried to the hilt.

It's probably a good thing we've used a condom up to this point. Otherwise, I would've proposed to her. Asked to take her last name and found a way to keep her in bed with me every hour of every day just so I could fuck her until my body gave out. The sensation is better than anything I've ever experienced.

There's a roar in my head when she drops her hand from the headboard so her nails can scratch my ass, urging me to fuck her deeper, *harder*, and I yield all my power to her. I'm unrelenting, every snap of my hips more aggressive than the last, and I wait for her to tell me it's too much. I wait for her to tell me to stop, that she needs a break, but she doesn't. Lexi squirms on the sheets, her chest heaving and eyes wide, gaze locked on me as she swallows down a gulp of air.

"What do you say?" I ask, and the right side of her mouth hitches up in a bold and beautiful smile.

"Thank you." She moves the hand not holding her underwear from my ass to her breast, pinching her nipple then rolling it between her thumb and finger. "Thank you, Riley, for making me feel so fucking good."

"You're mine," I say, and her face softens. There's a flash of fear behind her eyes before she blinks it away and arches her back off the bed. "My friend. My favorite person. *Mine*," I repeat.

"I've never been anyone's," she whispers, clenching around my cock. She closes her eyes and blows out an exhale. "But I think I am yours."

We don't say anything else, instead sinking into the rhythm of each other as we climb toward the edge of relief. I hold back, wanting her to go first, and she does when I touch her clit again. I talk her through it, telling her how strong she is. How well she's doing and how beautiful she is when she takes my cock. She whispers *thank you* over and over again until pleasure races up my spine. Until she cups my balls in her hand

and rubs her thumb over the shape of them, and I can't take it anymore.

I lose it too, my right leg almost giving out when I slam into her a final time and follow her over. I pulse inside her, my heart racing and a bead of sweat rolling down my cheek until I'm empty and delirious when it comes to anything but her pussy and how I never want to pull out of her.

"Fuck," Lexi says. She lets go of her underwear, the lace rubbing against my sensitive skin and making me jerk my hips again. "How was that ten times better than with a condom?"

"I don't know." I wipe my forehead with the back of my arm. "I could feel you the whole time though."

"And how did it feel?"

"Heaven on fucking earth," I say. She laughs, then winces when I pull out of her and leave a trail of cum on the inside of her thigh. I swipe my thumb through the sticky mess and bring it to her chest. I yank down the cups of her bra and circle her nipples until they're covered in my release too. "God. You're a vision."

"How do I look?"

"Perfect. Beautiful."

"We're never using a condom again."

"Never."

Her beam is a punch to the gut. "Come here, Mitchy."

I grimace as I move toward her, my right thigh throbbing from bending in a way it hasn't before. "I think we need to start covering sex positions in our sessions so I can strengthen the muscles I use when I fuck you."

"I'm sure Coach would love to come in and hear what we're doing when he asks what we've worked on for that day. I don't think that was included in our agreement."

"Coach can fuck off. He'd be a lot less uptight if he got laid." I settle next to her and she rests her head on my chest. "I can also add a treatment table to my place so we can work on things there."

"I'll do some research. We'll get you in tiptop shape, and your next friend with benefits won't know what hit them."

I frown as I wrap an arm around her shoulder. I can't imagine someone else being in Lexi's place. I don't *want* to imagine someone else in Lexi's place. I know we said no feelings and no emotions, but the things I feel for her stretch far outside the bedroom. They teeter toward *I think I might be falling in love with you* and *if you gave me your heart, I'd promise to protect it for as long as you wanted.*

At what point do I tell her what I'm thinking? Do I keep my mouth closed for the rest of eternity and suffer in silence? Do I risk mentioning it and pushing her away? I told myself I wanted her any way I could have her, and that's still true, but it feels like I'm lying to her the longer we keep this physical thing going between us, and that's the last thing I want to do.

"Cool," I say. "Sounds good to me."

"Maybe you'll meet a woman who's also an amputee. She'd understand what you've gone through."

"Maybe."

Lexi pulls away from me and frowns. "Are you okay?"

"I'm great. Just tired. Your pussy is something else, Lex."

"Right back at you. Well, not… you know what I mean," she says with a grin. "You had a bag earlier. Does that mean you're sleeping over?"

"Is it okay if I sleep over?"

"Yeah." She rolls her lips together, looking deep in thought. "That would be okay. I slept so well the night you stayed over when I was sick. It's like my body knows it's safe around you."

"You are safe around me." I play with the ends of her hair, and her frown turns up into a smile. "I brought clothes for our session tomorrow too, so I'll catch an Uber from here to the arena."

"Why would you do that? I'll drive you."

"You don't have to. I know you want to keep this just between us, and if we show up together, the guys might—"

"Think we're friends? So what? We are friends." She sits up straight and leans against the headboard. "I know we're sleeping together, but I also like… I like spending time with you, Riley, when we're not sleeping together."

"Yeah?" I sit up and mirror her pose. I can tell this is a lot to admit to me, that it goes against everything Lexi usually stands for, and I don't want her to think I'm not appreciative. "So do I."

"And maybe we can…" Lexi folds her hands over each other, and I swear I see a blush on her cheeks. "Do other things that aren't in the bedroom or a treatment table?"

I can't fight back my grin. I want to jump up and down and pump my fist in the air because that's promising. *Things outside the bedroom* is something I can work with, and holy hell does my heart gallop at the thought of hanging out with her wherever I want.

"Are you asking me on a date, Armstrong?" I tease, and she hits me in the face with a pillow. "Here I was thinking no one was ever going to want to date me again."

"*No.* It's not a date. It would just be… not in the bedroom," she says. "And plenty of people are going to want to date you. You're a catch, Mitchy."

"Ah. I love not bedrooms."

"I'm ignoring you." She tries to climb off the bed, but I grab her around her waist and pull her back to me. She squeals and tries to shove me off of her, but I don't budge. "Let me go!"

"Never, you stubborn woman," I murmur in her ear, dropping a kiss to her neck. "Where are we hanging out first?"

"I have a plan, but it's a surprise. You'll have to wait until our away game in New York to find out."

"Please don't tell me it's a tour of the hot dog carts in

Manhattan. I promised Ethan if I ever had the chance to do that, I'd do it with him."

"It's not hot dog carts." She laughs and relaxes into me, her back flush against my chest. "It's something else. Better than hot dogs."

"That's a bold statement."

"Most of the things I say are bold statements."

"You're going to make me wait a week and a half to find out? You're cruel."

"You like it," Lexi says.

"Maybe I do," I answer, and some flutter of hope I've never had before springs to life in my chest at the possibilities.

THIRTY-EIGHT
LEXI

GIRLS JUST WANT TO HAVE FUN(DAMENTAL RIGHTS) AND GOOD SEX

PIPER
New York, baby! And for multiple nights because we're doing a back-to-back with both NYC teams.

MADELINE
I think I need a job with the Stars. You all go to these amazing cities all the time, and I'm watching the rain in DC.

ME
Our equipment manager is retiring at the end of the season. Do you have any NHL experience?

MADELINE
I couldn't even tell you what equipment hockey players wear, Lex.

A jersey? And... socks?

HAT TRICK

EMMY

Close enough if you ask me.

MAVEN

Where are you today, Em?

EMMY

Right across the river in New Jersey. We're leaving for Denver later this afternoon, though. I'm grabbing dinner with Amelia Green who's the associate coach for the Goldminers.

ME

She's my ultimate girl crush.

PIPER

SAME. Her ability to ignore the commentary about her being a woman coaching men is astonishing. And her clothes? I'm so jealous. I want to raid her closet.

MAVEN

She gave me a tampon in the bathroom last season, and I think I fell in love with her.

EMMY

You know I love you all very much, but if we were going to add anyone to the group, I'd love for it to be her. She's an icon.

ME

Tell her she has a fan club in DC if she ever makes her way out east!

PIPER

Want to get dinner tonight, Lex and Mae?

ME

Sure. I can make reservations somewhere.

MAVEN

Sorry! No dinner for me. Dallas is also playing in New York this weekend, so we're doing a kid-free night of dinner and a Broadway show. You two have fun!

ME

Looks like we're going on a date, Piper.

PIPER

Can't wait!

RILEY

I'm excited for this surprise. When do I get it?

ME

Tomorrow after practice. I'm stealing you for the rest of the afternoon, Mitchy.

RILEY

Sounds promising. Are you still not telling me where we're going?

ME

Nope. You can be patient, right?

RILEY

Do I get something if I am?

ME

The rest of the day with me. And the night, if you want it.

RILEY

I definitely want.

ME

> Good answer. See you later ;)

"OKAY. This place is way too nice for the jeans I'm wearing." Piper opens her menu and scans the wine list. "I didn't think we'd be going to an upscale restaurant when I packed yesterday. There is a hole in the denim right above my knee."

"I don't think we're the most underdressed people here. Those tourists are wearing Statue of Liberty crowns on their heads."

Piper giggles. "Okay, fine. We don't look *that* out of place."

"Evening, ladies." Our server stops at our table and smiles at us. He's young, probably in his late twenties with tan skin and dark eyes. "Can I get you all started with something to drink?"

"I'll have your sauvignon blanc please," Piper says.

"Gin and tonic for me," I add, and the server nods.

"I'll be right back," he says, flashing me another smile.

"Okay." Piper puts her menu down and kicks my shin under the table. "He is *cute*. And flirting with you."

"What are you talking about?" I laugh and roll my eyes. "He asked if we wanted something to drink. That's his *job*, Piper."

"The extra smile he tacked on at the end probably isn't included in his job description."

"Maybe not. But who doesn't love some extra hospitality?"

"Are you going to give him your number?" she asks.

"Why would I give him my number? I'm here with you, and he's clearly busy with work."

"Wait a second." She drops her chin in her palm and narrows her eyes. "You're hiding something."

"I'm not hiding anything!" I exclaim.

"You so are and—" Piper gasps and moves my hair away from my neck. "Is that a hickey?"

"You are so nosy." I touch the mark Riley left on my skin two nights ago when he came over to watch a movie. We lasted thirty minutes on opposite ends of the couch before I was in his lap and his mouth was on my throat. A rough growl rumbled out of him when I said if he wasn't careful, he was going to make me bruise, and he sucked on my skin even harder. "It's not a hickey."

"It is so a hickey. Who are you sleeping with?"

"A guy I've seen a few times." I shrug, the lie easily rolling off me. "It's not serious."

"Not serious? Lexi Armstrong *never* goes back for seconds. He must be pretty special."

"Okay, look. I've gone back for seconds once or twice. I just don't like to. Why drive the same car when you can keep test driving better models until you find the one you like best?"

"Doesn't seem like you're test driving this one." She smiles. "How'd you meet him?"

"You know." I wave my hand and scan the restaurant, hoping the server is on his way back with our drinks. I could use some alcohol right about now. "Around."

I can't pinpoint why I'm hesitant to give Piper details. I know everything about my friends' dating histories and who they've been with, and no part of me thinks they would judge me for sharing it's *Riley* I'm sleeping with.

Deep down, I think I'm afraid. Nervous that if people find out about us, they'll put a label on something I don't want to define. They'll start asking questions, and it'll ruin the fun we're having. It'll put pressure on me, on *him* to make it something it's not, and the last thing I want is for someone to try to explain why there's an ache in my chest when he leaves my apartment in the morning and why I check my phone to see if I have a new message from him waiting for me.

That's all too deep, too personal, and I've never been that girl.

"Around," she repeats, then gasps again. "Oh my *god*. You like this guy."

"I like his dick," I clarify, blushing when the server returns and clears his throat.

"Sorry to interrupt," he says, setting the drinks on the table. "Are you ready to order?"

"I think we need some more time," I say, and he nods.

"Sure. I'll be back in a few."

When we're alone, Piper studies me. Her attention makes me itchy, and I hold my menu in front of my face so she can't scrutinize me.

"Lex," she says softly, and I peer at her over the top of the pasta offerings. "What's going on?"

"Nothing. I'm sleeping with someone I've slept with before. We enjoy spending time together, but it's never going to be something other than a physical relationship, and I'm okay with that."

"So, you do like him."

How could I *not* like him?

My mind races to Riley and the handful of times he's slept over at my place lately, an arm behind his head and a book open on his lap. In the early mornings before the sun rises and his hands slipping under my sleep shirt. Late at night when I'm curled around him and telling him about my day, his eyes half closed and on the edge of sleep but still fully engaged in my stories.

He's perfect. The antithesis of everything I ever thought a man could be, and for as much as I *do* like him, for as much as I want to spend my free time with him, I also hate him a little bit for making me so reliant on him.

"He's fine," I say.

"It's okay to have feelings for someone, Lex."

"Is it? Because usually when you're attracted to someone, bad things start to happen."

"Hey." Piper plucks the menu out of my grasp and sets it aside. She takes my hand in hers and squeezes my palm. "You're talking to the woman who got divorced before she reached thirty. I know firsthand what happens when you start to fall for someone, and it's absolutely terrifying. It's even more terrifying when you do it a second time after a disastrous first attempt."

"Fall for someone?" I laugh. "It's not like that. I'll admit I like him and I like spending time with him. I'll admit he's great and wonderful and everything a man should be. But I'm not *falling* for him. I'm not that girl. I never will be."

"What if the right guy makes you that girl?"

"I'm not changing for a man. Besides, he wouldn't want me to change. He likes me exactly how I am."

"Are you happy?" she asks.

I'm so happy I could fucking die, and it's the worst feeling in the world.

"Yeah," I answer. "I am."

"Poor Riley." Piper sighs. "He's going to be so disappointed to hear his crush is crushing on someone else."

"He doesn't like me *that* much."

"Sure he doesn't. That's why he looks at you nonstop. Because he doesn't like you."

I hide my smile behind a cough. He is always looking at me, and I like it when he does. Attention from him means more than attention from anyone else, and I hope he doesn't stop looking at me anytime soon.

"He'll get over it," I say. "I doubt he's losing any sleep over me."

"I hope not. That boy has been through enough, and it's good to see him so upbeat these days. Whatever he's doing seems to be working."

"It does, doesn't it?" I grab for my highball glass. "Are we finished with the interrogation about my personal life?"

"Yeah, yeah. I'm happy for you and the good dick you're getting."

"Thanks for your support. It is good dick."

"One day you'll confess, and until then, I'll keep pointing out the servers who are hitting on you. Oh, look. He's headed back this way."

"I'm not interested. For now, I'm a one-man woman."

"Lexi Armstrong. I never thought I'd see the day."

"Me either," I say. "But I kind of like it."

ME
Hey. Are we all set for tomorrow?

MAVERICK
Yup! Just got off the phone with the board of directors and made a generous donation to the NYC Department of Cultural Affairs. Everything should be up and running and fully staffed.

ME
Thank you so much for doing this, Maverick. I can't tell you how much it means to me.

MAVERICK
Don't mention it. I'm a little jealous I wasn't invited, but I'll let it slide.

You two have fun ;)

ME
I'm ignoring that winking face.

MAVERICK

And I'm ignoring the fact that people think I don't notice things. I see everything, Armstrong.

ME

There's nothing to see.

MAVERICK

Keep telling yourself that!

"A SUBWAY?" Riley laughs when I tap my phone against the machine and nudge him through the turnstiles. "This is the big surprise?"

"We have to take the subway to get to the surprise." I tap my phone a second time and follow behind him. "We're not there yet."

"Darn. I was looking forward to seeing all the boroughs."

"We can do that instead if you want."

"Nah." He drapes an arm over my shoulder and ruffles my hair. "I want to see what has you all fidgety."

"I'm not fidgety," I challenge, but it's a lie.

I'm so goddamn nervous about this surprise, and I have been since the idea came to me a couple of weeks ago. I've spent days exchanging phone calls and emails with important people, and even though Maverick told me everything is in place, I'm still holding on to the doubt that I won't be able to pull this off.

"Whatever you have to tell yourself, Lex."

The train comes and we find two seats next to each other. The hour ride passes quickly as we talk about tomorrow's game, and Riley lights up when he mentions the line switches he helped Coach make that have led to a two-game win streak.

A couple of people do a double take when they step on the subway and spot him, but no one approaches us. When we get close to our stop, I make him put on a pair of noise-canceling headphones so he can't hear station announcements. I lace my hand in his when we climb the stairs at the exit so we don't get separated, telling him to keep his eyes closed.

"Almost there," I say after a short walk in the March sunshine after I take his headphones off. It's warm out, the start of spring in the air, and I keep our fingers intertwined. "Sorry it's taking so long."

"I have gone over a hundred possibilities of what's about to happen, and I don't know which one to pick." Riley shuts his eyes and lets me lead him down the sidewalk, excitement pounding in my blood as I see the entrance gates. "I feel like a kid on Christmas."

"Okay." I stop us in front of the ticket booths. I loop my arm through his and put my head on his shoulder. "You can look."

He blinks and covers his face with his hand to block the sun from hitting his eyes. He squints and reads the words stretched across the welcome sign. "Coney Island? What the hell are we doing at Coney Island? Are they even open?"

"No. I, um, had Maverick pull some strings."

"What kind of strings?"

"A generous donation. He can afford it." I pause and swallow down the nerves sitting in my throat. "We wrote out a life list for you, and I want to help you check off some of the things you want to do because you deserve to be happy and have fun, Riley. You mentioned going on a roller coaster and screaming until your throat is sore. There was also discussion about carnival games, so. Two birds, one stone."

"You rented out an entire amusement park?" Riley spins so we're facing each other. "For me?"

"Yeah. I know it's not much, but with us having the afternoon free, I figured we could do something besides sit in our hotel rooms. The fresh air is nice. There won't be anyone else around, and if you're bored after two hours, we can leave and grab pizza somewhere."

"This is unbelievable." He holds my face in his hands and shakes his head. His glasses slide down his nose, and he smiles when I push them up for him. "I'm so excited."

"You are?"

"Of course I am. I get to spend the day with you. And on Maverick's dime? We're buying everything in the park."

I smile so hard my cheeks hurt. I tug on his arm, laughing when he lifts me up and spins me around. "Put me down, Mitchell. We have a busy day. We're starting on the Cyclone. It's been standing since nineteen twenty-seven, and it's three minutes long."

"Look at you being a theme park expert."

"I did a lot of research for today."

Riley sets me back on the ground, and I let him hold my hand as we walk toward the roller coaster. We pass photo booths and benches, the entire area deserted save for the occasional theme park worker. They wave to us but keep their distance, and when we make it to the entrance of the Cyclone, a bubbly blonde welcomes us.

"You must be Lexi and Riley." She smiles and gestures to the front row of an empty car. "Hop on in."

"I sure hope I don't lose my leg," he whispers to me, a hand on the small of my back as I climb in first. "Can you imagine how embarrassing that would be?"

"I bet it wouldn't be the first time." I yank him next to me and smile when he puts his arm around my shoulders. The car is a tight squeeze and our legs are pressed against each other, but I don't mind. "A lost prosthetic is probably infinitely better than two teenagers humping each other on the ride."

"Oh, we should try that. Forget about my leg."

"Keep your pants on, Mitchell."

I wave to the ride attendant. Our vehicle lurches forward, and I squeal when we roll out of the station and start up a hill.

"Jesus. The track isn't even straight." Riley holds me closer to his side. "And look at all those marks on the side. What if we go off the rails?"

"You need to live a little! That's the whole point of this. Look how high we are!" I lift my arms above my head as the beach comes into view ahead of us. "I better hear your scream, Mitchy."

We fly down the first hill, and Riley lets out a yelp next to me. He slides into me when we come around the first hill, elbow jabbing my side and making me burst out laughing. Our car shakes and rattles, and when we go down the second decline, he's screaming his head off.

"I feel so alive," he yells, and it's my turn to smash into him. He puts a hand on my thigh to keep me in place, and he howls with laughter. "Holy shit. I wouldn't care if we went flying off."

"That's what I'm talking about!" I yell back.

We match each other's screams for the duration of the ride. Tears are streaming down my face from how hard I'm cackling, and when we pull back into the station, I fall out of the vehicle and onto the platform in a fit of hysterical giggles.

"Ignore her," Riley says to the attendant who watches us like we've lost our minds. "This is normal behavior."

"I'm going to pee my pants. You sounded like a kindergartener playing dodgeball." A fresh wave of laughter hits me as he helps me to my feet and leads me down the ramp that dumps back into the park. My sides hurt, and I wipe under my eyes. "Can we please go again?"

"I think my throat is going to be sore for weeks." He coughs and touches his neck. "Am I twenty-six, or am I going through puberty?"

"You have to admit that was fun."

"It was insanely fun. What's next, Armstrong?"

"Carnival games! We're knocking things out left and right."

"I'm going to have to get Maverick a disgusting birthday gift to say thank you." Riley puts his arm on my shoulder and I loop my arm around his waist, my palm slipping into the back pocket of his jeans. "This is unreal. It's some apocalyptic shit walking around without anyone else here."

He picks a ring toss game first, ignoring the attendant's protest that everything's been paid for and slapping down a twenty-dollar bill. After fifty rings, he's nowhere near landing on the clear bottle for the grand prize, so we shift over to a water racer game where we sit side by side and try to hit the targets in front of us.

Riley reaches the top first, and he picks a giant stuffed ice cream cone as his prize that he hands over to me as soon as it's in his possession. We move to the lone hot dog stand that's open where we take a selfie that he sends in his group chat with the guys. His phone starts chiming immediately, and he blushes when he silences the text message notifications.

"You're a popular guy, Mitchy."

"Ethan is very happy we found the hot dogs, and everyone else has some commentary about how we're spending our day off."

"Good commentary?"

"Embarrassing commentary." He wipes a drop of mustard away from my mouth and smiles. "But fuck 'em."

"That's the spirit." I take another bite of my hot dog and gesture to the rest of the rides. "What else do you want to do? We have hours to go and so many options."

"The go-karts," he says.

I grin, not caring about the piece of bun stuck to my gums. "Our stomachs are going to be fucked up."

"Is there any other way to do a theme park?" He pops the last of his hot dog in his mouth and tugs on my arm. "Let's go, Lexi baby."

We spend the rest of the afternoon going from ride to ride. I kick his ass at go-karts, but he makes me pay for it by spinning us around the Tea Party attraction like a madman. After a visit to another roller coaster and a second ride on the Cyclone, we grab two ice cream cones and take our time walking down the boardwalk.

"Want to finish with the Ferris wheel?" I ask. "Technically it's part of a different amusement park, but Maverick paid for it too."

"Gift cards really aren't going to cut it for a gift this year." Riley stops us in the middle of the sidewalk and hooks his finger in the belt loop of my jeans. "Thank you for doing all of this for me. It means a lot, and this is the most fun I've had in a very long time."

"We'll get to some of the other things on your list." I give him a one-armed hug, but he pulls me close. Tips my chin back so our gazes meet, and the sun setting behind his head makes him look like he has a halo. "I'm glad you're having fun."

"Lexi." He rubs his thumb along the curve of my jaw. I sigh and turn my head so I can kiss the center of his palm. "Today was a very, very good day."

"Yeah?" I smile, heart leaping up to my throat when he rests his forehead against mine. "It was pretty great, wasn't it?"

"One for the books," he murmurs, nose bumping against mine. He bends his neck and kisses me soft and slow, out in the open where anyone could see, and I let him. "You're my favorite person in the entire world."

"You're not so bad yourself," I say, because I'm caught off guard by how natural and *right* all of this is; spending a full day together. Being affectionate out in public. Having fun and feeling free in a way I've never felt before. "Okay. I'm lying. Besides the girls, you're my favorite person in the entire world too."

"I'd never ask to be put above them. That's their rightful spot."

Something tender stirs inside me as he tosses his ice cream in the trash and kisses me again, a hand in my hair and the other back on my cheek. It's steady, heart-pounding, and I think my feet might be coming off the ground because I'm enjoying it so much. I think my heart might be skipping a beat when he laughs against my mouth and kisses me harder. I think the deepest parts of my soul might be healing when he throws me over his shoulder and ignores my complaints about riding the Sling Shot with a full stomach.

On the subway ride back to the hotel, I put my head on his shoulder and close my eyes, feeling like a goddamn liar.

Today wasn't pretty great.

It was the best day of my life.

THIRTY-NINE
RILEY

DAD
How're you doing, kid?

ME
Can't complain, really.

DAD
Saw you on the bench the other night. The suit and tie look good on you. Interesting how the team starts to win after Saunders puts you in a leadership role. He should've done that from the beginning.

ME
I'm glad he didn't. I wasn't ready for that yet. I am now, and I'm having fun.

DAD
Good. Don't let Minnesota get the W this weekend. I've always hated them.

ME
Ha. I only have so much say, but I'll do my best.

DAD

That's my boy.

EVERY MORNING I WAKE UP, I wait for the other shoe to drop and shit to hit the fan.

I'm waiting for things to start going wrong, because everything in my life seems too damn good to be true.

I've slipped into my role behind the bench much quicker than I thought I would, and the boys are moving up the standings with win after win. Lexi and I switch off where we have sleepovers when we're not on the road, and it's *so fucking good*. Some nights we don't even have sex, staying up and reading books we pick out for each other and spending half the night arguing over which characters we like and why.

Because of Lexi's hard work and thorough rehabilitation plan, I'm ahead of schedule with my recovery. Moving is easy these days. There are still exercises I struggle with, but I'm stronger. More agile too, and while I haven't tried getting back on the ice, I'm feeling more and more like who I was before the accident.

So, yeah.

I'm waiting for the big third-act conflict. The wrench that gets thrown into my plans and fucks everything up.

"We have a situation," Mikal Reynolds, our top assistant coach says as he barrels into the locker room before our away game in Minnesota. "Saunders isn't here."

"What do you mean Saunders isn't here?" Maverick looks up from his skates and frowns. "He was literally on the plane with us yesterday afternoon. Or did I dream up that whole flight?"

"Definitely happened. He yelled at me for having my phone out and took it away until we were back at the hotel." Ethan grins and fixes his shoulder pads. "Joke is on him. I have a burner one I use to troll people who shit on us in social media comments."

"There is a lot to unpack there." Hudson glances at Mikal. "Is Coach okay?"

"Don't know. He said something about was a family emergency and that he was getting on the first flight back to DC."

"Shit. I hope Olivia is okay," I say. "Coach hasn't missed a game since he took this job."

"He also went five seasons without missing a game when he was in the league." Grant jumps to his feet and wobbles on his skates. "This is a code red."

"We'll worry about Saunders in a minute. You're taking over for him, right Ren?" Maverick asks Mikal.

"I mean, I can, but I've been out for two weeks interviewing for head coaching positions. I've missed all of your practices, and I don't know what the hell kind of shifts you're running. It's going to take me more than the time we have before puck drop to watch some film and catch up. " Mikal eyes our other assistant coach, Parker Barnes. "And you've been out on paternity leave."

"Coach has been doing this shit by himself and putting up with all our stupid asses? Give that man the Jack Adams Award immediately," Ethan says.

"Hang on. Riley's been at every practice." Hudson turns his attention my way. "You haven't missed a morning skate in months."

"Whoa. Slow the fuck down." I hold up my hands and shake my head. "I don't like where this is going."

"Oh, fuck yeah, Mitchy," Grant cheers. "You have to do it."

"I don't know the first thing about coaching people who aren't five years old. And this is an important game," I rush out. "Every win this late in the year matters. You don't need someone like me in charge when a loss could tank our playoff chances."

"Team vote." Maverick stands and surveys the locker room. "All in favor of Mitchy taking on responsibilities tonight raise your hands." Twenty arms shoot up in the air, and I shove my glasses up my nose in a fit of nervousness. "Captain has the last say, and I say you're in. Welcome to the big leagues, Ri."

"When we lose, I can't be held responsible." I accept Coach's whiteboard from Mikal and stare at the triangles and marks on it. I've seen it a thousand times as a player, but looking at it now feels like I'm looking at a calculus problem I have no clue how to solve. "It's going to be all your fault."

"A decision I can live with." Maverick flashes me a grin and grabs his helmet. "Hands in, boys. Let's go snag a W for one of our best guys."

I don't stick around for the huddle, glaring at Mikal and Parker as I storm out of the locker room and head for the ice. This is too much responsibility for me to handle. I can sit on the bench just fine, but leading a team in enemy territory?

I'm going to shit my pants.

"Looking snazzy, Mitchy." Lexi waves at me from the end of the tunnel, a clipboard tucked under her arm and athletic tape shoved in her pocket. "What's with the scowl?"

"Coach had to fly home to DC for a family emergency, and guess who got put in charge over the two assistant coaches who are paid to work on shifts and penalty kill plays? *Me.* The guy who doesn't know shit about coaching."

"Wait, what? You're calling the shots tonight?"

"Apparently. Mikal and Parker both have excuses for why they don't feel comfortable, but at least they have experience in the role. I'm a fucking novice and they want yours truly to make the decisions against the best team in the league." I glare out at the ice and the Minnesota Vipers logo at center ice. "When ESPN does a whole segment on how I fucked up tonight, I'm putting out a statement that I was coerced into this."

"Okay, you're not being dramatic at all." Lexi's mouth twitches, and she walks toward me. "Take a breath, Mitchy. It's going to be okay. Who cares if they win or lose?"

"I do. I don't want them to fall out of the playoff hunt the day after I call the shots. Do you know how embarrassing that would be? I couldn't show my face in a barn again."

"It's not like you're out there hitting the puck and giving up goals, Riley. You can only do so much from on the bench. Whatever happens, happens. They need a leader, and tonight, that happens to be you. The guys respect you, it seems like the decision has been made, so you might as well have some fun with it."

"Why do you always have to be so rational?" I grumble. "Can't you be on my side?"

"Oh, I'm on your side. You'll get there eventually."

She pats my chest and turns for the ice. I follow behind her, careful as I walk around the curve of the rink to our bench on the other side of the arena. I wish she was allowed to sit with us over here during the game. I'd be more relaxed if she were nearby, but she has to hang out in the tunnel as soon as the puck drops.

The boys skate out to an arena full of boos, and my heart has never pounded so hard. The fear in my chest slowly shifts to adrenaline and excitement as they do a lap. The referee skates over and asks for the starting lineup, and I hand over our starting six with an apology for the delay so he can pass it along to the Vipers' coaching staff.

"Thanks for stepping up," Mikal says, and I scoff.

"I didn't have much of a choice, did I?" I cross my arms over my chest and watch Liam finish up his warmup in the goal. He looks locked in tonight, quick with his movements and tracking every puck that comes his way. "Let the shit show begin."

Someone from ESPN tries to grab me for an interview, but the PA announcer comes over the microphone and asks everyone to stand for the national anthem. I ignore the faint ache in my right leg and bend to adjust my prosthetic, hoping no one catches me on camera hunched over with my hands halfway up my thigh.

The buzzer sounds, starting lineups are introduced, and our first six skate down the bench in a line to get fist bumps from our teammates. When they reach me, they all put a hand on my head. Liam grunts in my direction and Maverick grins, pulling me into a hug.

"Relax," he says, laughing when I nudge his shoulder.

"Easy for you to say. You're out there with a stick."

"We really don't give a shit what happens, Ri. This season has had so many fucking highs and lows, and the fact that you're here right now is a major fucking win. Let's chirp some, show some heart, and we might get out of here with a win."

"Damn you, Maverick Miller," I say. "Get your ass to the face off."

"There he is." With another smile, he skates toward the puck drop. "See ya soon, Mitchy."

WE'RE up by four with three minutes left in the third.

I don't know how, but everything that needs to click does, and we're on fucking fire.

Our passes are smooth. We're aggressive on offense. Ryan Seymour made a spectacular dive to prevent a Vipers goal halfway through the second, and I ditched the whiteboard during the first intermission in favor of addressing the players directly.

"Coming up on two and a half minutes." I clap then put a hand on Grant's shoulder. "You're going in next shift, and I want to see those efficient passes we worked on at practice, yeah?"

"Sure thing, Coach. Sorry. I mean Mitchy."

He switches with Maverick during the next break in the offense, taking off to get in position for an open pass from Seymour.

"Even the rookies look good tonight." Maverick sprays his Bodyarmor in his mouth and stretches his neck from side to side. "You might have the magic touch, Ri."

"Shut up." I track the puck and make a mental note to praise Ethan on his face off win percentage tonight. He's sitting around sixty percent, a stellar stat from a guy who's been lazy from the get-go up until recently, and he's the kind of player who responds well to positive reinforcement. "I'm busy."

Time ticks down, two minutes going to one, and fans start clearing out of the arena. The boys don't get sloppy the last sixty seconds, and Grant sinks a five-hole that has me pumping my fist in the air just before the clock expires.

"Nice win," Mikal says with a hand on my shoulder. "I knew you could do it."

The final horn sounds, and our boys do a celly lap before skating over to the bench. I can't avoid an interview this time, and Piper wrangles me over for a couple of questions before the national media can get a hold of me.

"Riley. Tell us what it's like transitioning from player to coach. Is it difficult to see the ice from this perspective?" she asks, leaning the microphone in my direction.

"It's not difficult but different. When I'm on the bench in my uniform, I'm more focused on watching my position. Back here, I see the whole picture. I'm watching their tendy and their forwards, and you have to be quick to react if needed."

"How prepared did you feel stepping into this position tonight?"

"Not very," I laugh. "But the heart and hustle from the boys and the encouragement from the rest of the coaching staff made it manageable. We got the W, and that's what matters."

"Last question, then I'll let you go celebrate. Was tonight the start of a position you see yourself doing long-term?"

"Ah, shucks. I don't know. I had a good time. I love hockey. Being out here is a gift, ya know? Whether that's with skates on my feet or a lineup sheet in my hands, I'm blessed to do this."

"Thanks, Riley. Enjoy your 1-0 coaching record," Piper says, lowering her microphone and giving me a wide grin. "Sorry for the formalities, but holy shit, Ri. That was so fun to watch. I'm so proud of you. I bet your phone is going to start ringing with opportunities. Scouting maybe too."

"That's a discussion for another day. Right now, I need to get back to the hotel and get out of this leg. It's fucking killing me from the nonstop standing."

"Can I help with anything?"

"Nah, I'm good. You should—"

There's a round of raised voices and lots of yelling. I blink and turn around, trying to find the source of the noise, and I'm met with twenty water bottles full of sports drinks getting dumped on my head.

"Fuck yeah, Mitchy!"

"Coach Saunders is shaking in his fucking boots!"

"We have to go out and celebrate."

"Hot dogs for everyone!"

"Jesus Christ." I laugh and pull off my glasses, trying to wipe them clean on my suit jacket. "Everyone needs to chill the fuck out."

"C'mon, Mitchy." Hudson smiles and holds out his arm so I can step onto the ice and not slip. "You know we don't do anything half-assed."

"Never. It's always full ass. Full dicks, too. You all need to tone it the fuck down."

"Never!" Grant yells, squirting me with another splash of his drink. "We're loud and proud!"

The boys skate toward the locker room, and I hold the

boards as I make my way around the rink behind them. I step off the ice and into the tunnel, an undeniable smile still on my mouth.

"Pretty impressive stuff there, Mitchell," Lexi calls out. "I love being right."

"Don't gloat," I tell her, knocking her shoulder with mine. "It's not a cute look."

"Please." She grins. "I'm always cute."

"Debatable," I say, and she flips me off.

"You're going out to celebrate with the boys, right?"

"Probably not. I'm exhausted. That took a lot out of me physically, and I think I'm going to call it an early night."

"Do you want some company?" Lexi asks. "Or would you prefer to be alone?"

"Some company sounds nice," I tell her, and she smiles. "Especially if it's you."

"I'm so proud of you. I know this is different from the other areas in your life you've been working on, but you still deserve all the praise, Riley. I can't wait to see what you do next," she says, hooking her pinky in mine, and the praise means more from her than it does from anyone else.

FORTY
RILEY

PUCK KINGS

EASY E
If u could be any animal, what would u be?

SULLY
Something that helps you leanr to spell. How hard is it to spell out the word you? It's two more letters than what you're doing now.

G-MONEY
Ooooh, Goalie Daddy spelled a word wrong!!! Shame!!!

MAVVY
Don't poke the bear, Grant. You don't want to be on the receiving end of his wrath!

G-MONEY
Hush, Cap. We have a celebrity in our midst. Mitchy's been everywhere on Instagram and TikTok!!

ME

I have?

G-MONEY

Mhm. The girls loveeeeee you. Especially your slutty little glasses.

ME

They aren't slutty. I need them to see.

EASY E

They've ALWAYS been slutty glasses.

MAVVY

He's going to develop an ego. But he's cute so it's deserved!!!

HUDDY BOY

Who? Riley? He's the humblest guy I know.

ME

Okay. We don't need to make this conversation about me. In fact, I would prefer it if we didn't.

SULLY

Has anyone thought about shutting this godforsaken chat down for a day? Or a fucking year?

MAVVY

Nope. You're required to be in it. Captain's orders.

SULLY

Fuck your captain's orders.

G-MONEY

How is there not a line of women at your door, Mitchy? My god. I think even I'm attracted to you.

MAVVY

I really don't like losing the top spot on the team.

HUDDY BOY

You'll get over it.

THERE'S NOT a line of women at my door, but there is a knock at six thirty in the evening that confuses the hell out of me.

It's not a book club night. Team dinner isn't until tomorrow. None of the guys said they were stopping by, and thanks to two great back-to-back performances, Coach gave everyone the full day off.

Frowning, I push back from the bar stool I've been sitting on for the better part of an hour answering emails. I pad across the kitchen floor and into the foyer, smiling when I see Lexi on the other side of the door.

"Well"—I lean against the frame and cross my arms over my chest—"this is a nice surprise. To what do I owe the pleasure, Lex? Do you want me to put my head between your legs?"

"Tempting." Her grin is intoxicating and addictive. I could stare at her mouth for hours. I probably already do. "But we're going out tonight."

"Out? Where? I don't feel like going to a club or anything like that."

"To dinner, which is something both of us need because I'm guessing you haven't eaten yet."

"I haven't, and my fridge is bare as fuck after being on the road the last few days." I glance down at my joggers and black T-shirt. "Let me change really quick."

"We're not going anywhere fancy." Lexi grabs a paperback off my shelf and sits on the couch, relaxing against the cushions. "And take your time. I started reading this one on my Kindle. Could hardly put it down."

"Don't get too sucked in or we're never going to leave. You want a drink while you wait?"

"Nope." She flashes me a smile but doesn't look up from the page she's on. "I'm all set."

I stare at her for a minute. She looks perfectly in place there, with a blanket over her lap and her legs curled under her. I don't even mind that she didn't take her boots off. I'm too distracted picturing her like this every night: after a game, in one of my shirts, a mark on her neck that I left behind.

It's easy to imagine it. We've been spending more and more time together, and the fantasy is starting to dance around in my head. Loudly, obnoxiously, and it feels like I'm four seconds away from screaming *do you like me back? Yes or no?* just so I don't have to keep this inside anymore.

In a fit of spontaneity, I walk over to her. I touch her cheek, and she finally looks up at me.

"I'm glad you're here," I say to her, and her face softens. A smile pulls at one corner of her mouth, and I bend to kiss her right there, just so I can have the beam all for myself. "If you want to stay on the couch and read all night, I'll order us takeout."

"No. I'll happily put the book away for you." She grabs my shirt and tugs me toward her, kissing me again. There's the swipe of her tongue, the bite of her teeth on my lower lip. I sigh against her mouth, and she pulls away far too quickly. "Can't wait to see what you're going to wear, Mitchy."

"Don't get your hopes up."

"I don't need to. You always look great."

I blush, the compliment meaning more from her than it would from another woman. "Right back at you, Armstrong."

"Go." She swats at my arm, and I can't help but laugh. "You're distracting me from my reading."

"I'm going to get dressed extra slow just so you can finish that chapter."

"A man after my own heart." She winks, and I rub a hand over my chest.

It feels more and more like my heart isn't even my own anymore.

It's hers, and I think it's always going to be hers.

THE SPORTS BAR Lexi picks is loud and busy. I put my hand on the small of her back as we make our way through the crowded restaurant, not wanting her to get jostled by the group of drunk guys around the bar who are yelling about our shitty baseball team.

We find a table toward the back against the wall, and we slide onto the wooden barstools across from each other. Our knees are touching because of the small space, but I don't mind. I like her close to me. I like having the option to touch her if I wanted to, and *fuck*, do I want to.

"I'm not totally digging the ambience, but they apparently have good burgers. I'm hoping that will make up for the douchebags screaming at the TV. I'm glad the pitcher can't hear them. Sports fans are ruthless," she says.

"It's funny. I doubt any of them could throw a baseball more than four feet, but they're out here acting like they're the next Cy Young."

"Do you have anywhere you like to go in the city?"

"If I'm going out with someone, I prefer it to be somewhere more intimate. So I can hear what they're saying and hold a conversation, you know?"

"Oh." She sits up and grins. "Is this your romantic side?"

"It's the decent human side of me."

"I bet you'd be fun to go on a date with. You're probably all smooth moves and that whole *oh, you have something on your shoulder, let me get it for you* trick where you end up having your arms around her."

I snort. "The arm around the shoulder. Acting like I can't hear her, grabbing her stool, and scooting it closer. Pretending like she has something on her face, but it's really just an excuse to touch her. The perfect date hat trick."

"I want to see Date Riley," she says.

"No, you don't. I'm really not that exciting."

"Come on, Mitchy." Lexi sticks out her bottom lip in a pout. "Show me what you're like on a date."

"You never go on dates," I say. "I remember you being specifically anti-dates."

"Tonight I'm not. Tonight I *do* go on dates. I picked you up from your apartment. I'm wearing my nicest underwear. This is absolutely a date. Or, at the very least, a pretend date."

"Nicest underwear? I hope I get to see them later."

"Only if you answer my question," she teases.

"Fine." I grin. "I'd start the night by picking you up from your place with your favorite flowers."

"Tulips," she says. "Which is a frustrating choice, because they don't bloom up here until April. What's next?"

"I'd tell you how hot you look in your skirt and how much I like your boots."

"They're cute boots, aren't they?"

"Very cute." I put my hand on her leg and give her knee a gentle squeeze. It's only been two days since we last slept together, but I missed the feel of her skin, how warm and soft she is. "Next, I'd ask what you want to order for dinner."

"You wouldn't order for me?"

"Fuck no. You're an independent woman who can speak

for herself. And, on the off chance you don't like what you pick, I'd make sure to let you try some of my meal too."

"Shared custody of our french fries? I like where this is going." Lexi reaches for my collar and tugs on my shirt. Our faces are inches apart, and I can see the brightness in her eyes. "Give me more, Riley."

"Well"—I blush and clear my throat—"we'd talk. I'd ask about your job and your family. I'd compliment you and tell you how beautiful you look, which you do. You always do, with your strong legs and your pretty smile. I'd laugh at your jokes even if they weren't funny, and at the end, I'd pay for our meal, kiss your forehead, and text you when I got home."

"My forehead? That's a tease."

"Yup. You should always leave them wanting more."

"Where are the ropes?" she asks. "And the orgasm denials? And the blowjobs? You're holding out on me, Mitchy."

"Ah." I didn't think it was possible for my cheeks to get even redder, but here we are. "I only do that with people I know and trust. People I like."

"We do all of that." She smirks. "Must mean you like me."

I grab her chin and her eyes lock with mine. Her breath hitches when I say, "You have no idea, Lexi."

There's an underlying message there.

I like you so fucking much, but I also think I more than like you.

Do you think you could like me too?

Why can't we give it a chance?

I promise I'll make it good for you.

Lexi pulls back and tucks a piece of hair behind her ear. "Should we order some fries then? So I can steal some of yours?"

"I'll give you the whole damn plate, Lex, if it'll make you happy."

Her smile is soft, timid. Maybe I'm imagining it because it's what I want to see, but I swear she inches closer to me. I take matters into my own hands and drag the leg of her stool across the concrete floor, just like I said I would.

"When was the last time you went on a date?"

"Huh." I put my elbow on the table and frown. "I don't remember. Maybe a couple years ago? I've only had a handful of first dates. Nothing's ever stuck."

"Wait, *what?* That's a long time. I thought all the guys were playboys."

"You thought wrong. We're much more mellow than people think. Except for Ethan. Dude can't keep it in his pants."

"Now that I can believe. But don't change the subject! We're talking about you. Why hasn't anything stuck? You're a great guy." Her smile is wider now, and I like that she lights up when she talks about me. "A total catch."

"Shucks. You're going to make me blush, Lex."

"I'm serious! You have so many good qualities. A woman would be out of her mind to not want to see you a second time."

"Don't know." I shrug. "Maybe I have bad breath. Or my hands smell too gnarly from my gloves."

Lexi laughs at that, but I don't add in the other part: how every date I went on, I'd sit there and wonder what it would be like to be having dinner with her instead. It's not like she led me on and gave me some false hope of something we could be down the road.

It's more pathetic than that.

I took one look at her, and I was done for.

I haven't been able to get her out of my damn head, and I learned a long time ago that as long as we were on the same team, as long as we were in the same zip code and orbiting around each other, I had a shot. And I wasn't going to blow that shot by going on shitty date after shitty date with someone who wasn't *her*.

I rub a hand over my jaw knowing it's not fair to her to be

feeling these things and sleeping with her like everything is platonic between us. But I'm selfish.

I know when I tell her, that's going to be it, and I want to hold on to her for a little while longer.

"Let me see." Lexi takes my hands in hers and brings them to her nose. She pretends to gag then laughs again. "Just kidding. They smell very nice. Is that vanilla?"

"Yeah. It's some soap Hudson told all of us to buy. It's nice, isn't it?"

"I can't find hockey smells anywhere."

"Probably helps that I haven't worn any gear in months."

"You know what I mean."

I shrug. "I told you what I'm like on a date. What's Lexi Armstrong like?"

"I don't go on dates, remember? And if I did, it would include lackluster conversation, then an invitation back to my place to sleep together."

"I'm listening," I say. "You've never told me why you don't date. Did someone fuck up once upon a time? Are you secretly not a fan of places with a ton of options on their menus?"

She pauses. "Something like that."

The answer is stilted, and I can tell she doesn't want to talk about it, so I switch gears. "What else is on the agenda tonight?"

"Besides hoping all those dudes lose their parlays? I thought maybe we could go bowling or to see a late-night movie. My apartment is starting to feel lonely when I'm there by myself, and as much as I like to be alone, I don't like to be isolated and sad."

"My door is always open," I say, putting a hand back on her knee. "If you ever want company. Any time of day or night."

"Thanks, Mitchy. I'll keep that in mind." Her foot kicks mine, and it feels like we're the only people in the room. "Let's order eight rounds of french fries. Shared custody and all of that."

"Co-parenting. Very mature of us."

She laughs and so do I. We go through three baskets of fries and start making up stories about who we think the finance bros might be. Her theories make me cackle until my sides hurt, and we never make it to bowling. We close down the restaurant, only leaving when the server turns off the lights and kicks us out. On the walk back to my place, I do the cheesy shoulder trick on her so she's in my arms. I bend my neck to hear what she has to say and kiss her cheek. And when I drag her to my bed and pull her close, her thigh thrown over mine, I fuck her nice and slow until she's begging me for more, and it's the best non-date I've ever been on.

FORTY-ONE
RILEY

PUCK KINGS

> ME
> This is embarrassing, but is anyone free to help me with something this afternoon?

EASY E
> Uh oh. Did you get something stuck somewhere it shouldn't be stuck?
>
> Been there, man. Sucks.

> ME
> Uh, no.

G-MONEY
> Sometimes it amazes me you're just out there walking around with the rest of the population, Ethan.

EASY E
> I've made it 23 years. I'm doing justtttttt fine.

HUDDY BOY

Madeline and Lucy are having a girls' day, and I'd love to help.

MAVVY

Emmy is out of town, and if I sit around the apartment by myself for another second, I'm going to go out of my mind. Count me in.

HUDDY BOY

Liam?

SULLY

No.

MAVVY

Come on, Liam. It's Mitchy.

ME

Well, I feel pathetic. Thank you.

SULLY

Fine. You get me for an hour tops. And I reserve the right to complain the entire time.

G-MONEY

I don't like being left out!!! I want to come.

ME

Whoever wants to come can come. Be at my apartment at two.

EASY E

lol so secretive. What are you hiding, Mitchy??

SULLY

Your IQ.

EASY E
Damn. Goalie Daddy is on fire today!!!!

"IS THIS A SCAVENGER HUNT?" Maverick looks around my living room and frowns. "What exactly are we helping you with?"

"It's not housework, is it?" Grant groans. "Everyone thinks I know how to use a drill because I'm a guy, but the thing fucking terrifies me."

"Can y'all stop complaining and let Mitchy talk?" Hudson smiles at me from the couch. "We're here for whatever you need."

"Okay. You know I lost my right leg," I say, gesturing down at my joggers.

"We had no fucking idea," Liam draws out, and Hudson hits him with a pillow.

"Ignore him. Keep going, Ri."

"I haven't driven since the accident. I'm comfortable using my prosthetic in my day-to-day life, but if I want to get behind the wheel again, I'm going to have to use my left foot. Trying to get my brain to understand the pedals after years of being on autopilot is intimidating." I rub the back of my neck. "I was hoping, ah, you guys could be in the car with me while I try for the first time? In case something happens?"

"Fuck, yeah. It's *Grand Theft Auto* in real life." Grant jumps to his feet. "Where are your keys? I call dibs on shotgun."

"Okay, slow down there, G," Hudson says. "Let's plan this out."

"Always so fucking rational," Liam grumbles. "We're going to an empty parking lot."

"I like that idea," Maverick agrees. "How about the football stadium? The parking lot is massive, and it should be mostly deserted since the Titans are in their offseason."

"Does someone mind driving us there in my car?" I ask. "I've turned it on every few days to make sure the battery still works, but it hasn't moved since June."

"I don't trust any of you behind the wheel." Liam grabs the keys hanging from the wall in my foyer. "Except Hayes. He's the smartest one of the group. But I value my life too much to have Tweedledee and Tweedledum in charge," he says, pointing at Maverick and Grant.

"Someone pissed in his coffee this morning," Grant whispers.

"Let's go. Sully can drive us there like the good little chauffeur he is, and we'll figure this out together," Maverick says. "You have insurance, right?"

"Yeah, but I'd prefer it if we didn't crash my hundred-thousand-dollar vehicle." I bend my hips back to adjust my residual limb in my socket then straighten my leg. "I'm not in the mood for paperwork."

"I'm never in the mood for paperwork." Grant heads for the door and flings it open. "Come on, boys. Let's pretend like we're Princess Mia driving the Mustang."

"That's a good fucking movie," Maverick says.

"A great fucking movie," Hudson adds, and I follow them down the hall.

Twenty minutes later, we're parked in front of the DC Titans' football stadium. My hands are on my hips, and I stare at my SUV.

"How do you want to do this?" Hudson asks, a hand on my shoulder.

"We could crank the driver's seat back and have you sit in one of our laps?" Grant suggests, and I burst out laughing.

"That would be a fucking sight," I say.

"Damn. I was really hoping I'd get to have Mitchy in my lap. That's a dream of mine." Maverick taps his cheek. "How about one person in the passenger seat. Someone right behind you who can grab the wheel if you panic and another in the middle who could reach forward and tap the brakes if needed?"

"Whose arms are the longest?" Hudson asks, and Liam scoffs.

"My wingspan is the biggest on the team," our goalie challenges. "Have you seen me stop a puck?"

"You know what they say about goalies and wingspans." Grant winks. "He's also the most flexible one. Maybe he should be in the middle."

"Liam in the middle. Hudson up front because he's the most rational, and he'll definitely be the calmest. I'll go in the seat behind Riley and be on deck to take over the wheel. G-Money… you'll be the spectator in the back right seat," Maverick says.

"Not fair! Everyone else has a job." Grant pouts. "I'm good at things."

"You can be in charge of… navigation," I say, pulling something out of my ass. I don't want him to feel left out. "Tell me if I need to go left or right. You're great at reading the ice. You can help me avoid the concrete lampposts."

"This is an honor, Riley." He puts a hand on his chest and dips his head. "I will not let you down."

"Everyone get in the goddamn car," Liam says, climbing into the middle seat in the back. "If someone starts quoting *Spiderman* about power and responsibility, I'm out of here."

"Another great movie," Maverick whispers, and Grant nods sagely.

We get in our places, and I hold the steering wheel with a white-knuckle grip. I run my palms along the curve of the leather and take a deep breath. Glancing down, I stare at the pedals and frown.

"I'm trying to figure out how to position my legs," I say. "I think I'll keep my right foot where it would be if I had cruise control on, then stretch my left leg diagonally to reach the pedals."

"Probably easier than trying to tuck your right leg behind your left, yeah?" Hudson asks, and I nod.

"And uncomfortable. Safer too, I bet. I don't need another fucking surgery." I turn the key in the ignition and exhale. "Okay. Here we go."

"Give me some window privileges, Mitchy, so you can focus on your feet," Grant says, and when I roll down the back windows, he sticks his head out into the sunshine. "Forward, matey!"

Shifting the car into drive, I slowly ease my left foot onto the accelerator. The car jolts to life, and we roll across the empty parking spaces. I'm pretty sure I'm sweating. Everyone in the car is silent, and I try adding more pressure to the gas pedal.

"It's the same configuration," I tell myself. "Just a different angle."

"Try braking," Maverick says, and I nod.

I'm a little too firm when I move my foot to the left and tap on the brakes, because Liam goes flying forward and almost rolls over the center console. Grant screams and clutches the door to prevent himself from falling out the window. Maverick topples sideways, his head under Liam's ass, and Hudson cackles in the seat beside me.

"Sorry, sorry!" I apologize, being gentler the second time I try the brakes. The SUV slows to a stop, and I glance at my teammates. "Got a little excited there. Is everyone okay?"

Liam rubs his forehead. "I'm fucking concussed."

"I saw my life flash before my eyes," Grant says.

"Scary, isn't it?" I ask, and he nods.

"Liam, I swear to god if you sit down right now, I'm going to bite your ass," Maverick warns, trying to get himself upright. "Don't you fucking dare."

"I wish I had that on video." Hudson wheezes, the only one unaffected by my shitty first attempt. "I've never heard Grant scream like that before."

"Hey. I was *scared*, and this is a judgment-free zone. Watch yourself, Hayes," Grant says, bopping him on the back of the head. "I'm stronger than I look, and I'll fling you out of the window if you laugh at me again."

"If anyone wants to evacuate, they can," I say, checking to make sure everyone is okay. "But I'll be more careful next time."

And I am. I get us cruising up to twenty miles an hour, and I make a big lap around the perimeter of the parking lot. Grant keeps his head out of the window, guiding me left then right, and when I tap the brakes again, we roll to a gentle and complete stop without incident.

"Nice job, Ri," Hudson says. "That was smooth."

"Not as hard as I thought it would be," I say. "I just need to train my brain."

"Online it says you can buy something called a left foot gas pedal?" Maverick asks, looking up from his phone. "Have you thought about that?"

"Not really." I shrug. "People already treat me differently because of my leg, and I want to try to keep things as normal as I can. I wore shorts to the grocery store the other day, and you would've thought I had skin lesions all over my body. Someone asked if I needed a wheelchair, and while I'm sure some folks with prosthetics do, it was like they were only seeing my disability, not me as a whole person." I sigh. "It's frustrating. I don't want to be coddled. Do I need special accommodations sometimes? Yeah. Am I going to take the elevator instead of climbing five flights of stairs? Sure. But I'm still me."

"Shit. That was really powerful, man. I never thought of it that way," Grant says.

"When I was in the hospital and being transported back and forth in a wheelchair, no one talked to me. They only talked to the person pushing me. As if I stopped being an individual entity when I lost my leg. That's why I'm hesitant to show off my lower half. Not because I'm embarrassed. But because everyone always makes it a way bigger deal than it needs to be."

"It sucks that you're treated like that," Hudson says.

"You should partner with the league to do a disability awareness class," Maverick suggests. "Get some Paralympic athletes on board too."

"If anyone gives you problems, I'll kick their ass," Liam adds, and I laugh.

"Thanks, guys. And thanks for doing this with me. It was too intimidating to try by myself, but hearing Grant scream like that was worth bringing in reinforcements."

"Another lap." Maverick clasps my shoulder. "Try to get up to thirty miles an hour."

The next time around the parking lot is easier. I can tell I'm using my left leg, and there's the hint of discomfort in my right knee area, but overall, I'm happy with how I do. The tension leaves my shoulders when I complete a fourth lap at an even faster speed, safely parking in a spot and checking to make sure I'm within the lines.

"Next task is going to be tackling an actual road," I say, stretching out my legs. "I might panic and press the gas instead of the brakes."

"I bet you'll be more confident after another two practice rounds," Hudson says. "And we'll be here with you."

"I'll be wearing a helmet," Liam says, and I snort.

"Sorry, Sully. I didn't mean to mess up your pretty head."

A call comes through on my Bluetooth, and Lexi's name pops up on the car screen.

"Oooh, why is Lexi calling you?" Grant leans forward and smashes the green button before I can stop him. "Hey, sugar," he says. "What's cookin', good lookin'?"

"Okay, stop," I say, shoving him out of the way.

"Is that Grant?" Lexi asks.

"The one and only," he yells from the backseat.

"You're on speaker," I tell her. "We were having a driving lesson."

"That sounds fun. How did it go?"

"I'll be stopping by your office tomorrow before morning skate because Mitchell injured me," Liam says. "You can blame him for giving you extra work."

"I love extra work," she says. "Sorry to interrupt! I'll text you instead, Ri."

"Everything okay?" I ask, and another round of *oooohs* come from the back.

"Everything is great. Just wanted to say hi." I hear the smile in her voice and wonder what she's up to. If she's having a good day and doing anything fun. "I don't want to interrupt guy time."

"You're not interrupting. They all suck," I tell her, and Maverick gasps.

"Fucking *rude*," he mumbles. "We had a moment when I put my hands over yours on the wheel, Mitchy."

"Wow. I'm really bummed I missed out on this." Lexi laughs. "You all have fun. I'll talk to you later!"

Everyone except Liam yells out a goodbye, and when I hang up the call, Hudson is grinning at me.

"I don't want to hear it," I say.

"You're so down bad." Hudson smirks. "We've all been there."

"Except Grant. He's too young to understand love." Maverick ruffles my hair. "Have you told her how you feel?"

"Nope."

"Are you going to tell her how you feel?"

"Nope."

"Riley," Hudson says gently. "You went through a traumatic event that showed us how short life is. Wouldn't you rather get everything out in the open instead of hiding it? What if you never get the chance to let her know you're head over heels for her?"

"She doesn't want head over heels, so I keep my mouth shut."

"She might with you," Liam says, surprising me.

"I'll think about it." I put the car in drive, then purposely slam on the brakes to another round of screams. "And stop meddling in my personal life, you nosy assholes."

"Worst day *ever*," Liam growls, and I grin at him in the rearview mirror.

FORTY-TWO
LEXI

THERE'S a doughnut waiting for me on my desk when I get to work on Saturday morning. The boys have an afternoon skate and won't come in until later, so the arena is quiet to start the day, and I don't know who is lurking around. A quick check of my calendar tells me I have no appointments with any players until eleven, and I lift the treat to inspect it.

"I didn't poison it," Riley says from the entrance to the locker room, and I drop the pastry so I can lob a stapler at his head in an effort to protect myself. "Jesus Christ. It's just me, Lex."

"You cannot sneak up on a woman alone in her office without announcing yourself." I put a hand on my desk and take a deep breath, my heart skipping a beat when I realize it's him. "That's not nice."

"Did you forget about our session this morning?"

"Shit." I look at my calendar again and spot the little R in the right-hand corner of today's date. Our sessions have moved to twice a week instead of every day based on his improvements, and with the season ending in less than a month and our fight for the playoffs amping up, my brain is all over the place. "I did. I can't keep track of what day it is. Sorry."

"I should be the one apologizing. That was creepy of me to startle you."

I scoop the doughnut up and groan as I take a bite. "Apology accepted. This is the best thing I've ever had in my mouth."

Riley laughs and sits on the edge of the treatment table. "I would say I'm offended, but I had one on the way over, and I have to agree."

"Thank you for this." I lick a drop of jam away from the corner of my mouth and smile. "How did you know I needed something to get through the day?"

"I know everything." He takes off his sneakers and lets them fall to the floor. He stretches out on the table with his arms behind his head. "How do you want me today, Lex?"

"I'm going to defer to you. Is there anything in particular you want to work on?"

"Is napping an option?" He tosses me a rogue grin I feel in the center of my chest, and I have to tuck my chin to avoid him seeing my blush. "If not, anything that will require you putting your hands on me."

"This is a professional environment, Mitchy. Keep your dick in your pants."

"Says the girl who can't even look at me."

I roll my eyes and lift my gaze to meet his. "Better?"

"Much. I mean this in the least creepy way possible, but how about a massage then some time on the treadmill in the weight room? The strength and conditioning coaches have been working on building my speed back up, and I want to see how fast I can go today."

"I thought you hated running." I finish off the doughnut and wash my hands in the corner of the room. "How times have changed."

"I think it's because it was taken away from me. I've

missed it. I can't run in this prosthetic because it's too heavy, and I've been thinking about asking my doctor for a blade I can try. It's not hockey, but it's something."

"Really? That's awesome, Riley. It would be exciting to try something new."

"Yeah." He nods and pushes the button on his socket, waiting for the air to release. When he pops it off, he hands it to me, and I set it against the wall. "We'll see."

"Where do you want me to massage?"

"My left leg then my right one. If, ah, that doesn't gross you out."

"Why would it gross me out?"

"Because it's scarred and fucked up. The last time you, um, touched me like that was in a dark room." His throat bobs around a swallow. "You can see everything under these lights. Every mark. Every spot on my body from where they sewed me together. There's, uh, less places for me to hide in here, and I don't want you to feel uncomfortable with what I'm showing you."

"First of all, nothing about you is fucked up," I say, hoping he can hear the conviction behind my words. "And I don't care how bright it is in here. Would you prefer if I dimmed the lights? It could recreate the mood."

"No. I'm fine with it. I see my limb every day. I want to make sure you're okay with it," he says.

"I'm more than okay with it."

"Glad to hear it." He flips on his stomach and rests his arms at his side, blowing out a long breath. I grab a hot towel from the warmer and drape it over the back of his residual limb, smiling at his low groan. "That feels so fucking good."

"I haven't given anyone a massage in a while, so no making fun of how out of practice I am." I start on his left leg, working on the tendons in his hamstrings then down to his calves. "How was your night?"

We had plans to meet up yesterday, but he texted me an

hour before I was supposed to head to his place and asked to cancel. He was in a bad mood, overwhelmed after a frustrating day with his body and another adjustment at his prosthetist's office, and I agreed without a second thought.

I'm so glad I get to see him today.

I didn't realize how much I would miss him until I tried falling asleep last night. I kept getting distracted by the scent of his shampoo on the pillow he likes to sleep on. I cradled it to my chest and woke up this morning smelling like him, a fact I like way more than I should.

"I turned off my phone, did some painting, and started a new book. It was fine, but I probably would've been in a better mood if you had come over."

"Yeah, right. I'm sure I would've annoyed you."

"You never annoy me." He pauses when I move up the hem of his shorts, thumbs pressing along the lines of his muscles. "I missed you."

"I missed you too," I admit quietly, and it's scary to put that out into the universe. I never miss anyone besides my girlfriends, but when Riley's not around, his absence is noticeable. An ache in my chest carves itself out when we say goodbye after spending time together, and no matter what I do, I can't soothe the sting when he leaves. "A lot."

"Yeah?"

"Yeah."

Riley turns his hand right-side up, an invitation there. I hesitate for only a fraction of a second before I slide my palm against his and lace our fingers together. He relaxes the second our touches meet, and so do I.

He's warm and comforting, the swipe of his thumb over the curve of my knuckles a welcome display of affection.

When did I get so reliant on him making me feel good?

When did my happiness become intertwined with him being around?

When did I start smiling nonstop?

What if I never stop?

"Can I ask you a question?" Riley murmurs, and I look down at him.

"Sure."

"I want you to let me get it all out before you answer, okay?"

"Sounds like something I'm going to hate, but let's hear it."

"Hang on. I need to sit up for this." He takes his time flipping onto his back and sliding up the treatment table so we're facing each other. "Moment of honesty?"

"Yeah," I croak, afraid of what he's going to say next.

Does he not want to see me anymore?

Am I being too clingy by asking to spend time with him almost every day?

Has he noticed the shift between us, the start of something deeper than physical attraction brewing beneath the surface when we lie together, tangled up in sheets and sharing secrets we've never told anyone else?

"This friends with benefits thing has been amazing," he starts, and I'd be shocked if he couldn't hear my heart beating right now. "But what I feel for you isn't strictly physical anymore. It never was, and it was shitty of me to pretend otherwise. I-I want to go out to dinner and hold your hand in public. I want to go to bookstores together so we can argue over which books are best. I want to go to another amusement park and laugh until I cry. I want to take you out on a date—a real date—and I know that word might scare the shit out of you, but we can go slow and do things on your terms, because I'm sick of acting like I'm only interested in hanging out with you if it means I get to fuck you. I want so much more than that, and I think you might too."

The world stops moving, and I suck in a sharp breath. Riley is staring at me with gentle, kind eyes, and never, in my entire life, have I ever felt so vulnerable and off-balance, but also so seen and understood.

It's like he's staring into the depths of my soul, and if any other person on this earth said those things to me, I'd run. I'd be out the door and halfway to my car, but I can't seem to bring myself to move. I'm rooted here, in a way. Frozen in place while he waits to hear what I have to say with a patient smile and a soft pink blush on his cheeks.

"What… what would change?" I ask, voice shaking with fear. "Between us?"

"Nothing," he says automatically. "If you want things to stay the same, they'll stay the same. There's just more… heart to it all."

"Heart," I repeat. "And we can go slow?"

"As slow as you want."

"I don't know how good I'll be."

"Me either. But we can try together. If you want."

I want that more than I've ever wanted anything else, because Riley makes it sound easy and fun, but I'm terrified I'm going to mess up. I'm terrified I won't be good enough for him, and he deserves *so much good* after the shit he's been through.

"Can we still be friends if…" I trail off and wring my hands together. "If things don't work out?"

"Yes," he says. "Of course. You're my best friend, Lexi. Nothing will change that."

Every part of me that's been conditioned to shove men away and live happily ever after by myself wants to scream no. I've done just fine for so long, so why should I change things now?

But… it's *him*, and if it's going to work with anyone, it's going to be with the man who brings me doughnuts and tells me how capable I am. The man who listens to me and encourages me, and every wonderful thing he's done for me in the time we've spent together comes racing to the front of my mind. It's what makes me nod my head. What makes me huff out a laugh.

"Okay," I say, and I rewarded with his brightest smile yet. "We'll try,"

"Yeah?" he asks, and I nod again.

"Yeah," I say. "But only so we can argue about books and I can tell you why I'm right."

"What makes you think I won't let you win?"

"Because I'd be furious with you if you did."

"I know you would be." Riley tugs on my wrist, and I step close to him. "You're in charge, Lex. You're calling the shots, and I'm entirely at your mercy."

I've never had power like *this* before, and it makes me feel like I'm on top of the world. I give his shoulder a light shove, rolling my eyes when he lets out a laugh, then I pat the table.

"If that's the case, get on your stomach, Mitchell. You have work to do, and you shouldn't be flirting with the training staff. That goes against NATA's Code of Ethics."

"What the hell does that acronym mean?"

"It's the National Athletic Trainers Association. I, um, did some research when we started sleeping together regularly," I admit. "I wanted to cover my bases in case someone found out about us and tried to get me in trouble for spending time with you outside the arena."

"And?" Riley presses. "What did you find out?"

"It's all kind of vague. We're not supposed to engage in conduct that could be construed as a conflict of interest. We're also conduct ourselves in manner that doesn't compromise professional responsibilities."

"Wow." He blinks. "It's like you just threw a rulebook at me."

"I know. Sorry. I obviously didn't…" I tuck a strand of hair behind my ear. "I didn't see us getting this far because I *never* get this far with a guy, but after you took care of me when I was sick, I was curious. *Technically* you're not on the team, so *technically* I'm not breaking any rules. And nothing we're doing jeopardizes my credibility as an athletic trainer."

"Does that mean we're in the clear?"

"For now. If—when—you rejoin the team down the road, we're probably going to have to have a conversation with management, but we can tackle that as it comes."

"Darn. It would've been kind of fun to break the rules," Riley says.

"Please. You're not a rule breaker."

"I could be." The grin he flashes me is mischievous, bold. "For you."

I bite back my own laughter, not wanting him to see how much he affects me. Not wanting him to know how light I feel when he's around, how easy everything is when he smiles at me.

It feels like I've been flying for months now, and I'm terrified of finding out what happens when I land.

FORTY-THREE
RILEY

> **ME**
> I'm taking you on a date tonight, Lexi baby.

> **LEXI**
> I need a nickname for you. RiRi?

> **ME**
> That makes me sound like a dog.

> **LEXI**
> Well. You did crawl. Could I get you to bark too?

> **ME**
> Way to be a smart-ass. Guess the ropes will be getting some use tonight.

> **LEXI**
> If that's supposed to be a threat, it's not going to work on me!

> **ME**
> Clearly.

> **LEXI**
> Dinner sounds great. What should I wear?

> **ME**
> Something casual but warm. I figured we could walk.

> **LEXI**
> I'm excited.

> **ME**
> See you at 7, Armstrong.

> **LEXI**
> Looking forward to it, Mitchy.

I PACE in front of Lexi's door for three minutes before I finally decide to knock. I take a step back and wait for her to answer while I practically sweat through the hoodie I have on under my jacket.

I'm so fucking nervous.

This woman is a goddamn queen, and she can be with anyone she wants. The fact that she's picking *me* blows my mind, and I'm going to do everything in my power to prove I'm worthy of her time.

The door unlocks and flies open. I blink and Lexi is there in a pink sweater and jeans with her long dark hair framing her face, and yeah. I'm so fucking weak. I almost *whimper* when I see her because she's so beautiful.

"Hi," I say, and her smile is sly and sexy.

"Hi," she says, eyes bouncing to the flowers I'm holding. "What are those?"

"They're for you." I thrust the bouquet her way, and her

mouth pops open. She takes the flowers and holds them close to her chest. "Tulips, right?"

"Right. You remembered," she whispers, touching one of the petals. "Of course you did. Gosh. They're beautiful. Where did you find them out of bloom?"

"I pulled a few strings and might've used my name. It's not something I do frequently, but when the situation calls for it I will."

I shove my hands in my pockets and shrug, trying to look nonchalant when, really, I spent three days calling dozens of greenhouses across the Southeast to see if anyone had any tulips they could overnight me. I finally found a place in Florida, and a gruff, irritated-sounding dude assured me the flowers would be at my door by morning.

He wasn't lying, and I think I might believe in angels now.

"Do you want to come in? I'm going to put these in some water, then I'll be ready to go," she says, turning on her heel and gesturing me inside.

"Thanks." I shut the door behind me and follow her into the kitchen. I slide into a chair at her small kitchen table and watch her snip the ends of the stems and fill a vase up with water. "How was your day?"

"Busy. Two women I went to college with host a podcast about sports and women enjoying sports, and I recorded an episode with them about my favorite teams to make the NBA playoffs."

"No hockey talk?"

"No. It didn't feel right to talk about teams other than the Stars. I'm a biased fangirl through and through." She smiles at me over her shoulder. "We are going to make the playoffs though. I can feel it."

"I hope we do. The boys have been playing hard and putting in the work. Starting at the bottom of the Eastern conference but having the best record since the All-Star break is the momentum we—they—need heading into the last ten games of the season."

"And you'll be there coaching them." Lexi drops the flowers in the vase and arranges them in a neat order that doesn't look any different from before. "Am I dressed okay for tonight? I didn't want to be too fancy or too casual, and—"

"You look perfect." I stand and walk toward her so I can drop a kiss on her forehead. She wraps her arms around my waist and rests her head on my chest, and this, *this* is perfection to me: her in my hold, touching her anywhere I can reach. Listening to her let out a content sigh that tells me she likes it too. "You don't need to change a thing."

"Okay." I feel her smile against my hoodie, then she tugs on the drawstrings. "The chances are high I'm going to be stealing this sweatshirt from you too, Mitchell."

"Maybe getting you out of your clothes and into mine was my plan all along."

"You're sneaky." She kisses my jaw and pulls away, grabbing a purse and slinging it over her shoulder. "I'm ready for you to woo me on my first date ever."

"Get ready, Armstrong. I'm going to date your ass off."

TWO HOURS, a large pizza, and a couple of drinks later, we're side by side in front of a pool table at an arcade. The lighting is dim. The music is tolerable, and when Lexi grabs a cue and leans against it with a raised eyebrow, I give her a sheepish grin.

"Yes?" I ask.

"I'm surprised," she says. "You're a romantic guy. I was expecting something fancy and over the top. Book boyfriend level with a boombox on your shoulder and some groveling."

I spent hours trying to figure out where to take her, and everything I came up with didn't feel like *her*. Dinner at a restaurant on top of a hotel overlooking the city seemed too cheesy. Wandering around the museums after hours seemed too much like I was avoiding having a conversation with her. A black-tie fundraising event seemed like it would be boring as hell.

So, I decided to take her to do the things we'd do even if this *wasn't* a date. Dinner at a casual restaurant where we tried to make the most ridiculous pizza in existence before our walk to an underground arcade. And the night is young. There's plenty more on the agenda, but kicking her ass in pool is a good break in the action.

"You're a date virgin," I say. "I'm easing you into it. Being gentle, you know?"

"You're doing so good," she purrs, and I deserve a goddamn medal for not getting hard from her silky, smooth voice. "It's cute you think you're better than me at pool."

"You play?" I rack up the balls and grab my own cue. "I'm surprised."

"It's like you don't know me at all. Being good at things men think they're superior in is my quest in life."

"Care to make a bet?"

"You have my attention." Lexi leans over the edge of the table, and I'm distracted by her hand running over the felt, thinking about how much I'd like to pin her palms in place and fuck her until she screams my name. "What did you have in mind?"

I blink and clear my throat. "Another thing on my Life List." I step closer to her and slide a hand over her waist. Her sharp inhale tells me she's probably fantasizing about the same things I am, and I'm glad we're tucked away in a spot where no one can see us. "Tattoos."

"Are you going to put my name in a heart on your arm?" she teases.

"I was thinking more along the lines of the winner gets to pick what the loser puts on their body."

"Oh, those are some interesting stakes." She turns her head, a smirk pulling at her mouth. "Stipulations?"

"Nothing profane or vulgar. It has to be small—nothing bigger than a silver dollar coin. If it's something the loser really doesn't want, they're allowed a veto."

"Deal." Lexi sticks out her hand, and I shake it. "You're going down, Mitchell."

I let her break, and she sinks two stripes right off the bat. My first two turns result in not pocketing a damn thing, and I'm afraid I'm going to eat my words. Lexi tries to distract me by wiggling her ass and pulling her hair up in a high ponytail so I can see the line of her neck, but I persevere. I make six shots in a row and take the lead, laughing when she crosses her arms over her chest and pouts.

"Something wrong, Lexi baby?"

"I don't like losing. But I hate it even more when someone lets me win." She lines up a shot and misses knocking in her ball by a hair. "I'm kicking myself for being so cocky."

"Not everyone can be a winner." I sink my last ball in a corner pocket and point to the eight ball. "I'm trying for the left side pocket."

"How did you get so good at billiards?" she asks. "Weren't you too busy playing hockey to excel at anything else?"

"I was a talented child athlete with many skills." I knock the eight ball, but it spins off the edge of the table and comes to a stop in the middle of the felt. "But you can thank my dad. I traveled a lot for sports, obviously, and we'd always find a place to play no matter what city we were in. It was a good way for me to get my mind off the games I had ahead of me. When I was on the ice, I was locked in. Off the ice when I wasn't practicing, I did things other than hockey. It was sacrilegious to some of my teammates, but I think that's what helped me be as good as I used to be."

"That's smart." Lexi finally pockets another ball and

pumps her fist in the air. "And it's cute to imagine you in bars when you were eleven."

"I always ordered cheese fries and drank a Shirley Temple. I was living the dream."

"I'll say." She misses again and frowns. "You're up. This is for all the marbles."

"Left corner," I say, lining my cue up with the eight ball again. I close one eye and bite the tip of my tongue, grinning when the ball sinks straight into the pocket. "And that's the game."

"Well played, Mitchell." She puts her cue back on the rack and holds out her hand. "A valiant effort."

"And a worthy opponent." I give her palm a shake and keep our fingers interlocked. "C'mon. There's a tattoo parlor just up the road, and then we have one more stop to make after."

"This is an action-packed date. There hasn't been a dull moment."

"I aim to please, Armstrong."

The walk to the shop is quick. When we step inside the space, we're greeted and given an available slot. After filling out a shit ton of legal paperwork, the tattoo artist waves us over, and we head for the booth to the left of the shop.

"What's my punishment, sugar?" Lexi asks, grinning when I blush and run a hand through my hair. "Do I get to put your hockey number on the inside of my wrist? Maybe *Riley's girl* on my lower back?"

"All great ideas, but not on brand with who you are. And you haven't ever worn my number. Tattooing it on your body seems extreme."

"Do you want me to wear your number?"

"Seems silly now, doesn't it? I'm not going to wear a hockey jersey again. You shouldn't have to."

She hums and hops on the table. "Guess I'll have to find another Stars player I like. I wonder if Grant is available."

"No fucking way," I say, putting my hands on either side of her hips. "It's my jersey or no jersey, Lexi."

"Possessive Riley comes out. I like it." She tilts her chin back and laughs. "Fine. No one else's jersey."

"Good."

"Hey, folks. What are we getting done today? Do you want to see a sample of ideas, or do you have something in mind already?" the artist asks, and Lexi gestures my way.

"Whatever this guy decides. We just met at a bar, and he talked me into getting matching tattoos. I don't even know his name," she says, and I laugh.

"What's your ugliest tattoo?" I ask. "Something you'd be horrified to actually put on someone's body."

"I did a pile of shit once," he says. "Including flies."

"If you make me get shit on my body, I will murder you, Riley Mitchell," Lexi warns.

"No shit. I promise. I was thinking more like five hearts. Either connected or staggered above each other," I say. "And maybe a puck in the middle of them."

"Is this like a nine lives thing? Or how many hearts I've broken?"

"Do you really think I'd ask you to put something related to *a man* on your body? The five hearts are for you and the girls." I slide my hands up her thighs, and her eyes widen. "Your best friends and the loves of your life. I know they're important to you."

"That—" She bites her bottom lip and sniffs. A tear rolls down her cheek, but she wipes it away before it has time to dry. "I really like that idea."

"Yeah?"

"Yeah. It's… it's so me."

"I thought so too." I kiss her forehead. "When you're with me, Lex, I always want you to be you."

"Ah, so the stranger thing was a roleplaying bit." The artist nods and draws an outline of the design. When she gives her approval of the size and positioning, he grabs his tattoo gun, and I move out of the way. "Kinky."

Lexi huffs out a watery laugh. "Something like that."

I hold her left hand while the artist rolls up the sleeve of her sweater and tattoos the five hearts and a tiny puck right above her right elbow. The process takes less than an hour, and when he finishes, she examines the permanent ink with a wide smile.

"It's sexy," I murmur, careful when I touch the area around the marks. "I like it."

"So do I," she whispers. "It's perfect."

"Anything for you, man?" the artist asks, and Lexi lifts an eyebrow.

"You should get something. We can be tattoo twins."

"I'm not sure how five hearts would look on me. And there would be a huge fight over who each one represented. I don't have favorite teammates."

"Maverick, Hudson, Liam, Grant and… dare I say Ethan?" Lexi fills in for me, and I smile.

"Spot on, Armstrong."

"What about a tiny roller coaster? It could have a double meaning: something crossed off your list, yeah, but also a representation of life. Its ups and downs. Highs and lows. But you always pull into the station at the end, ready to ride again."

"Wow." I drag my thumb across my bottom lip, thinking. "That was deep as shit."

"Right?"

It could also commemorate the most perfect day I've had in a while. Our trip to Coney Island awakened something in me, and I wouldn't mind having the memory of it on my body for the rest of my life.

"Let's do it." I slip off my jacket and tug off my hoodie, laughing when Lexi grabs the sweatshirt and holds it to her chest. "I'll get it in the same spot as you so we really can be twins."

My tattoo takes a little longer, and when the artist puts a protective film over it, I turn my arm to the side to admire it.

"It looks great," Lexi says. "The perfect size."

"I can take a picture of them side by side," the artist says. "If you want."

"Yes, please!" She hands over her phone and lines our arms up. "I need a photo to remember this date by."

"You're not going to remember it by the art we just put on our bodies?" I ask, and she sticks her tongue out at me.

I give the artist a thousand bucks, which is way too much money for the cost of the pieces, but Lexi is smiling nonstop. She keeps snapping photos of the tiny hearts, and I'd pay a thousand more just to keep her happy like this.

"Ready for the last stop?" I ask, stealing my hoodie back and pulling it on.

"I don't see how tonight gets any better, but yeah. I am," she says, looping her arm through mine as we step onto the sidewalk. "Does it involve sex toys?"

"What?" I sputter. "No, it does not involve sex toys."

"You never know with you, Mitchy. I didn't think I'd find ropes in your dresser, but here we are."

"Okay, fair, but there are no sex toys scheduled for the rest of the night."

"Bummer. Whatever else you have planned is just as good, I'm sure."

"I'm starting to think you like busting my balls," I say.

"Starting to think that? Oh, Riley." Lexi flashes me a smile. "You're so naive."

We get to the ice cream shop, and she lights up. She orders a large cup of cookies and cream and I get a chocolate cone, making sure to grab a stack of napkins for us. We shuffle back outside and sit next to each other on a bench, taking a few bites before we talk again.

"This is the best date I've ever been on," she says.

"Isn't it the only date you've been on?"

"Technically? Yes. But it's still the best one. I don't remember the last time I had such a good time out with a guy."

"What do you mean?"

"All the socialization was to make sure they weren't a serial killer before going back to their place." She swallows down a bite of her ice cream and pauses. "No one's ever asked me questions about myself. No one has ever wanted to know."

"Do you mean how you're allergic to bees and you like cookies and cream ice cream the most, but only if it has lots of Oreo pieces in it?" I nudge her knee with mine. "I want to know these things."

"Even the boring stuff? Like that my favorite color is orange?"

"You're my best friend, Lexi. Of course I want to know all of that."

"I'm not glad you lost your leg and went through a world of pain, but I'm so glad our paths crossed in the way they did." She puts her head on my shoulder and sighs. "The girls might be the loves of my life, but you're my best friend too, Riley."

I've been broken for months. Half of who I used to be physically and mentally, but when I'm with her, it feels like I'm on my way to being whole again. Every laugh of hers is a stitch that sews the busted-up, ugly parts of me back together. Every smile is a balm to the aches that linger around, and little by little, I'm on my way to being who I used to be.

For a long time, I thought I wouldn't know what to do without hockey in my life, and now I have it figured out. I have a new purpose besides the sport I love. Something bigger and more important than hitting a puck and lacing up my skates. I can have two favorite things, because it involves proving to Lexi every goddamn day she's worthy of being treated right, worthy of being told she's special and brilliant and beautiful, and I won't stop until there's not an ounce of doubt in her mind that she's one in eight billion. One of a kind, my favorite person, and the woman I'm falling in love with.

So many things have been almost impossible for me since the night my life changed, but Lexi? Lexi is the easiest part of every day.

I turn to kiss the top of her head, everything in me calm and settled. "You want to come back to my place?"

"Yeah." Her nod is vigorous, certain, and I'm grinning like a goddamn fool. "I do."

"Today was a good day," I murmur.

"They're all good days with you, Riley," she whispers, and I hold that as close to chest as tight as I can.

FORTY-FOUR
LEXI

GIRLS JUST WANT TO HAVE FUN(DAMENTAL RIGHTS) AND GOOD SEX

ME
Do you like my new tattoo?

PIPER
Oooh, that's cute!

MADELINE
It's so tiny! I love it!

MAVEN
Was this a drunk decision, or is there meaning behind it?

ME
I lost a bet with Riley and had to get a tattoo that he picked out. He decided on five hearts which represent our group of friends. Because you all are the loves of my life.

EMMY

You fucking bitch.

Why are you making me cry?

PIPER

Oh my GOD. Lexi!!!! That is so sweet!! I love you all so much!!

MAVEN

Okay, I'm obsessed with it too, but are we glossing over the fact that you and Riley are making bets now?? What else are you two doing?

ME

I don't kiss and tell. Xoxo.

PIPER

Oh my FUCKING god. You cannot leave us hanging like that.

MADELINE

Does that mean what I think it means?

EMMY

I will literally come to your apartment and force it out of you.

MAVEN

You really are a bitch!!!!

RILEY'S BED is just as comfortable as I remember it being. So is the big purple T-shirt he gave me to slip on before and I curled up next to him with a book I picked off his shelf. There's one in his lap too, and I smile when he drapes an arm around me.

"Is this our life now? In bed by eleven and reading side by side?" I ask. "There goes my youth."

"It's the perfect night." Riley stifles a yawn and opens his paperback. "I've never been a big partier or someone who likes to go out. The athlete lifestyle isn't for me."

"You're wasting away your mid-twenties with someone who uses retinol. That's perfect?"

"Will you stop with the self-deprecating jabs?" He pinches my side, and I squeal. "I want to be here, and I want to be here with you. Deal with it, Armstrong."

I grin and bury my face in his chest.

I want to be here with him, too, and tonight was absolutely perfect. Fun beyond my wildest dreams, and I couldn't have dreamed up a better date if I tried.

And when he told me his idea for my tattoo, I wanted to burst into tears. I think I might've fallen a little bit in love with him, and the realization of my feelings is making my head spin. It's making me want to be honest, to share parts of myself I've never shared with a man before, and it's both fucking *scary* and exciting, too.

"Riley," I say, pulling away from his bare chest so I can look at him. "I want to tell you something."

"Okay." He puts his book down and gives me his full attention. "What's up?"

"You once asked me why I don't date, and given how things are going between us, I-I want to be honest with you about my past. About why I am the way I am, because you've been so honest with me."

"I'm all ears," he says, and I take a deep breath. "And I promise this is a safe space."

"My dad left when I was younger. I don't remember much about why he walked out on me and my mom—I might've been six or seven at the time—just that he never came back. As I got older, I started to crave attention from men because I wasn't getting any of it at home. I learned very quickly boys are visual and physical creatures, and kissing them, being intimate with them, was a surefire way to get what I wanted."

"I'm sorry to hear he left," Riley says softly, and he takes my hand in his. "That must've been tough."

"It was hard on my mom, but I saw how strong she was. She never put her trust in a man again, and I followed that attitude into my early twenties. It was sex, and just sex. There wasn't a chance they could walk out on me, because I walked out on them before anyone got attached." I swallow the lump in my throat and continue. "When I was twenty-four, I met a guy, and we hit it off. One night turned into two, then three. We kept coming back for more, and he made me feel *good*. Appreciated. It was mostly physical, but we'd fall asleep talking on the phone. We'd text all day, every day. It lasted a long time—over a year and a half—and it was the first time I thought I might have judged men too harshly."

"What happened?"

"He told me he had to go out of town for work, and something in my gut told me he was lying. I did a deep dive into his social media and found out he was married with kids. As fate would have it, the next day, a message from his wife popped up in my inbox. She accused me of being a homewrecker. Of being a whore who only wanted what she can't have, and she told me no man would ever want to date me. I was a temporary fix, a vessel for their pleasure and incapable of connecting with another human on a deeper level." I pause to take a breath and sneak a glance at him, hoping he's not about to bolt out of here. "And in a way... I think she was right."

"Whoa. Hold up. This guy was hiding a wife and children from you and *you* got blamed? That's fucking bullshit," Riley says, his rage on full display. "You wouldn't have done that if you knew he wasn't available."

"I like to think I wouldn't. I've always been a girl's girl—you know, a woman who supports other women? Anyway, it *hurt* to know I betrayed someone, even unknowingly. Ever since then, I've been adamant about not letting things get too far with a man. The second I feel like I'm getting attached or veering down a road that leads to something other than mindless sex, I get out." I pause and look up at him. "Until you."

"Come here, sweetheart," he murmurs, opening his arms, and I move to him like I'm being physically pulled his way. I climb in his lap, careful to avoid putting my weight on his residual limb, and stay there, my heartbeat syncing with his. "Thank you for telling me all of that. I know it doesn't mean much and I know you might not believe me—not yet—but I promise you can trust me. I promise I won't ever treat you like you're just a… a thing. Like you're not this incredible, magnificent woman. And yeah, you've made some mistakes, but who the fuck hasn't? I don't care about how many people you've slept with. I don't care about the guys who came before me, because I'm the one here with you right now. And I'm so fucking lucky."

"I haven't told the girls that story," I admit. "I always brush it off when they ask why I don't date and throw in a joke about men not being shit."

"We aren't shit."

I chuckle, then let out a sigh. "I don't want them to look at me differently because of things I've done in the past, especially now that most of them are married. I'd never—a thought like that hasn't ever crossed my mind, and I'd give up talking to men forever if it meant getting to keep them."

"They wouldn't look at you any different. I know they wouldn't." Riley rests his chin on top of my head, and it's freeing to put this out in the open. To let him hear the secret I've kept locked away for years, too afraid I'd be burned at the stake if it ever got out. "You're so strong, Lexi, and I'm so sorry someone took advantage of you. I don't know if it means much, but you've had my attention for years."

"Please." I squeeze his arm. "I have not."

"You don't believe me?" He untangles our limbs and frowns down at me. "Ask me what my tattoo means."

"The roller coaster? I know what it means. I was there when you—"

"No. The constellation."

I suck in a sharp breath and drop my gaze to the small cluster of stars on his left arm. I haven't been able to figure out what it might represent.

I lick my lips. Anticipation claws at the base of my spine, and with a shaky hand, I trace the design.

"What does your tattoo mean?" I whisper, and the room is so quiet, I can hear a car horn beeping from all the way across the street.

"It's the stars in the night sky the day I stepped foot into the arena for the first time. And, consequently, the day I met you."

"What?"

"Yeah. It was a big day for me." He folds his hand over mine and guides me to each individual star. There are probably close to two dozen of them, and my heart lurches in my chest. "I signed my ELC. A pretty girl said hello to me. You had a ribbon in your hair, and your smile was the brightest thing I had ever seen."

"You remember what I was wearing?"

"Down to your high-top sneakers. I wasn't kidding, Lexi. You've been on my mind from the second I locked eyes with you across the ice, and I'd had done just about anything to get you to look at me back then. To get you to *keep* looking at me."

"The girls would always tell me you had a crush on me, but I always shrugged it off."

"A crush?" Riley laughs like it's the most ridiculous thing in the world. "Please. There's a reason why I haven't dated anyone since I got to DC. I know not a goddamn one of them would ever compare to you."

Hell.

It's the sweetest, most wonderful thing I've ever heard, and I guess I must be a romantic now, because I'm climbing back into his lap. Straddling his waist and kissing his cheek, his neck and the soft curve of his mouth.

Knowing I've had his attention even when I was busy trying to get it from somewhere else makes me feel like a fool, like I've wasted *so many good moments* I could've had with him, but a part of me heals with his words. He's looking at my baggage. Sticking out his hand, saying *here. I can help.*

I've never felt safe enough with a man to let my guard down. I've never felt like I'm worthy enough to stop running and rest my head, but with Riley, I'm opening the gate. I'm inviting him in, asking him to stay. And a sob works its way up my throat when he hugs me tight.

"Sorry," I whisper. "This is a lot for me to process. You… you have the day we met tattooed on your body. All those times I looked at it during our sessions, and I had no idea."

"Now you do." He wipes my tears away with his thumbs and smiles. "And it's not just about you, Armstrong. It also represents the day I became a professional athlete. Let's not forget that."

"Ass." I nudge his shoulder, but he grabs my hand. He kisses my knuckles then my wrists and puts my palm against his cheek. "Sorry for being selfish for a minute."

God.

Is this what love feels like?

Like the first bit of sunshine peeking through the clouds after a rainstorm? Like a warm blanket on a cold day? Like a million stars lighting up a night sky? Like I might not be able to breathe if he isn't around, and like I'm taking my first deep breath in years when he's close?

I've never felt anything like this before. I've never tried to define it, never tried to wrangle it in so I could accept it, but here I am. Rushing toward it with open arms, desperate to yell out *I think I want to give this a chance!*

"Lexi." Riley kisses me again and brushes his nose against mine. He cups my face with both of his hands, and the world shakes with his heavy exhale. "How did I get so lucky to find you?"

I don't know how to answer that, so I kiss him back. I let him pull my shirt over my head and lay me on the mattress. When he holds himself above me, I tug off my underwear and look up at him. It's like I'm seeing him for the first time, shimmering and bright, and he's the most beautiful thing in existence.

"I want you to fuck me," I whisper. "Like I'm yours."

"Yeah?" He drags his fingers over my breasts then dances his touch down my body. "What else do you want?"

"I want you to use the ropes. I want to you to have complete control over me."

"Are you sure?"

I nod. "Positive. There's not anyone I trust more than you."

"I hate to make you do this, but it's going to be much faster if you get the rope." Riley gestures at his lower half. He took his prosthetic off when we got back to his place, and his crutches are on the other side of the room. "Do you mind?"

"Not at all." I slip out from under him and grin as I pad over to his dresser. I pull out the rope and walk back to the bed, handing it over. "Here you go."

"I'm only going to use it when I get you off. I want your hands to be free when I fuck you," he says.

"Okay." I climb back on the bed and hold out my wrists, smiling when he makes quick work of wrapping them together with a single column knot. I tug on the rope to test the resistance, a soft groan leaving me as he guides me onto the pillows and spreads my legs. "*Fuck*, Riley."

"Don't move," he tells me. "I won't let you come if you do."

I bob my head and close my eyes, resisting the urge to lift

my hips the second his knuckles graze over my entrance. He's teasing me, testing me, and I have a feeling I might fail miserably.

Riley grips my knee and pushes one finger inside me. A louder groan escapes me this time, and it takes everything in me to not squirm on the sheets.

"Stay still, Lexi baby. You want to come, don't you?"

"More than anything." I whine when he adds a second finger, the stretch blissful and perfect in a way only he can manage. "I can't believe you've been looking at me for years."

"Looking and looking and not touching. But I'm touching you now." A third finger, and an even more delicious stretch. I'm full, *needy*, and the thumb he presses on my clit almost makes me lose my mind. "Because you're mine."

"I want more, Riley."

"What do you want? Use your words."

"Your tongue," I blurt, not caring how desperate I sound. He's never shamed me for being so vocal, and I want him to know I'm happy for any and all of his attention. "Please."

"So polite." The weight on the mattress shifts, and I open my eyes. I find Riley between my legs, his other thumb stroking my knee and his mouth trailing hot kisses up my thigh. "You know I'll give you anything you want."

I cry out when his tongue flicks my clit, and the heavy arm he drapes across my stomach only makes me want to move more. I'm trapped with nowhere to go, nothing to do but sink into the bliss I know he can bring me.

He buries his tongue inside me and my mind goes blank, the slick glide of his fingers matching the rhythm of his mouth, and I can't take it anymore. I know I don't stand a chance of lasting long, and I pull on the ropes so hard, I know my wrists are going to be red for days.

"Lexi," he warns. "Don't move."

"I'm sorry. It's too much. I'm so close. You're—can you curl your fingers—*fuck*. Yeah. Just like that."

"I can't wait to taste you. Best part of my day."

"I didn't know you had an affinity for female orgasms," I pant.

"I don't." He pinches my hip—hard—and I whimper. "Just yours. Ride my face, Lex, and take what you need."

Just yours.

Because he hasn't looked at anybody except me in *years*.

How many times has he fallen asleep dreaming about me?

How many times has he touched himself to the thought of me?

How many times have we been in adjoining hotel rooms where I've been using a vibrator and he's been on the other side of the wall? Did he hear me? Did he listen?

A swell of pleasure builds inside me.

I reach for it, aching for release as I grind against his face. He answers me with a low moan that propels me forward, the understanding that he's enjoying this just as much as I am and he's not even being touched.

"I'm going to—"

"*Mine*," he growls, and the word and what it means makes me explode into a thousand pieces.

Riley is unrelenting, his fingers and tongue staying in me until I'm a writhing, squirming mess on the sheets with my legs tipped open wide and my arms loose above my head. He only stops by kissing me everywhere with his wet mouth, marking me and showing off how well he knows my body.

He works his way up my legs and my stomach. Across my ribs and my breasts where he stays for a few minutes, sucking on my nipples and making me wet all over again. He ghosts his mouth over mine and I arch my back off the mattress, needing him like I need air.

"Shit," I whisper when he kisses me. I taste myself on him, and his tongue bumps against mine so I don't miss any of the aftermath of what he did to me. "You are unbelievable."

He brushes the hair off my forehead, peeling it away from

the dried sweat clinging to my skin. "I'm going to let your wrists free, okay?"

"Okay," I rasp.

The second the ropes are off me, he's helping me sit up. He's reaching for the nightstand and handing over a glass of water so I can take a sip. He's kissing my hands and flexing my fingers to make sure I didn't lose circulation, and this fluttery, light feeling in the center of my chest has to be something so much stronger than lust.

I'm certain of it.

FORTY-FIVE
RILEY

IT TAKES Lexi a few minutes to calm down after her orgasm. She seems out of it, floating in some distant dreamland when I ease her onto the pillows and find her smiling up at me.

"You're so good at that," she mumbles, voice thick with exhaustion. She holds up her hands and looks at her wrists, her smile shifting to proud. "I'm doing better with the ropes, aren't I?"

"You are." I prop myself up on an elbow next to her, imagining what it would be like if I tied her ankles to the bed posts. If I made her stay like that until I was ready to have her and how long she would last. "I'm so proud of you."

"Thank you." She yawns and trails her touch down to the waistband of my pajama bottoms. "Take these off, please."

"You're literally falling asleep."

"I am not falling asleep, and I was promised a fuck. That's what I want."

I burst out laughing. "We can rest for a minute."

"I don't want to rest." Lexi shimmies out from beside me and yanks my pants down. My cock springs free, and she wraps her hand around my length. "I want you, Riley."

Who am I to tell her no when she's spitting on the head of

my cock and stroking me up and down in a torturous, cruel way like she's toying with me?

"Okay." I grip the sheets around me, my fingers curling into a fist. "You can have me."

"What position do you want to try tonight?"

"Something new." My hips buck when she swirls her tongue over my slit and laps up the pre-cum I know I'm leaking from watching her get off. "Can you get on all fours for me?"

"*Oh*." Her eyes widen, and she's quick to release me from her hold. "This is one of my favorites. We haven't done this before."

"I wasn't sure I could balance on just my left leg." I wait for her to get on her knees and put her hands out in front of her. Her ass lifts up in the air and I put a hand on her lower back, keeping her there. "But I've been practicing."

"Practicing? Are you fucking your pillows when I'm not here, Riley?" she asks, gasping when my other hand reaches out and closes around her throat. "Harder."

My fingers squeeze her windpipe, and she rocks her hips back, ass brushing against my cock. I take it as confirmation the pressure isn't too much, and I stay there for a count of ten, releasing her and wrapping her hair around my wrist when I let go.

"God. You take everything I give you, don't you?" I ask.

"Everything," she repeats, her cheek against the sheets. She turns her chin toward me so she can see, and there's a challenge behind her smile. "And more."

Lexi is perfect in every way, but she's goddamn exquisite in the bedroom. I couldn't dream up a better version of her if I tried as I drag the head of my cock through her pussy lips. She's still wet and I lean forward, almost folding my body over hers. It's the only way I can stay upright, and her hand resting on my left thigh gives me the added balance I didn't have when I tried some of these moves by myself.

"I like this angle." I thrust my hips and push inside her, rubbing a small circle on her back when she cries out. "I get to watch your ass bounce and I can get nice and deep. And I can touch your throat again if you want. You wear my hand as a necklace so well."

"C-can you do it right before you're all the way in?" she asks, the words racing out of her.

I nod even though she can't see me and snap my hips forward to bury another inch of my length. I'm thorough as I fuck her, pulling all the way out before rocking back in and finding a rhythm that gets progressively rougher with every thrust.

It's so easy to get lost in her. It's like time stands still with every one of her gasps, with every sharp graze of her fingernails, and it doesn't take long before I'm snaking my hand up her chest. Before I'm holding onto her neck and squeezing at the same time I drive into her, all the way to the hilt.

Her moan is muffled against the sheets, and I grab her chin and force her to turn her head so I can look at her.

"Every inch, Lexi baby," I say, and she tightens around me. "There you go. You're doing so well."

I hope one day I'm able to last longer than a few minutes with her. I have the stamina; she just feels *too fucking good* to try to hold back. She's wet, *hot*, and she does some sort of roll of her hips that has me seeing stars.

I bite into her shoulder and lose myself in her, knowing there will be plenty of times to fuck her nice and slow. To make love to her in the tender way I'm not sure she's ever experienced, but right now, it's nothing but raw need. It's animalistic and sweaty and loud, the sound of my hips slapping into hers filling the room.

"Harder," she begs. "My throat. My pussy. All of it."

I grunt in response, my rational thoughts deteriorating as she reaches her hand through her legs and cups my balls. My glasses slide off my face and land god knows where. She's a blurry, fuzzy shape in front of me, but I don't care. My chest presses into her back, my weight unintentionally resting entirely on her, but she doesn't protest. She doesn't fight back, instead meeting me thrust for thrust with the slam of her hips until she clenches around my cock like she never wants to let go.

"Lex." I groan. "I can only go through reciting so many presidents before I lose my fucking mind. How are you this tight? I just fucked you with my fingers."

"It's like my body knows it needs you," she pants, and I shutter my eyes closed. If I look down at her and see the sweat rolling down her back and the easy way I slide back into her pussy, it's game over. "I think I can come a second time. Is it okay if I—"

"I'd watch you fuck yourself with a toy if it meant getting another orgasm out of you. You do whatever you need to get there, sweetheart. This is a collaborative effort."

Her laugh is light, beautiful. Her hand bumps against mine, and I know she's touching her clit. Circling it in the way she likes, and her breathing hitches up half an octave.

"I want you to come in me." She gasps, rocking forward with a particularly hard thrust. "I want you to fill me up, Riley. I love your cum."

Jesus Christ and Satan too.

There's no way in hell I'm going to heaven after hearing that, because my balls tighten. Pleasure races up my spine and I let out an ear-splitting groan as I fall apart, my cock pulsing inside her until I don't have a fucking drop left.

She loves my cum, I think from some far-off realm in my rotten brain. *And I love her.*

Lexi tumbles over the edge next after she rubs her clit against the sheets, and I hold her in place until I know I'm finished doing exactly what she asked. Every part of my body is sensitive and alive, and I collapse forward when she wiggles out from underneath me and flops onto her stomach.

"Ten out of ten. Five stars. Would fuck again," I say, finding my glasses and putting them back on. She takes my hand in hers and I open an eye when I feel her moving my palm over her body. "I thought you finished. Do you need my fingers?"

"No." She guides my fingers to her pussy and works my pointer finger inside her. "I want you to feel what you did to me."

"Holy hell." I scramble across the sheets so I can get a better look, and I *can* feel what I did to her. The warm, sticky mess I made, and when I pull my finger out, I smear the cum clinging to my knuckle on the inside of her thigh. "Your sexuality is such a turn on."

"Some people have told me I'm too bold." Lexi brings my finger to her mouth and closes her lips around it. I whimper when she drags her tongue up to the tip, sucking the digit dry. "I like that I can be myself with you."

"You'll never be too bold. Ever. And if there's something you want to try, tell me, Lex. Because chances are, I want to try it too."

"Look how compatible we are, Mitchy." She rolls onto her side then hesitates, something weighing on her mind. "Are you my boyfriend now?"

I don't dare move a muscle, afraid this might be a trap. I suck in a slow, intentional breath, careful as I ask my next question even though my heart is about to beat out of my chest with excitement.

"Do you… want me to be your boyfriend? We don't have to put a label on anything."

"I said I'd give this a try, and that means calling you my boyfriend. Fuck buddy doesn't feel right anymore. Not when you do all these nice things for me."

"No." I tuck a piece of loose hair behind her ear. I'm probably grinning like a goddamn fool. "It doesn't."

"What do we do now?"

"We've had sleepovers before, Lex." I laugh. "Did you forget all the times I've fallen asleep at your apartment?"

"Yeah, at my apartment. I've never slept over at a boyfriend's place before. This is new territory for me."

"Okay, well, it's the exact same as it is at your place. And the other times you've dozed off here. Except my bathroom floors are heated, and I'm going to make us a grilled cheese after we take a bath."

"Really?" Lexi lights up. "We have to be careful with our tattoos. I don't want to ruin it already."

"We'll keep our arms over our heads. It's going to be great." I tug her toward me and kiss her. She swipes her tongue across my bottom lip and I open my mouth, the aftertaste of my cum still lingering on her tongue. "There are going to be french fries, too."

"I'm still thinking about that pizza we ordered earlier. The server probably thought we were high. Two types of onions, three types of peppers, and four types of meat? There's going to be a Reddit thread about us tomorrow."

I laugh and close my eyes. "Always have to keep them guessing is what I say."

"That's a good motto to have." She touches my chest, and I relax under the soft brush of her fingers against my skin. "Riley?"

"Hm?"

"Today was a really good day. And the best date I've ever had. I… I can't wait to see what we do on our second date."

"A really good day," I agree. "But they're all good days with you, Lexi baby."

FORTY-SIX
RILEY

> **ME**
> I think I'm ready to get back on the ice.

> **LEXI**
> Yeah?

> **ME**
> Yeah. Can that be our session today?

> **LEXI**
> Of course. Should I ask the guys to come?

> **ME**
> Not this time. I want to do this by myself. And with you.

> **LEXI**
> Meet you at the arena in an hour?

> **ME**
> See you there.

I DECIDED on hockey pants instead of jeans for my second attempt at skating, and I'm hoping if I dress the part, I'll be able to *do* the part.

Wishful fucking thinking, probably, after how disastrous last time was.

I've gone through the list of meditation exercises Dr. Ledlow gave me at my most recent therapy session, and I'm trying to visualize myself on the ice. I'm remembering what I looked like and how it felt when I was *good* at skating, but I'm not sure the positive reinforcements are going to stick.

"Hi," Lexi calls out from the bench, and I smile at the sound of her voice. "Sorry I'm late. With two weeks left in the regular season, everyone needs extra taping and foam rolling."

"What the hell are you carrying?" I point to the large bag in her arms. "Is there a body in there?"

"Something better." She sighs in relief when she sits next to me. "I did more research on the AHL player who had his leg amputated after going into cardiac arrest."

"Oh, yeah." I remember her mentioning him back at our first meeting with the team after my accident. I haven't let myself look him up, too worried if I do, I'll start creating unrealistic expectations for myself. I'll start comparing myself to him, and I've never liked putting myself up against other people. "Is *he* in the bag?"

"No, but the prosthetic that's identical to the one he uses is." Lexi pulls the trash bag off the top of the hidden object and throws it on the floor. "I don't know why I didn't think of it before. Once I did, I made some phone calls. I talked to some very smart people who outfit Paralympian speed skaters specifically, and they got to work. It's a leg that attaches to a streamlined skate blade. You won't have to lug around your heavy walking prosthetic, and this gives you more range of motion."

"Holy shit." I examine the prosthetic and lift it up. "It's so light."

"Right? Fair warning: it probably won't fit perfectly today. I went off your other prosthetic measurements, so we're probably going to have to do some adjusting, but I figured we'd try."

Excitement buzzes through me, and Lexi waits for me to strip down to my briefs. I pop off my usual leg and replace it with the lighter, more agile one with a flexible liner. I lean forward and turn my hips side to side, trying to get used to the feel and shape of the new addition.

The socket isn't as hard and rigid as what I'm used to, and it makes bending the knee easier. The pylon attached to the socket is slightly thinner, and at the bottom, instead of a foot, it's an attachable Tuuk blade, exactly what I'd find at the bottom of a skating boot.

"What do you think?" she asks after I've taken a few minutes to twist and turn.

"I'm not sure. I feel naked. I'm so used to dragging that clunky thing around, and it feels like I'm forgetting something. It also looks funny."

"I brought you some gym shorts. I know you were going to use your hockey pants, but these are going to allow for more movement." Lexi pulls a pair of black athletic shorts out of the bag next, and I snort. "Is something funny, Mitchy?"

"What else do you have in there?" I ask, accepting the shorts and slipping on my hoodie.

"Nothing you're going to get now." She takes off her skate guards and stands. "Want to take it for a spin?"

I stare out at the ice and take a deep breath. The quiet arena has become a welcome place for me lately. Even though I haven't laced up my skates and done so much as a lap around the rink since my epic fail of a first attempt, just being out here settles every racing thought in my head.

Today feels less monumental than the first time.

There's no fanfare. There's no one around to watch me

fail except Lexi, and she's seen me fail plenty of times. I've failed more times than I've succeeded, and she's stuck around.

I stand and hold onto the boards, already knowing I'm in a much better headspace than I was. I'm stronger both mentally and physically, and I nod, ready to give this thing another fucking shot.

"Do you think you can hold my hand?" I ask, and I don't care how weak it might sound. I can't do this without her. She's been there every step of my journey, and if *this* is the way to get back to doing what I love, I need her by my side. "Please?"

"Gosh, Mitchy. Stop flirting with me."

Lexi smiles and passes through the gate, holding out both her hands. I put my left skate on the ice first, then my right, exhaling when my legs shake. We stand there for a minute, stationary as I test out the weight and balance of the foreign prosthetic.

"Okay." I give her a nod, and she wraps an arm around my waist. She holds my left hand in hers and pushes off, starting us down the straightaway. "Holy shit."

"Does something hurt? The doctor said your residual limb might be uncomfortable in the new liner and socket. I brought some body oil if you need lubrication and—"

"I feel like I'm fucking flying." I glance down. I'm steady on both skates, blades pointed straight ahead, and I roll my shoulders back. "This was the missing piece."

"Yeah?" Lexi says, and her hold around my waist loosens. She grips my hip and lets out a squeal when I'm the one to push off the ice and move us forward. "Okay, speedster. Let's remember you don't have any protective equipment on and this is your first time using—"

She breaks off with a chuckle when I round the first corner, adrenaline pumping in my blood. I can't explain it, but this new equipment feels *natural*, like my leg is really there and it's the one doing the work, not relying on a piece of machinery. I'm balanced, centered. It's easier to make the turns, and my range of motion stretches wider than last time.

"It's so light. Nimble. Feels like it can support my weight better, too," I say.

"Do you want me to let go?" she asks. "I don't *want* to let go, but do you want to give it a try by yourself?"

"Okay." I swallow, throat thick with emotion as she carefully detaches herself from me. "Just one lap."

I take off, my body leaning into the prosthetic with all of my weight as I increase my speed. I wobble once or twice when my right skate gets stuck under me, but it's snappy. Easier to pick up and fucking *go*, and one lap turns into two. By lap number three I'm drenched in sweat, exerting myself in a way I haven't since last June, and I don't know if I want to laugh or cry.

On lap number four, I try skating backward. I lose my momentum, my left leg giving out from under me, and I cackle when my ass hits the ice. Lexi races over, touching my head and my shoulder, and I grab her hand so I can kiss the tops of her fingers.

"I'm fine," I pant. "Got a little showboaty there. I deserved to have my ass handed to me for going too fast too soon."

"Give me feedback. How's the weight and the dynamics of it? Does your limb fit in the socket?"

"I notice there's a touch of extra space. I'm rubbing against the liner when I get going, but when I'm moving more slowly, I can't tell. Holy fuck." I put my hands on the ice, not caring my palms are going numb, and stare down at the blade attachment. "This is fucking incredible, Lexi."

"I was hesitant to reach out to a new prosthetist. What you use in your day-to-day life is perfect, and your gait is exactly what it needs it to be. After I learned about a company that solely designs prosthetic limb attachments for athletes, I figured it was worth a shot. The doctor told me he's listened to your story, and he's honored to hopefully be a step in your journey. I told him I'd film you on the ice and send it his way. Maybe I can share it with the social media team too, so they can post it on the Stars' official accounts."

I roll my lips together.

This is far from a comeback.

I'm not donning a jersey anytime soon.

I can't make it more than a lap without getting winded and my upper body is still flailing around in preparation of a wipeout, but it's step one. A peek into what my post-recovery career as a professional hockey player might look like, and if it inspires other athletes or a kid out there who wants to give up because they look a little different than how they used to, I've done something good for the world.

"Okay," I say slowly, standing. "I'll let you record me, but I want to do something else first."

"Anything," she says automatically, and I gesture to the bench.

"Can you FaceTime my dad? I want him to see me skate. My passcode is 0813, and he should be near the top of my call log."

Lexi smiles and heads for my bag, riffling through the extra clothes I brought while I do another slow lap, coming to a stop in front of her. She holds up the phone so it faces me, and when the call connects, my dad's face fills the screen.

"Riley?" He squints and leans away from the camera. "Hey, son."

"Hi, Dad." I grin and put my hands on my hips. "Guess what?"

"What?"

"I'm fucking skating."

"No." Dad sits up in his recliner and fumbles with the glasses on top of his head. He shoves them up his nose and squints again. "You're fucking with me."

I look over the top of the phone and wink at Lexi before I

take off again, hugging the curve of the rink like I've done millions of times before. I drag my fingers across the ice, a holler and a laugh falling from me as I change directions mid-push, finishing the rest of the lap backward and with my head held high.

"Holy shit," Dad whistles. "And look at that blade. How does it work?"

"Attaches to the pylon." I hold onto the boards and lift my right leg so he can get a better look. "It's only a blade, not a skate, and it's so lightweight."

"Wow. Where'd you get that? It's a genius piece of equipment."

"Lexi." I take the phone from her and flip the camera around so we're both in the shot. "My athletic trainer."

"Hi, Mr. Mitchell," she says with a wave, and my dad's knowing smirk has me six seconds away from ending our call. "It's nice to meet you."

"And you. Are you the one who's been keeping Riley in line?" Dad asks.

"Yes, sir. We've been working together since September, and he's come a long way." Lexi puts a hand on my shoulder, and I don't miss the way my dad's smile grows. "I'm so proud of him."

"You and me both. Get some footage so I can show your mother. She's going to be so angry she missed this," he says.

"I'm going to do a lot of recording, and I'll make sure Riley sends it your way," Lexi adds. "Everyone should see this."

"I'm going to do another lap or two, Dad. I'll call you later," I say.

"Sounds good. Nice to meet you, Lexi. And Ri? I'm so proud of you."

I smile and end the call. Lexi is looking at me, and I join her on the bench.

"I'm so happy for you, Riley," she says.

"I'm happy too. And, hey. You were moving pretty quick out there when you were helping me along. When did you get so fast?"

"Oh." Lexi blushes and knocks my knee with hers. "I wanted to be ready to join you if and when you wanted to get back on the ice, so I've, um, been skating with Maverick and Hudson a couple times a month. I can go backward—but I'm not great at it—and I know how to come to a complete stop too."

"You did that for me?"

"All of this is for you." She gestures at the rink then down to my leg. "I'll make a hundred calls if it means finding something to get you back to the sport you love. I'll stay here every day after practice with you if it means helping you feel closer and closer to who you were before. I'll cheer you on even if you fall on your ass three hundred times in a row, because that smile of yours when you were out there was the greatest thing I've ever seen in my entire life."

"I spent weeks wishing I could go back to who I was before the accident," I start. "My new body didn't feel right. *I* wasn't right, and I was so fucking depressed. But if someone popped out of a time machine right now and offered me the chance to go back to the old Riley, the chance to have my old life back, I wouldn't take it. I might be down a leg. My spirit might be fucking bloodied and bruised, but look at what I have now: the opportunity to spread awareness about the need for accessible prosthetics for young athletes. The best friends a guy could ask for, who I'm closer with than before. And you. I have you, and that's the best thing of all."

"This is *not* supposed to be a sappy rom-com moment. It's supposed to be an adrenaline-filled workout session that leaves you in a tired heap on the ice because you've pushed yourself so hard. We can cross another thing off your Life List." Lexi wipes under her eyes then grabs a fistful of my hoodie. I laugh when she brings her mouth to mine, smiling when she kisses me once, then twice. "I'm glad I have you too."

"You know, Lex," I murmur, running my wet hand through her hair. She doesn't seem to mind. "I'm starting to think you might be the one who likes me."

"You have no idea how much I like you, Mitchy," she whispers back. "Even I can't comprehend it."

"Enough of this sappy shit," I say, and her exhale is a soft puff of a laugh against my cheeks. "Want to race?"

"You, the NHL superstar, wants to race me, the lowly athletic trainer who still has to reach for the boards to balance from time to time?"

"I'm down a leg, Lex. Pretty sure this is going to be an even playing field."

"Yeah?" There's a challenge in her eye when she elbows me gently. When she hops to her skates and stumbles forward, taking off for the goalie crease on the other side of the rink. "Loser is buying dinner."

I give her a head start before I chase her down and wrap my arms around her middle. She lets out a scream that turns into a cackle when we both fall back onto the ice, out of control and a mess of limbs and blades. After, she records me doing two easy laps at a slow and steady pace and passes along the video to our social media team.

Ten minutes later, the video gets posted on Instagram. A tidal wave of comments and notifications come in, but I don't give them any attention.

Today is day one. The start of something new, something fucking exciting, and I'm doing it with her by my side.

FORTY-SEVEN
LEXI

GIRLS JUST WANT TO HAVE FUN(DAMENTAL RIGHTS) AND GOOD SEX

ME
Last away game of the season!

MADELINE
Lucy and I are tagging along!

EMMY
I'll be there too.

Who doesn't love Chicago in April?

MAVEN
I can't tell if that's a joke.

EMMY
Not a joke at all. It's also the city where Maverick and I got together for the first time.

> **ME**
> Look at you being a romantic gal who remembers details like that! You've come so far.

> **PIPER**
> Says the woman who won't tell us what the hell is going on in her personal life.

> **ME**
> Lunch tomorrow after we land? Coach scheduled a later afternoon skate, so I'm free until four.

> **EMMY**
> I'm down.

> **MADELINE**
> Hudson said he'll watch Lucy, so I'm in.

> **PIPER**
> I have a meeting at three with the other commentators, but I'm free until then!

> **MAVEN**
> Count me in.

> **ME**
> Can't wait.

"I CAN'T BELIEVE the regular season is almost finished." Piper takes a sip of her water and leans back in her chair after we finish our lunches. "I know we have the playoffs, but this year has been a whirlwind, hasn't it?"

"I don't know how it's already April," I say. "It feels like it was just training camp."

"Time flies when you're having fun. And it's going to be even more fun when we kick the Stars' asses in the first round," Emmy says. "If you all lose tomorrow, you're facing off against Baltimore, and we have the home ice advantage."

"But if we win, we play Detroit. We've beaten them in all four matchups this season, and I like our odds," Madeline says, and we all stare at her. "What? I pay attention to sports sometimes." When I lift an eyebrow, she grins. "Okay, fine. Hudson has drilled these scenarios into my brain, and I can recite it from memory. I didn't do it on my own."

"Still. It only took you two years, but you're talking about sports," Maven says. "And I'm proud of you."

"Thanks." Madeline laughs. "How are the guys feeling, Lex? Are they all staying healthy?"

"Surprisingly, yes. Balancing the normal things I see during the season and Riley's rehabilitation has been exhausting, but also damn rewarding. I'm proud of myself for working so hard, and I'm proud of the guys for taking injury prevention seriously this year," I say. "We're the only team in the league who hasn't had a player miss a single game all season."

"One day people will acknowledge your team is held together by successful women," Emmy says. "And until then, we're going to order dessert and stuff our faces."

I beam at the compliment and sneak a glance at my phone. Riley is spending the afternoon with the guys, and he mentioned something about lunch and a movie-watching party. I smile when I see a text from him, then I drag my thumb across the screen to see what he has to say.

> RILEY
>
> Why did no one tell me The Fox and the Hound was the most depressing movie they'd ever seen?
>
> Grant is sobbing on the hotel ballroom floor.

> **I don't think Ethan is going to be able to play tomorrow.**
>
> **We're a goddamn mess.**

> ME
>
> Who the hell picked that as the movie for you all to watch?

> **RILEY**
>
> **Ethan did as a joke. He said he could get Liam to cry.**
>
> **Spoiler alert: he didn't cry, and I'm convinced he's a robot.**

> ME
>
> Poor baby. Are you okay?

> **RILEY**
>
> **Will you come kiss me and make it better?**

> ME
>
> Later tonight I will.

> **RILEY**
>
> **Good answer.**

> ME
>
> Talk to you soon, Mitchy ;)

"Is there something interesting on your phone, Lex?" Piper studies me. "You're *grinning*. And totally ignoring us."

"No, I'm not."

"You so are," Maven says.

"I don't want to talk about it." I lock my phone before anyone can see the photo that comes through of Riley with red-rimmed eyes. There are tears on the lenses of his glasses, his hair is a mess, but he's the cutest thing I've ever seen. "Someone else make this conversation about them."

"Maverick and I are serious about investing in a PWHL expansion team," Emmy says, and I perk up. "We're hoping to put in a proposal to the city of Detroit in the next few months, then we can get this ball rolling."

"Stop it." Maven claps. "That is incredible, Em."

"It's pretty cool, isn't it?" She smiles and drops her elbow to the table. "I'll always feel so fortunate I was the first female in the NHL. I'm glad that door is open if women want to go down the same path, and I'm also glad there's a market and demand for more women's sports leagues. I wouldn't trade my experience in the league for anything, but as someone who had to play on all-boys teams because there weren't options for me as a young girl, I'm sure it's so special to be surrounded by strong and powerful women training with the same goal in mind. You have athletic trainers who understand women's bodies," she says, glancing at me. I nod in agreement, knowing how different male and female athletes' skeletal structures are. "There are resources like locker rooms and showers and free feminine hygiene products, and a focus on mental health and family accessibility. There's sisterhood embedded in the competition, and I want every little girl out there who loves the sport to know she can play in the big leagues too."

"I didn't think I was going to cry at lunch, but here we are." Madeline dabs under her eye with her napkin. "What a time to be a woman."

"Would you move to Michigan?" Maven asks, and Emmy shakes her head.

"Michigan will always have my heart, but DC is home now. I know Maverick wants to retire with the Stars, and I'm hoping to sign another contract extension with the Sea Crabs. Besides"—Emmy pauses—"it took me thirty years to find a group of women I could call my friends. I'm not leaving without you all."

"This is why I love my tattoo." I push up the sleeve of my sweater and show off the small hearts that are healing on the curve of my arm. "So I can always carry you all with me."

I'm so close to telling them about Riley and gushing about how wonderful he is. They know almost everything else about me, but for some reason, I want him all to myself. I'm not embarrassed by him—god no. I never could be.

He's my best kept secret, and the second people find out we're seeing each other, he won't be just mine anymore.

And, gosh, do I love that he's just mine.

"We really need to start saving these heart-to-hearts for when we're having a glass of wine," Piper says. "Then I can blame my crying on the alcohol."

"Speaking of crying, the entire team is an emotional mess because of the movie they watched this afternoon. If they lose tomorrow, your darling husband is to blame," I tell Piper. "Does that man ever show any ounce of emotion besides being totally locked in during a game?"

"We went to the animal shelter last week because we've been thinking of getting Pico de Gato a sibling," she says, mentioning Liam's cat. "He held a senior cat that's been overlooked for months and burst into tears. When he tells you it was allergies, don't believe him."

I laugh. "Oh, I can't wait to give him shit about that tomorrow."

"Speaking of, I should get back." Madeline taps her phone screen and checks the time. "Hudson and Lucy have been at the museum, and she's begging for pizza. I said I'd join them for a second lunch."

"Tell Huddy Boy we say hi," Piper sings. "And give Lucy a big kiss for me."

"Will do." Madeline smiles. "I'll see you girls at the game tomorrow."

"I need to get going too. I have some ankles to tape, and god forbid anyone else on my team does their job." I stand

and pull out a twenty from my wallet to leave behind as a tip. "Everyone get back safe."

"You make me want to be a hockey player," Maven says. "Just so I can be under your care."

"Please. I'm not that special."

"I bet there's someone on the team who would disagree with that," Piper teases. "Maybe you've met him? He's six-two and wears glasses. Oh, and he blushes whenever you're around."

"Can't hear you," I say, sticking out my tongue and waltzing toward the exit of the restaurant.

ME
I know you said you wanted me to kiss you and make you feel better, but I have a better idea.

Attachment: 1 image

Meet me at the rooftop pool?

RILEY
Is that a goddamn string bikini?

ME
Get up here and find out.

THE HOTEL'S outdoor pool is warm when I dunk my head beneath the surface. My muscles unwind in the heated water, and my body is grateful for the moment of relaxation after an early morning and a long travel day. When I reemerge, Riley is standing on the pool deck in a hoodie and gym shorts.

"Hey." I smile and wipe the water from my eyes. "That was quick."

"You sent me a picture of your ass in a bathing suit. I haven't moved that fast since the playoffs last year."

I laugh and swim over to him. The water gets shallower, and I walk across the bottom until I reach the stairs. I shiver at the change in temperature, the cool night air making goosebumps pop up on my skin. "We should cross another item off your Life List."

"Yeah? And which one is that?"

"Skinny dipping." I pull the tie around my neck, the triangle piece falling into the water. Riley tips his head back and stares at the sky, and I throw the top of my bikini at him. "What do you think?"

"I think one of my teammates could see you naked, and then I'd have to kill them."

"Coach put tape on their doors. No one is going to risk sneaking out the night before one of the most important games of the season. They'd be benched for the playoffs."

Riley lowers his chin and rubs a hand over his jaw. He's staring at my chest and my pointed nipples, and when he drops his gaze to my stomach, I reach down to my waist and pull on the strings at my hips.

"Jesus," he mumbles. "You make me want to be reckless."

"Strip, Mitchell," I say, and his eyes dance with glee. "Let's live a little."

"I have to take off my prosthetic."

"We have all the time in the world."

"I might drown."

"I was a lifeguard one summer."

He laughs and pulls off his sweatshirt. I'm glad to see he's not wearing anything underneath it, and he drops it in a heap on the concrete. His glasses go next, landing beside the pile of clothes, and he puts his hands on his hips. "You drive a hard bargain, Armstrong."

"Come on in, Ri." I toss my bikini bottoms at his head. "The water is fine."

"Hang on." Riley drags a pool chair over to the door, blocking the entrance and keeping anyone from getting up here and finding us. He scans the deck, eyes gleaming when he finds what he's looking for. With a quick flick of his wrist, he flips a switch and the lights around us extinguish. "There. I'm sure this place has security cameras, and the last thing I need is our asses ending up on TMZ's website."

"You're so resourceful. What else can you do?"

"Give me a second and I'll show you."

Riley hooks his fingers in the waistband of his shorts and yanks them over his legs to reveal no underwear and his hard cock. He wraps a hand around his length and gives himself two jerks before he slowly lowers himself to the deck in a sitting position. There's no grimace on his face as he takes off his prosthetic, and when he slips into the water and grabs me by my waist, I can't help but giggle.

I've seen Riley naked dozens of times, but there's something about the way his body looks under the night sky that's intoxicating. It's beautiful, a testament to his perseverance and all the hard work he's put into his physical journey the last eight months.

But under all of that is his kind soul and his soft heart, and out of everything I've learned about him, those are the most magical parts that make me so wonderfully happy.

I wrap my legs around his waist and he rests his back against the pool ledge, staying in the shallow water so he can keep one foot on the ground.

"I'm waiting," I murmur, and he brings a wet hand to my hair. He drops my head back and presses a kiss to my neck, his tongue running up the length of my throat.

"I have a tough choice to make, Lexi baby. Do I get you off out here where anyone can see?" he asks, and I press my chest against his. "Or should I make you wait until I get you back to my room?"

"Both are good options." I sigh when he moves his hand down my throat and dips it below my collarbone. He snakes his palm across my body, between my legs, then shoves my thighs apart with a satisfied hum. "I can be patient."

"The last thing you are is patient." He pushes a finger inside me, and my nails dig into his shoulders. "We might need to add an addendum to the list: skinny dipping with orgasms. That's way better than just skinny dipping, don't you think?"

"Y-yes," I rasp, the syllable cracking when a second finger sneaks inside me and pumps my pussy. I arch my back and bite my bottom lip to hold back a moan. "Way better."

"Look at you." His mouth moves to my shoulder, and he laps up the water on my skin with his tongue. He sucks on my skin then finishes it off with a quick bite of his teeth, the sting sending a delicious roll of pleasure through my body. "You're so beautiful all the time, but I like you like this: no makeup. Your hair down. Naked. I like that it's the side of you only I get to see."

He forgot something on his list.

Exposed.

Split open with my heart in my hands.

Out here in the quiet, still night, I'm handing over pieces of myself I don't normally show during the day. I'm sinking into him, letting him possess me in new ways, and I wonder how it could *ever* be better than this.

"Riley," I whisper, putting both hands on his cheeks. "I'm glad I get to do your Life List with you."

His face softens. The intensity behind his eyes melts to hopeless, *loving*, and I swallow the lump in my throat when he kisses me slow and tender.

"There's no one I'd rather do it with," he says, and I don't know if he's talking about the list or the thumb he's pressing against my clit or something bigger that I've been trying to explain to myself for weeks but can't figure out.

He fucks me with his fingers lazily, like we have all the time in the world.

Maybe we do.

There's no hurry, no rush. Riley brings me to the edge of an orgasm then pulls back, smiling into the curve of my neck when I say *please* and whispering back *okay*. He transports me to some mystical place I'm not sure I could reach if we weren't out here, if I wasn't with him, the slick glide of our bodies against each other and my muffled moans buried in his shoulder when he finally, *finally*, plucks me apart with four fingers and a gentle laugh that makes my heart twist in my chest.

He eases me down from the high with a kiss everywhere he can reach: my forehead, my cheek, the curve of my jaw and the spot below my ear where I'm secretly ticklish. I can feel his body shaking, his muscles straining, the strength of holding me on one leg an excruciating task I don't take for granted. I shiver when I kiss him again then pull away, wanting to relieve him from the weight he's carrying.

"Can we go to your room?" I whisper against the corner of his mouth, and he nods.

"Yeah. It's going to take me a minute to get my leg back on, though. If you want to go ahead, I'll—"

"I'll grab us some towels." I slowly unravel from around his middle, limbs heavy, sated and satisfied. "And I'll help however I can."

"A towel would be great." Riley spins and puts his hands on the edge of the pool, hoisting himself out of the water as rivulets of chlorine roll over the sculpted muscles of his ass. "My liner won't go on if I'm wet."

I swim over to the stairs and step out of the pool, feeling his eyes on me as I grab a handful of towels and make my way over to him. He smiles when I hand him two, and he dries his hair and shoulders before tackling his lower half.

"Are any of the guys on your floor?" I ask, wrapping my towel around my body and scooping up my discarded bathing suit.

"Ethan is next to me. I heard him recording a video earlier, and I hope I never have to hear a conversation like that again." He laughs as he dries his residual limb. "It was vile."

"You need to download an app that does white noise. Or get some headphones."

"I already ordered a pair of noise-canceling ones." Riley puts his shorts back on but leaves his hoodie off. Clothed from the waist down, he assembles his prosthetic, then stands. "There we go. We're back in business." He holds out his hand, and I lace our fingers together. "Ready?"

"I'm ready for you to fuck me into oblivion, Mitchy," I say, and his laugh is loud enough to wake up the whole hotel.

FORTY-EIGHT
RILEY

WE LEAVE a trail of wet footprints behind us, and Lexi teases me the whole way back to my room. She roams her hands up my chest and down my back. She rests her head between my shoulders when we ride the elevator to the seventh floor and grazes her palm against the front of my shorts as we walk down the hall. She kisses my neck, and I fumble with my room key, practically throwing the door open and yanking her inside.

"I'm not sure how this is going to go." I unfasten her towel and let it drop to the floor, her naked body on display. "You're incapable of being quiet when I touch you. There's a good chance Ethan is going to hear you when I make you come again."

"Someone is sure of themselves. Maybe he's going to hear you when I make *you* come." Her hands rest on my bare chest, and she drags her nails down to my stomach. I'm instantly harder, and I have to tell myself not to thrust into her touch. "Do you want to crawl again, Riley?"

"I want you on the bed," I tell her, kissing her once and spinning her to face the mattress. Before she can walk away, I grab a handful of her ass cheek, her body toned and lean from hours of physical activity. "With your face in the pillows."

Lexi likes to pretend she's unaffected by things, but I hear the hitch in her breathing. I see her squeeze her thighs together before she walks to the bed, and I smile when she sneaks a hand between her legs to touch herself.

When we get home, I want to find some toys for us to try. I've always thought of them as tools, not deterrents, and I think I'd enjoy seeing her turn into a squirming mess at the hands of a vibrator.

She arranges herself into a comfortable position, her ass in the air and her breasts against the sheets, and it's a glorious sight. I hold off on joining her, wanting to commit this to memory so I can pull it out and jerk off to it when I have to spend a night alone and am missing her.

Just when I think she can't get any hotter, she reaches behind her and puts her palms on her ass cheeks, spreading herself open so I can see every part of her. I shove my glasses up my nose and take off like a lightning bolt. I grab her by the waist and spin her so she's facing the wall instead of the headboard. I kneel on the ground at the edge of the bed and put my mouth on her cunt, not wanting to go another second without tasting her.

"*Shit,*" she hisses when my tongue circles her clit. "It's supposed to be your turn, Riley."

"In a minute," I say, licking her like she's my salvation. I really think she might be. One drop, and I'm free from my sins. "I need to eat first."

I shove a hand down my shorts and grip my cock with a tight fist. There's pre-cum all over the head, and I drag my thumb across my slit so I can jerk myself up and down. I pump harder when she stifles a moan and grips my hair, tugging on the strands and trying to get me to bury my tongue deeper inside her.

"Where do you want to come, Lexi baby?" I ask, voice low. "On my tongue? Or on my cock?"

"Your cock," Lexi says, but I don't pull away just yet.

"I bet we can get both. What do you think?"

"That it's cute you're assuming you have magic fingers and genitalia. Three times in one night is a lot for me."

I laugh and give her ass a light smack. "It's going to be cute when I give you all three and you don't have to fake a single one."

I keep my mouth on her and add my fingers, matching them with the hand on my cock. Lexi starts to tighten around me, fighting back a groan when we get to three fingers, then four. She's doing so well with staying quiet, so well with taking what I'm giving to her, and the competitiveness that's been hiding away for months starts to peek its head out.

She doesn't think I can get her to the finish line, and I can't fucking wait to prove her wrong.

"*Please*," she whispers.

The word is magnified, consuming, and it does something to me. I know she's asking me to give her the pleasure she wants—and I will—but it feels like she's also asking me to take care of her in other ways; protecting her heart. Being careful and gentle with her. Going slow like I said I would.

And I plan to do all those things and more.

I let go of my cock and use my thumbs to spread her pussy open. I spit on her clit then circle the saliva with my tongue, and her body tenses. She claws at the sheets before covering her mouth with her hand, and a tear slides down her cheek. I crane my neck so I can watch her, mesmerized as she climbs higher and higher until her orgasm races through her.

"I've got you," I say, kissing the curve of her ass and slowly pulling my fingers out of her. They're soaked, and I dry them off on the inside of her thigh, only to pause and reach forward, unable to help myself, and slide my tongue through the mess. When I meet her gaze again, she's staring at me, eyes wide. "You did so well, Lexi. That was the second one, right? Only one to go. I know you can give me a third."

She collapses on the mattress, her nod feeble and her limbs heavy. She lifts her head to try to look at me, but her hair is sticking to her forehead and cheeks. Her eyes are glossy, and I stand on shaky legs. I all but rip off my shorts and shoes, making a split-second decision to leave my prosthetic on in a fit of sheer horniness.

I'm too worked up from touching her in the pool and making her come, and I don't want to have to wait to bury myself inside her. I need her like I need air, and I run a hand through my hair.

"I want to be on top." She clears her throat and props up on an elbow. "So I can watch you."

"Okay." I lick my lips. Her taste is still lingering on my mouth, and I hope I have the remnants of her orgasm all over my face. I want to wear it like a damn medal. "We can make that happen."

Her smile is a gut-wrenching, heart-piercing thing when she reaches for me and slides our palms together. I join her on the mattress and help her climb on top of me, a leg on either side of my waist and her hand on my chest. She smells like chlorine and sweat and sex, and it might be my new favorite scent.

I wonder if she can feel my heart racing. I wonder if she can tell it skips a beat when she leans forward to kiss me, tongue swiping over my lips like she wants to have a taste of her cum for herself. I wonder if she can hear my brain screaming *I love you* over and over again when she lines up the head of my cock with her entrance and takes me inch by fucking inch until we're joined together and I don't know where I end and she begins.

"Wow," Lexi breathes out. She drops her head back and rolls her hips in a circle. "I'm so full when you're inside me, Riley."

"Yeah?" I rasp. Rational thoughts are impossible. My dignity is flying out the window because she's lifting herself off of me. Slamming back down my length with her tight pussy and making my breath stutter out in a ragged exhale. Who am I? Where am I? This has to be heaven. "*Christ*, sweetheart. You're going to give me a heart attack."

"I thought you wanted to give me three. I need it fast, baby. Please."

Fuck my sanity.

She's being sweet and cute. She's lifting her arms above her head and twisting her body, showing off the swell of her tits and her stomach.

And something inside me snaps.

Mine, my brain roars. *I love you*, my heart yells, and I thrust into her without abandon. It's hard, *rough*, the most uncoordinated I've ever been, but she asked for something, and I'll be fucking damned if I can't give it to her.

"Like that?" I grit out mid-thrust, and her answer is a resounding moan the whole hotel can probably hear. My hand flies out and closes around her throat. I put pressure on her windpipe, and her smile turns greedy. "Yeah. I thought so."

My hips snap up and I fuck her exactly how she likes. The only part of my brain that's thinking straight remembers I'm wearing my prosthetic, so I cup her ass cheek to protect her skin from the lip of my socket. I'm barely in control of my limbs, and her safety is the most important thing to me.

After making her come for a third time, of course.

Her tits bounce, and her mouth parts. She rides me, and now she's close. She's on the precipice again, and my growl makes her eyes fly open.

"Touch your clit," I tell her, and she's quick to put a finger on herself. "So you can come on my cock."

"I'm so close. It's… it's right there." Lexi shuts her eyes again. She arches her back and rubs her clit in quick, small circles. "*Riley*."

Hearing her say my name does it for me. It's *always* going to do it for me, and I hold her hips still while I fill her with my cum. She tightens around me and squeezes my cock as her orgasm hits her at the same time. A laugh rumbles out of me when I regain consciousness, and I groan.

"Not only did you come three times when you didn't think you would," I pant, trying to catch my breath. "But you also did the incredibly romantic, totally unbelievable thing and finished at the same time as me."

"That was a coincidence. Total luck." Lexi rolls her hips one more time for good measure, and, yup, I could probably get hard again. "It doesn't mean anything."

"Means something." I yawn and scoop my hands under her ass so I can lift her up. My dick is sensitive. My heart is close to flatlining. My glasses are smudged. I need a bath and water and to sleep for ten hours with her wrapped around me, but all I do is arrange her next to me on the bed, brush her hair back, and tell her, "Don't ever doubt my bedroom capabilities, Lexi."

"I should tattoo *I'm getting the best dick of my life with a man I very much enjoy* on my forehead so the world knows."

I burst out laughing and she rolls over, her palm covering my mouth. "If you don't want me to make noise, you need to stop being so goddamn cute."

"I'm not cute."

"Oh, you're so fucking cute. And sexy." I touch her waist and rub my thumb over the shell tattoo on her hip. "You rocked my fucking world like you always do. I hope my teammates heard us. It would give me a chance to make them jealous for a change."

"Moment of honesty?"

"With you? Always."

"Do you think getting into a physical relationship helped your recovery? I don't mean that sex healed you, because that's not realistic. Just that… I don't know. I'm not sure how to word it."

"I understand what you're asking. Knowing you wanted to sleep with me was a big ego boost, and I was motivated to get stronger so I could be with you and not worry about being in pain or figuring out awkward positions. And, since we're being honest, I'm not sure I would've trusted anyone to be my first after the accident except you."

"Really?"

"This is the most vulnerable I've ever been physically and mentally, and, at the risk of sounding really fucking cheesy, it's been empowering to… reclaim myself in the bedroom? If that makes sense. And it's a relief to know if a part of my body stops working, if I'm in pain and need to take a breather, it's not going to be the end of the world. I'm with someone who would be patient enough to wait until we can try again, and they wouldn't be weirded out."

"Never. I don't… the sex is extra," Lexi says, her voice softening. "I'd be okay without it if it meant having you around."

"Yeah?"

"Yeah. There's never going to be any pressure with me, Ri, to act a certain way in the bedroom. We could go a month without having sex, and I'd still be so damn happy."

"My romantic ways are rubbing off on you, Armstrong."

"Seems that way." She rests her chin on my chest. "I'm glad I get to be here with you."

I love you, I love you, I love you, I think as I stroke her hair. We lie there for what feels like hours, only pulling apart to use the bathroom and rinse off. We drift back to each other minutes later and I turn off the lights. Our bodies slot together, and just before I lose consciousness to sleep, I throw up a prayer to whoever is listening that she loves me too.

FORTY-NINE
RILEY

COACH
Can you stop by my office today?

I want to talk to you about something.

ME
Sure thing. Everything okay?

COACH
We'll talk soon.

ME
Coach asked to see me in his office so I'm pretty sure I'm being sent to some club team in Alaska.

LEXI
Wow. Dramatic, much?

Did he tell you what the meeting was about?

> **ME**
> Nope. Vague as always, and I don't like when Coach is vague. Usually means there's bad news on the other end of things.

> **LEXI**
> Whatever it is, I'm sure it'll be fine. Call me after?

> **ME**
> I will. Kind of feels like I'm heading to the guillotine. Wish me luck.

> **LEXI**
> Good luck. Xoxo.

"HEY." I slip into Coach's office and shut the door behind me. "What's up?"

"Why do you look like you just saw the Grim Reaper?" he asks, glancing up from the whiteboard on his desk. "I'm not going to bite."

"Sorry, but you asking to see me is the equivalent of being sent to the principal's office." I laugh and take the chair across from him. "Is everything okay?"

"How are you feeling?" Coach caps the dry erase marker he's holding and stares at me. "Physically? Mentally?"

"I've been back on the ice five times now, and it feels like I never left. I'm going to my therapy sessions, the boys are in the playoffs, and, I don't know. Am I allowed to say things are pretty fucking great right now?"

"You are." He pauses and tips his chin to the tattoo on my bicep. "And how's Lexi?"

I hesitate before answering his question. It feels like a trap. A trick to get me to blurt out, *Oh, fucking fantastic. Have I mentioned I'm in love with her? Because I am. Head over heels, can't eat, can't sleep kind of love that makes all the bad shit seem irrelevant.*

I casually asked Maverick if he and Emmy got in trouble for starting their relationship back when she was on the team. They didn't, and she was traded shortly so they didn't have any other issues, but there's nothing in the team handbook that says Lexi and I can't be together. Add on the fact that my contract is murky right now and I don't *really* have a spot on the Stars' roster, and I'm ready to defend her if Coach starts talking about moving her to a different department.

"Fine," I say slowly. "Is there a reason why you're asking me when you can walk down the hall and ask her yourself?"

"Do you think you're the only one around here with secrets?" Coach snorts. "Please."

"She's, uh, yeah. I mean, we spent weeks together. I couldn't help—"

"I don't care about your personal relationships, Mitchell. It's not affecting either of your jobs, so I don't need to hear about how she makes your heart skip a beat and all that other shit."

"Wow. Not a softie, are you?"

"I got a phone call this morning," he says, switching gears and avoiding my interrogation. "From Minnesota."

"Is it about a trade? Am I even eligible for a trade? Oh, shit. Don't tell me you're sending Maverick away."

"Not exactly. They asked about bringing you on as a scout. They want to set up an interview."

I blink. "What?"

"Their amateur and college scout is heading to LA in a new role, and they're looking to fill the spot. They've been impressed with what you've done behind the bench, and with how strong of a collegiate player you were, they think you'd bring a lot to the table."

"How—is that even allowed?"

"Technically, yes. We'd have to void your contract with the

Stars, but unlike being a player, you have the power to turn this down if you don't want it."

"I don't… this is a lot to take in," I say. "I never… before I got behind the bench, a leadership position wasn't something I considered. I'm still not sure it's what I want to do because my heart belongs to skating, but this… it could let me still be around the sport I love. There's no guarantee I'll ever be able to play competitively again, even with the progress I've made, and this…" I trail off, at a loss for words. "I don't know."

"You don't need to make a decision today. Think about it. Our scouts are available if you want to talk to them. You can get some different perspectives and some pros and cons."

"What do you think I should do?" I ask. "If this decision was in front of you?"

"It was in front of me, and I went with the coaching route. Do I regret it?" Coach rubs his jaw and crosses his arms over his chest. "Sometimes, yeah. What if I had rehabbed differently? What if I had taken two years off from playing and stopped trying to rush my recovery? Would my body have healed more strongly? Could I have gotten back on the ice? Maybe. Maybe not. Coaching was a sure thing though, and in the moment, I was afraid to not have a sure thing. I loved the sport too much and I had given it too much of myself to it to walk away empty-handed."

"Yeah." I fiddle with the drawstrings on my joggers and stare at my thighs. "That makes sense."

"If I had the choice again today I don't know what I would do, but you have to think long-term. What makes you happy? What's going to get you up out of bed every morning, even on the days you don't want to? Because you and I both know you're going to have a fuck ton of those."

I had one yesterday. It was the worst I've had in a while. I pulled my covers over my head and massaged my residual limb as I told myself the pain would go away soon. Even breathing felt difficult, a pressure on my chest that stayed there for three hours. I had to actively fight back against the demons in my head that called me weak when I grabbed my crutches, but I persevered. I came out on top, and today is better.

Can I be a scout who doesn't know what kind of pain he's going to be in until he climbs out of bed? Can I really decide which players are worthy of a spot on an NHL roster when I'm not on one myself? Is that fair to their livelihood, the power of their futures in the hand of someone who can't skate for more than ten minutes before he has to stop?

"I need to think about it," I say. "I need to… I should talk to—"

"Lexi," he finishes for me. "I figured. It's a big decision. One you're not making for only yourself. I told Minnesota you'd have an answer by the time the postseason wrapped up, and with how all these series are going to game sevens, I can buy you until mid-June."

Mid-June. The one-year anniversary of the night that changed everything.

What a fucking coincidence.

I rub a hand over my chest and nod. "Okay. I'll, uh. Report back."

"Remember what we talked about, Riley. What would you tell your younger self if you found out you got a second chance at life, and you finally started fucking living again?"

I'd tell him he's going to have a lot of lows, the darkest hours he could ever imagine, but he's also going to have a lot of highs. A lot of new experiences that are going to change and shape him. I'd let him know he's skating again, that love still there even after it was almost snatched away from him.

And then I'd tell him about the girl.

The one he's madly, hopelessly, irrevocably in love with who flipped his world upside down. I'd tell him about the life they have, the quiet moments late at night when she tucks herself into his side and the louder, brighter ones during the day when she's giving him shit and making him laugh. I'd mention how perfect she is. How patient and kind and funny she is, and how every time he's with her, his broken pieces put themselves back together. Because she's the closest thing to an angel he'll ever find on earth.

"Thanks," I croak. "You've given me a lot to think about."

"This shit is never easy. If you want to bounce any ideas off of me, I'm around."

"What's with this new hospitality of yours?"

"Don't know, but don't push your luck by mocking me, Mitchell."

"I'd never." I stand and hold out my hand, smiling when he shakes it. "I appreciate you, Coach. And everything you've done for me."

"Enough with the dramatics. I have another meeting in ten minutes. Your time is up."

"Yes sir." I give him a nod and file into the hallway. I know Lexi's in the athletic trainer's room, and I make my way there.

I don't know what the fuck to do about this job opportunity. On one hand, it's the chance of a lifetime. I've always had an eye for good skating, and getting paid to watch hockey is a goddamn dream.

But accepting it means I'm not ever going to put on a jersey again. And, as far-fetched as the idea seems, I've been selfishly clinging to the idea of getting back out there one day, if even for a ceremonial puck drop.

I push the door open to the training room, covering my eyes when I see Liam's bare ass climbing off the treatment table.

"Jesus, man. Put a fucking towel on," I say.

"I'm getting treatment done on my sore body because everything fucking hurts, dickbag, not parading around for all the world to see."

"Treatment on what? Your balls?"

"You're lucky I don't have a free hand right now," he growls, and I peek through my fingers to find him glaring at me with a palm over his dick. "Or I'd have you against a wall."

"I'm telling Piper about your violent tendencies," I say, and his eyes go wide. "And then you'll be in big trouble."

"Are you two done acting like you're five years old and on the playground?" Lexi draws out. "Liam, you're finished. Go get in the ice bath. I don't want your muscles to cramp up, and I've had enough of your hairy ass."

"Fine," he grumbles. "And my ass isn't hairy."

"It's definitely hairy," I say when he leaves, and Lexi smiles my way.

"Hey. How'd it go with Coach?"

"Interesting." I sit on the treatment table next to her stool then think better of it, imagining Liam's bare skin rubbing against the leather. "He told me Minnesota wants to set up an interview with me."

"An *interview?* For what?"

"Their open scout position."

"What?" She stands. "Riley that's… wow. What did you say?"

"I said I'd have to think about it. There's a lot to consider."

"It sounds like an incredible opportunity."

"Yeah." I touch her cheek and stroke my thumb over her jaw. "But it would mean moving away from DC. Having to do long distance with you."

"Oh." Her smile drops to a frown, and she takes a step back. "Right."

"I don't have to decide anything now. I just wanted to tell you what was going on."

"It would let you still be involved in the league." Lexi starts to pace around the room. I can already feel her nervous energy radiating from her. "You'd have health insurance and benefits, which you're going to need for caring for your prosthetic. That's important."

"You're important too."

"Come on." Her laugh is brittle, sharp. "You can't really be considering not taking a job because of me."

"Why wouldn't I?" I challenge. "You're the most important thing in my life. DC is my home. *You* are my home."

"This is your career we're talking about, Riley! Your future! A chance to keep doing what you love without wondering if you'll ever have a shot at making a team somewhere down the road." She pauses and snaps her mouth shut for a beat. "You should do it. You should go."

"Ah. I see what's happening here."

"Nothing is happening here."

"Really?" I step toward her, not stopping until our chests are pressed together. "You're not trying to push me away when things are getting serious between us? You're not taking this as a sign I'm going to leave you and hurt you when I go, because everyone else has? You want to run because you're scared. Because it's never been like this for you before, and I get it. But guess what, Lexi? It doesn't matter if I'm here, or if I'm in Minnesota, or any other fucking team in the league. I'm not letting you go even if you push back and try to tell me all the reasons I shouldn't stay."

"Why not?" Tears pool in her eyes, and she wipes her cheek. "Why are you different? Why should I believe you?"

"Because I *love you*," I tell her, and she freezes. Her shoulders shake, but I keep going. "I love you so much it fucking *hurts*, and I know that scares the shit out of you. It scares me too, because how can things be *this fucking good* with you when the rest of my life is in shambles?"

Her chest heaves. Her eyes are wet, and her mouth is halfway open, like she has something she wants to say.

"You want to know why I've had all those good days? Because you were there. Because I've been an idiotic, pathetic mess of a man since the first day I saw you. I can't think straight when you're around. I can't walk right when you smile at me. I can't... I can't fucking *breathe* unless you're looking at me. And everything in your past might have fallen apart, but we won't. We can't, because deep down, I know you love me too," I say.

Lexi's bottom lip quivers. "I-I need some air," she whispers. "I need to get out of here."

"If you want to run, I'll chase you. If you want to build a wall to keep me out, I'll climb it. If you need time, I'll give it to you. I'm patient, Lexi. I'm going to be waiting for you when you come back. However long that takes."

She touches my cheek with a soft graze of her fingers, and I melt. I don't know whether it's the last time I'll get to feel her on my skin or the start of something new, so I savor it. I turn my cheek and kiss the center of her palm, the curve of her knuckles, and she pulls away.

"I love you," I repeat, my voice hoarse and throat raw. It feels like I've been screaming underwater for hours. It also feels like someone is digging a screwdriver into my chest. "And I'm going to love you for as long as you'll let me."

I kiss her forehead and hop on the treatment table. I can't be the one to leave. It has to be her, and with a heavy breath, she shuffles to the door. She wraps her fingers around the handle and looks back at me, something else on the tip of her tongue.

But she doesn't say it. She disappears into the hall and I stay there, ready to wait for the rest of my life, if that's what it takes.

FIFTY
RILEY

"THIS MONTH'S BOOK SUCKED," Grant groans. "A third act breakup? *Miscommunication?* Read the fucking room, bro. No one wants to read that shit."

"I don't mind miscommunication," Connor says. "It's realistic. People miscommunicate all the time."

"It's not hard to just open your fucking mouth and say what you're feeling," Maverick argues.

"Look who's a relationship guru now," Liam draws out. "As if you didn't keep your mouth closed after all your one-night stands then make Hayes do your cleanup work."

"There was a lot of cleanup work," Hudson agrees.

"Hey. Don't talk about my past. I'm a changed man these days. A one-woman-for-the-rest-of-my-life married asshole who's never been happier." Maverick snaps his fingers in front of my face, and I blink. "Earth to Mitchy. You haven't contributed to our conversation all night. It's like talking to a wall."

"Because he hated the book too," Ethan says. "That ending was fucking horrible."

"I didn't hate it." I put my paperback on Liam and Piper's

coffee table and take a sip of my beer. "I have a lot on my mind."

"Ah, pensive Riley." Grant nods. "Heavy is the head that wears a crown."

"What does that even mean?" Ethan asks.

"Like, responsibility? A heavy burden? I don't fucking know. That's not important. What *is* important is what happened. You okay, Mitchy?" Grant asks.

"I..." I trail off and take another sip from the bottle. "I don't know."

It's been a week since I spilled my guts to Lexi. She's dodged me on the team plane on our flights to and from Detroit, and I can't find her in the tunnel during games. I keep checking my phone, hoping there will be a message from her, but it's been silent.

I'm starting to think I fucked up.

Majorly.

I'm pretty sure I came on way too strong with that whole *I love you* speech, but I do. I do love her, and I'm not going to let her push me away without a fight.

Unless that's what she wants.

And the more days that pass where I don't hear from her, the more I'm starting to think I read this entire situation wrong.

"You can tell us anything," Hudson says.

"Is it about your leg?" Maverick asks, and I shake my head.

"Does it have to do with skating?" Ethan chimes in. "Those videos the team posted of you are fucking sick."

"No. It's, ah, more personal than that."

"A girl," Liam rumbles out, and I jerk my head up in surprise. "*The* girl."

There's a chorus of *ohhh*s from around the room. Grant jumps up and runs to the kitchen, returning with half a dozen beers he sets on the table. Ethan grabs the bowl of popcorn and puts it in his lap after shoving a fistful in his mouth. Hudson leans back on the couch and drapes his arms across the cushions, and everyone stares at me.

"You all know?" I ask.

"That you're in love with Lexi? Uh, yeah." Maverick snorts. "Keep up, Mitchy."

"Why don't you tell us the whole story?" Hudson asks, and I do.

I launch into what I was working on in my rehab and the time we kissed in my hotel room. The second time we kissed, then the third. How we've been spending day after day together and going on dates without anyone knowing. Grant screams when I mention the skinny dipping. Ethan throws the bowl of popcorn in the air when I give them the play-by-play of my confession after the job offer, and Maverick gasps when I share the real meaning of my constellation tattoo.

"Oh, shit. You're so fucked," my captain murmurs.

"Yup." I down the rest of my beer. "Thoroughly."

"And you haven't heard from her in a week?" Grant confirms, and I nod.

"Seven days. She won't look at me when I get on the plane. When I go to the training room, she's not there. She's avoiding me, and I know what that means. She's trying to find a way to let me down easy without disrupting the entire dynamic of our team." I scrub a hand over my face and sigh. "Maybe I should go to Minnesota. The last thing I want is for her to be uncomfortable."

"We need a diagram." Maverick snaps and points at Liam. "Where's that whiteboard of yours, Sully? The one we used for our fantasy football draft?"

"In my office," he answers.

Grant sprints down the hall and returns with a three-by-five whiteboard on wheels, proudly rolling it to the center of the room.

"We don't need to do this," I say. "It's going to make me feel worse."

"Let's analyze this like we would a romance book." Maverick snatches my glasses off my face and slides them up his own nose. "Hell, Mitchy. How do you see with these things?"

"I can't see *anything* since you stole them, bastard."

He waves me off and scribbles out a handful of words on the board, using a candlestick as a pointer. "Lexi doesn't date, but she's spending all her time with you. We all know she's never been shy about expressing her feelings, yet when you dropped the *I love you* bomb on her, she's gone quiet."

"I don't see how any of that helps," I say.

"I see where Maverick is going." Hudson joins him at the board, and I have to squint to read what he writes. "If she didn't love you too, she would've already told you. She wouldn't care about your feelings."

"She's exactly like Emmy," Maverick adds. "Rough around the edges. A hard exterior to crack. Using sarcasm as a method to hide what she's really feeling so it looks like she doesn't care. And, as someone who finally learned how to get under her skin, I can tell you it takes women like them a lot longer to come around to the idea of giving up their independence. Men in their past have treated them like shit," he says, his grip on the candlestick tightening. I know he's thinking about Emmy's ex and all the horrible things he said to her. "They're strong and capable on their own, so they don't see *why* they should rely on a man."

"Women like Piper love easily," Liam says, and I stare at him, flabbergasted that he's actively participating. "And they love everyone. Even the people who don't deserve their love. They'll share their feelings with you any chance they can get, and that's different from how Lexi's been conditioned to act. She doesn't think she is lovable, because no one's loved her before."

"Which is why it's so hard for her to admit she loves *you*," Grant summarizes.

"Are you… is this some fucking PhD class on women's emotional intelligence?" I ask. "When the fuck did you all get so deep and insightful?"

"My mama raised me right," Hudson says. "Women are complicated creatures. They're not as easy to read, but they're the only reason any of us are on the paths we're on right now."

There's a murmur of agreement, and I stand. I walk to the board and tap the points they made. "Wait. She loves me?"

"Of course she fucking loves you!" Maverick exclaims. "I know you've been looking at her for years, but now she's looking at you."

"What the fuck do I do? Do I bust down her door? Do I buy her flowers or chocolates or jewelry?" My skin is itchy. My cheeks are hot. I fan my face and have to do a lap around the living room. "Someone help me."

"No, you idiot. You don't do any of that. Haven't you heard anything these saps have told you?" Ethan scoffs. "You wait. You wait until it's time for her to come to you. Then, and only then, do you repeat to her how you feel. That's when she'll say it back."

"The earth is officially ending. *Ethan* is doling out advice," I say, and he flips me off.

"I read books. I know a thing or two about women besides how to get them off."

"I said I would be patient, but it's killing me not to do anything. I just want her to know everything is okay."

"She knows that," Hudson reassures me. "You've done plenty over the last few months to show her that."

"Uh, not to diminish this whole big revelation, but can we talk about the elephant in the room? What are you going to do about the scouting job?" Grant asks.

"I don't know," I answer honestly. "I see the pros and cons to both sides, and I'm not sure which way I'm leaning. I love DC. I love you guys and being here. You're my family. The brothers I never had, and leaving what we've built together would break my fucking heart. I don't know what's best for me, and that's what I'm struggling with."

"Do you want to play? Or do you want to have an active role in a player's development and journey to the NHL?" Maverick asks. "That's what it comes down to."

"My heart tells me I want to play. But I don't know if my body can take it. This sport is ruthless when you have all of your limbs. It's even more excruciating when you're missing one, and I don't know if I can justify throwing away a once-in-a-lifetime shot on the possibility of a maybe." I sigh and take my glasses back from Maverick. "It's a tough decision to make."

"Coaching and scouting will always be there," Hudson says. "Playing might not be. You're young right now. You're the healthiest you're ever going to be, and it's only going to get harder the more years that pass."

"True." I nod. "I might go out there and just talk with them. Maybe that will tell me everything I need to know."

"You're always going to have a home here," Maverick says. "On the team. In the stands. We are brothers. And brothers stick together until the end."

"Fucking hell." I pinch the bridge of my nose. "We really need to stop letting book club get so deep. You're going to make the waterworks start, Cap."

"Group hug," he yells, and I laugh when they all tackle me.

We fall on the floor and Ethan yells about my foot being in his ass. Liam tries to pull away, but Grant climbs on his back and keeps him there. It's chaotic and insane but also exactly what I need.

"You just have to be patient a little longer, man," Hudson says. "The best things are always worth the wait."

"Yeah." I grin. I think about Lexi and me ten years down the road. The smirk she's tossing me and the way she'll still have my heart. She's still taping up ankles and I'm there, happy to just be around her. "They are."

FIFTY-ONE
LEXI

AFTER A WEEK and a half of thinking about what Riley said to me—that big, emphatic *I love you* that stole my breath away—I decide I need reinforcements.

"I love a girls' night." Piper takes the charcuterie board from me and sets it in the middle of the kitchen table. "And I need a break from the playoff stress."

The Stars are one win away from advancing to the next round in the playoffs, and tensions are high. They've done the impossible this season, coming back from an abysmal start to shake up the Eastern conference, and everyone who counted us out before the All-Star break is eating their words.

"I'm sorry you all lost, Em," Madeline says gently, and Emmy sighs.

"Me too. We had all the components to go far this year, but it didn't happen. Guess it's back to cheering for the Stars and my obnoxious husband who thinks the world revolves around him."

"You're quiet tonight, Lex." Maven rests her head on my shoulder. "Are you okay?"

What a fucking loaded question that is.

No, I'm not okay. The nicest and most supportive man in the world loves me. Isn't that the most devastating thing you've ever heard?

"I, um, need some relationship advice," I mutter, and my kitchen goes silent. "Before I give up the best thing that's ever happened to me."

"Okay," Piper says slowly. "Do you want to tell us what's going on?"

"Riley and I have been sleeping together for months, and he told me he loves me. I think I love him too, but I've never loved anyone before, so I can't be sure I'm doing it right. And I'm really, really scared."

"Whoa," Madeline whispers.

"Holy shit. Maverick is going to owe me *a lot* of money," Emmy cheers.

"I figured you two were up to something because of the tattoos and the goddamn hickeys on your neck, but *love?* That's a big word, Lex," Maven says.

"Minnesota wants him to interview for an open scouting position, and I kind of pushed him away when I told him he should take it. I put up the barrier I *always* put up, and that's when he told me he loves me."

I can still hear his words ringing in my ears. They've followed me around every single day that's passed, a reminder of what I could have if I just accepted it.

Half of me has hoped he'd reach out. I constantly check my phone to see if he's messaged me, but he's sticking to his word. He's letting me decide how this moves forward, and that makes everything swirling in my head even more convoluted and complicated.

"How do you feel about him?" Piper asks, and I shrug.

"The sex is great," I say, and she puts her hand over mine.

"How do you feel when he's around?" she asks instead, and that makes me pause.

Like I'm on top of the world.

Like I could jump off a building and fly.

Like I could climb the highest mountain and scale the rockiest cliff without breaking a sweat.

Like I've finally found somewhere I can stay for longer than a night. Somewhere I feel safe, secure, and taken care of, and I swallow down the lump in my throat.

"You know the first day of spring after the snow melts?" I croak. "The afternoon where you step outside and tip your chin up to the sky and let out a deep breath? I feel like that every single time he hugs me. It's never-ending warmth. Constant sunshine, even on the dark days, and I-I don't know how any of it is real."

"Just because you haven't experienced it doesn't mean it doesn't exist," Madeline says. "You don't have to see it to believe it."

"Can it always be this good though? The charm has to wear off eventually, right? Do I have rose-tinted glasses on? Am I only feeling this way because it's new and fun and something I haven't done before? People… people aren't this happy all the time, are they?" I ask.

"I am," Emmy says. "And as someone who spent many, many years *not* happy, it's such a relief when you finally stop fighting it."

"So, what? If he does go to Minnesota, would I follow him? Would I chase after him and put my career on hold for his? Would we do long distance? Break up?" I challenge. "How would any of this work?"

"If one of us came to you and asked for advice, what would you say?" Madeline asks, and I weigh her question.

"I would say you should never give up on your dreams for someone else. And your own happiness has to come before someone else's." I pause and blink away tears. "But I'd also ask when was the last time you were ever this happy."

"You two are adults. Adults make it work," Maven says.

"Even when it's hard. Even when it feels like the odds are stacked against you."

"What if it doesn't work? What if I give everything I have to this relationship and I come out on the other side alone like I always do? Alone."

"What if you don't?" Emmy counters, and from the woman who never wanted to settle down, it speaks volumes. "What if it's the best thing that could ever happen to you?"

"I feel like a total bitch." I wipe under my eyes. "I walked away from him. He poured his heart out to me, and I was the one who left. How could he ever want me after that?"

"He wants you because he *knows* you, Lex," Piper says. "And he knows you need time to figure out what you want."

I want him. Because I love him too.

How did this happen?

The thought races through me, and I have to grip the table to steady myself. I take a deep breath, the culmination of the last eight months playing in my mind like a movie, and I see it there.

In the doughnuts on my desk and his mumbled curses when I give him a difficult exercise to do. In a rooftop pool at a Chicago hotel, no one in the world but us, and his confession to me about how he wanted to end his life.

It's also in the times when he'd hook his pinky around mine before he took the ice in his nice suits. When he'd throw me over his shoulder then toss me on the bed. The nights when he'd listen to me talk about my day and the mornings where I'd wake up, his arms wrapped around me like he wanted to keep me in his bed forever.

It might've been there all along, back when I saw the broken boy in our meeting after his accident, sunken cheeks and hate in his eyes. Before that, at the very beginning and the very first day we met, his sweaty palm shaking mine as he stammered out his name.

I love him.

I love him, I love him, I love him.

"I need to go." I stand and push my chair back. "Right now."

"Is this the moment?" Piper claps. "Our girl is finally going to get her happily ever after."

"Can someone lock up? I—" I gesture around the kitchen. "I don't care what you all do in here."

"*Go*," Madeline says. "We'll be fine."

I nod and race down the hall, only stopping to slip on a pair of sneakers and grab my purse. I pull out my phone, thumbs shaking as I type out a text to my pinned contact at the top of my messages.

ME
Hi. Are you free?

His reply comes back seconds later, as if he's pacing around his kitchen holding his phone, waiting to hear from me.

RILEY
As a bird.

ME
Can I come over?

RILEY
Door is unlocked, sweetheart.

I grab an Uber, not trusting myself to drive. I'm still shaking. I feel a little dizzy. My heart is dangerously close to falling out of my chest, and when I make it to his apartment building and take the elevator up to his floor, he's there. Standing in the doorway with a bouquet of tulips and the brightest smile on his face, and I lose it.

"I'm sorry," I sob, my arms around his neck and my face

buried in his shirt. "I'm so sorry I made you wait so long. That was horrible of me."

"I told you to take your time." He strokes my hair then moves his palm to my back, rubbing small circles between my shoulder blades, and the tension leaves my body. "Did you have a good week?"

"No. It was miserable." I wipe my nose with the back of my hand, not caring about the snot or mascara I'm sure I'm leaving behind. "You weren't there, and I hated every second of it."

"Come inside, sweetheart, so you can rest."

I let him lead me into his apartment and over to the living room couch. He unties my sneakers and slips them off my feet. I don't put up a fight when he arranges me in his lap and kisses my forehead, a sigh loosening its way from the depths of my soul.

Finally, I think.

"I'm sorry for trying to push you away," I whisper. "You should do whatever is going to make you happy, no matter where that is. If that means going to Minnesota, I'll support you. Maybe they have a job opening, or I can look into the PWHL team. Or we can do long distance and go back and forth every other weekend. I know I want to—"

"I turned down the interview. I'm going to stay in DC," he says, interrupting me, and I pull away so I can look at him. "If I want to coach or scout, I can do that in ten years. But I want to skate. Odds are I'll never make another team. No one is going to want to take a chance on me. I'm a liability on the ice, and I'm not even sure my prosthetic is legal according to the rulebook, but I want to fucking try because I've come this far. And I want to try with you."

"Are you sure? You're always going to have your Stanley Cup rings and statistics. Scouting could be fun. It's something new, and you'd be so good at it."

"I'm sure. This is where I want to be. I've made DC my home, and I'm not ready to say goodbye yet."

"I have to tell you something," I say.

"Yeah? What's that, Lexi baby?"

"It's really important."

"I can't wait to hear."

I wring my hands together, and he waits patiently for me to continue. He doesn't rush me. He doesn't try to guess what I'm going to say, but he knows, because his smile is widening. His eyes are crinkling in the corners, and I can't keep it in anymore.

"I love you," I whisper. "I love you so much, and I hope you still love me too."

"I never stopped. And I don't plan on stopping anytime soon."

"I'm scared, and I need your help. You're going to have to remind me to express my feelings. You're going to have to tell me if I'm not showing you enough affection or if I'm too demanding by asking for space every once in a while. I might freak out about some things, like when you—"

Riley cuts me off with a kiss. It's searing, *grounding*. He puts everything he has behind it, and I meet him halfway, every feeling of elation I've had recently in the press of my mouth. In my hands roaming up his arms and across his shoulder and the soft sigh I let myself breathe out when he holds me tight to his chest.

"I love you, Lexi. And everything that comes with being with you," he says, and I start to cry again. They're the most beautiful, sure words I've ever heard. "You can be scared with me. I promise I'll take care of you."

I've been told a lot of promises throughout my life, and this is the first time I actually believe it. Riley *will* take care of me, and I'm the luckiest girl in the world because of it.

"RiRi?"

"Ah. We settled on that as a nickname?"

"Until I think of something else."

"What is it, Lexi baby?"

"Today…" I sniff. I laugh and trace over the stars on his arm, every one just as perfect as the one before it. "Today has been a very, very good day."

"The best I've had in a while," he agrees. "Ever, I think."

"Until tomorrow," I say. "I think tomorrow is going to be just as nice."

FIFTY-TWO
RILEY

I DON'T KNOW how Lexi does it, but I fall more in love with her every day. I walk into a room and she's there, a book in her lap and a blanket wrapped around her shoulders, and it's a lightning bolt to the chest. A flashing neon sign that says *there's the love of your life,* and it's true.

The boys made it to the Eastern conference finals after clawing back from a 0-2 deficit in the semifinals, and we're having one last team dinner at Maverick and Emmy's before we head to Miami to see if we can make it back to the Stanley Cup finals.

"You know they're going to lose their minds when we go in there holding hands, right?" Lexi asks, peering up at me as we stand outside the door. "If there's not a champagne shower, I'm going to be shocked."

"Please." I snort and roll my eyes. "They know I've been obsessed with you for years. And they gave me some good advice recently that I took to heart. There was a whiteboard. Liam even participated. The world might be ending."

"Wow. So everyone knew about your feelings for me except me?" Lexi grabs my collar and tugs my mouth to hers. "I don't like missing out on secrets."

"It's not a secret anymore." I kiss her then pull away with a smile. "But we should take bets on who says the weirdest shit to us."

"Ethan," she announces without a second thought. "You know he's going to be the one who will give us his honest opinion without holding back."

We step into the foyer and take off our shoes, walking into the living room where my teammates are spread out on the couches. I rub my thumb over Lexi's knuckles, smiling when she rests her head on my shoulder and surveys the room.

"Hey," she calls out, and two dozen pairs of eyes look our way. "Who won the bet?"

"What bet?" Grant asks innocently, and I have to hand it to him. His fake surprised face has come a long way. I almost believe that he's caught off guard by us showing up together. "Is there something you want to share with us, Lex?"

"Nope." She stands on her toes and kisses my cheek, flipping everyone off when a round of *aww*s echo in the room.

Everyone settles in, handing over plates and silverware and water bottles. Hudson doles out the lasagna Madeline made. Ethan helps slice the sourdough loaf he cooked all by himself after he shows Lexi the forty-seven photos he took of himself with his starter, and I'm not sure I've ever seen him so proud.

"You know, I've never been the jealous type, but it's pretty unfair that all of you are walking around and showing off how happy and in love you are," Grant says after we all finish our food. "Is there any justice for us single people?"

"We're young, G," Ethan says, shoving a hot dog in his mouth. "We can't spend all our time settled down. Where's the fun in that?"

"It's plenty of fun," Hudson says.

"I can have sex whenever I want," Maverick adds, and Emmy hits him in the face with a pillow.

"Not tonight you're not," she says, and Lexi bursts out laughing beside me.

"That is a nice perk," she murmurs to me. "Maybe after the playoffs are finished, you can have book club at your place. You can tie me to your bed and make me wait there while you and the boys talk about your favorite parts of the novel, and none of them will ever know."

"Jesus, Lex." I blush and take a long sip of my water. "I need some warning before you say those kinds of things."

"You put a blindfold on me last night and smiled while you did it. Me tied to your bed is where you draw the line?"

"When I'm around my nosy fucking teammates who are probably eavesdropping? Yes." I put my hand under her thigh and drag her across the couch to me. "You know I'm pathetic when it comes to you."

"Yeah." Her grin is sharp and sly. "I do."

"What are we talking about?" Ethan asks, leaning on my shoulders from behind the couch. "Anything good?"

"Mind your business, Richardson, or I'm going to use the massage gun that hurts when you get on my table tomorrow," Lexi says, and he pulls away.

"Yes ma'am," he hurries to say, and I laugh.

"Great. Now you've scared him."

"He'll be fine."

"Listen up," Maverick calls out. "One of the people in the social media department wants us to take a group photo. She said the fans are requesting more behind the scenes access, and since they're not getting into the locker room, a quick snapshot of us all together will appease the masses. Everyone off your asses."

"They should post a photo of you in your smock when you're painting," Lexi teases, and I pinch her hip.

"You told me it was cute."

"It is cute."

"I have to go in front. I'm short," Grant says, and Piper moves to the first row with him. "Who else is a short king?"

"I'm the tallest on the team," Maverick declares. "So I'm going front and center. Get in here, Emmy girl."

"God. Not this again," I groan.

"Is this an ongoing debate?" Lexi asks.

"For years now. No one can make up their damn mind." I wrap my arm around her and stare at the camera Maverick positioned on the fireplace. Lexi rests her head on my shoulder, and I smile. "It's funny to hear their reasoning."

"Can everyone see the camera? Cool, let me press this nifty little button here and... perfect. It's counting down," Maverick says. "Man. Technology is amazing."

"Ethan. Stop flipping off Grant," Madeline warns.

"Liam, can you *please* smile?" Hudson asks. "You're freaking me out, and we don't need to feed into that conspiracy theory that's floating around about you being a contract killer."

"How about instead of arguing..." Maverick reaches into his pocket and unfolds a piece of paper, handing it off to Emmy. "Everyone say *Guess what? We're going to be aunts and uncles to the coolest baby girl in the whole fucking world who will be here by Christmas!*"

I can't hear myself think. Someone screams. A lamp goes flying off the side table, and Grant climbs onto Connor's back so he can get a better look at the sonogram photos. There's pushing and shoving and Maverick lifts Emmy up and spins her around.

"Surprise," Emmy says, her cheeks as red as her hair. "Baby Hartwell-Miller is on her way. It was impossible to keep a secret from you all, but we wanted to be sure things were looking good before we put it out in the open."

Lexi pulls away from me and crashes into her best friend with a hug. I grab Maverick and yank him toward me in a fierce embrace.

"Congratulations, Mavvy," I say, and his shoulders shake with laugher. "I'm so happy for you."

"It's unbelievable, isn't it? Me? A *dad?* I'm going to have two beautiful girls in my house, and I'm the luckiest fucker in the world." He pats my chest and looks at me. "I'm so glad you're here to be a part of it, man."

"Me too." I nod, and he laughs again, tears on his cheeks.

"That night in the hospital waiting room after your accident was the worst night of my life. When we go back for Baby H's birth, it's going to be the greatest night of my life. And you're going to be by my side."

"Fuck, dude." I pull off my glasses and rub my eyes. "I'm going to be the best uncle that girl has ever seen. I'll work my ass off to take the top spot."

"It's going to be a tough competition. I weirdly think Ethan might be the underdog."

We exchange another hug, and after a celebratory toast, Lexi sidles up next to me.

"Wow. How exciting." She fans her face and grins. "More babies to spoil. I love being an aunt."

"The best part is we can hand them back whenever we want." I sit back down and pat the spot next to me. Lexi smiles and joins me, taking a sip of water after another wave of tears roll down her face. "Those two are going to be the best parents."

"Tell us the story about Baby Girl Hartwell!" Grant calls out.

"Baby Girl Hartwell-Miller," Maverick corrects, and Emmy taps her cheek.

"You know what? Baby Girl Hartwell sounds way better," she teases, and the man is such a sap, he puts his head on her shoulder and buries his face in her hair, not bothering to argue.

"Well, G-Money, when a man loves a woman—" Ethan starts, and Hudson slaps a hand over his mouth.

"I'm so happy for you, Em," Piper says, and Liam keeps

handing her napkins to wipe her eyes. "I know you've been trying for *so* long."

"Are you going to play next season?" Grant asks, bouncing on the balls of his feet. "How are you feeling? Do you have any morning sickness?"

"I feel great. I played in our playoff series, but I'm taking next season off." Emmy glances up at Maverick. "Mav is undecided about what he wants to do. He has four more years on his contract, but he said he'd be fine retiring tomorrow."

"*Retiring?*" Ethan almost yells. "Seriously?"

"We'll see." Maverick shrugs and rubs his hand up and down Emmy's arm. "We all love this sport, but when you see what else is out there…" He trails off and smiles. "I don't know. Being home every night with my girls sounds like a dream. I think I'll know when the time is right."

The sonogram photos get passed around again, and when they reach, Lexi, she sighs.

"I can't believe that's a baby. With parents like hers, she's going to have unbelievable genes," she says.

"I hope she gets Emmy's looks. Maverick's nose is weird," I joke.

Her laugh is soft, and she keeps the photos moving down the line. When her hands are free, she touches my cheek and meets my gaze. "Have I told you today how much I love you?"

She has. Once this morning when I handed over a cup of coffee while she was still in bed. Again this afternoon when I woke her up from a nap. When we hopped in the car on our way here, the three words slipping out of her like she's been saying them to me for years.

I'm still giddy every time I hear them. I have to pinch myself to make sure I'm not dreaming, because a year ago, I would've laughed in someone's face if they told me this is how things worked out.

"I'm not sure you did. Could I hear it again?" I ask, and she smiles when she kisses me.

"I love you," Lexi murmurs. "So very much, Riley."

"I love you too, Lexi baby." I move my mouth to her forehead and kiss her there too. "Today's been a pretty good day, huh?"

"No." Her arms wrap around my waist, steady and safe. *Home.* "It's been the best day."

EPILOGUE
RILEY

Eight months later

"HOW ARE YOU FEELING?"

I look up from lacing my skates and smile at Lexi standing in the entrance to the Comets' locker room.

"You're not supposed to be in here." I sit up straight. I open my arms and sigh in relief when she marches toward me and drops in my lap. "You're a rule breaker, Armstrong."

"Girlfriend privileges. And I cleared it with Coach Thompson," she tells me, mentioning the AHL team's head coach. "Plus, you know I haven't followed the rules a day in my life."

"You haven't, and that's why I love you." I rest my chin on her shoulder and wrap my arms around her waist. "You asked how I'm feeling, and it's embarrassing to admit I'm fucking terrified. I don't know why. I've played in more important games than this. It's the AHL, not game seven in a playoff series."

After months of intense strength training, skating every morning and every night, and getting reacquainted with the ice, Marcus renegotiated my contract to become on loan as part of a minor league conditioning assignment. It lets me swing between the AHL and NHL—which I doubt I'll see again—and tonight, I'm making my debut with our affiliate team.

I've scrimmaged with my new teammates. I've been going to practice. Lexi stays at the rink with me until midnight while I work on speed drills and shooting on an empty net, but none of it is as important as this.

"You're going to be great." She reaches for my helmet and gently sets it on my head. "You've worked so hard for this, Ri, and you're already a winner in my eyes. You always will be, even if you never play again."

"Promise not to laugh if I trip jumping over the boards?"

"I promise."

"You can laugh if my leg becomes detached during the game though."

The prosthetic blade she had designed for me has worked well up to this point with its state-of-the-art technology, but I've never tested it in an intense scenario like game play. There's a chance I could run into issues if I get slammed into the boards too many times, and I don't want the boys to be assessed a bench minor because I have to fix the technology that's allowing me to skate.

Lexi laughs at that, and she buries her face in my jersey. "I'm sorry. I'm picturing the logistics of that, and I don't know what I'd do if that happened."

"It would be the funniest fucking thing. The meme accounts would have a field day." I run my fingers up her spine and trace over the letters stretched across her shoulders. "Nice jersey, by the way."

It's my first time seeing her in it, and yeah. My friends are right. Seeing the woman you love rock your name on her back like she's claiming you is hot as hell.

"I had to steal one from your closet because the merchandise store is sold out. The fight strap is annoying as hell. And it smells like death. Do you ever do laundry?"

"You should've worn some of my pants for the full effect."

"Is that a scene you want to act out? Me in all your gear?"

I slip my hand under the front of her jersey and stroke my thumb across her stomach. She shivers under my touch, and I grin. "It might be. You'd have to keep still while I took every piece of equipment off of you. I'd go slow, Lex, just to torture you. To see how well you can behave."

"You know I can behave," Lexi whispers, and her eyes flutter closed. "But if we're talking about fantasies, you in your gear is extremely hot. Maybe later tonight you can fuck me while you wear your helmet."

"I'll do you one better and wear the goalie mask I stole from Liam last year."

"You have my attention, Mitchell." Lexi kisses my neck and wiggles off my lap. "But you have a game to play first."

Nerves sit in the pit of my stomach. I close my eyes and run through Dr. Ledlow's meditation exercises, but I'm still jittery. Full of adrenaline and fear like I've never experienced before.

"What if they treat me differently because of my leg? What if they go easy on me because they're afraid they're going to hurt me? What if I'm fucking terrible and fall flat on my face?" I ask.

"Hey." Lexi tugs on my arm and helps me stand on my skates. My legs feel like Jell-O, but when she rests her head on my chest, I'm steady and settled. At ease, like I'm landing on solid ground. It's always like this with her. "If you don't want to do this, you don't have to, baby. I'll sneak you through the hallway in the back, and no one will know. But I want you to know it's okay to be afraid. This is a big step and something new. No one is going to fault you for being nervous."

I stroke her hair while my heart races. "That helps to hear. I just don't want to let anyone down. Especially the team after all the money they've invested in me and you for all the work you've done with me. You've put so much time and energy into my rehab, Lex, and I want to make you proud."

She frowns, and I pull down on her bottom lip with my thumb. "I am always proud of you," she says.

"I guess it's good our AHL team's attendance is shitty. No one can see me fail." I kiss the top of her head and grab my stick. "And I'm glad the boys aren't getting back from their road trip until tomorrow. They won't be able to chirp me for being slow."

"Mitchell," Coach Thompson calls out from the office attached to the locker room. "Let's go."

"Good luck." Lexi stands on her toes and kisses my cheek, right above my chin strap. "I love you so much."

"I love you too, Lexi baby." I bend down and check my socks, smiling when my fingers brush against the folded paper shoved down near my skate. "I'll see you out there."

She disappears with a wave, and I join the team out in the hallway. A couple players bump my knuckles, and a few knock their helmets against mine. It's not easy being the new guy on a squad that has a lot of camaraderie and friendships, but I'm starting to click with them.

I stare down the tunnel at the ice, and that fear turns to excitement. I spin my stick in my glove and nod at Dusty Pembroke, our goalie.

"Ready?" he asks me.

"As I'll ever be."

"Protect my net, and we won't have any problems."

I laugh and tap his pads with the blade of my stick. He and Liam would get along just fine. "You got it, man."

He leads the team down the hall and I bring up the rear. When I skate onto the ice and check out my surroundings, I freeze.

The arena is packed. Full to the brim with spectators from

the front row all the way up to the nosebleeds, and I see dozens and dozens of fans lining the glass with signs.

WELCOME BACK, MITCHY.

WE MISSED YOU.

LIFE'S A BITCH, BUT WE HAVE MITCH!!!

"What the fuck?" I look around. "What are all these people doing here?"

"They're here for you." Brock Sidell, the Comets' defenseman, grins. "You thought people would miss your comeback? Please. This is going to go down like Jordan's flu game in sports history."

My eyes prickle with tears. I squeeze them shut, and when I open them, I see twenty-six familiar faces right behind the Comets' bench, all wearing my jersey.

There's Grant and Ethan. Liam with Piper on his shoulders and Maverick with his arm around Emmy and their little girl resting against her chest. Hudson and Madeline and Coach. My parents, Marcus, and Lamar with his son. They're all banging on the glass, and I can't help it.

I let out a sob and skate over to them. A team official gestures for them to fill in the box, and they do, squeezing shoulder to shoulder until the entire team is there, with Lexi right in the middle.

"There's our boy!" Grant screams, jumping up and down.

"What the hell are you all doing here? You're supposed to be in California."

I know Lexi got the okay to leave early after the Stars' game yesterday afternoon, but everyone else wasn't due back until tomorrow.

"We took the redeye home last night," Hudson explains.

"Did you *really* think we'd miss your AHL debut?" Maverick smirks. "Fuck no."

"It was Liam's idea." Ethan pinches his cheek, and Liam scowls. "Practically demanded the pilots get us back to the East Coast with whatever shortcuts they could find."

"I don't know what the fuck you're talking about," Liam grumbles.

"Wow. I can't believe you all are here." I pull off my glove and wipe under my eyes. I glance over at Lexi, and she's beaming. "You knew about this?"

"Why do you think I pretended to have cramps last night and slept in the spare bedroom? I was texting Piper nonstop to make sure they were getting in on time," she says.

"You're sneaky, Armstrong."

"It's for a good cause." She reaches for my hand and gives me a reassuring squeeze. "Everyone wanted to be here to support you, and no matter what happens, we're all going to have your back."

"I love you." I look down the bench at the players I've gone to battle with. At my brothers and sisters who helped pick me up when all I wanted to do was crawl in a hole and not come out. At the friends who believed in me when I didn't believe in myself. "I love all of you. I'm a lucky bastard."

"Give them hell, Mitchy," Emmy says, and I pop in my mouthguard, ready to get to work.

I'VE ONLY PLAYED six minutes, but it's the greatest night of my professional career. Skating fast, chasing the puck, scooping up rebounds and setting up an assist that leads to a game-tying goal feels like I'm on top of the world, and I hope this elation never goes away.

My body aches in ways I've never experienced before. My right leg feels like it's seconds away from giving out. My eyes burn with sweat, but every time my blades touch the ice, I tell myself Riley from a year ago wouldn't believe how far I've come, and I push even harder.

I'm doing it for him and the demons he faced in the hospital bed. For the nights when he wanted to give up and give in to the pain, and when an opponent cross-checks me into the boards directly in front of where my friends are all sitting, I can't help but laugh.

The final buzzer sounds, and we win three to two. After a quick huddle with the team at center ice, I tap my blade on the logo and skate to the locker room.

"Mitchell," someone calls out, and a Comets' team official is gesturing for me to stop. "You're the first star tonight."

"What?" I sputter. "I barely played. I did the least amount of work."

"You worked harder than everyone." He spins his finger in a circle, and I make a U-turn back to the barn. "Get out there."

I hold up my hand to a roaring round of applause, thanking the fans and laughing when Lexi blows a kiss my way. I pretend to catch it midair, and she grins when I tuck it in my pocket.

As the spectators starts to leave, my Stars teammates step onto the ice. Coach Saunders gives Coach Thompson a handshake, and Hudson puts a hand on my shoulder.

"You looked sharp out there, Ri," he says. "How are you feeling?"

"Like I need to soak in an ice bath for days." I hold on to his waist while I adjust my prosthetic. Everything is out of alignment after those hits, but I'll worry about that tomorrow. I'm glad to know no one took it easy on me tonight. "How was my stick handling?"

"Still infinitely better than Ethan's," Maverick calls out, and Ethan gasps.

"So fucking rude, Cap. But you're right. That was pretty to watch, Mitchy."

"Thanks, guys." I turn my attention to Lamar and skate up to him and his son. "Hey, man. Thank you so much for being here."

"That was something else." We clasp hands and pull each other into an embrace. "You were so fun to watch."

"You should've seen me last year. I was much faster. But I'll get there." I glance down at his son and smile. "How're you Mikey?"

"This was my first hockey game!" he exclaims, waving a foam finger. "I can't wait to come back."

"I might've created a monster. Sorry," I say to Lamar, and he brushes me off.

"Don't worry about it. I'm just glad we got to see you."

"How's Aliyah? And Destiny?"

"Both healthy and beautiful. She wishes she could be here, but I told her I'd have you over for dinner soon."

"I'd love that. Anytime." We exchange another embrace. "I can't thank you enough for saving my life that night. I wouldn't be here today without you."

"I didn't do anything except call the ambulance and then your friends."

"You stayed with me. You stuck around when you didn't have to. You didn't try to sell the story to a media outlet, and I'm forever indebted to you."

"We have to take care of each other, you know? Too much shit going on in this world to not have love in our hearts," Lamar says.

"Amen to that, brother. You two get home safe," I say.

I give my parents a quick hug and shake Marcus's hand before I get bombarded with Lexi jumping into my arms. We almost topple over, but Liam catches us at the last second, and I hold her tight to my chest so she doesn't get hurt.

"You did it," Lexi squeals. "Oh my *god*, Riley. You really, really did it."

"Thank you," I say into her hair. "For not letting me give up that first day in the training room. You're the only reason I got this far."

"You would've always gotten this far." She kisses me, and I set her down. "Grilled cheeses and milkshakes to celebrate?"

"Hang on. I have to do something first."

I dig in my skate and pull out the small plastic bag I hid when I was getting dressed earlier. I open it, unfold the napkin that's inside, and hand it over to her.

"What's this?" she asks.

"My Life List. It needs some updating."

We've added to it over the last eight months, and I can barely fit anything new on it these days with all we've accomplished. There are small wishes like being able to squat two times my body weight and running a mile. Bigger ones like flying her out to Chicago to spend a week with my parents and going to Florida to visit her mom. Other things we haven't done quite yet, like helping her open a Pilates studio where one class a day is modified and designed for individuals with disabilities, but I know one day we will.

"What do you need to update?" she asks, and I tap her hand so she knows to turn it over.

"Playing in a professional game. Do you have a pen?"

"Of course I have a pen." She pulls one out from the pocket in her jeans and takes the cap off with her teeth. "Okay. Playing in a professional game. Check."

"Can you read the last three things I have on there?"

"Sure. Let's see. *Get Lexi to like me. Get Lexi to fall in love with me. Get Lexi to spend the*—'" She jerks her chin up to look at me. "Riley."

"Hm?"

"What does this say?"

"I don't know." I shrug and fight off my grin. "Read the whole thing."

Her hand shakes, and she tries again. "*Get Lexi to spend the rest of her life with me*," she whispers.

"It's not a proposal. It's not a ring, and I'm not going to get on one knee. Ever, if that's what you want. But it is a promise I will be here by your side for as long as you'll have me. It's a vow that I'm not going anywhere unless you're coming with me. I love you, Lex, and you have my word."

She leaps into my arms again, legs wrapping around my waist. I stroke her hair and kiss her forehead, grinning like a goddamn fool who's lost his mind.

"What do you say?" I ask.

"Yes," she whispers.

"Yes to which one?"

"All three. To liking you. To loving you. To spending the rest of my life with you, however that might look for us. I want all of that, Riley, and more."

"That's a hat trick, Lexi baby, and that means I win."

"Win?" She wrinkles her nose, and I kiss away her frown. "What the hell do you win?"

"You, obviously," I say. "I don't need anything else."

COMING SOON

The DC Stars will be back with more stories soon! Here's who else is getting a book:

Coach Saunders (one night stand, player's sister, age gap where he's older)
Grant (off-limits woman, age gap where she's older, secret relationship)
Ethan (accidental pregnancy, forced proximity)

ACKNOWLEDGMENTS

In May 2024, I published Face Off, book one in a new hockey series. It did okay its first couple of months out in the world, but then, because of some incredible content creators, it took off.

The last twelve months have been nothing short of amazing, and sometimes I have to pinch myself that this is my life. I know people read my books, but it still blows my mind people read my books and *enjoy* them.

Thank you, from the bottom of my heart, for reading Hat Trick. This team of boys and the women they love have been the most unexpected surprise and my greatest joy. I get emotional when I think about your constant love and support for too long, but please know your enthusiasm for my books is beyond my wildest dreams.

An immense thank you to my beta read team, as always, and my sensitivity readers. Every comment, every suggestion, every critique is so impactful, and your hard work is the reason this book exists today.

Thank you to Hannah, my editor and, even more importantly, my friend. Thank you for making me laugh and sitting across from me at Waterstones when this was a fraction of what it is today. I'm so grateful we get to work together.

Britt. These stories wouldn't be what they are without you. From the very beginning you've been in my corner, and I hope you know how valued your feedback is. You're incredible at what you do, and I can't wait to keep making magic with you.

Thank you to Chloe for another fantastic cover. This one is my absolute favorite, and you brought the love Lexi and Riley have for each other to life in the best possible way.

To M & R: My favorite guys. I love you.

And, again, to every BookToker, every Bookstagrammer, every reviewer and reader… thank you. I get to live out my dreams because of you. Please never stop shouting about the books you love. You're the glue that holds this community together, the reason so many of us keep writing, and your infectious love of reading is the bright spot in a world that so often feels dark.

ABOUT THE AUTHOR

Chelsea is a flight attendant and romance author who writes fun, fresh, and flirty love stories with plenty of spice. When she's not making fictional characters banter for twenty chapters before they finally kiss or serving chicken or pasta on an airplane, you can find her trying to pet as many dogs as she can.

Stay up to date by signing up for her newsletter: https://authorchelseacurto.myflodesk.com/newsletter

- instagram.com/authorchelseacurto
- amazon.com/author/chelseacurto
- tiktok.com/@chelseareadsandwrites
- threads.net/@authorchelseacurto

ALSO BY CHELSEA CURTO

D.C. Stars series
Face Off

Power Play

Slap Shot

Love Through a Lens series
Camera Chemistry

Caught on Camera

Behind the Camera

Off Camera

Holiday Novellas
Dashing All The Way

Boston series
An Unexpected Paradise

The Companion Project

Road Trip to Forever

Park Cove series
Booked for the Holidays

Made in the USA
Middletown, DE
11 June 2025